These Affli

People whose minds
challenged, severely

by Bruce Alway

Contact: BruceAlway23@gmail.com

Portions of contents under © 2017 by Bruce Alway. All contents registered with WGA #1951844

Story and Pages

A Storm of Design

Son, the true story that I'm giving you is more than one just about my youth; it's mostly a confession that I'm finishing with my slow, shaky hand as I lay here dying in my hospital bed.

There's a secret in our family that has been held for decades and carefully guarded by three people. My Ma passed away years ago, having never remarried. And my sister Mary died recently. Now I can say what I need to say because they were the other two holding the secret. We agreed that the last one of the three of us would share the secret with you. I haven't got much time left and can't imagine this old, sick body ever rising from this bed again. The years have etched wrinkles over my face: one for every pain and smile. Now, time is ready to collect its toll, and I must unstrap the weight of the secret off my back. Right or wrong, justified or not, I have lived my life with the burden of this story. At the end of it all, what I want to believe is simply that a stranger saved our Ma's life and gave the three of us a new one, and that's enough for me. I love you, son, as I have told you many times. You have always been my pride and joy. I hope that after reading this story, you won't rush to judgment. Instead, I trust that you will carefully consider everything I've written. Having said all of that, this letter will finally tell you why you never knew your grandpa. Perhaps a greater power in play was the reason or maybe it was just plain human nature. Please forgive us for not telling you the truth until now.

I was fourteen years old the day the stranger pulled his buckboard wagon up to our humble and remote farmhouse. Fourteen in those unsettled days of hard work and responsibility, was very near being a man.

Calling where we lived a 'house' wouldn't be accurate. It was more like a large shack with a small kitchen built on the left side. It took Pa and me a full year to build the house and barn with unpainted and mismatched boards. We planted our large garden close to the house. Pigs were kept next to the milking cow, and all of these were separated by split rail fences which we cut and split from the trees we had cut down.

Some days the wind would squeeze through narrow spaces between some of the boards; whistling highs and lows with the changing force, and sometimes bringing small amounts of snow inside the house to lay it in careful, narrow lines on the bare wood floor. When it rained, the roof leaked in places, so we had to gather all the pots and buckets to catch the water; having to empty and move them often. The wooden floor was worn smooth from the dirt we brought in on our feet or boots, and some of the boards dipped slightly in places when we stepped on them, having never been nailed down properly. Wooden pegs had been driven into the upright beams where lanterns, two iron skillets, Ma's stained apron, and a few miscellaneous items were hung. The stone fireplace was the center of the home. Old worn chairs, some covered with handmade quilts, were positioned around it.

Ma did most of the cooking on a wood burning cook stove in the small kitchen. The house had only three windows; one in the front, one in the back, and one in the kitchen; strategically placed for cross drafts in the summer and to shoot out of if attacked which could have happened at any time.

My little sister, Mary and I climbed up the wooden ladder each night to the small loft where our beds were separated by an old hanging blanket.

Our parents slept in the narrow bed downstairs so Pa could tend the fireplace in the night and to be ready with his rifle in case anyone came along like "Outlaws, savages, or other vermin," as he put it.

It was widely rumored that Indians were in the area and had been known to attack and burn settler's homes, leaving no men alive; just women or children, but only if the Indians wanted to take them. It was also a lawless time of bandits when men who weren't able to find work or didn't want to, grouped together to rob and steal. Every settler had to fend for themselves and work hard to provide and protect even the meager necessities needed to survive.

Our Pa was fit for this way of living. He wasn't given to much cursing, and he never drank, but he was a mean man, quietly angry and devoid of compassion or gentleness. To his credit, he was a man of his word; his word was one of the few possessions he had.

He often said to me, "A man gathers all his honor on his tongue when he gives his word."

His soul, born pure and innocent like all new souls, must have been forged hard with struggle and constant work at an early age. I assume that his Pa was the same way; denying his children demonstrations of love, warmth, and sensitivity. Probably I shouldn't make that assessment since my Pa never spoke about him.

Another one of my Pa's few sayings was, "Ya don't get no thanks fer do'in what yer supposed to do, fer not do'in what ya should'a done, or fer just say'in what yer gonna do."

Ma did the laundry in a large pot by hand, once a month in the winter and twice a month in the summer. Between washings, we wore the same dirty clothes every day. Pa's shirt might have been nice a long time ago, but the constant work he did around our little farm took its toll on it. He wore old suspenders but had a leather belt hung on a nail inside the door for the often beatings he would give to Ma, me, and my little sister, Mary. Its presence was a constant reminder of Pa's strict expectations. Rarely did we get a visitor out to our remote little farm because we were so far from any neighbors.

One cold winter day everything was being covered with small falling snowflakes suggesting that the coming storm was going to be a big one. Pa and I were sawing logs next to the house when I noticed two brown horses in the distance coming our way through the fields and trees, slowly pulling a buckboard wagon with one figure leading it as he sang.

"Pa, someone's com'in," I announced, standing there holding an armful of split wood.

Pa turned to stare out at the wagon. As it got closer, he walked over to the porch and took his rifle and pointed it from his hip in the direction of the stranger. His usual state of mind was mistrust or at least suspicion.

He snapped out an order to me, "Pick up the ax boy and get ready."

We had rehearsed times like this. I dropped the wood from my arms, picked up the ax, and took a few steps toward the approaching wagon. I was young but determined to use the ax as a weapon if need be.

As the stranger approached, he waved his hand as a friendly salute, but my father just stared, standing stoically. He had a grandfatherly appearance, as his black and white bushy beard and eyebrows suggested that he was an older man. His flat rimmed brown leather hat dusted with snow was pulled down just above his eyes as he sat hunched in a heavy tan overcoat and scarf. He pulled back the reins and stopped his wagon, facing our house. It was then that we noticed an arrow sticking in the side of the wagon.

"Hello," he said, smiling. "The name is Charles."

"What do ya want?" Pa sternly asked with the rifle still pointing toward the stranger. He waited until then to pull the hammer back for the 'click,' to emphasize his frame of mind. But the casual stranger seemed not to be alarmed.

3

"Well I meant to just pass by, but I saw smoke from your chimney. There's a big storm brewing, so I'm hoping to find refuge for the night if you allow me to."

"We ain't got no room. Ya best be moving on," Pa answered without apology.

Charles pointed to the small plain barn and said, "That will do fine for my horses and me. I have blankets. I'd be happy to bed down in their so I won't be a bother. To earn my keep, I'll help you with that pile of firewood."

He looked innocent enough, I thought. I glanced at the back of the wagon to see a large snow-covered horse blanket protecting what must have been a few bags and two larger items.

"Alright, you can sleep in the barn." Pointing to the woodpile, Pa added, "The split'in ax is right there after you tend to your horses."

"Much obliged friend." Charles smiled. He never seemed to feel threatened. Although Pa had the rifle, Charles always seemed to be in control.

Ma heard the conversation from inside the house and stepped out onto the porch with my little sister. Both of them looked un-kept. It must have seemed obvious to the stranger that their pinned-up hair hadn't been washed or brushed for some time, and their dresses were old, but the little lines of hand stitching indicated that they did their best with what they had. Charles noticed the fading green bruise on Ma's cheek. And after seeing the red welts on my sister's arms and my swollen lip, he must have determined that Pa must have beaten us regularly, which he had.

Charles tipped his hat to Ma. "Ma'am. My name is Charles."

"I'm Sarah," Ma introduced herself with a smile. "Ezra, I'd like to invite this gentleman in for suppa this eve'nin if it's alright with you," she said with a slight pleading tone while wiping her hands on a stained kitchen towel. "We ain't had company for so long."

Behind Ma's request to allow Charles to stay was her need for civility and neighborliness. She remembered her parents having company and entertaining friends. Right then she needed a social occasion to contradict their basic current life as pioneers that some might say was primitive.

Pa began to sternly reply, "We ain't got enough for nobody else so..."

Charles, who seemed to know how to maneuver around Pa's resistance with subtle agility, interrupted, "I have food to share: a

4

wonderful beef roast. It's frozen, but it will make a nice supper in the hands of a good cook." So as not to sound like he was being charitable to a proud man, he quickly added, "It will help to earn my keep."

Pa lowered the barrel of his rifle toward the ground and slowly brought the hammer down with his thumb. "That's acceptable."

I always wondered if, to Pa, the arrow in the side of the wagon influenced him to allow the stranger to stay for the night. Maybe there was a hint of compassion and approval for anyone who had come that close to death and was able to escape it, and therefore should be given at least basic accommodations.

Charles slowly stepped down off the wagon, humming so as not to cause alarm, and walked stiffly to the back as anyone would do who had been riding for a long time in the cold.

"When I had a younger man's body, I moved much quicker."

He lifted the corner of the snow-covered wool blankets and moved things around while Pa kept a close suspicious eye on him. Finally, Charles stepped around the front of the horses with a burlap bag and walked up to the porch.

"Ma'am, I have to lighten my load to pull the wagon through the snow in the morning, so I hope you can use some of these items." He looked into the bag. "In here is the meat, a bag of flour, a little coffee, yeast, lard, sugar, and salt. Oh, and a bag of beans, some molasses, and a little honey. Son, why don't you take these in for your Ma? I'll get my horses in the barn then get started on that pile of firewood."

I looked at Pa for permission. He nodded. I was already looking forward to the meal and having company. Tonight, there wouldn't be the same old pork, boiled cabbage, and carrots, or my least favorite meal when things got especially hard, potato soup.

"My name is Caleb, sir."

Charles leaned forward with a smile and a compliment. "Caleb, you look like a very strong and capable young man. It is a pleasure to meet you."

I smiled, walked over to the burlap bag and carefully and took it inside.

The stranger took his wagon to the barn and began to unhitch the horses. Pa, seeing that we had another set of hands for the firewood, walked over and began to fix the fences that our cow often used to rub against.

Soon, Charles came back and began splitting the short sections of the logs that Paw and I had sawed with the old two-man crosscut saw. Maybe because he was a little thicker around the waist, he grunted when he bent over, so I offered to place the logs on the stump for him to split. We didn't break any speed records for splitting and stacking firewood because of the little stories he told and the questions I asked him. If it makes sense to say, I could feel the depth of his experiences, his wisdom, and his refined strength. He was a gentleman and a traveler. And by the way he talked, I suspected he had some real education. The 'stranger,' Charles, immediately began to invite me to like him.

"Sir, I couldn't help but notice the arrow stuck in the side of your wagon."

"Ah, that was just a mistake, son."

"Sir? A mistake?"

"Yes. While the group of Indians were riding toward me and yelling, one of them shot an arrow at me before he got close enough to see who I was."

"Then what happened?"

"They saw who I was, stopped, and turned back. They always do."

"Wh…why? Who are…"?

Pa yelled over from the fence, "Boy! Too much talk and not enough work!" The conversation gave way to the sound of the short logs being split before the pieces jumped off the stump.

The evening inside the house was pleasant for the most part. The fireplace was bright and warm. Delicious but unfamiliar smells of the cooking and baking slowly and painfully announced the forthcoming meal. Pa had relaxed a bit in his chair, and Ma and little sister were busy getting dinner ready. Ma was singing as she walked back and forth from the kitchen to the table. I hadn't heard her hum or sing for a long time, and I loved it whenever she did. Although Charles tried several times to start up a conversation as they sat, Pa never returned a full sentence. But it wasn't because Pa was unrefined or uneducated which he was, it was because he was unpleasant. It soon became evident to all, that our guest was a charming man. And he was kind, learned, and well spoken.

"Dinner is ready if you three men would like to come to the table," Ma instructed. "Charles, you can sit right there on the bench."

"Thank you, ma'am."

"I wanna sit next to Mr. Charles!" little Mary exclaimed, taking Charles by his arm and leading him to his seat.

With everyone seated, Charles asked, "Any idea how much snow we're going to get?"

"We'll get what we get," Pa replied.

With the thought of snow, Mary exclaimed, "I'm gonna make a snowman tomorrow!"

Pa rebuked her. "You ain't doin' nothin' til all your chores are done."

"Yes, sir," Sister replied dryly, with the standard answer in our house.

Dinner was delicious. With the items that Charles gave us, Ma served the beef roast, potatoes and gravy, fresh bread, and some warm, sweet pastries. Pa never lifted a finger to help or gave a 'thank you' or any kind of compliment to Ma although he ate his meal with controlled passion. He ordered seconds by planting his elbow on the table, lifting his plate eye-level, and silently staring at Ma seated across the table until she noticed. She quickly got up from her own meal, took his plate into the kitchen, refilled it, and placed it in front of him.

"Anyone else?" she offered with the smile of the hostess that she obviously enjoyed being.

"Ma'am, I don't think I could eat one more bite even if I pushed it down with my shortest finger. No thank you," Charles replied with a satisfied smile as he patted his belly.

Ma smiled. "Charles, you may call me Miss Sarah now that we're properly acquainted."

"Thank you. I'm from a different generation, so by instinct, I might slip and call you 'ma'am' again."

"If ya do, I'll try to forgive ya," Ma replied, smiling.

"Children, what do you think of your ma's cooking?" Charles asked.

Mary was happy to reply. "It was real good! And I helped too!"

A big smile formed on Charles' face. He put his hand on Mary's head.

"You sure did darling! Well, you worked like a busy little beaver!"

He followed his compliment with a chuckle that caused his whole portly body to tremble gently. He seemed to love people and didn't think it a demotion to speak to young Mary as a friend. Ma and I smiled at the human warmth.

"Mr. Charles, what's a beaver?"

"Miss Mary, a beaver is an animal that chews down trees to make a home."

Pa interrupted the rare happy moment. "Boy, go fetch some wood and don't leave that door open too long. It's snowing hard."

My given name is Caleb, but Pa rarely used it. In keeping with his ways, he usually called our Ma 'woman.' And he often referred to Mary as 'the brat' or 'runt' which the rest of us privately hated.

"Yes, sir. Ma, supper was real good," I said, stopping to kiss her on the cheek, then patted my sister's hair as I walked to the door.

The only other person who hadn't expressed appreciation was Pa. Although there was ample space in the conversation for a compliment, he never said a word of appreciation.

"Thank you, Caleb," Ma answered.

I came back into the house with both arms cradling firewood. After closing the door with my foot, I wiped my feet on the old rag then carried the wood to the fireplace.

"Why don't you men move to the chairs by the fireplace? Mary and I will clear the table," Ma suggested.

Charles stood. "Thank you, ma'am. I'll be right there. But first I have to lighten my wagon as much as I possibly can." He glanced out the window. "It's snowing harder. The horses are going to have a hard-enough time just pulling me and the empty wagon especially after that wonderful meal," he said with a chuckle. "I have to go out to my wagon to lighten the load. Would you excuse me for a minute?"

"Why, of course," Ma replied.

After taking his hat and coat off from the wooden pegs and putting them on, Charles opened the door against the wind and snow, stepped out, then quickly closed it.

The chairs near the fireplace were placed in a semi-circle. From the kitchen, Sister slowly and carefully brought old mismatched cups and chipped saucers one at a time, staring down at the empty cup to make sure it didn't drop. Ma brought the hot iron kettle over to us, filled Pa's cup and offered me coffee which made me feel like one of the grownups. I didn't like it but drank it anyway, not wishing to risk looking like a child, and only after adding plenty of sugar and milk.

Charles came back through the door with another burlap bag which he placed on the floor between his legs, as he sat in a chair near the fireplace. Ma and Mary joined us in curiosity.

"If you'll allow me, I have to give a few things away." We all watched him as he reached into the bag moving things around. "Ezra, here's something that you might like."

He pulled out a new polished cherry-wood smoking pipe and a large pouch of tobacco and handed it to Pa took who them and immediately placed them on the little table beside his chair without looking at them. He just stared at Charles without so much as a 'thank you.'

"It's a flat-bottomed pipe so you can set it on the table or a fence post. That will reduce my load by a pound or two. A relaxing thing to do on the porch in the evenings."

"I ain't got no use fer it," Pa replied.

Charles continued, "These next items are a little heavier." He reached back into the bag again and pulled out a hand-held, framed looking glass, hairbrush, and a spool of yellow ribbon. "Miss Sarah, if you could take these from me before I break something, I would appreciate it. I've got no use for them anyway. I saw my face in a looking glass once. It nearly scared me to death, and that was the last time I did that, let me tell you. I once knew a young woman so vain that she wore holes plumb through one just by looking at herself so often."

I grinned at his humor and glanced at Pa hoping he would too, but he didn't. Our guest brought refreshing levity to our home that was usually governed by tension caused by Pa's stern expectations.

Ma's face lit up when she saw the items. "Oh, I suppose there's no sense in break'in something like this," Ma said coyly, as she gladly accepted the items that Charles reached out to her. "Much obliged."

"It's the least I can do for your warm hospitality."

To my little sister, Charles said, "Mary darling, this item isn't heavy but it needs a special little girl to take care of it, and I'm not the one for the job."

Charles pulled out a little bundle wrapped in a pink blanket and reached it out to my sister kneeling on the floor. She took the bundle and carefully unwrapped the blanket to discover a beautiful baby rag doll in a little dress with long yarn hair. Its eyes were pretty buttons, and a permanent smile was stitched with red thread.

"Would you like to take care of her?" Charles asked. "She really needs a little mommy."

"Oh look, Mary. A baby-doll!" Ma exclaimed, with extra excitement to add more fun to the moment.

Little Mary's face lit up. She smiled at the doll and nodded before she brought the doll up to her neck, cradled it, hugged, and kissed it. Adjusting its hair, she said to the doll, "My name is Mary, but you can call me 'mommy.' I love you."

"Mary?"

"Thank you, Mr. Charles," Sister said, after Ma's gentle reminder of her manners.

"You're welcome little mommy," Charles replied with a satisfied grandfatherly smile. Mary stood up and walked over to Charles and gave him a big hug. Pa, who never invited his daughter's affection or offered his own, glared.

While we sipped our coffee, Ma and my sister enjoyed brushing each other's hair and seeing themselves in the looking glass, seeming to be mesmerized by their reflections. Ma complained about the little wrinkles around her eyes. Sister made faces and giggled, having never seen herself before and of course she fussed over her baby doll and played with her.

"Oh, by the way, your baby doll needs a name," Charles told her.

"Mary, you can take yer time think'in of the very best name. Every mommy does," Ma added.

"Ma, I already know. Her name is Elizabeth."

"How sweet! Elizabeth is my middle name!"

"Yep. I already know'd that too," Mary replied, matter-of-factly.

Sister immediately walked around to each family member and proudly introduced Elizabeth; briefly explaining to her who each of us was and what we did for chores.

Charles lifted his head from looking into the bag. "This next item is for Caleb. It comes with a lot of responsibility. Ladies, if you'll please excuse us for a few minutes."

"Oh certainly," Ma replied, standing up and taking my sister's hand. "Come with me to the kitchen little darl'in and help me clean the supper dishes."

"Can I bring my baby?"

"Well, a course ya can. I'm bringing you ain't I? Cuz you're *my* baby."

Mary looked up at Ma as they walked to the kitchen. "Ma? Are you a grandma now?" We all laughed at the cute question, except for Pa.

"Ya might say that cept we won't be use'in the word, 'grandma' just yet."

Charles, who had spoken in a friendly and humble way since he arrived, now spoke with a serious tone of the senior man that he was.

"Ezra, this last item in the bag is meant for your son. I'm going to take it out of the bag. Before I offer it to him, I'll make you a promise; I'll ask you to make a promise and ask your son to make one too."

"What if I won't?" Pa asked with subtle defiance.

"If either of you won't make a promise, the item goes back into the bag, and I'll take it with me in the morning."

Charles reached into the bag and carefully pulled out a brown polished leather gun belt that held cartridges in small leather loops. At the end of the belt was a holster, holding a real six-shooter, slightly used but nice enough. I silently gasped as he held it.

"Now my solemn promise to you Ezra, is that one day your son will save your wife's life with this gun. I promise you that as the moon and stars are my witnesses. Now the promise I need from you is you will always allow your son to wear this gun or have it ready within his arms reach and never take it from him. Can you promise me that?"

Pa looked at the gun, then at me, before answering, "Yep."

"Do I have your word then?"

Pa nodded then said, "Yep. Ya have my word. But how do ya know he'll have to use it to save his Ma's life?"

Charles locked his eyes with Pa's eyes, and he leaned slightly forward. His expression changed to that of a proud man of integrity whose word was too easily disregarded.

"Believe me, I know. Your son *will* take the life of a man to save his Ma."

His sober and confident prediction made me afraid. There was authority and warning in his voice, and fear, as if a dark cloud passed over our heads. I swear, the room became gray for a few moments before the oil lamp on the small table next to Pa suddenly dimmed. He simply reached over and raised the wick, never considering the coincidence; the same coincidence that made my scalp tingle. Whether all of that was evil or good, I didn't know and still don't to this day.

Charles turned to look at me in the same stern way. "Now Caleb, I need a promise from you too. Will you be man enough and careful enough with this gun and keep it clean and dry? One day you will save your Ma's life with it. Caleb…, you will kill a man with this, so it will need to be ready at all times for the unfortunate, but necessary occasion."

"Yes, sir. I promise," I answered against the tears and the eerie, unsettling feeling that evil was gathering outside in the dark woods to attack our small farmhouse.

"Will you wear it like a man and be brave enough to shoot it when the time comes?"

"Well, yes sir. A'specially for my Ma. I will be brave enough. But sir, can ya tell me what's gonna happen?"

"I can't tell you, son. If you knew, you wouldn't be watching out for what else you weren't expecting. Right?"

"Yes, sir. Sir... do *you* know?"

Charles ignored my question, but it seemed to me as if he was sent, dispatched with orders from the future to help prevent a crime.

"On your word as a man and with a handshake?" He said as he stood up extending his hand to me.

I also stood and walked the few steps to him.

"Yes sir, on my word."

I reached out my hand, and we shook on it. I realized that I had never shaken hands as a guarantee between men and wondered if the act made me a man. It felt as if Charles intended for me to consider myself a man.

"Very well then. Here, take it. It's yours."

He reached the gun-belt out to me, and I took it. It was heavier than I expected. My eyes and fingers ran over the features.

"Thank you, sir."

"You're welcome. It's yours now. Your Ma is more than worth saving. And don't you ever forget it. And don't hesitate when the time comes."

"No, sir. I won't."

"It's not loaded right now, but keep it loaded except when you're cleaning it. Now, I'll head out to the barn and get some sleep. Before I leave in the morning, I'll teach you how to aim and shoot it. Keep it unloaded until then. You won't need it tonight while I'm here."

"Why sir? Do you have a gun too?"

"Quiet, boy. Ya ask too many questions," Pa said.

Charles shook his head slightly. "No, Caleb. I don't have a gun. Never needed one. You might have to put a new hole in the belt so it will fit you. You'll want the gun's handle to be against the palm of your hand when your arm is straight down at your side. And tie that thin leather strap around your leg so the holster won't lift when you pull the gun out. If you have to be out in the rain, buckle the belt and put it over your head with gun opposite your shooting hand, tie the strap to your belt, then put your coat over it. You'll figure it out. Good night, gentlemen."

"Good night, sir."

He walked to the door and put on his coat and hat, then turned toward the kitchen. "Thank you for supper, Miss Sarah and Mary. Goodnight."

"Good night, Charles," Ma said smiling as she turned around wiping a plate.

"Good night, Mr. Charles! Elizabeth says good night too!" Mary replied.

"Goodnight Elizabeth." Charles stopped and looked around the three-room farmhouse as if to make a quick assessment before stepping out into the heavily falling snow.

Sometimes out of the corner of my eye I would see Pa looking at my gun belt which I rarely took off. The gun belt and six-shooter would be envied by most any grown man, but Pa was restrained from taking it or making me take it off by having given his word, which meant everything to him. When a man has nothing else, he will always have his word.

It seemed to me that Pa didn't appreciate any of the items that Charles gave us or even Charles himself, for that matter. I wondered if it was because Charles gave us things that Pa couldn't or wouldn't give us. Or, maybe because Pa privately admired Charles as the kind of man he wanted to be but couldn't. Maybe he knew that he wasn't the man his family needed him to be. It seemed that Pa didn't like it that Ma enjoyed the stranger's company as much as she did, or that she smiled a lot when he was on the farm. I could tell that Pa didn't like it that Mary didn't hesitate to jump up on Charles's lap but mostly kept her usual distance from him. Was Pa jealous or was he hurt? Or was there something else deep in his mind, behind that expressionless face? I could never tell.

Charles woke on a pile of hay the next morning, covered with blankets. He labored to push out the barn doors against the snow piled against them. As he stepped out, he discovered that the snow had finally stopped falling, but it was much deeper – just at his knees. But the sun was shining, and the air was warming. He decided there was absolutely no way he could take the wagon. Pa and I were digging firewood out of the snow.

"Good morning!" Charles called.

"Good morning, sir!" I replied. Pa didn't return the greeting.

Charles began to trudge over to the wood pile. "Son, if you can take a break, I'll show you how to aim that six-shooter before I leave."

Pa said, "He ain't got no time with all this damn snow."

"I understand," Charles replied.

He went back to the barn and came back leading just one saddled horse. Ma and Mary came out of the house and stood on the porch.

"Folks, there is no way I can pull my wagon through this deep snow, but I have to get going. Ezra I'll have to ask a favor of you. May I leave the wagon and one horse here for your use? That will allow me to saddle up the other horse and get on my way. I don't know when I'll be back but consider them your own until I return. If I don't return within six months, you may keep them or sell them if you like and keep the money."

"That's a fair arrangement," Pa dryly replied. "If ya do come back, you'll get straight to the horse and wagon and get directly on your way. And don't bring nothing else to give out."

Charles looked at me. "Caleb, they say if you put arrowheads around your house the Indians won't bother you."

"I'll do that! I found some!" I replied.

Pa scolded me. "Ya ain't putting no damn arrowheads around the house!"

"Yes, sir," I humbly answered.

"Thank you, all. And now I must be on my way." The leather covered saddle squeaked as Charles placed his boot into the stirrup, grabbed the horn, and pulled himself up. "I appreciate your hospitality, friends." Turning to me he said, "Son, I imagine that you will take care of the horse. Walk her around or ride her every few days. She's a worker. Use her to pull logs or stack the wagon with firewood or just go for a nice wagon ride after some of this snow melts. Of course, everyone can ride her. There are a saddle and the tack under the blanket in the back of the wagon. I'm sure your Pa can show you how to put the saddle on." Then he sat up straight and looked down at me like a general giving his last order to hold the fort while his silent gaze brought me to the point of discomfort. "Remember your man-to-man promises son. Be ready. A broken promise makes a broken man."

"Yes sir," I answered and reached down to pat my six-shooter for assurance.

"Load it the next chance you get. So long, for now, everyone."

Ma and Mary waved from the porch. Pa just stared. Charles pulled the reigns, and the horse circled around. Immediately, he began to sing, the same way he did when he arrived the morning before.

After Charles left, I felt like the sheriff; always watching the woods and investigating strange sounds. I even went outside in the dark and frequently checked the barn. There wasn't any way that robbers or Indians were going to harm my Ma. They would have to get past me and my six-shooter first.

Pa routinely hit or gave beatings to all of us, but about a week after Charles left, he had an awful spell of uncontrolled rage and violence. I believe we all could feel it coming because he was in an especially dark mood since Charles arrived.

One morning, still in the happy spirit Charles left us, Ma wanted to surprise Pa, so she brushed out her long hair real nice and my sister's hair too. Afterward, she tied little yellow ribbons in their hair and even put one in the baby doll's hair.

Heavy footsteps were heard coming to the house, so Ma and sister quickly lined up next to each other, smiling. Mary had the doll in her arms. Pa walked in, saw the ribbons and the smiles, then clenched his teeth with almost a growl.

"Woman, get that off your head. Ya, look like a whore."

Ma's smile dropped. She reached up and pulled the ribbon out of her hair, then removed my sister's ribbon from her hair.

"Ma, what's a whore?" Mary innocently asked.

Pa hurried over to sister and slapped her hard across the face knocking her to the floor. She laid there screaming and clutching her doll.

"Don't you ever use that word again!" Pa yelled.

Ma, who never challenged her husband, knelt down to comfort my sister saying, "Ezra did you have to hit her right on her face? She don't know what that word means. She ain't never heard it afore."

"Woman, I'll teach you never to question me!"

Pa quaked with anger. Mary took her doll, ran to a corner, and buried her face. Just at this moment, I walked into the house to see Pa grab Ma by her hair in a rage and stand her on her feet. He backhanded her three times then threw her to the floor. Ma was dazed and bleeding but managed to stumble away. Pa threw aside furniture to trap her against the wall and hit her again with his fist. I nervously stepped forward to let Pa know that I was watching. Ma fell to the floor. He stood over her with his fist clenched.

"Pa! Stop! You're gonna kill her!"

Pa turned to me in cold anger. "And yer next, boy."

He looked down at Ma and drew back his fist again but never got the punch in because suddenly, there was a terribly loud BOOM followed by hazy smelly smoke that hung in the air in front of me. Pa fell to the floor next to Ma. Neither one of them moved. I looked in front of me and saw that my gun was raised, and my ears were ringing. I stood there confused as to what had just happened until my brain was able to organize it all. Then it hit me; I had shot my Pa. Mary was still screaming with her hands over her ears as she hid in the corner. I hurried the short distance to kneel down to check on Pa and then Ma.

"Ma?" She didn't respond. "Ma?"

Her face was bloody and already red and beginning to swell. Her eyes were barely open, and all that was showing was the white part, which twitched.

"You're alive," I whispered. I took a pillow off their bed and placed it under her head. "Don't move."

I ran outside and took a handful of snow wrapped it in a cloth and returned. After gently applying it to the swelling on her face, I threw a rug over the puddle of blood coming from Pa's body.

After about an hour Ma was barely even able to stand to her feet. With my help, she managed to step around the rug and walk a few steps and sit in a chair. Mary stopped crying and uncovered her face but remained facing the corner, talking to Elizabeth.

I whispered in Ma's ear, "Ma, Pa is… dead. I'm going to hitch the horse to the wagon, tie the cow to the back, and bring them up to the house. You just sit here for a while." She nodded slightly, not able to open her swollen tearful eyes.

When I came back inside, Ma's face was very swollen, but she had wiped away some of the blood with the cloth which was now red. I knelt down again next to the chair.

"Ma, stay put and relax. This is what we're gonna do; I'll gather everything we need and pack it in the wagon."

I did the packing as Ma sat and mumbled directions as to what she wanted to take. My sister had calmed enough, and we let her focus on playing with her doll as I moved around. Ma and I spoke as calmly as we could.

When Mary finally turned from the corner and looked at Ma, she began to cry again and walked over to her. "Ma, what happened to yer face?"

"Honey, don't fret. I got stung by some wasps, but I'll be alright in time. Just let me be."

Sister calmed a bit and just stared at Ma, then at Pa. "Is Pa sleep'in?"

"Yes," Ma answered, as tears ran down her swollen cheeks.

"Shhhh… Let him rest, sweetie."

"Ma, why is he sleep'in on the floor?" sister whispered back.

"I guess he was just too dog-tired to make it to his bed," Ma said, in-between gasps.

"Is it gonna rain? I heard loud thunder," sister whispered as, with her gentle and forgiving spirit, took a blanket from a chair and covered her Pa. She then turned her attention back to her doll. Ma didn't answer.

Again, I knelt at Ma's chair and whispered, "The horse is hitched, and the wagon is packed. I tied Betsy to the back of the wagon. Now get yer warm clothes on and take sister on a ride in the wagon. Make sure she has a blanket over her head and sits still so she won't be look'in back. Stop and wait for me at the old Maple tree and I'll meet you there in just a little while. I'll take care of things here."

I'm certain that Ma did her best to answer sister's questions as they sat on the wagon seat and pulled away with all our things in the back. It seemed peculiar to me as I watched them leave, that the wagon with all the weight of our belongings pulled through the snow fairly well and with just one horse.

I stood there staring at our little farm; wondering what to do. Deciding that we couldn't take the two pigs, I just opened the gate and told them, "You're on your own now."

Entering the empty little house, I looked down at my dead Pa knowing in my heart and mind I would have a lot of things to sort out, but right then wasn't the time. Suddenly, I had to be the man of the house and take care of things. I took all three kerosene lamps and broke them on the floor; one of them next to Pa's body. The extra oil from the spare bottle, I poured around the walls. Since almost everything we had was made of wood, I knew there wouldn't be much left after the fire. Standing in the doorway, I watched the the burning wooden match fall from my fingers into the oil. After waiting for the flame slowly but eagerly spread across the wooden floor, I closed the door and left before the fire got to my Pa's body.

Remembering the Indian arrowheads, I ran to the barn to get them, then scattered around the burning house. I didn't want any Indians coming around trying to find whatever might be left.

Shortly after I started the hour-long walk to the Maple tree, our two freed pigs following me, found places to stop and root in search of food. And I had a chance to think more about the stranger who called himself Charles. We never asked his last name, and we didn't know where he came from or where he went after he left our farm. He just came one day and left the next; changing our lives forever. I wondered if it was just coincidence that he had to leave the wagon and horse which seemed he could have taken through the snow. I wondered about the stern promise I had to make to protect my Ma with my gun. Charles never said who I would have to protect her from, but I always wondered if he knew and if he was sent. At the time, I wasn't thinking that I was planting false evidence to make it look like Indians had attacked our little farm, killed Pa and took the rest of us, but whoever came upon the burned down little house probably came to that conclusion, leaving us free to leave without suspicion. I wondered if Charles had that figured out. Maybe the whole thing was evil, and Charles was sent to make Pa jealous and anger him to the point where he almost killed Ma while giving me no other choice but to shoot him. Or maybe the whole thing was good, and Charles was simply sent to be the means of saving our Ma. I couldn't have saved her without the six-shooter. Or, maybe it was all without any influence, but just human nature acting out in the ways it can. Also, I wonder to this day if I was a killer or a savior. Does killing a guilty person to save an innocent one, make the person a murderer? All I knew is if I had to do it all over again, I would have done the same thing to save our Ma.

"Stranger? Who's the stranger now?" I asked myself, barely recognizing the man I had become over the last two weeks.

Ma and my sister slid over as I climbed up on the seat and took the reins. That was when I noticed a buckboard wagon on the nearby hill.

"Ma, look over yonder."

Two brown horses were hitched to it, and a single bearded figure with his flat-rimmed brown leather hat pulled down, sat in the seat singing and looking out at the pillar of smoke from our burning farmhouse.

"Mr. Charles!" I shouted while waving my arm but the man didn't look or wave back.

"How'd he git anotha buckboard wagon and horses azackly like this one so quick?" Ma wondered out loud.

"Mr. Charles!" Mary exclaimed as she stood and waved.

Maybe he didn't have a concern with us and just wanted to make sure his plan worked. The familiar figure glanced our way, snapped the reins, and turned toward another dark storm forming in the distant sky. If we had any doubt that the man was Charles, as the wagon turned, we saw the arrow sticking out of the side which drew our attention to the one still stuck in ours. Maybe he knew of another poor farm where he would ask if he could take shelter for a night in exchange for some chores and two bags of gifts. Maybe another life needed to be saved or taken. The three of us, Elizabeth, and the cow pulled away to find our new life together.

Two days after we began our travels, I whispered to Ma, "Ma do you think it would be wrong if I smoked the pipe that Charles gave to…Pa?"

"Charles may have offered it to yer Pa but yer Pa never really accepted or touched it a second time, so it belongs to you." She patted my knee and looked at me. "You're the man of the house now… and son thank you… for everything."

Fresh tears trickled down her cheeks as she leaned over and hugged me. Her saying that to me, lifted much of the weight off my soul and my eyes filled with tears. I pulled the pipe and pouch of tobacco out of my jacket. When I opened the pouch, it gave a sweet woodsy smell. After taking a pinch and pushing it into the bowl, I lit it, coughed a few times, and smoked it as I led the wagon down the road. We all sat quietly which gave me more time to think.

"Ma, why did ya marry him?"

"Son, when we were court'in he was nice to me and strong, determined, and confident. He was a hard worker, and I knew he would be a good provider for me and the young'ins we would have."

"Did ya love him?"

Ma paused to search for the truth in her heart. "In a way I did. But, after we were married things changed; we needed one another to survive, and survival was mostly what we had to think about. Caleb try not to judge him too harshly."

After having gone far enough away that no one knew us, we finally settled in a peaceful little town, rented a small house, and started a new life. With the tools from the farm, the food we brought, and the small amount of money my parents had saved away, we made a new start. I sold the cow at a decent price as soon as I found a buyer.

Ma avoided people for almost a month, giving her and Mary's face a chance to heal. Whenever anyone asked about the absence of a Pa or husband, we agreed to stick with the story that Pa had fallen ill and died.

With my tools and skills, I managed to get work on a cattle ranch, building fences, barns, and outbuildings. Ma worked as a clerk at the mercantile, and my sister went to school for the first time. I never left the house or went to bed without telling Ma and Mary that I loved them. For the rest of Ma's life, I never had another need to lift my gun from its holster to save her from another man.

I love you son.

———

Caleb struggled to sit up in his hospital bed and slowly folded the thick letter with his trembling hands then put it in an envelope. As the nurse walked in, he spoke slowly, straining to make himself understood through his labored breathing and fragmented sentences.

"Nurse, would you be kind enough to give this envelope to my son if I pass before he arrives? He's coming to visit soon."

"Of course, Caleb," she said with a smile while she gave him his pain medicine and held a small glass of water to his lips. "But I'm sure you'll be able to give it to him yourself." Her tone wasn't convincing, but it had compassion.

Caleb's son walked into the hospital later that evening and introduced himself to the nurse going over papers at her desk.

"I'm so sorry sir, but your father passed about two hours ago. We haven't disturbed him yet because we were waiting for you. I'll give you all the time you need with him. You may follow me."

The nurse walked him to the room and left. The envelope with his son's name was on Caleb's chest. His son spent a few quiet minutes looking at his father. He kissed his Pa on his forehead and dried his eyes. Next to his bed on a little table, he recognized the old worn cherry wood pipe. Picking up the pipe and smelling the bowl, he remembered the many times as a boy he sat on his Pa's lap to have bedtime stories read to him while his Pa smoked the pipe. He noticed the worn inscription etched on the bottom: 'Man of the House' and wondered who had etched it there. Finally, he sat down in the chair next to the bed and read the letter while holding the pipe with its familiar scent.

Present in Absentia

The old farm once active with livestock and crops had been mostly unattended for the last ten years. There was an outhouse, and electricity wouldn't be brought down the dirt road for a few more years. After having labored for decades on the property, the rusting red tractor now sat idle with an old tin can over its exhaust pipe and tall weeds around it. The barn had long been vacant of the large herd of cows it used to hold and the trucks that had come for the cows had no more business there. Only a few things were still in use: some chickens in the old coop, the flower garden at the back of the house, a clothesline, and the rope-swing with a board made to seat two. White birdhouses built on metal poles were scattered around the yard that always seemed to need mowing. The empty silo that stood within the barbed-wire fence around an overgrown pasture had begun to lean.

With each group of cows they had sold, and each hired hand they let go, the couple's world slowly contracted from the one-hundred-acre cattle farm to a small circle around the modest old house. The only things just outside of that small circle were the two gravestones just beyond the backyard under a solitary tree, waiting to welcome the future residents: James Mitchell and Ethel Mitchell.

The main room of the farmhouse was the largest and covered with old wallpaper. The fireplace, with soot-blackened stones at the top, sat in the middle of the outside wall on the right. Two matching wooden rocking chairs with the finish on the arms worn off were positioned on either side of the phonograph, sitting against the wall. A hutch with windows displaying 'the good dishes' for special meals, sat next to the kitchen at the far end. Old pictures and a few potted plants had kept their places for years, being occasionally lifted for weekly watering or dusting. The single bedroom consisted of a metal framed, quilt-covered bed, matching nightstands, and two oak dressers. Oil lanterns had their places throughout the house, waiting for dusk to give them purpose. The kitchen was in the front, and although closest to the dirt road, had no entrance to the outside. It was separated from the other rooms by a large arched entrance in the center of the wall. Inside the kitchen sat a black woodstove trimmed with white porcelain knobs, close to the small cloth-covered wooden table with four chairs where the couple ate their meals. A hand pump on the countertop provided water for cooking and their weekly baths in the blanket-covered claw-foot bathtub against the wall.

The happy old childless couple; James and Ethel Mitchell had lived here since they were married. They loved their farm and the life they shared. Always in love, they had remained best friends.

When two people have been in love for that many years, it becomes more than a feeling or familiarity. There is a merging of souls toward the formation of one. Each person remains distinctly different while being a large part of the other.

Moving slower in those latter days of their lives, they held hands as they sat together on the large tree-swing in the afternoon drinking iced tea. A long time ago the young husband had carved their initials on the trees surrounded by a heart, but the bark of the growing tree has scabbed over most of the letters. Traditionally, because of his long legs, it was Mr. Mitchell's job to keep the swing gently swaying. The small dog laid in the shade of the tree, and the cat's attention was grabbed by every bird that flew by. The gentle, quiet creaking of the rope swing provided them hypnotic permission to return to the past.

Ethel took a deep, gentle breath. "I love this old place. And I love having spent all these years with you, James."

"You made it a happy home. I love you for that and many other reasons. You know, I can barely remember when we built the house."

"You were twenty, and I was eighteen." Ethel paused. "I wonder how our lives would have been if we were able to have children."

"Me too. But it wasn't our choice. It was fun trying, however."

James turned his face away to hide his smirk as he waited for the response he knew was coming. Ethel playfully slapped her husband's leg.

"James Mitchell!"

James kissed the side of his wife's gray head. They both laughed.

In front of the fireplace, the happy couple often slowly danced to the music from the old phonograph. His right hand was on her lower back, and his left hand held her right hand. She looked up smiling at him and said, "I love you, James Mitchell."

"We should get married and spend our lives together," he replied with a wink.

"Are you proposing to me?" she asked, acting surprised.

"Yes, Ethel. Will you marry me?"

"Yes, I will."

James continued, "Will you stay with me even when we get old and gray?"

"There are already well over fifty years between, 'I do' and 'I have.'"

One afternoon from inside the house, standing at the large window facing the backyard, James watched his wife outside kneeling in the garden, planting flowers. He gently tapped the window. Ethel lifted her head to look at her husband from under the broad rim of her sunbonnet and smiled. James kissed the window, leaving a print. Ethel blew a kiss back. James winked at her.

It was early morning and still dark. Ethel woke with her husband's arm around her as her head rested on his chest. She became aware that his heart that had lulled her to sleep for decades wasn't beating. Or maybe she woke because his rhythmic breathing that had soothed her over the length of their marriage had stopped. Instantly, she was overwhelmed by his death. After kissing him on his lips, she laid her gray head back on his chest as the tears rolled down over her wrinkled cheek onto his pajama top. Her heart was broken, but she reached over to hold her husband's cool hand until the morning light came; still expecting him to speak or move while hoping that she would die too. She believed dying together would be the perfect end to a long life with her husband. For the rest of her life, she'll expect to hear her husband say something, walk into the house, flirt, or push the swing.

The neighbors, George and Harriet, regularly drove their Model T the half-mile trip to the Mitchell farm to check on their friends and have coffee or iced tea. That morning was one of those times. Ethel stood in her nightgown leaning against the outside door-jam as the car pulled into the dirt driveway around to the back of the farmhouse. The car stopped. Harriet got out holding a small basket.

"Good morning Ethel! I brought some fresh blueberry... Is there something wrong?"

"It's James. He's gone. My James is dead," she replied softly and trance-like.

George and Harriet hurried over to Ethel.

"Oh, my Lord," Harriet exclaimed.

"May we come in?"

"Of course, George."

The three of them stepped into the house. Ethel led them inside but stopped in front of the only bedroom on the left. James' body laid peacefully on the bed. His white hair was wet and freshly combed.

Harriet put her arm around her newly widowed friend and said, "Come on Ethel. I'll make you some tea."

In the kitchen, Harriet went to the hand pump near the sink and pumped water into the teapot then lit a burner on the stove with a wooden match. Ethel sat numbly at the small table next to the wood stove.

"Ethel, I'll go into town and take care of things for James."

"Thank you, George," she replied, looking up at him with sad red eyes before he walked out and got into his car.

"Harriet, I want to go back to James."

"Of course, dear."

The two ladies went to the bedroom and stood at the side of the bed holding tissues under their noses.

"What am I going to do now?" Ethel sobbed. "He was my whole life."

"I know he was. He was a good and loving man and a dear friend of ours. We know you're thankful to have had all those wonderful years with him."

"I'll never get used to being without him," Ethel said, as she carefully brushed the back of her fingers over his cheek. "Never."

Harriet paused. "Give it some time. You'll never get over a death of someone you loved, but you can learn to live with it if you try. If you don't mind, I'll go check on the kettle."

"Thank you. I'll wait here with James," she replied without looking away from her husband's ashen face. Harriet left Ethel alone with her husband's body. Ethel placed her cheek against her husband's cheek and whispered in his ear, "James come back. Please come back to me. Or, take me with you." She burst into sobbing and placed her head on his chest. "Don't you leave me all alone, James Mitchell."

In the late afternoon, through the bedroom window, Ethel and Harriet watched George pull into the driveway, followed by a black hearse. The Undertaker and his assistant got out of the hearse, walked around to the back doors, and took out a stretcher. Holding hands, Ethel and Harriet came out of the house.

The assistant tipped his hat to Ethel. "Ma'am."

The Undertaker said, "We're sorry for your loss, Mrs. Mitchell." Ethel replied with a gentle nod.

"Ethel, let me take them in. You ladies can wait out here," George said. Ethel nodded again.

"Follow me, gentlemen." George led the way into the house as the two men brought the stretcher behind him.

Minutes later, George came out the door followed by the two men carrying James' body on the stretcher. They stopped momentarily in front of Ethel and Harriet.

The Undertaker gently said, "Again, we are very sorry, Mrs. Mitchell. We'll take good care of him."

Ethel walked alongside the stretcher as the men carried it to the hearse; fussing over her husband's pajamas and hair all the way. She adjusted his pajama collar and steadied his head with one hand while holding his hand with her other hand. The stretcher stopped at the back of the waiting hearse. Ethel stared at the opened doors which looked like a mouth to her, and the floor like a flat tongue that they were going to place her husband on.

"Mrs. Mitchell please, you'll have to let go of his hand," the Undertaker said with compassion.

Confused by the remark, Ethel looked down to realize that she was tightly gripping her husband's hand. Shaking her head, she insisted, "No... I can't. I don't want to! Don't ask me to let him go. I'll go with him. It's my time too! Please take me!"

Harriet gingerly said, "Dear, it's not your time. You really must release his hand. He has to go now. They'll bring him back for the funeral."

She placed her hand on Ethel's. The new widow slowly slid her shaking hand back and erupted in sorrow. As Harriet put her arm around her shoulder, Ethel collapsed in Harriet's arms, crying. Standing together in the dirt driveway, the three of them watched the back doors close before the hearse turned around in the driveway and pulled around the front to fade into the dusty country road.

"Ethel, what can we do now? How can we help?" George asked.

Harriet added, "We've been your neighbors for years, and we're just a half mile away. How about I spend the night with you?"

"Thank you, but no. I'll be fine. I would like to be alone."

"Okay, but we'll check on you in the morning," her friends assured her.

Harriet hugged her before she and George got in their car, drove around to the front of the house, and headed home.

Stepping back over the threshold into the house, Ethel, still drying her tears, paused to study the room. Memories crowded her mind; holidays, special dinners, and her husband building the house as a strong young man so many years ago. Standing there feeling very alone, she wiped the tears streaming down her face and felt afraid to take the first step into the large emptiness waiting like a thick fog to engulf her. Her eyes stopped at the photograph of their wedding picture on the fireplace mantle.

"James, I'm not sorry for one moment since that day." She looked at the matching rocking chairs. "I miss you. I miss you, my love. Why aren't you still sitting in your chair?"

The next morning, Ethel, George, and Harriet had tea at Ethel's kitchen table. Harriet asked, "Ethel dear, did you get any sleep last night?"

"Not a wink. I laid there without my good-night kiss. I caught myself reaching over to touch him. Finally, I leaned our wedding picture against his pillow. It helped a little."

"I hate to bring this up," George said with care, "but the funeral is in two days. Is there anything we can do for you?"

"Just be there for me."

Harriet replied, "We will. With all our love, as usual."

That night it rained. In the light from an oil lamp, Ethel noticed the print of her husband's kiss still on the window. Remembering that day and James standing in the very spot, for the first time since his death, she smiled. A surprising giggle even managed to squeeze past the sobs.

"Kiss me my darling like you always do," she whispered, tilting her head up, closing her eyes, and pursing her lips.

On the morning of the funeral, the hearse pulled into the driveway and parked in the back of the farmhouse. By the time Ethel, George, and Harriet came out of the house, the polished wooden casket was out of the hearse, and sat on metal stands behind the open backdoors. The assistant stood silently with respect.

"Hello, everyone," the Undertaker said. "Mrs. Mitchell, I was wondering if you might want to see your husband before the funeral service."

Ethel looked at him with confusion. "How? Where is he?"

Harriet nodded toward the casket. "Darling, he's right there. You should look. It will help."

"He's got a nice suit on. He looks very handsome," George said. "Go ahead and open it, fellas."

The two men lifted the lid and held it open. Harriet gently nudged her friend, "Go ahead and step up to it, Ethel darling."

Harriet put her arm around Ethel and walked her over to the casket. Ethel's eyes dropped down into the casket.

"That's not my James! This man is dead! George, make them close it!" Harriet and George glanced at each other.

"Go ahead and close it, fellas," George instructed.

A few chairs were set up in the recently mowed grass under the solitary tree. The minister gave his thoughts, quoted his Bible verses, and prayed his prayers before the small group dispersed, after dropping their flowers down on the casket. After the 'Amen,' the undertakers collected the chairs and carried them back to the hearse. They returned with shovels and began to fill dirt into the hole as the minister shook hands with the mourners. Ethel stood and watched the casket being covered with dirt until the minister went over to speak briefly with her. Finally, George and Harriet escorted her away from the grave and back to the house.

Ethel had looked at her husband for almost sixty years and couldn't help but visualize him everywhere around the farm. Carrying their wedding picture around the house, she placed it down almost everywhere she stopped and wondered if he really was gone because it felt to her like he wasn't. Their picture laid on the swing next to her as she sat with her sweet tea and rested it on his pillow at night. For days, the dog looked at her with compassion, offering little whimpers, seeming to also feel the loss.

One late morning, the new widow opened a window for fresh air which allowed a waiting breeze into the room that gently pushed the curtains aside and very gently rocked the closest rocking chair – her husband's. Ethel was both alarmed and hopeful that James might be sitting there again. The breeze subsided but was followed by a stronger one that stirred the smoldering ashes in the fireplace so that the coals glowed red before small flames arose. Her eyes darted back and forth from the rocking chair to the fireplace.

"James is that you? Say something, my love… Show me something."

Two nights later, the dog sleeping on the rug in the living room quickly came to attention and ran to the kitchen, excitedly wagging its tail.

"Darling?" Ethel called out while staring into the dark kitchen. She sat up in her chair looking and listening in vain for her husband's voice to reply.

One afternoon, the cat lying on the rug in front of the fireplace cleaning her fur, suddenly stared over into the bedroom, ran, and jumped up on the husband's side of the bed with her tail straight up, and began to look around, purring. Mrs. Mitchell stared from her rocking chair before she stood and walked into the bedroom wondering if her cat could also sense her husband lying there.

"Where is he Tabby? Do you see him? James, sweetheart, are you here?"

On a quiet afternoon, a bird flew through the open window and landed on the bedpost on her husband's side and looked at Ethel while she made the bed. It then flew over to the fireplace mantle next to the picture of James and chirped before flying back out the window.

"Yes, I know. I do know," Ethel said. "Thank you."

Convinced more than ever that her husband was still in the house, in the evenings Ethel cranked up the phonograph and danced with the memory of her husband. She was certain she could feel his right hand on her lower back, and his hand in hers before she slowly began to waltz.

"This has always been our favorite song, hasn't it, James?" She looked up. "I love when you wink at me."

Each time her neighbors visited, Ethel, excitedly told them 'about any new, what she called 'signs.' She was convinced that these occurrences proved her husband was still there. Also, she informed them that she often talked to him throughout the day. George and Harriet tried to dismiss the events as coincidences.

"But have you actually seen him?" George asked.

"No. But I know James is still here. Tabby and Sport see him!" she exclaimed, smiling. "Can either of you feel him right now? You can, can't you?" She looked at them expectantly, nodding her head.

"We're sorry Ethel, but we can't. James has passed you know," Harriet replied.

"And just what does having passed mean? Passed doesn't have to mean that loved ones have altogether left us!"

"Do you ever actually hear his voice?" George inquired, blandly.

"Yes," she answered, with a confident tone. "My husband speaks to me in my head, and sometimes I think he whispers to me."

"Our dear Ethel," Harriet said, "you simply must see a doctor."

"No thank you." Ethel suddenly retracted her excitement. "I appreciate you coming over and checking on me, but we would like to be alone now."

George noticed the word 'we' and wanted to believe that she was referring to herself and the pets.

"Good night then, Ethel. We'll be back in a day or two," Harriet said, as she and George stood and left.

Naturally, George and Harriet were very gentle with her. They understood that she was in a lot of pain and said everything they could to ease her into reality but were careful to try not to contradict her. Privately, her loving neighbors understood that Ethel didn't want to let go, but they just wouldn't be convinced that her husband was still there. They were very sad for her; a new widow who didn't seem to accept her husband was dead. Further, George and Harriet feared Ethel had become delusional in her grief. They believed that her anxious imagination was protecting her failing mind, but they hoped that she would gradually accept the truth and try to move on the best she could.

Ethel guarded her belief over the next couple of weeks with so much passion and conviction that her neighbors visited her less often. They found it increasingly difficult to talk to her about anything else because she was obsessed with what she believed was her dead husband's presence. Finally, in desperation, Harriet pleaded again with her to see a doctor.

"Our dear Ethel you simply must see a doctor. He will give you something to calm you and help you to understand and accept what really has happened."

"And that is, your husband and our beloved friend, has died. Now please! We'll take you," George insisted.

"No. You must understand that he's still here! He hasn't gone anywhere! He just left his body that's all." Ethel shook her head, smiling.

The two visitors stood to leave. George pleaded with her, "Think about our offer Ethel. We'll take you to see the doctor the day after tomorrow. We'll see you then. Good-bye."

George took his hat from the table. Harriet kissed the top of Ethel's head as she walked by.

That night, as usual, Ethel laid in bed holding the wedding picture on her chest and smiling. Tears ran down her temples. Her eyes closed and her face relaxed. The gentle grip she held on the picture frame loosened.

The dog and cat stayed at her side for the next two days until her body was discovered by George and Harriet on a still morning. They knocked on the door, but Ethel didn't answer.

"Ethel? Ethel, dear?" Harriet gently called out from the open door.

George and Harriet took a few careful steps inside and looked in the bedroom, then at each other.

"Ethel, are you awake?" Harriet asked. The loving neighbors entered the bedroom and stood next to the bed. Ethel's ashen face confirmed that she too had passed. Harriet removed a tissue from her purse and cried, "Oh, dear God."

The same two Undertakers that took her husband arrived to take Ethel's old body away. "We're very sorry for the loss of your friends. We'll take good care of her," the Undertaker assured them.

The assistant added, "Someone will contact you about the arrangements."

George silently nodded.

After the Undertakers carefully placed her body on the stretcher and into the hearse, they drove out of the driveway and back down the dusty road.

The same small group of mourners attended the funeral service under the solitary tree. They too, left flowers on the newest casket before they slowly walked back through the grass to their cars. The Undertaker and his assistant carried the chairs back to the hearse and returned to the freshest grave with shovels. The dash after Ethel's birth date patiently waited for the stone carver to complete the span of her life, just as James' dash had.

After the last car left the driveway, George said, "Harriet, let's go back inside and take care of things. We don't know how long the house will be vacant."

Once inside the Mitchell's house, George and Harriet watered the plants, closed the windows, and disposed of perishable foods. While preparing to take the dog and cat to their own home, they wondered whom to contact.

Harriet stood at the back window facing the garden ready to close the curtains where she noticed the print of a kiss on the window facing the garden in the backyard.

"Oh, how sweet! George, come and look at this."

George walked over from the kitchen. "What is it?"

"Look here," Harriet replied. "It looks as if James had kissed the window. Ethel must have been outside. How darling."

As they looked at the kiss-print, a smaller kiss-print slowly overlapped it. The swing in the backyard began to move drawing attention to the breeze-less day. George and Harriet looked at each other wide-eyed. Harriet snapped the curtains together. They both quickly left with the pets, never saying a word to the Undertakers who were placing their shovels in the back of the hearse.

The neighbors would never speak of what they saw, even among themselves, and never enter the Mitchell farmhouse again; always staying comfortably outside to check on things until they no longer could.

A few years have passed. The old Mitchel farmhouse still sits back off the road; unvisited and largely unnoticed within the tall grass and the wild crowding bushes. The windows are boarded up. Far in the back, two completed headstones peak just above the tall grass around the solitary tree.

Inside the farmhouse, dim light from the setting sun squeezes through the narrow spaces between the boards on the window, barely illuminating the front room. A slice of light temporarily rests on the framed photograph of the Mitchell's on their wedding day, sitting on the mantle. The phonograph plays their favorite song as twenty-year-old James places his right hand on eighteen-year-old Ethel's lower back. He softly takes her other hand. The newlyweds slowly dance. Ethel looks up at James and smiles. James looks down at his young wife, smiles, and winks.

The Face Behind Me

Within wars are battles. Within battles, a man fights. Within the fight is his heart. As the soldier's heart goes, so goes his fight, so goes his battle, so goes his war.

My enemy came from behind me on the crowded battlefield, struck me to the ground, and took me, prisoner. As I laid face down in the dirt, wounded and tired, my enemy placed the tip of his sword against the back of my neck and said with scorn, *"It is easier to conquer defeated men than to slay the dead."*

This enemy made me stand to my feet and stayed behind me with the tip of his sword pressed against my back, all the while and promising that if I ever turned around, I would die. Then he drove my soul to a muddy road which separated into many paths and pushed me on through fog and frequent rain never allowing me to see his face. I felt I was all but dead.

We trudged along to an unknown end down the muddy path where gloomy days and murky nights blended together. The passing of one could scarcely be determined from the beginning of the other. The sun had turned its face away, and the birds had taken their songs to another land. Dark thoughts and gloom resided in the deep folds of my mind, nesting depression, and despair. On this path, the clouds seemed unnaturally thick, dark, and low. The air which I breathed was rich with gloom and filled with dense anguish.

Eventually, we came upon a town that had a familiar feel, and I was certain that I had been there before. My enemy stopped me. It seemed at first, there was nothing to be seen, but I searched the mist until I saw a group of men who had just finished digging a deep hole, then another group of men came behind them and began to fill it back in. The first group of men dug and then the second filled, and the endless process continued around the large circle.

My adversary said, *"These are men without hope of gain trying hard to earn a good wage but gaining just under enough to sustain their families. Note the deeply worn ruts in the ground which connects their hard labor to their humble homes. They live to work and not work to live."*

"Yet they live and work with honor and pride," I replied. "And they are free."

"Are they indeed? Of course, they have free will but is anyone truly free? Children must do what is expected of them. Adults must do what is required of them. Old people can only do what they can. People are free to obey and free to travel just to the edge of their near limitations. They

are free to use the little wisdom we have acquired free to understand with our limited perspective, free to choose without the knowing the future, free to guess without the ability to look into the hearts and minds of others, and free to maneuver through life's unexpected changes. Yes, we are free; free to think to believe and decide within the small space of our minds. Both Men and ox toil in yokes; the ox by nature and man by curse. A life of labor is the essence of their worth. The very ground we walk on is cursed. Man must toil all of his days to sustain his earthly needs at the expense of having the time to lie in the grass at night and search the eternal heavens or to quietly sit at the edge of a vast ocean and completely lose himself as the waves move up and back to cleanse his thoughts. These times allow the soul to grow, but there is often little occasion or thought to answer the part of him that desires to explore, create, dream, and imagine because labor and thoughts of labor consume him. Mostly we are free to do what we have to do at the expense of what we want to do. We all are whores. Whores know they are not loved by their customers, but they give them what they want and get what they can. One day, we will all be old whores; used up and unwanted, sitting alone in silence with no one to hear us cry."

I pitied the men in this yoke and sympathized with them; knowing myself the nagging pain of quickly passing years in redundant and fruitless labor which denies the inherent wonder and joy of being fully alive. They worked to buy shovels to work to buy shovels.

The long line of these old men with heavy eyes and muddy shovels walked slowly to the next hole, making it feel like a funeral procession wherein life itself had passed away. And like pallbearers, the laborers bore the weight of the death of life upon their hearts. A low painful monastic groan began to build and with it came a high eerie and unnatural wail of suffering and mourning swaying above the moan like a long weed at the bottom of a troubled sea. I could not determine the source of the sorrowful cry, but it seemed to come from their very souls through unparted lips. The moan and the cry receded and settled at times for the men to speak the verses without measure or rhyme.

The first man said, "Yesterday was a moment ago and tomorrow eagerly waits in the dawn to pounce upon it then will quickly drag it into the night."

In unison, the other men returned, "The night has pulled another day away."

As they slowly arrived at the hole, they looked down into it and considered the meaningless task as each man pushed the end of his shovel into the dirt piled around it.

The low groan swelled again, and the sorrowful wail pushed its way up through and slowly fell back onto itself to near silence for another man to speak the next verse. "Family members and good friends will be taken one by one."

The other men responded as they dumped their dirt into the hole, "We just watch them go. Taken one by one."

The groan increased, and the mournful wail rose above it again, then became quieter for the next verse as another laborer called out, "The bright flame in the heart grows dimmer with each passing year as does the spark of life in the eye."

The men agreed together, "The flame's a grow'in dimmer and dimmer."

The groan lifted itself to its level then the mournful cry from their souls slowly erupted then faded.

The next man spoke, "Life will slowly reclaim your youth your strength and your health."

The other men replied together, "It's coming. It's coming to take them like sand being pulled back into the sea."

The moan got loud again, and the weeping wail rose above it then fell. One of the men turned his sullen face to look at me.

"Build your dreams while you are young and live with vigor while your eyes are bright and full of visions. Your early life is but a loan and time will have it repaid."

All of the men turned to look at me, and echoed several times, "Time will have it repaid."

Again, the painful moan swelled, and the wail of the mourning souls grew out of it until they reached their next hole and began to dig.

An old gray-haired man with a limp whose back was bent forward from years of labor stiffly walked over to me and said, "On a sunny spring day when I was young, I sat down in the shaded green grass under a tree and excitedly began to plan my life. When I lifted my eyes, I was old, and the sky was cold, angry, and gray. The tree was bare. And I had used my days."

He turned, put his shovel over his shoulder, and limped back to the hole as a different man shouted at me, "Do not believe that you possess that which you hold so tightly!"

My enemy pushed me on saying, *"Can't you see?! That's the deal!*

All that lives must shake the hand of time and make an accord. We are loaned the best of life first. Then as we grow old life begins to call back what we have found, built and gained; yea what we love and value. It sincerely is a cruel arrangement. We are born with nothing and die with even less. To never have had is better than to have it all taken, so to never have been born is better than to have lived."

He spoke nothing more, and we trudged on through the rain. For a moment, the distant thunder kindly drew me away and reminded me that there is perhaps something out there more than my world of captivity.

We walked through the darkness until our grimy path hurriedly changed to a clean red brick road. The clouds pulled themselves away like the curtains of a window, allowing the sun to shine warm and bright. My eyes quickly turned away not being used to the brightness until I was able to see the fancy sign reading, 'The Settlement of Prosperity.'

As I staggered, my muddy and tattered clothes insulted me, and I wanted to hide in embarrassment, but my enemy pushed me slowly forward through this ornate and fruitful place serving only to contrast my infertile life.

"*Stop and look!*" My foe demanded, extending his pointed finger over my shoulder.

Large beautiful estates sat proudly in immaculate settings stretching out on smooth, green sloping hilltops, the likes of which I have not seen nor shall ever have. Marble fountains, colorfully flowered pathways, and luscious gardens were kept secure by fancy iron fences and tall majestic gates. Everywhere there were lawn parties with nicely dressed guests sending polite carefree laughter in the air while being well attended by handsomely dressed servants carrying glistening silver trays of delicate cups, sparkling silverware, crystal glasses, and fine foods; offering them to each guest who had the given right to ignore the servants. Women in beautiful dresses waited until the sun touched their diamonds that they pretended not to be wearing until, by obligation, another woman pointed out the sparkling jewelry making sure to spend sufficient time adoring and complimenting while expecting to have the compliments returned because proper decorum insisted on it. The men had formed themselves in small groups smoking expensive cigars talking about hunting trips to Africa and investments while their egos vied for the next place in the conversation yet some yielded, recognizing their lesser social status.

"*Look at them!*" My enemy hissed over my shoulder. "*They are men of your age and younger. Most of them were born into money. The constant breeze that pushes their full sails through the smooth sea is family money. Their children will marry one another's children. These wealthy families pass their wealth to the next generation; money and land along with every advantage and any luxury that catches their eye! Are not kings made this way by just by being born into the lineage by no merit of their own? All babies are born through the loins of their mother; the children of the poor are wrapped in thin rags but the offspring of the rich in smooth velvet and silk."*

I felt indignation and heard judgment in my voice as I glared with disdain at them. "A title makes none worthy, a weapon makes not a true ruler, and a bloodline makes none noble."

"So true. Yet each one stands there in haughty pride sincerely believing that they made something of themselves and achieved great things."

"But they have not!" I snapped back in protest. "No one is born great, or all are. Without a doubt, they have great things, but there is among them a drought of doing great things. They waste and laugh while the poor cry in their lack and the rich fill themselves while others suffer."

"And you have done great things, my captive?"

"Yes, I have," I slowly replied. But the memories and the feeling have faded in my mind and in the minds of those who benefited." I heard my voice become slow and distant. "I was once like a green leaf that lived happily and high in the tree, enjoying the warm sun. But a cold season of sorrow came, and I wilted and fell to lie brown, dry, and spent on the dark forest floor… A time I determined not to remember yet I speak of it now because of you."

"And really you have achieved nothing great since…so many wasted years." My adversary's voice taunted me with the subtly of a serpent as he leaned forward to whisper in my ear. *"Those wealthy people pretend not to see you. It's apparent that you were no favorite child of good fortune. You were not born with this perfect arrangement, this great advantage, were you? Truthfully you were born far from it. Prosperity is generous with bestowing choices of comforts and pleasures but you, poor man, did not have many of each, did you?"*

"The place I was put in life remains a bitter taste in my mouth and sits in my belly like spoiled meat. My best end would be to die in some heroic way. Since my residency is shameful, let my eviction be memorable. Perhaps the last thought of me will be good, standing above all the bad. Why am I imprisoned in mediocrity? Where is the greatness in my life? Where is the power to rule in righteousness, justice, and love? Where is my prosperity that I may share with the poor? I would deliver the poor and judge the evil man, yet I stand here poor. If we are truly greater than the sparrow, why am I not free as one nor fly to wherever I choose. Hers is a life of adventure. How am I greater? My life is a poor existence. I am embarrassed and wish to keep it a secret from the sparrow lest it mocks me or offers some well-meaning but impotent encouragement. When the soul of a sparrow is placed into the bosom of an ox that ox resists the yoke and pulls the plow in a wandering line. Life whips the beast of burden for looking out to the forest colors and up to the passing clouds as he longs to fly. My life is below my dignity and unworthy of me. Who thought to place me here? Who matched my great soul with human life? I will throw it off, turn, and curse it as the droppings of a bird upon my head. Silent glory veiled by soiled garments and labor. Hidden royalty as the gem lying under the ground never to be awed. I reject this meager cursed existence. Who thought it best to place me here and give me this form of life?!"

I wondered what kind of man this was, my enemy. Certainly, he was devoid of compassion, and it seemed with the single mindset to secure my demise.

"How do you know so much about me?"

"*I am your enemy,*" he replied. "*Believe me when I say I know everything about you.*"

He nudged me forward as the muddy path appeared again and the dark clouds eagerly came together to cover the sun. A heavy fog closed in.

"*Tell me some lyrics, my captive. Entertain me with some thoughts from your troubled mind.*"

I reached into my memories and recalled a writing that I had penned in a time of darkness; a complaint told to no one.

"The whole kingdom waited for their prince to be born, but in an ill womb, he died. Taken from his mother and forgotten by his father after he was quietly buried in the night without ceremony or mourners. This prince was stillborn, an arrow never shot. His passing steed shall never hush a silent crowd with heads bowed. Let his sword never to be drawn in battle lay at his side in his hidden grave then place in his arms a scepter never to be raised. He shall also keep his jeweled crown there in his dark crypt among the good and righteous decrees he never had occasion to proclaim. Give his royal ring to his mother that she may bind it around her neck to lie against lonely breasts."

"*You speak of yourself. You believe you are that prince.*"

I am uncertain how he entered the depths of my soul to know this.

"Yes," I answered. "Providence in a moment of confusion mislaid me in a poor man's life, denying me of the means to relieve suffering. Although the fault is not my own, life suffers no protests nor admits to its mistakes. It is a tragedy when the lives of those who are called to do great things are carelessly placed in front of the blind eye of destiny."

My enemy laughed and asked, "*Ah high-minded fool, what right do you have to even consider such fantasy especially now as you draw near to your end?*"

"None, I suppose… none at all. In my life, I seem smaller than I am. At my death, I'll be greater than I was."

He prodded me along with the tip of his sword until we came upon the peaceful Kingdom of the Shepherd where joyful and content people sat at His feet on lush green grass, next to a beautiful calm lake, as He talked with them with loving smiles. My heart leaped! Often in my mind, I had seated myself among these blessed citizens whose souls have been restored and labored to keep the vision fresh in my bosom. I too longed to have my soul restored and healed!

My enemy pointed to the white skin on my arm where leprosy had planted itself. "*You are a leper so you must shout it!*" he ordered. "*It is written in the law.*"

Loudly, I said, "Leper."

"*Louder!*" he ordered. "*You cannot go near them, and they will not come near you!*"

"I am a leper!" I shouted, then cried with deep sobbing with my face buried in my hands. I was forced to stay away. The Shepherd turned to look at me, but His smile quickly faded. His children silently stood without expressions to watch me walk by. I ached for another smile, a single word, or even an invitation to return. My head twisted around to its extent, quietly pleading to catch a private wink or subtle nod from the Shepherd who would refresh my soul like a cool spring in a desert, but He granted me nothing. As I turned to flee to Him, my foe struck me violently so that I cried out in pain, and he forced me to keep walking down the sloppy, muddy path as the children began to sing. I listened until the sweet and joyful melody faded into silence. For a moment, I saw my reflection in a pool of water and remembered who I was. My enemy kicked a rock into the pool, and my image was disfigured.

He leaned forward to place his face on my shoulder and whispered into my ear, "*It must be that your sins are too abhorrent even for Him to bear.*"

For the first time, I found a weakness in his indictments. "No. You are a liar," I replied with a confidence that surprised even me. "Of this I am sure; there are no sins however vile and deeply stained within the darkest heart that He cannot forgive."

"*So, then you are left with just one simple conclusion; you have broken His heart too often, so He no longer prefers your company. Well, of course, He is compelled to forgive you because you are among His creation and His love has been cast over all, but you are an unnoticed spec among them. And although He may not have rejected you as a sinner it seems clear that He has not accepted you as a child, does it not? Or else you would be blessed as a father blesses his son, yet you barely exist on the crumbs under His table.*"

"There is much that I cannot answer, yet I do know that I am under His table and live from His hand. Therefore, it would seem that I am in His household; perhaps as a son or perhaps as a servant, but as either, I am blessed."

"*Are you indeed? I shall speak more directly. It would appear to any honest onlooker that He has little interest in you or that you have much value to Him. One might think of you as an orphan. Or, perhaps you are a child of God but a difficult one to be seen or heard among the vast flock, therefore unnoticed and forgotten by the Shepherd. All other heads raised above yours, and all other voices louder and sweeter. You must admit, even as a lamb you are not comely.*"

"Perhaps not. Perhaps all that you say has some truth. Yet I am somewhere in His flock and comforted by it, and the Shepherd knows each name."

Before I was taken captive, I had often been tormented with these thoughts within myself and sorrow flowed from deep within my heart and overflowed to my mind. I was broken and felt a great weight of rejection. My innermost parts were wounded such that I truly believed that I would never recover except if the Shepherd Himself should leave His flock and pursue me in the night as if I were a lamb who strayed into the dangerous forest, like the one I found myself in. But He did not leave

His flock or call out my name or follow after me.

The voice behind me did not relent. "*I look at the likes of you and ask, 'Where is the honor and glory of the sons of God? His weak and carnal children are a hideous reflection of Him. What is there to be praised about the nature of those like you who so easily succumb to the baser desires? He has lifted you up high yet you have settled back down to pursue by choice what the lesser creatures are governed to do by instinct. Even with humankind's higher intelligence, they succumb to their primitive ways which if whittled down are not unlike those of our fellow inhabitants the animals. Man's bend toward violence, dominance, survival, and mating, though painted with sophistication, polished with learning, adorned with their reasoning, and attired with justification, still controls them and will ultimately be their demise. The animal is true to its nature, but humanity likes to believe himself to be better. So then are people not then below the animal and farther from virtues? Where in you is the magnificence of which the angels sang at humanity's creation?! Shouldn't there be even a small trait of He who breathed His own breath into you? And why do not your eyes still brighten when you reminiscence of the morning walks in the garden? The fragrance of myrrh has long ago faded from your neck. Yes, you know the answers to these questions and what I speak is true. Perhaps these are the reasons the world is mostly ignored and unattended by the divine and more likely altogether forgotten. There is really and truly nothing for you here except glances of pity to a poor stranger passing by. So, march on.*"

The pain of each accusation and question pierced me deeply. "You have given me much to consider. I shall deeply think on these things."

The quivering in my voice betrayed my failed attempt to hold back a new wind of sorrow, and my mind was imprisoned... until I whispered to myself, 'I saw the Shepherd, and He saw me.'

My enemy exclaimed with delight, "*You have little time to meditate on anything, and the time it will take to find the answers to your questions would exceed a hundred full lifetimes. It is simply too late to find your answers; too late for anything. Twilight is settling upon you.*"

I thought within myself how it made me happy that for even a moment the Shepherd smiled at me, mistaking me for someone He knew; someone He favored. So, for my remaining time upon this earth I will remember that the Shepherd once smiled at me; however briefly, however, misplaced... but He said nothing. I mumbled to myself, "God speaks, or men die."

My enemy heard me and said, *"Unbelievers say there is no God. Believers disagree, and some of them defend the existence of God as if they were the very ones to secure God in his place. In both claims, there is no God. The jury no longer cares to hear the arguments and God chooses not to take the stand. Will he not show himself? You have decided that religion will do when God is absent. So, perfect your doctrine and music. Organize your faith intellectually, study foreign words, and polish the pews. Study the ology when the theo is not present."*

In this, my enemy became my mentor, and his questions became my prayers.

As far as the thick mist allowed, I saw another captive wearing a silver helmet of peculiar shape trudging along another path and driven forward by his own enemy behind him. The captive was a stranger to me as we had never met, but it felt like he was a brother as he had found himself on the same kind of dreadful path as I.

He looked in my direction, so I opened my mouth and filled my chest with breath to call out to him, but paused, for no salutation or words of encouragement came from my mind although I desired to give him both for pity's sake. What words are fitting for a defeated man on his way to die with no remedy to rescue him? Shall I encourage him to continue on to further torment and embrace a futile hope, or shall I urge him to stop and embrace courage without a chance to prevail? My heart yearned to free him, but the blade at my back reminded me of my own state of hopelessness while I mysteriously had the will to continue walking. There were no means I possessed to free him for I myself was not free. He disappeared behind the trees and into the fog, stumbling and splashing along with his enemy holding a sword to his back while speaking to him words broken by the trees and muffled by the distance; words I was sure, to weaken him and words to break him.

"I notice that there are no other footprints along the path I walk. Has no other man walked on this path?" I asked.

"You are yet a man of little understanding. How should any other captive walk on this path? This is your personal path and yours alone. And that man you saw walks his own path. Every defeated man and woman walk in private pain on their own path to haunted and familiar places they have created. And every one of them has an enemy to escort them. So, you see, only the free can walk on a path with his captive."

"So, these places are not real?"

"Oh, you can be sure that they are very real. They are real to you are they not? You remember them."

We walked on until we saw three figures sitting together and talking at a small wooden table; a woman soon to give birth and two old men. My enemy seemed both curious and surprised at this, ordered me to stop. We listened unnoticed as the three figures talked.

The young woman asked for advice and insight for the unborn baby she carried. "Gentlemen you have lived many years. Your wisdom is beyond my own, and your eyes have seen a greater part of life. It is as if you have brought up gems from the deep having slowly quarried them over the years; the gems of wisdom, knowledge, and perspective. I beg you to share what you can with my unborn child."

The first old man began quickly, with a deep frown that looked as if he ever bore it, "Little child where you are is safe and warm. Remain there if you can never to feel the coldness of a fire-less stove or see the face of one filled with anger. Do not chance the pain of an empty stomach."

The second old man smiled and said, "Nay, but come forth and feel the warmth. When the fire does come, the former chill makes the flame fonder. And let it be your purpose to make that face cheery with your smile. Hunger has been felt by all to make the heart more thankful for the next portion."

The first old man spoke again with the flavor of pain, "Oh, stay for what blessed peace there is in the assuring heartbeat of your mother. Remain there always to be joined as one by the blessed cord that unites your beings."

The second old man replied, "Yes, it is true of the cord of which he speaks, little one. But what is your mother's face but a treasure to your eyes? And what of her kiss that which brings healing to wound and worry?"

The first old man spoke coldly, "Remain where you are never to feel a sharp word of hate piercing your heart, or one you love not returning love leaving you empty except for the pain of heart that becomes your closest companion and long abiding."

The second old man answered, "If this happens, cast away that wayfaring fellow and fill the void with family and friends, with children laughing, with ocean breeze, with newly fallen snow, with doe and fawn. Surround your heart with those who love you; truly and fortress strong and a tower high they shall be to you."

He turned to the first man and said, "Speak not of such pain, my man. You cannot lift your eyes above your hurts to see life as it should be; joyful like a happy brook giggling around rocks, smiling at the fish, sparkling under the sun, offering its gentle melody to the woods and the animals while it flows on its way to the sea where all gather."

My enemy seemed taken back by the last man's view and became angry, speaking quickly and loudly.

"Foolish chatter! There are only two times in life where one is shown moments of compassion: right after birth and at the door of death; at birth because of helplessness and at death because of hopelessness! I am showing you what life truly is in between those moments - shallow and stupid! Life is a fatal condition without a cure, and there's no one to blame or thank for it! Walk, my captive! We have more to see before your end!"

I staggered forth in front of the wretch behind me until I looked up and noticed a man standing on a cliff facing the ocean that I could not see. The sound of waves seemed to be far below as if in a trance he stared into the distance. He was alone without an enemy.

"Sir!" I shouted with my hands cupped around my mouth.

He turned to look down at me as his graying hair was blown by the gentle salty air.

"Sir, why are you standing there!? You are too close to the edge!"

"To take in this final moment of victory before I die!" he replied, while carefully stepping down some rocks to speak with me.

"Where is your enemy that has pushed you to this dreadful moment?"

"Enemy? I have no enemy! And life has not prevailed over me! I will prevail by refusing it! Why should I remain in this low existence another day? Being satisfied here is a conflict of my dignity. Being content and happy here is actually an embarrassment to my soul. To feel that discontent and failure has been mine suggests that my spirit knows it is above such carnality and doesn't seek to grasp what others kill and die for. Since hoarding seems to indicate ultimate success to most humans then I don't want to stay. Why would I crawl when in another form of existence, I might fly? When I look over the landscape of humanity I am not satisfied and wonder why so many others are. What rank have I achieved even if I become the best-looking monkey in the cage? No. I am leaving with my dignity; proud to say that I don't fit, glad to admit that I am a higher being than what life in mortal flesh suggests I am. And if there is no higher existence for me, then I am simply done, and my last thought will be that I was better than all of this. I have owned my life and have decided to own my death having watched a dozen people I knew, die deaths that most of them would not have chosen. While most people my age are beginning to watch their health, memories, and senses fade, I have decided not to let myself watch while I dissolve. Why wait for all of that?! You might believe that I am depressed or even ill. After paying the tolls for the miles I have traveled, I simply looked around and decided that I am finished living. If ever a person can be sane and mentally healthy while planning his own death, I am he. Why try to stop a person like me? What logic can be placed in front of I who am logical? What promises could be presented to me? That my life will get better? That I will become mentally sharper, healthier, and in control? I watched my parents fade at the slow hand of a fatal disease and wonder if they would agree with me now. I will stay in this life just until the time I know I am done; at the peak of my best self. I'm not willing to someday look back and see my apex in the distance while trying to remember those best days. I refuse to die from old age after my memories and eyes are dimmed by time, or I have to battle some disease that will take pieces of my mind and body before I finally succumb. No. Not me!"

His next words were whispered in unison by my enemy as the man spoke them. "Why do accidents, age, and disease get to decide? I will choose to exit in the place, time, and way that I decide. Goodbye."

The man turned and climbed back up the rocks as my enemy pushed me on.

Eventually, we came to a small town which had but one street of what at first glance appeared to be lovely and happy homes lining both sides. But it soon became clear as we approached that the houses were not solid at all, but one-wall facades with one front door and painted on windows. The single front walls were supported behind by long shaky boards. Behind the colorful and detailed walls resided some of the saddest most miserable looking people I had ever seen; arguing, complaining, or weeping alone. Some walls had painted castle stones; others had painted columns and lovely trimmed shutters, brightly painted flowers, gardens, and fruit trees. Other walls had painted figures holding motionless smiles and raised hands of greeting. However, the focus was mostly on the painted-on windows with the images of the happiest people.

In the middle of the busy street, the residents stood pointing to their houses asking each other, "Do you approve? Do you like what you see? Please say yes. But don't get too close. Are you impressed?"

Every person to whom these questions were asked replied, "Oh yes. I can see your happy and beautiful family through the window! How successful you must be!"

The resident to whom this reply was given, turned to their great fancy facade and shouted back, "They approve! They like what they see! Everyone is impressed!"

One resident had just finished painting a fancy chandelier on her window. With her wet paintbrush still in hand, she rushed over to another resident standing in the street.

"How do you like my new chandelier?" she asked with excitement.

Her neighbor replied, "Oh, I just adore your lovely chandelier hanging in your glorious parlor!"

"Thank you! It was a gift from my darling husband to celebrate our perfectly happy marriage!" She shouted back to the painted image of a happy looking husband smiling in the painted window, "She approves! She loves it!"

Although the scene at first appeared polite, happy, and neighborly, it became apparent that madness was its mayor. We continued to watch the residents do their utmost to impress upon each other the lies of contentment and happiness while the truth of being unhappy, disjointed, and broken-hearted was securely hidden in private lives, behind private walls, and secured by public lies.

Neither my enemy nor I spoke until I screamed out the folly to all of the residents. "You shallow, stupid fools! Why do you live your lives to impress the kind of people who are impressed by such things?!"

After the momentary stares at me and rare seconds of silence, the citizens on the street of this vain little town erupted back into their normal activity of laboring to create, and nurture lies about their lives. My enemy pushed the tip of his sword into my back, and we walked on through the mud.

The next stop on my dark path was named, The Town of Despair. This name was etched on a crooked old board nailed to a dead tree. My enemy hastened to explain, *"Here is where slumped shouldered men are never again proven to know their best nor do they again try. Defeated men whose souls now will not fly, whose legs will not climb, and whose downcast eyes will never again dare to look at the horizon. They will live and die without realizing the fullness of who they truly are while leaving only a brief mention of their modest accomplishments as their eulogy which will soon to be forgotten. This is the place where dreams are buried, and dreamers go on to die, and faith quickly fades away like the morning dew. Confidence and hope have been altogether banished from here."*

I looked at them and wondered if they had accepted their lot in life until I heard whispers of weeping from the shadows of their souls; whispers perhaps that their minds could not hear. Old prison buildings held good men and women whose pride and dignity reached out with thin arms through rusted bars while their muffled voices cried in private despair after having been overthrown by life. Other weak and shamed men cowered behind large rocks, and some ran among the trees peering out like hiding prey.

"They are the broken who have hoped tried and failed too many times, so their strength and fight has left them, leaving little of their former selves. Formerly brave bold and spirited souls who would have conquered life were eventually conquered by it. They once stood looking up at the top of a mountain and sought to take it but were cast back down a final time and settled to remain at the bottom until their days are over, having never looked up again. This is where I should leave you among these empty, heartless others," My enemy says with contempt. *"A fitting citizen you are. Perhaps you should be the governor. Here is where you belong except you have another destination and a final one at that."*

I longed to run and join these kindred souls, yet I would rather have been alone among them.

"Walk on, you shell of a man," he commanded. *"Whereas life has not welcomed you, death surely will."*

I stumbled along as ordered, feeling that my strength was fading more, toward a destiny not of my choice.

For miles, we went through the sucking sloppy mire while the rain fell on my matted hair and together with my tears, ran down my somber face to drip off my chin onto my path of pain.

"There is no suffering like a fool's suffering. It is because you are a fool; born for nothing and proven to be of little use!" My enemy spit on my back.

"And so, it seems," I admitted.

My soul was a sad, restless, and terrified soul; afraid that my strength would expire before I did, afraid that one day I would be trapped in a corner as an old man, and there I will slump down covering my face while helplessly realizing that my mind was departing from the heat of sorrow and age.

"*Turn your head, you feeble wretch. Look straight on… and walk. We are almost there.*"

I was broken and had accepted my fate completely as had the people who lived back there. I staggered on against my will, yet my will prevented me from falling a final time.

Shadowy forms lined my muddy path like merchants as we entered the Hamlet of Regrets. My enemy ordered me to stop as those whom I had hurt stepped out of the foggy darkness to confront me. In anger, they held up torches and lists of my selfish sins like merchandise, eagerly displaying them while knowing that I could never pay my debt for the harm I caused, or right my wrongs. Their voices shouted my sins as if they were calling out to them to resurrect them from a faraway place, but they did not realize that I clearly still saw and felt the memories of my transgressions that harassed me like circling stinging bees. The people came closer and all at once justly scorned me, mocking my weakness and angrily jabbing stiff fingers into my wounded conscious that had not healed. Hard fists pummeled me to my knees. Some of the people displayed their wounds inflicted by my selfish and reckless hand, demanding that I look at them. I begged for forgiveness and pardon as I have so often had done, but none of them would grant it.

My enemy pulled me to my feet, and the sharp pain from his sword in my back pushed me forward.

"*You were born into humanity with grand expectations, but you will leave the world worse off. Oh, you shall have your pitiful eulogy, but you will not leave a good legacy, of that you can be certain. You began good and strong… but you will end in dishonor.*"

I had no rebuttal, and to even explain the reasons for my sins would have felt like justifying them. My exhausted and depleted soul wept in shame as we continued down our muddy route.

"My sin revealed was my death announced. Perhaps when I die my past good deeds will be a credit to me," I feebly replied.

"*Perhaps. And your ill deeds and broken promises will be placed on the other side of the scale. But the final balance will not be in your favor. As it is said, 'scales do not lie.' Failure is not just doing what one should not have done but also not having done what one should have.*"

I spoke aloud to myself, "How shall I be presented before the presence of such a God? Perhaps I will be granted a second chance."

"*For some mistakes, there is no second chance. Once a man steps over some lines there is no stepping back, and that which was done cannot be undone. One single mistake can change a course and yield a great burden of regrets which shall be carried all the way to the grave. There is no second chance for you. Look at yourself. What can grow from dead wood, dry bones, and old scars?*"

I mustered the strength to say, "An acorn on top of a rock will not grow, but when the wind blows it off, and it settles next to the rock, the acorn will take root and overturn the rock."

But the uncertainty in my voice negated my weak answer so that my enemy needed not to further rebuke me.

My enemy taunted me further along my path, "*Do you yet smell the vile odor of death?*"

To which I answered, "Death a vile odor? No. Other men might perceive it as such, but to me, the thought is a welcoming fragrance on the summer breeze not unlike the rose. I do not fear the Reaper. He is my escort, a friend I have yet to meet, and an angel ready to take me out of this troubled life. When he appears, I will not flee or beg, but step forward and gently push aside his sickle to embrace him and whisper thanks into his ear, for I will be ready, and he will be welcomed; sent to harvest me from the vast fields of suffering humanity. What sweet being would I choose to behold at my end? Who will step forward to catch me as I fall? My soul thinks of a lady angel. Her wings would cover me, and we would lie together and weep."

My enemy spoke for the first time with a voice of compassion, yet I knew goodwill was not in him. "*You are among the misunderstood souls who do not want to die but do not want to live the life they never fit into and cannot escape. Not made for this world, you would rather have not been born than to live a life you never asked for. And no matter where you go or what you do, you soon realize that you have again been misplaced. You speak for all troubled souls who have been given suffering for their lot and question why they were born. What will you do? How can you go on? How will you end this suffering? When will you?*"

"Our lives are years of struggle and pain; some of which we freely admit is from our ill choices and some from the hand of bad fortune. Nonetheless, we secretly dream of another life that we have privately chosen and dwell there most of the time but regretfully wake to our own. We look over our shoulder and ask ourselves if 'that' was life. Is this it? Then we look ahead to the future as far as we can see and ask the same questions. But once we were child-like; calling out to life to come out and sing and dance with us and play a simple happy game. But what came out was a hard and bitter old man who chased us away with cursing. I raise my hands to the sky and plead, 'Come angelic reaper and thrust in your sickle! I am ready to go. Harvest me from this cursed earth!' Until I sleep my final sleep what choice do I have except to struggle and wait for the Usher? So, you see that the event of my death that you present to me as something to be feared and dreaded has only served to recall to my mind that blessed day. Thank you. You have lifted my spirits reminding me that there is an end to this stage of mislabeled existence that is not qualified to be called 'life,' and one day I get to die. My troubling thoughts will end, and the questions and voices will become silent."

My enemy's voice became almost like that of a friend. "*You may always end your cursed life at any time in mercy by your own hand.*"

"You speak with the voice of an ally, but your words are that of the foe you are."

My adversary realized that I was aware of his motive and kicked the back of my leg. I limped forward.

Out loud, I spoke of the moments before my welcomed death.

"I shall guide death's hand to my smiling face.
Sweet elixir poured through parted lips.
Death's sweet potion upon my tongue.
Death's sweet potion upon my tongue.
Lay my head down, then say what you will."

Later, desiring to break the redundant sound of wet and labored footsteps, my captor sought to gain the advantage of my muddled mind.

He said, "*I will offer you a riddle. A deer being chased by a wolf passes by a carefree cow grazing within its fenced pasture, but unaware of its approaching day with the butcher. Which animal's life is better; the cow which has a safe and comfortable life but its fate is determined, or the deer living free but unprotected from danger? Muse over this then answer me. But I warn you do not let a long wait bore me.*"

49

After a few silent moments, I answered, "The cow having enjoyed a life of security and care will surely meet its death by the same hand that tended to it. The deer might escape from the wolf that day or it might not, but still, it lives always free; even if free only to flee from its pursuer and so it has the better life. Further, the cow that discovers a way out through the fence finds itself in the woods and not having protection to survive there will, in fact, become prey to the wolf. And if the deer is captured and held in the fence, it will surely resist until it either finds a way out or dies trying, ever intent on being free."

"*So, what are most men?*"

"Every man may choose to live according to his nature. Some men are the like the deer; living free knowing the risks of life and chance while being guided by the attractions of choice and adventure. Other men like the cow prefer the security and routine of the familiar fence which they become fond of while understanding that they have been given an appointed day to die, and on that day, they yield with sadness, yet they yield."

"*So, what am I?*" he asked.

"You my captor are neither the butcher, or the wolf, or the deer although you may think yourself to be one of them. I am the deer in the fence and would quickly choose a quick death in freedom over a long slow one in any other way. You, however, are the cow in the woods and will someday fall prey. And if justice resolves such affairs, I shall be the wolf that brings you down."

Suddenly, the flat side of his sword was laid hard against the back of my neck with such force that I cried out and fell to the mud.

"*Get up cow and walk to the butcher!*"

In defiance, I grit my teeth, painfully stood, and promised, "If I had a sword I would turn and take your head."

My adversary replied, "*But you have nothing to defeat me with so I remain your enemy, and you remain my captive, and so it is.*"

"One of us must soon die. I cannot bear your miserable company much longer."

"*But I rather enjoy your company. You are a good listener.*"

"And I grow weary listening to you. Your words are death. I will sing within and think of things that bring joy and strength to my heart and will dream my dreams while I walk through this mud."

We walked and walked in the dimness on my twisted trail through a patch infested with briers, and all the time I wondered where to. My soul begged that the march would not be much longer and I hoped to soon find my end.

As we continued for what seemed like hours, my wounded enemy ordered me to stop. There were many other paths there, all leading to that one place. Next to me was a large pile of mixed swords mostly dented and dulled after long battles, thrown together like sticks of wood. They laid next to a heap of discarded shields of different colors and emblems, having been fiercely assaulted and damaged by heavy, brutal swords. These armaments took my attention before I gazed down into a deep pit in front of me where the dead lay. Their disheartened and drained souls had already taken their hurried leave after they found themselves at the edge of the pit as now do I. Lifeless faces on stiff thin bodies with fixed cloudy eyes stared out from underneath the pile. Some souls frozen in expressionless stares testified to their final state of mind. Like the door of a burning house thrown open by a man fleeing to escape the flames, the mouths of other souls remained wide open after their last cry burst out. Hardened weeping faces remained on other victims who lay tangled in this pit. Together they looked like a heap of worn and discarded statutes taken from a devilish nightmare. I imagined that at their end few of them resisted or struggled against their enemy. Instead, they yielded, welcoming their end as their souls without complaint, fell into the pit. After being broken and driven they had no will to oppose.

My enemy explained with new cruelty in his voice. "*Each one held themselves in chilling moments at the edge to understand that they were about to die. Each in a moment became aware that they are truly body and soul before feeling their very life pulling away in the terrifying uncertainty of their soul's fate. Each captive decided at the last moment what was worse; to no longer be alive or to soon be dead.*"

"The death of the body is not death, but death is that of the soul," I replied. "So... to this horrifying end is where you have driven me."

On top of the mound of souls sat the same silver helmet of peculiar shape that I saw on the man near my path, laying near the dead man beside it. Anger and compassion flooded inside me then gave way to a sense of my own finality.

"Is a prisoner granted a last request?" I asked my captor, still standing behind me.

"*What is it?*" He snarled. "*Do you wish to plead for mercy or do you wish to send a message of your death to friends and loved ones who then must then bear the burden of your grief which you would no longer bear but selfishly place upon them? I grant you neither!*"

"And I ask for neither. I request to finally see the face of my enemy before I die."

He answered sharply, "*You will not! Who I am is of no consequence!*"

In defiance, I quickly turned to face my mysterious enemy; to look into the eyes of the one holding the sword against me that had pushed me along speaking cruelly to me. My enemy wore my very same face! He was I! It was I who defeated me after the long battle and prodded me on this march. All the time it was I who spoke dark thoughts to me told me lies and cast over my mind a dark hood of depression. It was I who pushed me down the muddy path to the cruel places and finally to the edge of this pit. How I wish I had turned to look at this face long ago and spared myself this journey! Looking down again into the pit, my weary body swayed, and my head was unsteady. Fearing that I would fall, I confessed to myself that I did not want to die. I gathered my very last reserve of strength and shook my head to dislodge my dormant senses to live, pulling them up from deep within. Awakening from the spell I had cast on myself, my mind thrust forward a promise written by my hand long ago when strength was in me. I spoke it out loud to my soul.

"If I am awake before I die and have the chance to reflect, I will remember my kin and friends who have walked with me through parts of my life and carefully thank God for each one of them but reserve my last moments for myself. I will talk within like an old friend whose hand I hold; smile, and say, 'You were faithful true and good. There has never been a closer or sweeter companion. Death is not a lonely passing for I am right here with me. My loyal friend, thank you for the years and the journey. I would not have chosen to walk with another.' Then, I will compose my own beautiful eulogy and sing it within and look myself in the eye and love the reflection as I lie peacefully within my own warm embrace, charmed by my own approving wink and consoled by the pardon I will grant to myself. Lastly, with closed eyes, I will place a flirty kiss on my cheek and fade away with a smile in my soul and whisper, 'Thank you, my old friend. I have loved you more dearly than all. It was good to be me."

This pledge spoken in my own voice awakened me further, returned my dignity, and granted me new determination. That day will come, and the delight will be mine, but that day is not this day.

I took the courage to turn again to fight my enemy, considering that he was now wounded while admitting that I had but a small chance to win, but knowing it was my last and only choice. There, I decided that my enemy's words, "*Who I am is of no consequence*," should be his last. My enemy's face revealed weakness and pain as if he would negotiate his own life and his sword hung heavy at his side.

He tried to speak softly, pleading as if to negotiate his life, but I shouted over him, "I will not return to places I should not go! I will not relive my sins that you force me to remember! I will not listen to your dark lies! You will handle me no more!"

Without further pause, I wrenched the sword from his hand and easily slew him. Thinking first to cast him in the pit but deciding that he was unworthy to lie among the memories of those good people who once lived with honor and respect, I buried my foe and piled heavy rocks upon his grave so that he should never be uncovered.

Looking out into the distance, I was surprised to see the very battlefield from which I was first taken. The heated struggle still raged on. Fresh pride and new purpose swelled within me! I took the sharpest sword and the strongest shield from their piles, restored to them their honor, and christened them, 'My Consorts.' Courage and hope filled me with added strength. New and strong emotions erupted from within so that I shouted to the battlefield to warn the adversary that I shall fall upon them! With my sword raised high and shield held tight, I ran to slay the enemies of my captive brothers and sisters now that my own enemy had been slain and I was free and wiser.

Off to the side of the battlefield, walked defeated men and women taken captive, staggering along with their heavy eyes looking to the ground, each being prodded from behind by their own twin enemy. Brutally, my sword struck a brother's foe but my blade had no effect. It was then that I understood that each man and woman must slay their own enemy.

Running frantically along the long line, I shouted to the captives, "Do not continue on! Stop! Turn and look! Turn and look at the face of your enemy!"

Some of them heeded my plea, turned, and slew their captors. But others too weary, having lost all heart and hope, continued down their fatal paths toward delusions and fallacies they must never be allowed to see.

Those that did turn and slay their enemy followed me as our feet flew to each captive still walking. Passionately, we seized our brothers and sisters by their shoulders and turned them around, lifting their heavy chins, so their tired red eyes would see who it was that had defeated them, thus granting to each the truth needed to slay their own enemy.

I ran to the top of a hill to look out over the battle. From that position, I saw a sister walking in the far distance whose enemy escaped unnoticed with her and forced her onto her private path toward the dark woods. With haste, I ran to her shouting and splashing through the mud and fog with such fervor that my chest heaved and burned until I was well along her winding path. Finally, I came upon her to find that her enemy had already slain her and vanished. She laid dead, still embracing a new gravestone posted at the head of a fresh grave in a small cemetery. Throwing aside my shield and sword, I knelt at her side and wept, cradling her. The loss of my sister was too great for me to hold and my heart felt like it would rupture. Pressing her head against my chest, I kissed her lifeless face. Her path and her enemy were not mine so I will never know what dark persuasive utterances were whispered to her that she would make her end here. There was nothing left to do for her. She was gone.

Immediately, through the woods, I saw the gray shadow of a man being prodded along by his enemy. I gathered my sword and shield and ran ahead of him and waited behind a tree. As he arrived where I was, I stepped out onto his path and ordered him to stop.

He stopped, slowly lifted his head, looked at me with swollen eyes, and slowly asked, "Has my time come? Will I now die on this dark and quiet path? Perhaps it is best that this is my end."

His enemy interrupted and said to me, "Who are you? You have no right to be here. You have no business with him."

"I will not explain myself to you or justify my presence here," I replied with authority. "I am a free man and only the free can walk on a path with a captive. My 'former' enemy told me so."

I looked at my captive brother and said, "Unlike the one behind you, I am not your enemy. I am your brother and here to help you."

The captive replied as if still standing in a past time, "I have been driven to dreadful places and have seen images; images as if designed and built by the very cruelest heart. I was held in a deep cold dungeon, where those I know and those I love, visited me just to reveal their hatred for me; my wife among them. My death will mean less to her now that our relationship is far apart, and more to me because of it. Further, my enemy forced me into the darkest woods wherein I was lost and wandered in fear and then..."

"Enough!" I demanded. "Why would you relive such things? Even though you are not presently at those places still you revisit them in your mind as if you were still there, so the pain returns. Would you rid yourself of your enemy if given the chance?"

"Yes, but I have no means, much less the strength."

His enemy said to me, "Neither you nor your sword will have an effect on me."

"True. 'my' sword will not, although I eagerly wish I could fall upon you myself and rid you like I rid my enemy."

I placed my hand on the shoulder of my brother and looked into his eyes. "Allow me to be your means and strength. Here I give you this sword. It is now 'your' sword."

He looked at the sword I extended to him then slowly took it, fitting his fingers around the hilt.

"My enemy said that if I ever turned around, I would die," the nervous captive said.

"The truth is that *unless* you turn around you will die. He will drive you on to an untimely and tragic end. You must face the enemy behind you so that you may live again. I know who he is as you do. You will be surprised when you see him."

After briefly looking into my eyes for final assurance, the man turned and stared at his enemy until his mind grasped the truth.

"You? Me?! I should have recognized the voice, and now I see the face. Liar!" He continued in anger, "You stole precious time from me and divided my family! No more dark words from you, and I will not walk one more, weary step with you!"

With a quick slash, his enemy lay dead, and we buried him there under heavy stones.

We left his path and walked back in silence to the top of the hill until the man asked, "My brother how is it that we were overcome by our enemies and forced on our woeful paths?"

I replied, "Understanding the path has become clear to me. To some captives, their paths are sorrowful journeys to the regretful past, and to others, dread and fear about the present and future. To different people, their path is pleasant and happy, but with others their path is frightful; being populated with their distorted beliefs, unanswerable questions, and regretful memories. My insight about our enemies is that they were not always our enemies. Once they were but innocent thoughts and healthy questions that grew into pain and fear. Eventually the pain and fear became a voice, and the voice became like another person walking behind us; at first an adviser, but then an enemy. One might say the dark side of us. That voice became stronger the more we listened to it until one day it conquered us. My brother when you look at the reflection of your face in still water then drop a pebble into the water, it causes ripples, and your reflection becomes distorted. But in fact, is your face distorted? No. So, we should not believe we are the image that is reflected back to us. But sometimes we choose to believe that distorted truth is real; about us; what we know and what we believe. And in doing so, we push aside the power of truth about our beauty and worth."

The man paused to think for a moment and said, "The truth is not in the pebble or the ripples. Pebbles can be dropped into our puddle by ourselves or by other people, but still, the real image remains the truth and the truth we must guard."

I placed my hand on his shoulder. "My brother, you have it!"

He smiled and said, "Walking next to a brother is far better than walking in front of an enemy!" Thinking for a moment, he asked, "Who was it that finally rescued you?"

"I scarcely survived what I perceived as rejections. And I barely endured the wrenching questions, the sharp insults, and the threats while almost crumbling under the weight of sorrow and all of the rest. I was nearly depleted and actually gave up until at last my dreams emerged onto my gloomy path and wounded my enemy sufficiently so that I was eventually able to overcome him. Beautiful things my dreams are. They help keep me alive; therefore, I now keep them nearer."

"Where are they now?"

"Oh, they are never far off. Do you also have dreams?"

My new friend answered, "I once did, as did my wife. But in time and toil, we gave less attention to them. Now we can hardly hear their voices."

"See to it my friend that you call them back and keep them close."

We arrived at the top of the hill to see vast mounds of piled stones where people were burying their enemies. They waited there together for others to pass who might also have been taken in battle by their enemy. The man with me suddenly saw his wife down among the others who freed themselves. He ran down the hill shouting her name. She looked up with joy and ran to meet him. They embraced; kissing and weeping. I smiled.

Mind Invasions

The large windows of the psychiatric hospital's common room gave clear views to the peaceful flowered grounds outside. But inside the room, it was a scene of benign chaos in slow-motion. The imaginary conversations were generally quiet with only occasional outbursts and disruptions. Even the orderlies and medical staff who came and went, did so in erratic patterns, stopping to have hushed conversations with patients and visitors. Most of the visitors were seated watching their loved ones after deciding with every visit that an intelligent dialogue was not going to happen.

Julie Albert and her older brother, Geoff were in their early twenties. They watched their mother with sadness as she leaned with her back against a wall in her pajamas, slowly slapping the air in front of her, stopping only to push away an imaginary threatening figure.

"I don't know what happened to her. She was just parked on the side of the road, and they found her like this. Why? How?" Julie asked, staring at her mother.

Geoff slowly shook his head. "Every time we come it gets harder to watch. She doesn't even know we're here."

"God, Geoff. Just like that. One day she's fine and the next day… this."

"The worst part is that they have no idea what happened or how to help her. No idea."

"All the tests came back, okay. It isn't a medical issue, they say," Julie said.

Fifteen years later, the jury was seated, and the courtroom was full. Dr. Julie Albert was on the witness stand.

"Your Honor, if it pleases the court, I would like to ask Dr. Albert to summarize this science for the jury."

"Granted. You may proceed," the curious judge ordered, as she sat watching. There was no fidgeting in the courtroom or private conversations, as everyone's attention was focused.

The defense lawyer began, "Dr. Albert, what is your new technology called?"

"Intimate Mind Access."

"In basic terms, what exactly happens?" the lawyer asked.

"We tap into the subconscious mind of the patient. What we see is viewed and recorded from a monitor. Or, in some cases, we enter the mind."

"Dr. Albert, is IMA more accurate than polygraphs?"

"Polygraphs are, to a degree, susceptible to interpretation and manipulation."

"Doctor, is IMA better than DNA testing?"

"IMA is different," Dr. Albert explained. "It displays and records memories and images from the mind."

The defense lawyer turned to the judge. "Your Honor, at this time I would like to introduce into evidence the video from the IMA done on my client."

"So, noted. You may proceed."

A large monitor on the wall began to play the video. The scene unfolded through the defendant's own eyes as he was walking on a sidewalk at night. He saw a body lying in the entrance of an alley. He stopped at the body and knelt down. The victim's head was bloody and a metal pipe laid nearby. The voice of the defendant could be heard saying, "Damn, man. You okay?" On the video, police sirens were heard approaching while the red and blue lights pulsed on the buildings next to the alley. The police car stopped hard with its headlights on the defendant. The doors quickly opened, the police officers drew their weapons, and shouted, "Freeze! Get down on the ground!" The video stopped.

"Thank you, your honor," the defense lawyer said. "Nothing further."

"Do the people have any questions?" the judge asked.

"Yes, Your Honor." Another suited man stood from a different table and walked to the witness stand. "Dr. Albert, how are we to know that the defendant didn't simply kill the victim prior, and come back to the scene of the crime?"

"We thoroughly checked his memories. The account we just viewed was the only one associated with this incident."

The prosecutor announced, "No further questions your Honor." He returned to his seat and sat down.

"Your Honor with no incriminating evidence, along with the IMA video, I would like to move to dismiss the charge against my client."

"Do the people object?"

The prosecutor stood at his seat. "No objection, your Honor."

The judge announced, "case dismissed" and slammed down the gavel.

The defendant slumped in his seat with relief as those around him gave him hugs and pats on the back.

In the laboratory of Invasive Mind Access, a coma patient lay on a gurney with dozens of sensors attached to his head and back of his neck. The sensors were bundled together, running across the floor, leading back to computers where two technicians stood adjusting and monitoring them. From those stations, two computer cables lay on the floor; one connecting to the large monitor on the wall, and the other to Tim, Dr. Albert's senior assistant, standing behind the master computer in front.

Dr. Albert watched the video screen. "Okay, Tim. Let's see if there are any changes after a month with the new drug."

Tim tapped a few times on his keyboard as she watched the patient's vital signs as the monitor came on. Blurry swirling images and disjointed faces and scenes moved in and out.

"It's a little better than last month but not much," Dr. Albert noted.

"A little clearer and a bit more frequent," Tim added.

Dr. Albert gave a small sigh. "Okay. Let's hope next month is even better. Send a copy of the video to the neurologists."

"Yes, doctor."

Mr. and Mrs. Rodriguez and their eight-year-old daughter, Carmen sat with Dr. Albert and Tim in the conference room. Mrs. Rodriquez tearfully shared the problem. "She squirms and then screams. She can't remember anything."

Carmen's father added, "She's been to specialists. They say they're night terrors. She has them almost every night."

"In cases where medications and counseling aren't enough, I can personally enter the mind, "Dr. Albert offered.

"Why can't you just watch what happens on the monitor?" Mrs. Rodriquez asked.

"Because your daughter needs direct advocate intervention – someone to be with her during an episode."

Mrs. Rodriquez looked at her husband with concern. "I think we should do this."

Mr. Rodriquez closed his teary eyes and nodded.

Dr. Albert looked at Carmen with a smile. "Carmen, you're getting to be a big girl. Is it okay that I come into your dreams with you?"

Carmen nodded. "Daddy and mommy are scared and sad when I

wake up."

With a tone of assurance and confidence Dr. Albert replied, "Well, you and I are going to see what this is all about."

Two days later in the laboratory, Carmen's parents were standing next to each other with their arms around each other waiting to see what the monitor on the wall would reveal about their daughter's nightmares.

The lights were low. Quiet tapping and whispering from the two technicians added to the gentle atmosphere of the room. Carmen's head was raised as she slept on her gurney, even with the multiple sensors stuck to her head and upper spine. Her stuffed animal seemed very content to be at her side. Dr. Albert covered in the same way with sensors, lay with her head elevated on her own gurney next to Carmen. She gave a thumbs-up to Tim who wore a headset with a small microphone boom. He turned and whispered to the nervous parents, "If you must speak, please do so in whispers."

Mr. and Mrs. Rodriquez nodded.

Tim tapped keys on his computer before the video went from blurry to revealing Carmen's bedroom. Dr. Albert stood next to Carmen's empty bed.

"That's her bedroom!" Carmen's mother whispered.

"Carmen?" Dr. Albert gently called out with a whisper. "Carmen? Where are you?" She noticed a small foot sticking out from under the bed.

"Carmen, you can come out. It's me, Dr. Albert. I told you I would come and be with you."

Carmen's face slowly appeared. She looked up from the floor at Dr. Albert and whispered, "I can't come out. I'm hiding."

"From what?"

Carmen's eyes grew big. "The monster is coming!" She pulled her head back under the bed and whispered, "Shhhhhh. Don't move."

Carmen's body became restless on her gurney, and she cried in her sleep.

On the monitor, Dr. Albert turned and looked around the bedroom. A dark shadowy figure wearing a hat stepped out of the closet and approached Carmen's bed. Dr. Albert took a step back.

"Oh, my God!" Mr. Rodriquez whispered as she tightens her arm around her husband.

Staring at the monitor, Carmen's parents and Tim watched the dark figure stop at the side of the bed. Dr. Albert glanced back down at the bed then looked at the figure. She stepped up and violently grabbed it. The mysterious figure collapsed in her grip, and the hat fell to the floor.

"That's my overcoat and hat! I hung them in Carmen's closet because I didn't have room in mine," Mr. Rodriquez exclaimed.

Dr. Albert picked the hat up and stood holding the coat. "Carmen, you can come out now. It's not a silly monster. It's just an old funny coat. Do you want to see it?"

Carmen cautiously crawled out. Dr. Albert took her hand and helped her stand up.

"It's not a monster?"

"No, not at all," the doctor answered.

On her gurney, Carmen stopped crying and relaxed.

Dr. Albert asked, "Have you seen this coat and hat before?"

"In my closet. It scares me. It looks like a bad monster after daddy and mommy turn the lights out and leave."

"Hey, let's have some fun," Dr. Albert offered. "We'll play dress-up! Put the coat on, and I'll put the hat on!"

Carmen slid her arms into the sleeves of the big overcoat and smiled. "It smells like my daddy!"

"You look like your daddy! Hello, daddy!" the doctor, playfully exclaimed. Carmen laughed.

"Now get into your bed and rest."

Carmen climbed into her bed wearing her daddy's coat. Dr. Albert took off the hat and put it on Carmen's head. She giggled and closed her eyes.

"We're done here, Tim."

"Got it, doctor."

Tim clicked keys on his computer. Dr. Albert disappeared from the monitor, and the screen went blank. Mr. and Mrs. Rodriquez hugged each other with teary eyes.

A new patient, Norman, was just seated at the table with his doctor, Dr. Patel, Dr. Albert, and Tim in the conference room. Norman looked disheveled and exhausted as he sat fidgeting. His unshaven face, messy hair, and puffy red eyes revealed that he had lost many recent battles trying to get enough sleep.

Dr. Patel began. "Dr. Albert we've tried everything. Norman just can't stay asleep for very long much less soundly. You are our last hope."

"Norman, what do you feel when you are trying to sleep?" Dr. Albert asked.

"Well just as I'm about to go get into a deep sleep, I get afraid and wake up hot and sweating."

"I'm sure that Dr. Patel explained what we do," Dr. Albert said.

"Yeah," Norman replied. "You go into my mind while I'm sleeping."

"That's right. We hope to see what your subconscious mind sees."

Norman jumped up and burst back with a pointed finger, "I don't want you to see my memories!"

Dr. Albert calmly answered, "We're not probing for memories, but there is a chance that we may see some."

"No! Forget it! I ain't doing it!"

Dr. Patel intervened. "Norman, do you want to continue living without enough sleep and being terrified when you do sleep?"

"You gonna tell anyone what you see?"

"What you tell us and what we see is held in doctor-patient confidence."

Norman sat back down in his chair and buried his face in his hands.

"Oh God, I need some sleep."

Dr. Albert took some forms out of a folder and handed a pen to Norman. "Norman, sign here, here, and here, where it's highlighted with yellow."

Norman scribbled his name on the forms, dropped the pen on the table, and rubbed his tired eyes.

The lights were low in the laboratory. Norman was reclined on a gurney. It was obvious by his fidgeting that he didn't like all the wires attached to him. His nervous eyes darted around at the two technicians standing back at the high-tech machines, softly mumbling to each other. His eyes followed the cable laying on the floor, starting from Tim's computer. One cable ended near his head, fanning out the dozens of smaller cables that were attached to his head and back of his neck. Next to Norman, Dr. Albert lay on her gurney with her own wires and sensors.

Tim raised his head from his computer. "We're ready, doctor."

Dr. Albert carefully turned her head toward Norman. "Norman, remember we talked about the injection of the sedative? Tim is going to do that now."

Tim walked over to Norman and gave him a shot in his arm. Norman watched him squeeze the syringe as the plunger pushed the liquid into his vein. A wave of sleep overtook him before he let out a relaxing groan.

"Doctor, the patient is unconscious. We're ready."

"Proceed." Dr. Albert gave the order with a relaxed tone, but inside she was nervous and dreadful about what she might find inside the mind of a person like Norman, whom she suspected had dark secrets.

Tim walked back to his computer. He put his headphones on and tapped some keys on his computer. The large wall monitor turned from black to gray as it formed the scene. Dr. Albert stood in gray swirls and shadows. Her professional demeanor quickly gave way to wide, nervous eyes. She began to walk slowly, but her eyes were moving quickly as she took in everything she could see. The grayness around her started to clear revealing thick darkness on her left, right, and above her. With her next careful step, she felt something thick under her foot and looked down to the gray mist to see fingers extending out from under one side of her shoe and an arm extending out on the other side from the darkness. She quickly pulled her foot up. "Oh, my God!" she whispered, taking a few quick steps back. After taking a deep breath, Dr. Albert stepped around the arm and carefully walked forward. "Norman?" she called in a quiet voice. More body parts lay in between the gray haze on the floor and the darkness. She stared at each for a moment but continued walking.

In the distance, Dr. Albert saw a small dancing light. With each step, the details became clearer. The light was a small campfire. Against her fear, she subconsciously ordered both of her feet to move closer. Norman was tied up sitting on the right side against a dark wall. A bloody knife was stuck in the wall above him. What appeared to be a demon, sat in front of the fire, jabbing Norman with a flaming stick. With each poke, Norman pushed himself against the wall, trying in vain to avoid the flames and the pain. Dr. Albert stopped. She was frightened but gathered the courage to proceed.

"Doctor, I'm getting you out of there!" Tim said as he brought his hands to his keyboard.

Dr. Albert whispered back, "No. Wait."

A demon with tight, reddish-brown skin, claws, and short canine teeth turned toward the doctor at the sound of her whisper and stood as she approached.

"You shouldn't have come here," the demon hissed. "It's a very dangerous place."

"Why are you here?" Dr. Albert asked, with trembling in her voice.

The demon jabbed Norman again with the burning stick. "The fool's door was wide open."

Dr. Albert asked, "Norman can you hear me?"

The demon hit Norman over the head with the stick. Burning embers fell on him and onto the floor. Norman tried frantically to brush them off but, his arms were tied.

"Shut up!" he ordered Norman, as he approached the doctor.

"Doctor!" Tim exclaimed.

Dr. Albert pointed her trembling index finger up, signaling for Tim to wait.

"I'm not afraid of you," she said to the demon.

The demon hissed back, "I could kill you! But it's not just me that you should fear – it's my master, and he's coming!"

Suddenly, a large roaring demon with glowing yellow eyes entered from behind the fire's light. He saw Dr. Albert and ran at her through the fire, knocking over the first demon as it tried to scramble away. Terrified, Norman pressed himself harder against the wall. The two supporting technicians looked shocked. Dr. Albert turned around and ran.

"Tim! Now!"

Tim jabbed a key on his keyboard a moment before Dr. Albert disappeared from the monitor, then hurried over to the doctor and began to take off her sensors.

"Are you alright?!"

"Yes," she replied as she got her bearings. "Scared to death but otherwise okay. My God! We have to get some help."

Tim said, "I'm an atheist and never believed that demons are real."

"Neither did I. But those weren't just dream images."

"What do want to be done with Norman?" Tim asked as he helped the doctor get to her feet.

"Take his sensors off and put him in restraints. I'll get him admitted."

Dr. Albert, Tim, Father Mitchell, and Father Perez stood attentively in front of the monitor in the laboratory.

"Fathers, this is the video recording that we talked about on the phone," Dr. Albert said. "Go ahead, Tim."

Tim started the video. The small audience silently watched as the doctor walked through Norman's mind and encountered the first demon.

"Tim, stop here." The video stopped. Dr. Albert said, "This is the first demon I encountered."

The priests studied the image of the demon. Father Perez began.
"That's a common demon – small, lower level."

"They have some power but are mostly noise, lies, threats, and some violence," Father Mitchell added.

Dr. Albert said, "We had a short conversation. Go ahead, Tim." The video moved forward to where Norman was tied up.

"Stop," Father Perez said. "Your patient has got himself into a really bad situation.

"The first demon told me that Norman's door was wide open. Whatever that means."

Father Perez answered, "In spiritual terms, the 'door' refers to resistance or security. Some people's doors are locked some are closed but not locked."

"And some are left open meaning a virtual invitation to whatever might want to come in. Go ahead and start," Father Mitchell said.

The video advanced to the entrance of the large demon.

"Stop. Now, that's a problem," Father Perez noted. The two priests glanced at each other. "Is that Lucious?"

"Yes. I think it is," Father Mitchell answered. "He has been around a very long time. His image is in some of the oldest manuscripts in the Vatican's library."

"Why would 'he' be there? I'll say this; he's up to something very big."

Father Mitchell looked at his fellow priest. "And we have to find out what that 'something' is."

Father Perez asked, "Tim can you go back to the beginning, please? I want to take a closer look at the body parts on the floor."

"Sure, Father." Tim reversed the video and slowed it.

Pointing up to the monitor, Father Mitchell said, "A sneaker. Right there."

Father Perez noted, "That man has a beard and a gold loop earring."

"That looks like someone's back wearing a striped sweater," Dr. Albert said.

Father Mitchell exclaimed, "Look! That's a woman's face right there. It's clear. She's wearing diamond cluster earrings."

Tim observed, "There's a hand with a turquoise bracelet."

Dr. Albert asked, "Tim can you take still pictures of all of these and print them?" "Absolutely doctor. And I think I can add more resolution to them."

"Go back and get a picture of that knife stuck in the wall as well."

"You got it, doctor."

Father Perez asked Dr. Albert, "What kind of danger is there if we go in?"

"If things go badly, Tim can get you out in a flash," she replied.

Father Mitchell said to Father Perez, "We'll have to get the bishop's permission. Then we'll fast, pray, and go to confession."

Father Perez turned to Dr. Albert. "It will take a few days. We need to attempt a traditional exorcism first. We will need a private empty room."

"We'll get you the room here," Dr. Albert assured them.

Dr. Albert and Tim thanked the priests before they left.

Four days later, in an empty room in the facility's basement, Norman was sitting upright and strapped to a gurney. His eyes glowed yellow. Father Mitchell and Father Perez wore their surplice and purple stoles standing in front of Norman. The two priests traced the cross over Norman, themselves, Dr. Albert, and Tim. Then, sprinkled everyone with holy water. Norman was last to be sprinkled.

The first demon's panicked voice hissed through Norman. "No! No! No!" The demon screamed. Norman's body heaved.

"The first demon has left," Father Perez announced.

Norman snapped his head around. With a deeper and louder voice, Lucious shouted, "You coward! I will drag you to hell myself!"

Father Mitchell told Lucious, "We know you, foul spirit. You are Lucious."

"Then you also know that you cannot cast me out! His darkness opened the door. His evil called to us. He is mine!"

Father Perez opened his book and read out loud, "We cast you out every unclean spirit every satanic power every onslaught of the infernal adversary every legion every diabolical group and sect in the name of and by the power of Our Lord Jesus Christ. We command you be gone…"

"Little priests, I have the right to be here!" Lucious laughed hideously as the priests looked at each other, turned, and left.

In the conference room, Father Mitchell told Dr. Albert and Tim, "We couldn't cast Lucious out."

"You might say, spiritually speaking he has a legal standing to be there."

Father Perez added, "This isn't a normal possession. He has a strong hold on Norman."

Dr. Albert announced, "Then we will go back in and find that reason." The priests looked at each other and nodded.

"Dr. Albert, Father Perez and I will go in by ourselves. There is no reason you should go this time."

"Okay. Yeah, I'm not trained to handle demons. Tim and I will stand by at the computers," Tim quickly agreed with a deep nod.

The tension was high in the laboratory. Norman was on his gurney heavily restrained and drugged. Through small slits, his eyes glow yellow while he drooled. Covered with sensors, the two priests were on gurneys on either side of Norman, wearing crucifixes. They crossed themselves. Dr. Albert checked Norman's iv bag.

Lucious slowly mumbled, "I will kill every one of you."

"We're ready doctor," Father Mitchell announced.

"God be with us," Father Perez added with a nervous tone.

Tim turned and asked the two technicians," Are you guys ready back there?" They both nodded.

Tim's fingers found the keystrokes on his computer. The large monitor on the wall revealed swirling grayness. The priests appeared, standing as Lucious was dragging two bodies from the edge of the darkness toward the small fire. He held one body by a foot and the other by an arm. In front of the fire, Lucious picked each body off the floor and dropped them on three other bodies already there. Norman was tied up and sitting in the same place against the dark wall.

With his back still toward the priests, Lucious growled, "I knew you would come here, foolish little priests."

The priests walked to the fire. Father Mitchell declared, "We are servants of God. You will answer our questions."

Lucious turned around to face the priests. His eyes glowed yellow. "You want to know about these bodies. They are victims of Norman's murderous heart."

"You are a deceiver," said Father Perez. "It may be that he had murder in his heart, but it was you who pushed him to the acts."

Lucious replied, "I simply gave him an expression of his desire to murder. It did not take much."

Father Mitchell asked Norman, "My son do you have a confession?"

"You will not speak to him! He's mine!" The priests stepped closer and held out their crucifixes.

"We are priests of God!" Father Perez shouted. "We will not be silent! I rebuke you in the name of God!"

Again, Father Mitchell asked Norman, "Norman do you have a confession?"

Norman cried. "Yes! I killed these people. Father forgive me for I have sinned." He looked at Lucious. "He made me do it!"

Father Mitchell replied, "You are forgiven, my son. We'll talk about your penance later."

"You no longer have a hold on him." Father Perez announced. "Leave now in the name of the Father…"

Lucious screamed and dashed between the priests, pushing them aside. As he passed between the crucifixes, his skin smoked. "You cannot defeat me! I am Lucious!"

Dr. Albert and Tim watched as Norman's body heaved against the restraints. Sensor wires moved on Norman's head. A dark spot traveled along them through the bundle on the floor and up into Tim's computer. The dark spot flashed across the computer screen then into Tim's finger resting on a key. The lights in the laboratory went off. The dim emergency lights came on. Tim's body jolted as his back arched. The two technicians dived for cover under a table. His eyes glowed yellow. He knocked over the computers and pushed Dr. Albert down before running out the door. Dr. Albert slowly got off the floor walked to the priests laying on their gurneys and took off their sensors.

Father Perez looked around at the damage. "What happened?"

Dr. Albert was shaken. "It seems that Lucious is inside of Tim now. He ran out."

Father Mitchell asked, "Which way did he go?"

"He went left," she answered, still trying to regain her composure.

The two priests quickly gathered their prayer books and holy water and ran out the laboratory door into the dim hall toward the sounds of people yelling. They found a fire evacuation plan on a wall. Father Mitchell traced his finger over the layout of the halls.

"Father, you go that way, and I'll go this way! Let's try to corner him!"

Father Perez excitedly replied, "Got it!" The two priests ran in opposite directions.

Tim, with his glowing yellow eyes, ran down dimly lit halls, knocking aside doctors and staff. Nurses dashed back into rooms having

68

stepped out to investigate the commotion. A security guard was thrown through the air after confronting him.

Father Mitchell turned a corner as he ran toward the most recent shouting. Far down the hall, Father Perez walked toward him. Norman was between them. He turned from the direction of Father Perez and began to head in the opposite direction until he saw Father Mitchell coming toward him. As the priests moved in, Norman looked for a place to flee. He saw a door and ran through it while failing to notice the sign 'Chapel' over the door.

The two priests arrived at the chapel door within moments of each other. They crossed themselves, opened the door, and stepped into the dim chapel. Father Perez applied holy water to the door they closed behind them. Glowing yellow eyes stared from across the room.

"Fitting, that your demise will happen in a place of prayer, Lucious," Father Mitchell said.

"No. You are the ones that will die here," Lucious replied.

The lights flickered on then off again. As the lights flickered on again, the priests suddenly saw a pew flying through the air at them. They jumped out of the way just as the pew crashed on the last row of pews.

Father Perez shouted, "We bind you in the name of Christ!"

"You have no hold on him!" Father Mitchell yelled.

Lucious warned, "I'll kill him if you don't leave."

The priests slowly walked up the middle aisle. "We cast you out, offspring of Satan," said Father Perez.

Father Mitchell ordered, "We command you to leave him. We send you to hell."

Near Lucious, on the carpeted floor, a large circle began to smoke. Lucious looked at it and began to panic and couldn't move. The circle on the floor turned orange then red. Moments later the circle became a hole that burned through the floor. As smoke rushed up to the ceiling, the water sprinklers came on. Lucious was pulled from Tim's body and forced into the hole. Tim fell to the floor unconscious. Lucious fought his eviction by hanging from the edge of the hole by his claws while trying to climb out. The priests walked up near the hole. Father Perez sprinkled Lucious with holy water. Lucious fell down the hole, screaming.

Father Mitchell looked at Father Perez. "Why not?" He dropped his bottle of holy water down the hole.

Father Perez smiled. He took the cap off his bottle poured the holy water into the hole and dropped the empty bottle too. "It might freshen up the smell a bit." The hole closed.

Tim sat up, now himself. "What a nightmare," he said, rubbing his scalp.

Dr. Albert burst through the chapel doors and walked up the center aisle. "Is it gone?"

"Yes. Back to where it came from," Father Mitchell answered.

"And with some third-degree burns," Father Perez added.

Father Mitchell, Father Perez, Dr. Albert, and Tim left the chapel and made their way through the busy halls of broken conversations, rumors, and chaos as firefighters, maintenance employees, and staff buzzed around.

Dr. Albert pushed open the door to the laboratory with the priests and Tim following. The two technicians were still putting equipment back on tables while Norman peacefully snored on his gurney.

"He's a mass-murderer. What will we do with him now?" Tim asked.

Dr. Albert answered, "He's protected by doctor-patient and clergy confidentiality."

"That's way too convenient if you ask me." Tim shook his head and stared at Norman.

A week later, seated in the conference room, Norman looked better. "Thanks for getting rid of that… thing," he said.

"It wasn't easy," Dr. Albert replied. "How are you sleeping?"

Norman nodded his head. "A lot better. But I can still see the bodies on the floor. I wish they would leave too."

"Norman," Dr. Albert said, "I'll help you with those images on one condition."

"And what's that?"

"You go to the police and tell them what you did."

"Why?! The priests forgave me!"

Father Perez noted, "Confession cleanses the sin. Penance helps close the door."

"Norman, you murdered five people," Dr. Albert said. "God may have forgiven you, but you are still responsible."

"And still vulnerable," Father Mitchell warned.

Dr. Albert opened the folder in front of her and took out photos one-by-one. "You are responsible for these. She took out the first photo and placed it in front of Norman. "This is Josh Sweeny. He was seventeen. You killed him while he was walking home from basketball practice." The doctor flipped out another photo. "This man with the beard was Mr. Wooley, a father of two small girls." Dr. Albert flipped another photo onto the table. "This is Mrs. Lopez with the bloody stripped sweater. She was a bank vice-president."

Norman put his hand up. "Alright, that's enough."

"Oh no, it's not," Tim said with aggravation. "There are two more."

Dr. Albert continued by flipping out the fourth photo and sliding it in front of Norman. "This was a college student, Ms. Green. Remember the diamond cluster earrings?"

"She was about my age, ass-wipe," Tim told Norman.

"And this one was Steve Myers. He and his wife have five grandchildren." Dr. Albert said as she slid the photo across the desk to Norman.

"Tim said, "I'm surprised you didn't take his bracelet."

"And," Dr. Albert added, "this is the knife you murdered them all with." She dropped the last photo on top of the pile. Norman looked at the photos without expression.

Dr. Albert promised, "The Fathers and I will testify on your behalf. Once they see the video, the judge will understand."

Father Mitchell said, "Norman, you still need to do your penance."

"Forget it!" Norman raised his voice. "I'm done with all that!"

"Norman, there are always demons searching for people with open doors, just like you," Father Perez explained.

Norman was alarmed. "How do you know all about these people, anyway?"

Dr. Albert answered, "Because we found your memories as we were probing your mind."

"And they have been recorded," Tim said, pointing his finger close to Norman's face.

"I'd rather see the bodies than go back to prison!" Norman growled before he stood and walked out.

The flames and screams below, reflected up on the rocks as a very determined Lucious slowly climbed his way up the walls of hell. Dividing his attention, he looked for cracks to dig his pointed nails of his long fingers in, while looking down through the rising smoke with caution, like an escaping criminal.

It was night time in the city. Norman passed by an alley as he walked along a sidewalk. A set of yellow eyes glowed, then started to move forward toward the sidewalk.

Later, the same night, police officers in a circle wrote on small notebooks as they stood around a middle-aged man in a suit, lying on the sidewalk. Flashes of cameras illuminated a large amount of blood on the victim's chest. The ghost of the man sat up unseen and looked up into the distance and walked away with determination.

It was dark in Norman's small fourth-floor apartment. Lights from the city were just enough to see the streaks of blood on the light switch just inside the door. On the edge of his small table sat a bloody knife he had dropped there on his way to his bed. Norman slept fitfully in his clothes on top of the covers of his small bed. His hands were bloody. Glowing yellow showed through narrowly open eyes.

The ghost of Mr. Wooley passed through the outside wall. A female ghost wearing a striped sweater walked through the closed door from the hall. The young-looking female ghost of Ms. Green, wearing cluster diamond earrings, moved in through the closed window. The ghost of Steve Myers, still wearing a turquoise bracelet, came in from an inside wall. Up from the middle of the floor, the ghost of Josh, the teenage boy rose to stand among the others.

The five ghosts gathered around Norman's bed and looked down at him. He began to breath frosty air. Each ghost reached into Norman's body. Their arms struggled as Lucious resisted. But Lucious' resistance was in vain as he was slowly pulled out from Norman's body. Norman's body relaxed, and the glowing yellow from his eyes instantly faded out.

The ghost of Ms. Green held Lucious by the throat. The demon tried to speak but couldn't. She blew cold air on the demon's face which frosted it. The other ghosts blew frosty air on Lucious' body as they kept firm grips on his arms. The helpless demon trembled then stiffened before beginning to freeze. He turned black moments before he turned into ashes and disintegrated.

Josh's ghost moved to guard the door. Mrs. Lopez's ghost moved to block the phone. The ghost of Ms. Green kicked Norman's bed. He woke up startled and looked around in terror at the ghosts then turned over and buried his face in the mattress. Suddenly, the ghost of the middle-aged man in a suit came in angrily through the closed door. The other ghosts watched as he moved directly to Norman's bed and picked him up. He resisted and tried to pull away, but the ghost in the suit picked him up over his head. Norman screamed and thrashed as the other ghosts watched. The ghost took Norman to the window and threw him through the glass.

Norman's limp body was folded over the top of a fire hydrant, surrounded by broken frosted glass. Blood dripped from his head. The smashed window on the fourth floor above was vacant except for frost which slowly dissipated from the remaining jagged glass around the frame.

Dr. Albert was called by the coroner and a detective to meet them at the morgue.

"Thanks for coming doctor. This is Detective Jones." The doctor and the detective shook hands.

"Dr. Albert. I believe I have one of your patients. If you'll follow me, please."

The three of them walked down the hall together to the autopsy room. Norman's body was on a stainless-steel table, covered by a sheet from his feet to his neck.

"Yes. That's one of mine. Norman. What killed him?"

The coroner replied, "Blunt trauma to the spine."

"Doctor, I didn't call you just to identify him. I also want to show you something very unusual."

The coroner pulled the sheet down to Norman's waist. "Frostbites on the sides of his abdomen in the shape of hands. But it gets weirder. Most of the pressure was from the thumbs on the back of him. They left heavy bruises. But the finger marks on his front left lighter bruises."

"What does that tell you?"

The coroner re-enacted the assault with an imaginary body. "Norman was lifted up from being on his stomach, probably over someone's head. Then he was thrown through his apartment window with such force that he went over the sidewalk and landed on a fire hydrant near the curb. Frostbites... I can't explain them."

Detective Jones offered, "Well, the bloody knife we found on Norman's table might be connected to some cold case murders. We're checking DNA on it."

"He committed exactly five murders with that knife," Dr. Albert said, closing her eyes briefly.

The coroner and detective looked confused. "Doctor, how would you know this?" the detective asked.

"I have them all recorded through Norman's own eyes."

The detective looked at the doctor in disbelief. "You have them all recorded?"

"Yes, detective. We recently found Norman's memories of the murders while we were probing his mind. Do the names: Josh Sweeny, George Wooley, Maria Lopez, Julian Green, and Steve Myers sound familiar?"

"Yeah. I've heard a few of those names."

"Norman's work," The doctor said, as she stared at Norman's face.

Julie Albert and her brother, Geoff, sat at a little outside table at a café, drinking coffee.

"Geoff, I know we have talked about this before, but I want to bring mom to the laboratory."

"God, not this again. There are things that parents don't want their children to know; things they might have done that young people do. And there's always the possibility that you'll stumble onto them or some family secrets we would rather not have known about. I still think she should have her privacy."

"And her insanity? Geoff, would you rather take a chance on finding out something embarrassing about mom, or keep her in the state she's in? What do you think she would say; protect my privacy or try to free me from my illness so I can live out the rest of my life normally and happy?"

"I still won't sign the consent forms."

Dr. Albert sighed. "Your approval isn't necessary anymore. I petitioned for power of attorney, and it was granted."

"You did what?!"

"It's my decision, and I'm doing it! I'm going into mom's mind and find out just what the hell is wrong with her. And I would like you to go with me."

"If you're going in, then so am I."

Geoff and Julie sat up on gurneys in the laboratory, on either side of their mom. All three had sensors attached to their heads and backs of their necks. Their mom was sedated.

"Tim, we're ready," Dr. Albert said.

"Okay. Here we go," Tim replied just before he tapped the last few keys on the keyboard to start the sibling's journey.

Geoff and Julie appeared on the monitor. Their mother's mind was bright, organized, and clean. Thousands of faded still images and moving ones, floated in the air like small clouds. Some were quiet conversations. The siblings realized that they were in their mother's earliest memories. They held hands and began to walk slowly together through the memories, stopping briefly to laugh, smile, and cry.

"I could stay here for months," Geoff said, with wonderment in his eyes.

"Me too. Let's look at as much as we can, even briefly. It's all being recorded so we can review them later. Right now, we need to get to finding mom's issue."

They walked on together through their mom's newer and clearer memories. Finally, they recognize that they were entering the area of their mom's mind holding her last memories. Looking to the end, where there are no more memories, Geoff saw that the area was dim.

"Sis, look up ahead. That's where the problem is."

Without looking at the last few memories, the two of them hurried to the dense, black, hazy sphere on the ground.

"Mom?" Julie asked.

"Mom, it's us, Geoff and Julie."

Julie knelt down in front of the smoky blob. "Mom? Are you in there?"

Geoff squatted down next to his sister and waved his hand to fan the black fog. As the fog moved away, a human form began to appear. They fanned their hands faster until they confirmed that the figure was their mom. She was on her knees with her face to the floor, covering her ears with her hands. Julie reached her hand out, took her mother's arm, and gently pulled.

"She's not moving. She's too stiff."

Geoff and Julie stood up. "We have to turn around and try to find her last memories," Geoff said.

They walked back to the end of the memories. Immediately, it became obvious what caused their mother's condition. The brother and sister team stood in front of a floating memory and watched as the scene played out.

Their mother was driving at night. As she came around a bend, she suddenly saw a man walking in the road. With no time to even apply the brake, her car slammed into the man. He was hurled far through the air and landed in the pond along the side of the road. She screamed frantically, pulled her care over to the side, threw the door open, and hurried toward the water. The angry ghost of the man emerged from the water, walked to the shore, and came toward her. She turned and ran back to the car. After getting in the car, she slammed the door and locked it. As she watched in terror, the angry ghost arrived at her window and banged on it with his fist with his face pressed against the glass.

"That's it," Geoff said as he continued to stare at the memory.

"Tim, can you remove just that incident from her memories, please?"

"Yes, but it'll take about an hour to trace the synapses and zap the right neurons."

"Okay," Dr. Albert replied. "Start on that as soon as possible, please."

"Yes, doctor."

"Let's wait here," Geoff suggested. "We'll look around some more."

The two of them backtracked; looked at more memories and learned more about their mom.

An hour later, they returned to their mother just as Tim announced, "Doctor, we found the neurons, and we're ready to sever. Standby and monitor the memory that caused her condition."

"Thanks, Tim. Proceed when ready." Geoff and Lisa stepped back to the small cloud-like memory. Moments later, the tragic scene disappeared. Immediately, they returned to their mother. They reached into the dark cloud and gently grasp their mother's arm. Her body relaxed.

"Mom, it's your children; Lisa and Geoff."

Geoff coaxed her, "Come on, mom. Look at us." She slowly removed her hands from over her ears and turned her face toward them.

"Try to stand up," Dr. Albert said as she gently pulled her mom's arm. Together, they managed to stand her to her feet. After a few moments of confusion, their mother recognized her children. The three of them embraced.

"Tim, we're done here."

"Yes, doctor. Disconnecting you now."

The large monitor on the wall went blank. Dr. Albert and Geoff opened their eyes. Tim walked over to the gurneys and began to remove their sensors.

"Your mother should be out of anesthesia in about thirty minutes," Tim said.

"While we wait, I'll monitor her vitals and hope," Dr. Albert said, as she looked at the monitors.

Half an hour later, Mrs. Albert opened her sleepy eyes and looked around the room. "Where am I?" She gazed at Tim standing next to her gurney. "Who are you?"

Tim answered with a smile, "I'm Tim, your daughter's lab assistant."

"My daughter?" In wonder, she slowly turned her head to looked over at her daughter and son crying on the other side of her gurney. Reaching her arms toward them, she cried saying, "My God! Come here!"

A Henry Kind of Gift

It was the late 1970's when the Newsome house was snuggled together with other middle/lower-class homes on the tree-lined street. Another Elementary School day had Henry's mother in her routine of kneeling down in the bathroom putting gel in her son's hair. He held his small baseball cap and tried not to wiggle.

"Henry, did you eat your cereal yet?"

"Yes, mommy. And I drank all my milk! And I made my bed!"

"Thank you, Henry. You're such a good boy!"

"After school, I'm going to build the model airplane you bought me!"

"Would you like to build it together? Maybe you can teach me."

"Okay, mommy! We gotta put newspapers down and not use too much glue."

"You just turned eight, and already you're so smart!"

Little Henry threw his arms out like an airplane and leaned from side to side making airplane sounds

Henry's mother laughed as she said, "Hold still, you little wiggly worm! I'm trying to comb your hair!"

She parted Henry's hair on the side, finished combing it, then kissed him on his cheek. "Do you know I love you more than anything else in the world? It's our secret."

She offered her pinky finger to her son. Henry locked his pinky finger with hers.

"Yes. I love you too! You're my best friend in the whole wide world! Forever!"

"Forever," Henry's mother echoed with a loving smile.

"Hurry up and get your kid ready! If he misses the damn bus, I'm not taking him to school! Henry, get your butt out here!" The rough voice of Henry's step-father came from the living room.

Henry gave his mother a hug and a kiss then ran out of the bathroom with his arms out like an airplane while making his airplane sounds.

"Love you!"

In the front room, Henry grabbed his brown paper lunch bag with his name on it, from the dining table, and ran past his stepfather, sitting in a recliner, drinking a beer and watching TV.

"Don't let that door slam!"

Henry stopped running. When he got to the front door, he opened it carefully, stepped out onto the porch then carefully closed the door. After Jumping off the steps he threw his arms out, made airplane sounds while running toward the slowly approaching school bus.

The school bus doors opened, and Henry was greeted with a wide smile from the driver.

"Good morning, Henry."

"Good morning!"

Henry climbed up the steps then stretched his arms out over the heads of the other children while making airplane sounds as he walked down the aisle to find a seat.

In their front yard, Henry and his mother played hide and seek. With her eyes covered, Henry's mom called out, "You better hide! I'm coming to get you!"

Henry frantically ran back and forth, while he kept looking back at his Mother.

"10,9,8,7,6,5, Find a good place! 4,3,2,1 Here I come!" She began to search around the yard for Henry. "I'm coming! I'm getting closer!"

Henry was hiding behind a tree, but his shoulder was sticking out. His mother saw it but walked right by as if she hadn't.

"You found a really good place to hide! I can't find you! I give up!"

"I'm right behind you! I won!" Little Henry proclaimed as he jumped out.

"But I'm still going to get you, so you better run! Last one to the door is a rotten egg!"

She chased her laughing son all the way to the door and let him arrive first.

It was an evening in the Newsome house as Henry, and his mother sat at the dining table coloring in coloring books. His model airplane, crayons, glasses of milk, and cookies were scattered around the table. Henry's mother noticed that he was coloring outside of the black outlined balloons.

"Henry, what are you doing? You're supposed to color 'inside' the balloons."

"I know, mommy. Sometimes I like to do things different. All the other kids at school color inside the pictures."

"That's what your teacher told me. She said you took chalk from your classroom and drew more squares on the hopscotch on the sidewalk too."

"Yeah. Made it more fun. I always like to think of doing things other ways," Henry replied as he kept coloring. "The kids liked it. Johnny said he wished he thought about doing it."

"Your teacher also said that you sometimes sleep at your desk."

"No, mommy. I just like to close my eyes and think about other things when she gets boring."

"Well, just remember how it looks to her and the other children. Think about that for a while."

"Okay."

Henry's stepfather came through the door and announced, "I'm home, and I'm hungry. Get me a beer."

"Right away, dear," she said as she immediately left her seat for the kitchen.

He turned the TV on and sat in his chair.

"Dinner will be ready soon," she said as she handed him the beer then sat back at the table with Henry.

"Better be."

"Mommy?" Henry quietly asked as he picked up his model airplane. "Yes?"

"Do you think someday you and me could fly away together? Maybe go to heaven?"

"You and I will be in heaven someday. But we have a lot of living to do before we go there. Think about that for a while."

Henry was tucked in his bed. His mother sat on his bed and closed the book she had just finished reading to him under the light from the lamp.

"Okay, young man. Time for sleep."

"Mommy, why do we have to live with him?"

"Mommy doesn't have enough money to give you our own home and pay the bills. You'll understand someday." She kissed him then they locked pinkies. "I love you more than anyone in the whole world. Our secret."

"Our secret," he promised.

She turned off the lamp and left the room. Henry laid there with his eyes opened, deep in thought.

The Newsome family car was traveling too fast, leaning sharply on the curves as its headlights slashed at the dark country night. Henry's stepfather had been drinking.

In the back-seat, Henry had to hold on as he was forced to lean with every turn of the car. He held his baseball cap on but had to stop flying his model airplane.

"Honey, you're probably drunk, and you're driving way too fast!"

"I might be a little drunk, but I can still take these country roads."

"You're going to get us all killed if you don't slow down!" She turned to look back at Henry. "Sweetie, make sure your seatbelt is on."

"Okay, mommy." After a small metallic click Henry said, "It's on now, mommy."

"Thank you, sweetie."

The car screeched around a sharp curve as Henry's mother fumbled trying to fasten her seat belt. Suddenly, the car left the pavement. As it bounced onto the shoulder, Henry's mother quickly dropped the buckles of her seat belt and reached her arm to the back seat to brace her son as she shouted, "Henry!!!"

The front of the car smashed into a tree. Steam poured out from under the crumpled hood, yet the headlights remained on. A small fire appeared on the engine. The windshield on driver's side had a large hole in it. Henry's stepfather was motionless and slumped forward on the steering wheel, with blood dripping down from his face. Henry's mother's bloody head was tilted back, motionless. A metallic-sounding click of a seat belt being unfastened in back seat broke the stillness. Henry's face slowly rose over the front seat. His hat was gone, and front of his gelled hair was pushed back. He looked over at his stepfather and his mother then found his baseball cap and put it on. And he searched his seat and the floor for his model airplane until he found it. Henry pushed his door open and got out with his model airplane. The passenger side door was opened in the impact. Henry balled up in his lifeless mother's lap, reached up and touched her bruised face, and stared trance-like through the broken windshield at the slowly growing flames from the engine.

Another car approached from behind and pulled onto the shoulder. Bouncing headlights shined on the Newsome family car before it stopped. The driver's side car door quickly opened, and a man ran up to the burning car. The passerby reached through the broken passenger window and picked up Henry and his model airplane from off his mother's lap after checking for a pulse.

"I got ya, little fella. I got ya. Come on."

He hurriedly carried limp Henry back to his car and opened the passenger door saying, "Honey, get in the driver's seat and take this boy to the hospital! He can't see any more of this."

The woman jumped out and hurried around to the driver's side. The man placed Henry on the passenger seat, put his model airplane on his lap, and fastened his seat belt.

"Is he okay?!"

"He hit his face pretty hard. I think he's in shock. Hurry! You gotta hurry!"

"I'll call the police at the hospital."

"I'll go back and see if the driver is alive. Go!"

Henry curled up on the passenger seat as the car turned around and spun away. The man ran back to Newsome family car, checked the pulses of Henry's stepfather then re-checked his mother and shook his head. He began to pull the bodies out of the car.

"No little boy should have to grow up without his mother."

He laid the bodies in the grass, away from the burning car.

After screeching to a stop by the entrance of the emergency room, the kind woman hurriedly got out and ran inside.

"Help! I've got a little boy in my car. He's been in a car accident!"

A passing doctor flew out the emergency entrance door with the woman trailing close behind. The doctor quickly checked Henry and carried him inside.

Henry sat on the treatment table with his baseball cap and model airplane at his side. The doctor shined a small flashlight in his eyes.

"I want my mommy." Tears ran down his cheeks.

Ms. Parks walked in, stopped to look over at Henry, and took a deep breath. The attending nurse stepped over to her.

"Hi. That's Henry. We found his grandparent's information in his little wallet. They should be here any minute."

"Thanks. I got here as soon as I could. My God. Why do these things happen?"

Ms. Parks walked over to the doctor. "Doctor, how is Henry?"

"He hit his face on something. There's swelling, but nothing is broken. Be careful. His seat belt left quite a bruise, but it saved his life."

"Anything else?"

"Yes," the doctor answered. "He's been through a lot. Too much."

"How do you tell an eight-year-old boy that his mother and her husband are dead?"

Ms. Parks took a deep breath and walked and over to Henry.

"Hi, Henry. My name is Ms. Parks. I'm a social worker. Let me help you get down."

Ms. Parks picked up Henry and placed him on the floor, took his hand, and lead him by his hand to some chairs.

"Henry, let's sit in these chairs. I need to talk to you." Ms. Parks and Henry sat. "I need to talk to you about your father and mother"

Henry's grandpa and grandma suddenly rushed in, out of breath. They looked over at Henry. Henry's grandma put her hand over her heart, reached for Henry's grandpa to support herself, then fell to the floor. The doctor and nurse rushed over to her.

"Stat!"

Ms. Parks guided Henry and his grandpa to the side.

"Get the crash cart!"

"Let's wait out in the hall. Henry has seen too much already," Ms. Parks said to Henry's grandpa.

Ms. Parks, Henry and his grandpa left the room. Henry twisted his head around, looking back at his grandma.

Moments later a gurney quickly came out of the emergency room with Henry's grandma on it, assisted by the doctor, the nurse, and an orderly. The gurney disappeared down the hall.

Three caskets were lined up under the outside canopy, nicely dressed mourners sat in rows of chairs. Cars lined the roads in the cemetery. Henry sat in a suit, wearing his baseball cap and held his model airplane on his lap sitting next to his grandpa, and aunt. His eyes stared disconnected.

"Henry, do you want to come and live with me?" his grandpa asked. Then he looked up at the caskets and sobbed. "We both need someone."

Henry didn't respond. His aunt hugged him and his grandpa.

In the front room of his grandpa's house, Henry and his grandpa sat together on a couch.

"It's Saturday, Henry. What would you like to do?"

Henry was holding his airplane on his lap. He looked up at his grandpa momentarily and shrugged his shoulders slightly.

"I don't know," he mumbled.

"How about we go fishing?! Have you ever caught yourself a fish?! It's a lot of fun!"

Henry dropped his eyes to his airplane eyes in silence.

"Hey. I know. Let's go to the movies and have popcorn and candy!"

Henry remained silent.

"Cartoons again?"

Henry gently nodded.

His grandpa looked disappointed as he got up and walked over to the TV.

Two months later Henry was sitting on his bed. He could hear his grandpa on the telephone.

"Hi, darling. Listen, Henry needs a livelier home. I'm old now. You've got kids. How about you take him for a while?"

Henry dropped his eyes to the airplane on his lap.

Henry sat quietly on an old couch in the dirty, cluttered living room of his aunt and uncle's house. He looked around without expression, holding his model airplane. Two loud toddlers played aggressively on the dirty floor. The TV was on, but no one was watching it.

Henry listened to the argument upstairs as his uncle said, "It's hard enough just feeding 'our' own kids! We can't feed a kid who will barely even talk!"

Henry looked toward the staircase.

"He's my sister's kid for God's sake! We can't just throw him out! He's family!"

"You call that Parks lady and tell her to come and get him! Henry doesn't fit in with our family!"

Henry looked down at his model airplane and gently touched it.

Jim and Rebecca were foster parents and waited excitedly on their porch for the arrival of Ms. Parks and Henry who was a little older now. He had already been through a list of new homes and families.

Henry held his model airplane as he and Ms. Parks climbed the steps. Jim and Rebecca greeted them with smiles. Jim took Henry's small suitcase from Ms. Parks.

"Hello, again," Ms. Parks said. As we discussed on the phone, this is Henry. Henry, this is Jim and Rebecca, your new foster parents!"

"Hi, Henry. You're a handsome young buck. Hey, do you like baseball?" Jim asked.

Henry answered with only a slight shrug. Rebecca knelt down so that her face was even with Henry's face. Henry looked at her. His eyes began to well with tears.

"I bet you would like a peanut butter and jelly sandwich with a glass of milk. Right?"

Henry nodded gently.

"Thank you so much," Ms. Parks said. "I'll give you a call in a few days."

Jim opened the door and escorted Rebecca and Henry inside the house.

The beach was sunny, lovely and breezy. Jim was excited about the kite he brought.

"Okay, Henry. We need to run with the kite into the breeze until it begins to rise to the sky. Like this."

Jim ran in the wet sand with the kite. Henry looked up at the sky staring at an airplane far up.

Jim saw that Henry wasn't watching. He stopped running and looked at Rebecca with disappointment.

"Henry, are you okay?" Rebecca asked.

"I want to be in heaven with my mommy."

Six months later in their kitchen, Jim stood talking on the Telephone, "Ms. Parks, I know he's already been to other foster families, but we're sorry. Henry has issues deeper than what we can handle. We can't reach him."

Henry's bedroom door was open. He listened as he sat on his bed with his eyes closed.

In his tenth-grade English class, Henry sat with his eyes closed with a small piece of cardboard, a pencil and a book on his desk.

The teacher said to the class, "Remember, your short essays are due on Friday. Now let's turn to chapter ten."

Henry placed the cardboard and pencil in his shirt pocket, stood up, left his book on his desk, and walked toward the door. Other students turned to watch. The teacher paused and asked, "Henry, where are you going?"

"Retard," came a voice from the class.

"That's enough name calling!" the teacher said.

That was the last day of Henry Newsome's formal education.

The grocery store was busy as Henry, now a young man, was bagging groceries at a checkout. The store manager walked up to Henry.

"C'mon, Henry. I tell you the same thing every day. You've got to speed it up!"

"Yes, sir," he quietly replied.

The store manager pushed Henry aside and began quickly filling a shopping bag with groceries. "This is how you do it. Not in slow motion! Get it?! Now move!"

Henry took a bag and began to fill it with groceries.

"And as soon as you can, go out and collect the carts. Chop chop. Pronto!"

Minutes later, the store manager returned to the checkout. Henry wasn't there. He looked out into the parking lot. Henry wasn't there either.

"Where the heck is Henry?" he asked the cashier.

The cashier pointed to the end of the counter where Henry's smock laid with his name tag. He picked up the smock, shook his head, and promised, "That kid will never amount to anything."

Even as an adult, Henry couldn't keep a job for very long. It seemed he was often dropping keys on a manager's desks or handing his uniforms back to someone. But usually, he was simply fired. Although when things got stressful, and he felt the job wasn't worth it, he simply walked out.

Henry Newsome, an adult in his late-forties, walked to the park bench where he liked to close his eyes and think. Carrying a dirty plastic bag, his hair was long and messy, and his clothes were old and dirty. His face hadn't been shaved for months. He was homeless. When he arrived at the bench, he sat and placed a small piece of cardboard and a pencil on his lap then closed his eyes.

Mr. Banes, also in his late forties and Ginny his assistant, carried small bags from a local restaurant through the park as they often did, looking for the homeless. They saw Henry. He was exactly what they were looking for, so they sat down on the bench with him.

"Hello, friend. Here, has some breakfast," Mr. Banes said.

Henry, slightly startled, opened his eyes. His cardboard and pencil slid off his knee onto the grass. Avoiding eye contact, he graciously accepted the cup of coffee that Ginny extended to him. Smiling, Mr. Banes handed Henry a bag with a breakfast sandwich.

"Thank you."

"See that motel over there?" Mr. Banes asked. "We already paid for your room for two months. You're in number five."

"Here's a couple of hundred dollars to get the things you need," Ginny said, extending to Henry a small envelope.

"Thank you. My friends and I here are not what we seem to be. Think about that for a while."

"I'm sure that's true," Mr. Banes replied. "Your room is ready any time you want to take it. We already put some groceries in there."

"I'll have someone come and check on you and see if you need anything," Ginny said.

"Thank you."

Mr. Banes and Ginny stood and left. Henry took a sip of coffee, opened the bag and looked over at the budget motel.

A week later Henry quietly sat with his eyes closed on his bed in his little budget room. He was freshly shaved, his hair was combed, parted at the side, and held in place with sheen gel. He had purchased his old suit and tie at a local thrift store that he always wore. His room was cluttered but neat and organized. An old picture of Henry's mother with Henry at the age of eight was displayed on the wall next to a small baseball cap. His model airplane was suspended with strings over his neat bed. Often, it was the last thing he saw and thought about before sleeping.

It was in the morning, when a woman in business casual attire, knocked on door number five. Henry went to the door and opened it as far as the security chain would allow.

She smiled through the narrow opening. "Hello. Are you Henry?"

"Yes."

"My name is Martha. I'm a social worker. Some of your friends asked me to check on you. They said you might need a job."

"No. I'm not a good worker."

"Maybe you just haven't been in the 'right kind' of job. Here's my card." She held it in the narrow gap. Henry took it. "I'll come pick you up tomorrow morning at nine."

"Why?"

"Let's spend some time finding out what you like to do and are good at."

Henry slid the security chain and opened his door. "Okay. I'm sorry about your relationship."

Martha, confused at first, looked at the faint mark on her ring finger of her raised hand that held the business card. "Thanks. See you tomorrow, 9:00," she said before withdrawing her hand and covering it with the other.

Two days later, Henry walked into the public library as was his habit of doing several times a week. A torn piece of cardboard and pencil stuck out of his suit pocket.

"Hello, sir. Welcome. If you need anything, please just ask. Can I get you a library card?" the librarian asked quietly.

"Thank you," Henry politely and stiffly replied. "I know my way around. I have a card. I come here a lot."

The librarian looked closely at him. "Henry?"

"Yes." He took out his library card from his pocket and offered it to her.

"No, Henry. I know you! You look great! Oh, my word!" she whispered with delight.

"Thank you," he replied without a smile.

"What changed?"

"Some people cared."

As usual, Henry stayed the whole day sitting at a computer. He placed several magazines and opened books around the computer. The only break he took was lunch when he went outside with his paper lunch bag with his name written on it.

At the end of the day, there were only a couple of other people in the library. The same woman who greeted Henry that morning walked over to his table.

"Henry, it's almost time to close. You've been here all day. Why don't you go home now?"

"Okay." He logged off the computer, stood, and began to walk towards the door. "Good night."

"Good night, Henry. See you soon. Again, I want to say how good you look!"

"Thank you," he awkwardly replied. "You look good too."

Mr. Banes stood at the front of a large table in the conference room at an advertising agency. Seven people were seated at the long table. Five of them were team leaders. The sixth was the vice-president, and the seventh was Ginny, Mr. Bane's Operations Manager. The weekly meeting was already in progress.

"So, our revenues are still down, and the executive board isn't happy about it. Team leaders, we need to ratchet things up."

Kevin Gillam, the vice-president, added, "Longer hours, or whatever else. Just tell me what you need to sign some more contracts. We need more contracts."

"Is there anything else, Ginny?"

"Yes, Mr. Banes There's just one other item."

"Go ahead."

"The state's unemployment office asked us to consider bringing on a man whom they labeled, 'unemployable but gifted.'"

"Unemployable?" Kevin echoed with a frown.

Ginny read from a piece of paper in front of her. "He often has daydreams, loses interest, and sometimes suddenly walks out. He has more lows than highs."

"What? Wait. What are we doing here?" Kevin asked, spreading his arms. "Are we branching off to do rehabs?"

Ginny continued, "That's the bad news."

Kevin asked, "How can there be any good news after that?"

"There is a small tax credit for us and some very good PR. He was matched to an occupation requiring creativity."

"God knows we can use a little PR help right now," Mr. Banes said.

Ginny continued, "The state office asked if he could shadow and maybe even participate in our process."

"For how long?" Mr. Banes asked.

"Thirty days."

"And after that?"

"We can send him back or hire him."

"Sounds like we'll be sending that guy right back. He's just going to get in the way," Kevin complained.

"Okay. We'll do it."

Kevin turned his head away and rolled his eyes.

"Great," Ginny said. "He can start Monday. He'll be in the morning meeting."

Cartoons played on the TV in motel budget room number five. Henry was wearing the same neat, but old suit and tie as he stood at the kitchenette and put an almost empty jar of jelly in the mini refrigerator and scraped the inside of a jar of peanut butter with a plastic knife before putting the jar in the trash. He wrote his name on a brown paper lunch bag and rolled up the top, turned off the cartoons, and walked toward the door. Finally, he put a small piece of torn cardboard and a pencil in his suit's breast pocket and walked out the door.

Henry walked from his motel room door and through the parking lot with his brown paper lunch bag. Continuing down the sidewalk, he eventually came to a street rally where people were holding signs demanding that democracy and freedom be established in every country. A demonstrator approached Henry with a pen and clipboard.

"Sir, would you mind signing your name to get Congress to push harder for international democracy?"

Henry stopped. "You're another one thinking that democracy will save us."

"What do you mean?"

"Human nature with absolute freedom of expression? No thank you."

"What's wrong with human nature?" the demonstrator asked, looking surprised.

"Wars, poverty, crime, violence, and greed constantly dominate the headlines. Why do you think this is?"

"Okay, I'll give you that. But doesn't human nature have a good side?"

"Yes," Henry answered. "But it's not nearly as potent as the bad side. The good side is the only reason the human race has survived so far. But it has peaked its evolutionary arch, and now it's on the way down."

"Dude, that's gloomy."

"Go home and think about that for a while. I will not sign my name and neither should you." Henry brushed past the demonstrator and walked through the others.

Several blocks later, Henry walked with the crowd of morning pedestrians. Stopping to look up at the high-rise building where he was scheduled to be, he noticed an airplane flying overhead which took his thoughts away. He watched it until a pedestrian bumped into him. Henry apologized then went inside.

Once in the lobby, Henry walked over to check wall directory. Then he stepped into an empty elevator, pushed a button, and stood back in the corner holding his lunch bag in front of himself.

Moments later Henry went through a door and walked up to the receptionist's desk.

With a boyish mannerism, he said, "Hello, ma'am. My name is Henry Newsome. I'm supposed to ask for Ms. Ginny."

"Well hello Mr. Newsome," she said with a smile. "I'm Ginny. Welcome. The morning meeting is about to begin. Let me take you to the conference room."

"Just, 'Henry' please, and thank you."

"Then, 'Henry' it is. And please call me just, Ginny."

"Okay, Ginny."

Henry walked behind Ginny as she escorted him to the open door of the conference room and stopped. Henry waited submissively behind her and listened.

In the conference room, sat a stack of portfolios on the table near five of the people.

"By the way, has anyone got the 'thank you' ad suggestion yet for the charity that just met its fund-raising goal?" Mr. Banes asked. Blank faces from the people seated at the table looked at him. "I know it's a pro bono thing, but I need an idea from everyone by the end of the day. It's good community relations."

"Come on. You're team leaders. It'll count as half an ad for your team. Most of you need it badly," Kevin said.

"Plus, an easy hundred dollars for the ad that gets selected," Mr. Banes added.

Ginny knocked on the open door and escorted Henry into the meeting. "Everyone, this is Henry Newsome. Henry, this is Mr. Banes our president, Kevin Gillam, our vice-president, and our five team leaders. Henry is here to learn about what we do and maybe participate in some ad creations."

The smiling team offered hellos. Kevin just looked at Henry's expressionless face.

"Hello," Henry replied.

"Welcome, Henry," Mr. Banes said. "Please have a seat."

Henry sat and placed his lunch bag on his lap with his hands slightly gripping the arms of the chair as he stiffly followed the conversation with his eyes.

"What kind of education or experience do you have, Henry?" Stan asked.

"Tenth grade. But I read a lot."

Kevin mouthed the words, 'tenth grade' and rolled his eyes.

"So, you've never been to college or earned an online degree?" Karen asked.

"No."

Lee asked, "Are you good with computers?"

"Yes. I spend a lot of time at the library."

"I don't mean to pry," Karen said, "but don't you think an education might help you?

"Which is better; to study and memorize other people's thoughts and work, or to create your own?"

"Good question," Marcel answered.

Henry continued, "Which is the higher intelligence: to copy or create? To mimic or evolve? Think about that for a while."

Ginny looked at Mr. Banes who looked at her. Henry took out the small piece of cardboard and the pencil from his jacket pocket and put them on his lap.

Mr. Banes saw the cardboard, squinted his eyes, and looked at Ginny who was already looking at him.

Henry added, "Imagination and inspiration trump information... a paraphrase from Einstein."

"You've got something there," John replied. "But an education can change a person and help their future."

Henry looked up from writing on the cardboard. "For some. My grandpa used to say, 'Give an idiot an education and you'll have an educated idiot.' He thought there was nothing worse." Quiet chuckles but filled the room but Henry didn't smile. "He said most of them end up in politics."

There came another wave of quiet laughter. Henry didn't smile.

"But you're not an idiot, are you, Henry?" Kevin asked. Some team members looked at Kevin with frowns.

"Some people call me an idiot. The specialists often seem confused even when they finally decide on a new diagnosis for me."

The team members tried not to smirk. Henry looked down at his lap and wrote. "Some of the wisest people I know, sleep on park benches and eat out of dumpsters."

Kevin smirked. "Friends of yours?"

"Yes. Some failures and some wounded. People who have given up on the world or vice versa." Henry looked up from writing on the cardboard.

"Okay team," Mr. Banes said, "we have one week to design an ad for a top-shelf car company. All of you have your portfolios."

"The ad that gets selected comes with a bonus from me on top of the commission," Kevin added.

"Ginny, please see that Henry gets set up in the empty cubicle."

"Of course, Mr. Banes."

"So, Henry, what kinds of talent do you have?" Kevin asked.

"I know something about human nature. And sometimes I can see things that other people can't."

Kevin smirked again. "Like ghosts?"

"No."

John asked, "What do you mean, Henry?"

Henry answered as he looked down to write on the cardboard again, "It's not what you look at that matters, it's what you see."

"What should people see?" Kevin asked, still looking for a way to embarrass Henry.

Henry looked up again. "Whatever is there."

"That sounds cyclical," Pete noted.

"That just sounds plain *silly*," Kevin added.

"That sounded like a quote by Henry David Thoreau," Ginny said with a grin.

"That's right, Ginny," Henry answered. "You look until you see. You ask until it answers. You listen until you hear."

The of the team leaders just stared at Henry.

"All right, team. Let's get to it," Mr. Banes said.

Everyone began to stand and leave. Henry slid the cardboard note across the table to Mr. Banes who picked it up and read it to himself.

"Hold on for a moment everyone. Hold it. I want to read this to you. We just might have our pro bono ad."

The team members stood in place, watching and listening as Mr. Banes read Henry's cardboard note out loud.

"We reached our fund-raising goal. Some say it was an answered prayer. Several say it was karma; others believed that it was hard work, and sacrifice. A few say it was the benevolent hand of the universe. To everyone and everything we say, Thank You!"

Mr. Banes smiled and spread his arms. "Our new friend has just relieved all of you! This is excellent, Henry! I'll call the charity myself, today."

"Looks like Henry gets the hundred dollars," Ginny announced, smiling at Henry.

"Now, all of you are dismissed. You have work to do," Kevin ordered, displeased with what had just happened.

"Ginny, please get Henry a portfolio for the car company."

Ginny smiled at Henry. "Yes, Mr. Banes."

The team leaders shook Henry's hand before leaving the room. Kevin looked disgusted at Henry and walked directly out of the room.

"Henry, would you mind waiting in the lobby for just a minute?" Mr. Banes asked.

"No," Henry answered before he walked out the room. Only Mr. Banes and Ginny remained.

"Ginny, that's one of the people from the park that we got a room for!"

"I think he is! He doesn't seem to recognize us."

"Let's not say anything to anyone. Give him his hundred dollars today from petty cash."

"Happily."

Henry was alone in the bathroom as he stood at the last urinal, next to a wall. Kevin walked in and looked over at him before walking to the first urinal.

"Hello, Kevin."

Kevin silently stared at the wall in front of him. Henry finished at the urinal, walked to a sink, and began to wash his hands. Kevin finished at the urinal, walked to the sink next to Henry and washed his hands.

"I like my cubicle," Henry said.

Kevin quickly stepped in front of Henry to take paper towels from the dispenser. He dried his hands, balled up the paper towels, and threw them hard at the metal waste receptacle. He laughed at Henry before he walked out the door.

It was night as Henry slept restlessly on his small bed. Shifting eyes moved erratically under their lids as his face glowed with perspiration from his reoccurring nightmare. It was always a slow-motion scene of his mother reaching her arm into the back seat of the Newsome family car and her face of panic just before it hit the tree. Her loud echoing, "Henry!!!" quickly jolted him awake. He sat up with rapid breathing and cried.

At his cubicle. Henry took items out of a box and placed them on his desk and cubicle walls: a vase with a dead flower and a fresh flower, a blank white picture labeled 'snow storm', a picture of a chicken standing next to an egg labeled with a question mark, a picture of a horse pushing a cart, a picture of a white sky with black dots, small model cars, and plastic toy soldiers.

The team leaders were seated with three clients from the auto company. The clients were prepared to see what each team leader offered for a commercial. Mr. Banes, Kevin, and Henry mostly observed. Another commercial from a team leader was ending on the big screen on the wall. The clients made comments.

"Classy."

"Uh huh."

"Very nice."

"Thanks, Lee," Kevin said. "And lastly, we have our temp, Henry."

Everyone had subtle nervous expressions as Ginny started the video. The first video segment was outside on a parked car in the darkening late afternoon. The second segment showed a close up of a man's eyes in the lighted visor mirror above the steering wheel.

Narrator: "In the mirror, he sees a gracefully aging man. Slight wrinkles and graying hair frame his lively eyes just like his middle-aged body frames his younger soul. He searches the face and looks into eyes that no longer turn away. This man has lost and won and now wears a warm and confident smile. He earned his wisdom and has acquired the fortunes of both his successes and his failures, yet he still believes, and laughs, and dreams. Because... he's one of the people that doesn't just live... he is still fully alive."

The third segment gave a close-up view of the driver's hand as he put the car in gear.

The Fourth video segment was a close up of the brand name on the back of the car before it drove off toward the ocean side city landscape.

As the commercial ended, the clients clapped which startled Henry. They gave their evaluations.

"Fabulous! I really felt that! It's rich and deep. There's a strong and silent attention to the car, and it's not even mentioned in the narrative."

"It has perspective. It felt real and sincere. And this kind of person is the kind that drives our car. A lot of people are like that guy. Heck, *I'm* like him!"

"It makes me want to be that guy, to have those things said of me and drive the kind of car he's driving. And it was interesting, real, and relevant! I love it!"

One of the clients turned to the other two auto clients. "I don't know about you two, but I think this last ad is the one."

The other two clients nodded and smiled.

"That last ad gets my vote."

"Mine too."

Unnoticed, Kevin closed his eyes for a few seconds.

"Wonderful!" Mr. Banes exclaimed. "We'll get the contract ready, spruce up the ad, and present the final version the minute it's done."

"Fine. But don't change a thing with the essence or wording."

"I think it's perfect just the way it is."

The third client pointed to Henry. "And please keep this man around. We might need him again. Thank you, Henry. Great work!"

The clients all walked over to Henry. He began to stand, dropped his cardboard note, picked it up, and awkwardly shook hands but didn't smile.

"Thank you. You're welcome."

After the clients left the room, Karen said, "I recognize those eyes in the mirror. Mr. Baaaaanes?!"

"Yes, Karen. That was me. I volunteered. Henry deserves all the credit. He was the writer, producer, director, and editor."

"This is a good example of why we offer to help you in any we can.

95

If even Henry can do it, any of you can."

Mr. Banes gave a side-glance to Kevin, obviously not pleased with the comment.

Henry was alone in the break room with his wrinkled brown lunch bag, a sandwich wrapped in wax paper, a few cookies, an apple, a small carton of milk, and a paper napkin; all spread out in front of him. Mr. Banes walked in, went over to the coffee maker, and poured himself a cup of coffee.

"Hi, Henry. Everyone is still talking about your winning ad for the car company."

"Hello, Mr. Banes," Henry replied without looking up.

"We've got quite an ad crew here, don't we?"

"I'm a lonely boy standing on dark rainy street waiting for the school bus that never comes. I still dream that sometimes. Then I look behind me and my house is gone."

"God, Henry, where did that come from? The universe is a friendly place you know."

Henry stared at his lunch items. "No, Mr. Banes, the universe is not friendly. Neither is the wild beast, the streets, or death."

"But..."

"The augend and the addends must equal the sum. Think about that for a while."

"But Henry, can't we help make the unfriendly things, friendly? Isn't that why we're all here?"

"The universe doesn't cooperate or care. How can we say that the universe is friendly when the things that it produces are not? Even space is cold and silent." Henry slumped and became still before mumbling, "I hate that my childhood is gone."

He gently shook, crying. Then he buried his face in his folded arms resting on the table.

Mr. Banes looked at Henry with compassion, walked over to him, and put his hand on Henry's shoulder.

"Are you going to be all right, my friend?"

Henry took a deep stuttered breath, stopped crying, and nodded.

Mr. Banes began to leave. "Take the rest of the day off. Go to the park and enjoy yourself. See you tomorrow?"

Henry slowly stood and put his lunch items back into his lunch bag.

"Yes. See you tomorrow."

Ginny was seated at the front desk as Henry walked in with an opened envelope.

"Hello, Henry. How are you?" she asked with a smile.

"Hello, Ginny. I'm well. How are you?" He extended the opened envelope to Ginny.

"I'm fine. What do you have here?"

"There's a mistake in my paycheck."

"Okay. Let me take a look." Ginny opened the envelope and looked at the check before tapping keys on her computer. "No. There's no mistake."

"It's a lot of money."

Ginny handed the check back to Henry who looked at it again. "It's the commission you earned from the automobile account."

"It's a lot of money."

"Yes, it is. It's all yours and you deserve it."

"Okay. Thank you."

Henry walked past the receptionist's desk and down the hall. Ginny smiled, watching Henry make his way to his cubicle.

Mr. Banes, Kevin, Ginny, and Henry were seated in Mr. Banes office.

"Well, Henry you've been here almost thirty days. What do you think our agency?" Mr. Banes asked.

"I like being here. I've made some friends."

"You've done great work. I'd like to offer you a job here. But Kevin doesn't think the timing is right."

Kevin said, "Henry, I need to see you blend in better. You know, become more outward and less... different."

"You mean, less unique," Henry replied.

"No. I mean less 'weird', if you want the truth."

"Henry," Mr. Banes said, "personally, most everyone likes you. Professionally, you're making money for this agency. Those are what matter to me."

"They matter to me too."

"So, I'm offering you a job here because I feel you'll continue to do well."

"What do you think?" Henry asked Ginny.

"I'd like to keep having you around. And I bet you have a great smile. Can't wait to see it."

"Okay. I'll work here."

"Great," Mr. Banes said. "Welcome aboard!"

Mr. Banes stood first and stepped over to Henry and shook his hand. Ginny shook his hand with enthusiasm. Kevin reluctantly shook his hand.

Mr. Banes and Kevin stepped into Henry's cubicle. Mr. Banes was carrying a stack of portfolios. Henry sat in his chair with his eyes closed.

"Hello, Henry," Mr. Banes said. Henry didn't respond.

Kevin looked at Henry. "Earth to Henry. Come in Henry. Are you sleeping?"

Henry opened his eyes. "Hello. No. I was thinking."

"Henry, I need to shake things up here. I'm giving you your own team and office."

Kevin said, "I picked one member from each of the other teams for you. You'll have to meet in the Supply Room. It's all we have left."

Mr. Banes handed Henry the stack of portfolios. "Every team has the week to come up with an ad for a women's clothing line. Henry, I know you can do this."

"The Supply Room is a mess, but there are a table and chairs. You might want to take a look at it as soon as you can," Kevin said.

"Thank you."

Mr. Banes and Kevin turned and left. Henry stared at the stack of portfolios before he reached over, took one, and opened it.

Henry walked into his new supply-room office. It had full shelves of supplies and boxes were stacked on the floor along with cleaning products, a handcart, mop and bucket, stacked chairs, and miscellaneous items. A table was folded up against the wall. Henry spent most of the say organizing and cleaning.

At the end of the day, Henry walked into Mr. Banes office.

"Hello, Mr. Banes."

"Hello, Henry. What do you have there?"

"I need your opinion. I'm developing two short commercials for a company emphasizing unity and agreement. And I'd like you to look at them."

Mr. Banes reached out his hand and took the two papers. "Sure," he said before reading them out loud. "An old secluded gas station in the desert with a sign next to the door, 'Voted best gas station within 20 miles. A car pulls up to the rusty pumps. The driver sees the sign.

"How far is the next one," the driver asked the old man in the chair in front of the gas station.

"Bout twenty-five miles.

The driver asked, "So, how many people voted?"

"Just two." My wife was in charge of the vot'in, and I made the sign."

Mr. Banes laughed before reading the second one.

"It was their first date. In the restaurant, they sat across the table from each other, smiling.

She tells him, "I like you. And I hope you don't mind that I don't shave my legs or under my arms."

He replies, "I like you too. And I hope you don't mind that I don't brush my teeth or floss."

They stare at each other, each slightly taken back by the other.

Narrator: "For most things to work, agreements need to be made."

Mr. Banes laughed again. Henry's face remained expressionless.

"You know, I can't decide," he said chuckling. "Maybe you should offer both of them and let the client decide. You might find that they want them both; one for now and the other for a future ad.

"Okay, thank you."

An easel stood near a table with chairs at Henry's first team meeting. Henry's new team wearing name tags walked in and seated themselves at the table. Henry hadn't arrived yet.

"It's come down to this, huh?" Rick said, looking around.

"Must be the last place people go before getting fired," Cecilia added.

"The Supply Room. Really?" Steve asked.

Henry walked in, stood at the empty place at the table, opened a large paper bag and took out an aerosol can. Without expression, he sprayed his team members with a stringy stream of colored gel. His team jumped to their feet with alarmed and angry looks. Noisy complaints followed. Henry quickly took out more cans of spray gel and slid them across the table to everyone. The team members jumped out of their chairs laughing as they sprayed each other and Henry.

Kevin happened to be walking by the room and stopped to watch through the door's window. He immediately left for Mr. Banes office.

As he stepped through Mr. Banes office door, Keven exclaimed, "I just walked by Henry's Supply Room office. It's like they're having a party in there!"

"Kevin, you haven't liked Henry from the first day. We're probably standing on a gold mine. Are you able to see that?"

"Maybe so, but there's a whole lot of dirt on top and whatever psycho issues he has."

"And we need to be willing to take the time, patience, and effort to dig and see what we can find. I haven't said that about any other new employee."

Small bits of gel were still on the laughing team members as everyone cleaned up. Henry stood near the large easel as his team members seated themselves. Each one had a portfolio in front of them.

"So, why the spray gel?" Cecilia asked

"To break your mental pattern. I had to re-set your minds and emotions."

"Well, you sure did that," Cathy replied.

"You all have the client's portfolio. What is our commercial about?"

"Women's clothing," Steve answered.

"No, Steve. Not clothes."

Steve laughed sarcastically. "Yeah, I read the portfolio, and I'm pretty sure it's about women's clothes."

Henry replied, "Selling often has little to do with what's for sale. We are selling emotions and imagination. You don't sell the 'what,' you sell the 'why.' When people feel the value in the 'why,' they'll buy the 'what.'"

"C'mon. We're not exactly TV pitchmen, here," Rick complained.

"Yes, we are, Rick. We are pitchmen in slower motion. Pitch me a thingy. Go ahead."

"But wait! If you order today, we'll include a second thingy for free!"

"Cecilia, how easy will it be to pay for the thingy that people, ten seconds ago, didn't even know existed, but now can't live without?"

"Just three easy payments?"

"Don't say it - pitch it. I hate clichés, but you're not selling the steak, you're selling the sizzle and the smell."

"For just three easy payments!!" Cecilia exclaimed with enthusiasm.

"Notice the words 'just' and 'easy' and how they settle on the mind.

Think about that for a while."

Ramon shook his head. "I'm not so sure about this."

"Ramon, who gets paid more - educators or entertainers?"

"Yeah. I guess you're right."

Henry asked his team, "Who is our target audience for this ad?"

"Middle-age women," Becky replied.

"No, Becky."

She flipped open her portfolio and put the tip of her finger on the page. "Yeah. It says right here, women aged between..."

"Our target is middle-aged woman who want romance, who want style, who still want to feel beautiful, and prove they're strong.

"Ah, I think I'm starting to get this," Rick said with a grin.

"What do we want women to think when they see this line of clothing?"

Cathy raised her hand. "That if they buy this line of clothing, they will look beautiful and stylish?"

"No. We don't want them to 'think' nearly as much as we want them to 'feel' and to..." He waited as he looked around at the team member's blank faces. "Remember, we're selling emotion and..."

"Imagination?" Steve asked.

"Exactly. We want them to 'feel' the commercial and 'imagine' themselves in it."

"They need to hear the sizzle and smell the steak," Steve said, pleased that he was really getting it. The team members nodded.

"It's not enough to know your customer demographics and needs. You must also enter their dreams."

"Hot buttons," Ramon said.

"Maybe deeper than that. Look at buying motives as 'living' motives." He leaned over, placed his hands on the table, and looked around at the faces. "Our goal is to whisper a warm, breathy message right into the heart of women." He stood up straight and spread his arms. "So, what's the message?"

Steve was quick to offer, "She needs to believe that she can rise to the place where she is admired and adored!"

Cecilia squeezed her answer in, "We will help release her and give her that 'look' and confidence so she will know she will be desired."

"Lately, she's been feeling that she's ready for a brand-new chapter in her life," Ramon added.

Rick said, "She wants to explore and expand. Maybe she wants to start over and reset her life!"

"We want to help empower her to act on her dream to be stronger, smarter, and sexier," Becky offered with a giggle.

Cathy offered, "The women must feel romance, change, and success in the wind."

"Whoa. I didn't know I was going to get the 'best' people in the company!" Henry exclaimed. Light chuckles and smiles came from the team members.

Cecilia's tone changed. "Actually, the opposite is true. Most of us have one foot out the door. The team members rolled their eyes and nodded.

"We know this Supply Room is our last place before we're gone," Ramon complained.

"Do I have to spray you all with gel again?" Henry reached for the bag.

All the team members put their hands up and laughed. "No!"

Henry declared, "This is Supply Room is the place where you're going to start winning. Who is our A/V person?"

"I often do that!" Becky said.

"Good Becky. On Thursday take Cathy with you and some equipment. Plan on shooting some video."

"You got it!"

"We need a special tone in the voice of the narrator. Cathy, you have a nice voice. Find one that is calm, low, soothing, and honest."

"I can do that."

Henry paused and dropped his eyes. He faintly said, "My mother had a nice voice." The team looked at Henry and waited.

"Henry?" Becky said with concern.

Henry jolted slightly and cleared his voice. "Cathy, I want your voice to blend into Rick's voice halfway through the narrative. Rick, we need the same voice from you."

"Sure. I'll be fun!"

"Cecilia and Cathy are our models. Get a few of our client's outfits. Ask Ginny for a company credit card. Be ready to easily change your hairstyle and accessories between scenes."

"I'll get all my stuff together!" Cecilia promised.

"Cathy, you do the same. We edit Friday and Saturday."

"Saturday?!" Steve complained. "I have a volleyball game!"

"There are three kinds of people: those who won't fight, those who fight not to lose, and those who fight to win," Henry said.

"And those who won't get to play volleyball this Saturday. All right. I'll be here on Saturday."

"Because we're going to win this ad, all of you can mentally pull your foot back inside the door. We're going to make sure that happens." He took a marker and moved closer to the flip chart. "Okay, team, let's put this all together."

The hall was empty except for Kevin walking down the middle and Henry walking toward him. As they met, Kevin didn't move to either side until Henry moved to one side and pressed himself against the wall. Kevin suddenly changed his course toward Henry and bumped into him causing him to drop his binder. Papers scattered on the floor.

Kevin didn't turn around. He just laughed and quietly said, "Oops."

In the presentation room, three reps from the women's clothing line sat at the long table with the seven team leaders. Mr. Banes and Kevin sat with them. The large video monitor was on. A commercial ended.

Mr. Banes said, "Thank you, John."

"That was nice too. I like it."

"Yeah. Kind of classy."

"It was nice. Sure."

"Ladies, we have one more from Henry," Mr. Banes said as he pointed the remote at the monitor.

Quiet, playful music began. Cathy's voice began just after the first scene did: "Confident, enchanting to the heart, and captivating to the eye. She isn't flashy, hot, or cute, but holds the title scarcely granted to a woman; she is beautifully strong and elegant."

A suited man at a cafe table watched smiling Cecilia gracefully walking down a city sidewalk, looking like she was having fun. Two women turned from the front desk to watch Cathy as she glided through a fancy hotel lobby.

In a different outfit, Cecilia confidently leads a discussion in a conference room.

Restaurant staff noticed Cathy as she was being seated to join a pleased-looking gentleman who stood to admire and welcome her. He kissed her on the cheek then waited for her to sit before he did.

Rick's voice overlapped Cathy's as her voice ended. "Her poise demands that glimpses turn into stares. Casual glances try to look away then fight to look back. She wears the presence of joy and loveliness."

Cathy turned and joyfully smiled at the camera before she turned back to her happy handsome man.

The brand name rested unassumingly at the bottom of the screen with the phrase, "For every season. You pick the reason. Classy or Sassy?" The video ended.

"Oh, my gosh! I hate them! I'm so jealous!" the first client exclaimed. "Confident femininity!"

"Look at the attention they're getting, and they're not really doing anything but being 'beautifully elegant' wearing our clothes!"

"I love the motion and positive life feeling. It feels like they're really happy with themselves and their lives.

"It's so wonderfully strong yet subtle. Henry, what if we wanted something, say, in our lingerie line?"

Henry answered, "A model standing in the doorway, looking into a bedroom. A voice-over says, "Maybe she's ready. Maybe you need to make sure."

The client's mouths dropped open as they looked at each other.

A different client enthusiastically asked, "And for bathing suits?"

"A model walking along the beach with a voice-over saying, "Maybe she didn't plan on being a distraction. Maybe now she wants to."

The client danced in her seat. "Ahhhh! I love it! Oooh-wee! We should use those!"

"Can you imagine seeing that with captions on a billboard in Time Square?!"

She turned to her partners. "Yes?"

They all answered, "Yes!"

"We want to thank all the presenters for their great ads and Henry for his winning ad. We have our ad and it's a deal!"

"The thanks go to my team. They're the best," Henry said.

Kevin folded his arms and sighed. Mr. Banes noticed.

"You'll be hearing from us again!"

"Soon!" another rep declared.

The clients danced their way out of the room.

"Henry, you took some under-performing people and did a great job," Mr. Banes said.

"They're actually very talented. A seed is a seed. It just depends on where it's planted."

Marcel asked, "Henry, how did you know they were going to ask about lingerie and bathing suits?"

"I didn't."

Stan asked, "So, you just thought them up on the fly?"

"Yes," Henry answered with the same expressionless face.

Mr. Banes' grin stayed for a while.

The door of Henry's office was open as he stood studying a painting on the wall. Cathy knocked on the door jam.

"Hello. May I come in?"

Henry turned toward Cathy. "Sure, Cathy. Please come in."

"Henry, I just want to tell you how happy I am to be on your team. And for you putting me in the commercial. It was so much fun."

"I'm also happy to have you on my team. You have a nice voice and a pretty face. You gave life to those outfits, and that was the goal."

"Uh, could we have coffee together some time?"

"Sure. There's coffee in the break room. C'mon." Henry began to walk toward the door.

"No. I mean somewhere else - like a, like a date."

Henry stopped abruptly and turned back to Cathy. "I've never been on a date."

"On dates, people talk, go to movies, eat dinner, take walks together. Stuff like that."

"Sure. I like those. We can go on dates."

Henry came into the lobby and turned toward the receptionist's desk holding up an envelope.

Ginny looked at him with a smile. "It's right, Henry."

"It's a lot of money," he replied as he changed directions and went through the doorway toward his office.

Henry and Cathy stood with bags and shook hands with unshaven people wearing dirty clothes in the park.

"Cathy, these are my friends. You might say, they're my family too. Friends, this is Cathy. We're on a date."

Sincere greetings were returned by the men and women.

Cathy spread a blanket out on the grass. Henry put the bags on the blanket. Everyone seated themselves on the blanket and shared the food.

Kevin walked into Mr. Banes' office. "Hey, I'm thinking about strolling down to see how Henry is doing. Want to come?"

"Sure. I have a few minutes."

Henry's office had a lot of different kinds of items: a set of keys with the ends broken off, a small vase with a dead rose and a fresh one, sat on his desk. A clock with the hands replaced with strings, limply winding around the center, was on the wall. A mouse trap that had captured a small toy elephant and an old radio sat on a table beside him. Single light bulbs were scattered around the room. Henry, sat at his desk, covering his face with both hands, gently crying in front of a small standing picture frame.

Mr. Banes and Kevin walked in.

Mr. Banes asked, "How's it going? Henry?... Henry?"

Henry looked up and cleared his voice. "It's going well."

"Did we come at a bad time?" Kevin asked. "It seems like you're too sad to work."

"No. I'm fine. I'm fine." He dried his eyes with his hand.

Mr. Banes and Kevin pulled chairs over and sat in front of Henry's desk as he took a sip of water and cleared his throat again.

"Congratulations to you and your team. You may have spared some of their jobs. Do have everything you need?" Mr. Banes asked.

"Thank you. Yes."

Kevin said, "Henry if you don't mind, you've got some strange items on your desk and walls. May I ask why you have them?"

Henry looked around. "I need contradictions, opposites, mysteries, questions, and odd things to stimulate creativity."

"Henry, why is being creative, important to you?" Mr. Banes asked.

"Personally, it expands my mind. Professionally, no one buys old thoughts, worn clichés, or used concepts."

"You're right about that."

"You have a lot of light bulbs around here," Kevin noted.

Henry turned and picked up one of the light bulbs and looked at it. "They're looking for placement in a metaphorical socket. Each bulb has an idea or thought taped to it."

Mr. Banes said, "Henry, I'd like to ask about the picture frame with a plant growing inside."

"Would you ever think that a plant should be growing in a picture frame?"

"No. I sure wouldn't."

"That's why it's on my desk. One isn't expected to be paired with the other. Henry leaned forward to the picture frame and touched the glass softly saying, "I like to watch the plant's roots grow against the glass. I had an ant farm when I was a boy."

"Yeah. Me too," Kevin said.

"Think about that for a while. A colony of ants living in a modified picture frame that changed a one-dimensional still view into an active, three-dimensional living one."

Mr. Banes smiled. "I know your point is coming."

"Everyone had picture frames and knew about ants. Someone put them together. Millions of people bought the ant farm and they're still selling them."

"Very creative."

"And profitable," Henry added.

Kevin reached out and took the framed picture off Henry's desk. "Is this a picture of you and your mom? You look a little like her."

Henry stood and grabbed the picture from Kevin and laid it back on his desk faced down. He sat, keeping his hand on it. "She will not be a part of this conversation," Henry sternly exclaimed.

Kevin spread his hands and sat back. "Wow! Look at him!"

Henry looked at Kevin with anger. "My mother will not be an item in this conversation!"

"My apologies Henry. It's just that most people are happy to share memories about their loved ones."

"It's none of your business!"

"Are you sure you don't want to tell us something nice about her?"

Henry stood and held his fists at his waist. "I said, that's the end of it!

"He's getting violent!"

Mr. Banes reached over and put his hand on Kevin's arm. "Kevin, stop. Right now."

Kevin quickly pulled his arm away.

Mr. Banes looked to calm things down. He asked, "Henry, what about that picture of the photographer with his camera pointed at us?"

Henry sat down, took a deep breath, calmed himself, and turned his eyes slowly from Kevin to the picture. "It's a picture of a man taking a picture of a man watching him from the other side of the frame. I often ask myself, 'What else can this mean'?"

Mr. Banes stood. "I think I'm beginning to get all of this. Thanks,

Henry. If you need anything else, just ask Ginny or me."

Mr. Banes and Kevin walked out.

Henry lifted his mother's picture and looked at it. His chin quivered. He extended his pinky finger and whispered, "Our secret. Forever."

Moments later as Mr. Banes and Kevin were walking down the hall, Kevin asked, "Did you see that?! Something's very wrong with that guy. I thought he was going to punch me!"

"You would have deserved it. Kevin, Henry is different, but we don't know what his past has been."

"I recommend that we end this little experiment and forget about the tax credit and the PR. It's not worth having a problem child around here."

"Henry has a special kind of gift, a creative intelligence that if nothing else, produces signed contracts which we desperately need. He, for the most part, is keeping us afloat and saving our jobs."

"Well, I don't have to like him."

"Everyone knows you don't. But you do have to treat him well. This needs to stop now. I'm serious."

"I hear you. He just doesn't fit. He's not like everyone else who works here."

"No. He isn't. That's why he's still here and signing big contracts. He's taken a lot of corporate pressure off you and me."

Kevin whispered in anger, "How can an idiot make more money than a vice-president!"

"From now on, Henry doesn't answer to you. He answers directly to me. Go home. Come back tomorrow with a better attitude." Mr. Banes lifted his head toward the hall. "Go."

Kevin shook his head and quickly walked down the hall with heavy steps.

The break room was empty except for Cathy sitting alone at a table, eating her lunch. Henry walked in with his lunch bag.

"Hello, Cathy. It's kind of crowded in here. May I sit with you?"

She smiled. "Sure. You can have the last empty chair at this table."

Henry seated himself across from Cathy.

In a whisper, Cathy said, "Thanks for the movie last night."

"That was fun," Henry whispered. "Cathy, how would you like to be my very first girlfriend?"

She smiled. "Yes. I would very much like that. But we can't tell anyone here because of the rules. It's our secret." She reached out her hand with her pinky finger extended.

Henry paused, stared at Cathy's pinky finger, and slowly joined his pinky to Cathy's.

"Our secret," he mumbled as his eyes began to water.

"Henry, are you okay?"

"Yes. Thanks. I'm fine. It's... well, nothing."

Henry quickly unfolded the top of his brown paper lunch bag and took out the lunch items. Something began to change inside him. His stiff posture began to relax and expressions began to appear on his usual blank face.

In the presentation room Mr. Banes, Kevin, all the team leaders, Senator Fry, and his aide, stood watching a video playing on the screen. Kevin pointed the remote at the monitor on the screen. The video stopped. Senator Fry looked around the room. "All right. You're the pros. What do you think of my speech?"

Heads nodded with polite smiles. Henry was the only one that didn't respond, and Senator Fry noticed.

"Well, 'you' haven't offered anything yet. What's your evaluation?"

"Senator Fry, I really don't think Henry will have much to offer. He's new and well, you know, kind of..." Kevin began to say.

"No. I want to hear what 'everyone' thinks, even the new guy."

Everyone went silent and stared at Henry who answered, "You spoke like you were reading from a shop manual. Your methodical flat words were like metal parts dropping off the end of a sluggish conveyor belt."

Senator Fry smiled. "So, you think I..."

"Your speech was void of feeling, image, poetry, and engagement."

Kevin interrupted, "Henry, that's enough."

"No. Please continue, Henry," the senator demanded.

"Did you notice in their eyes, that their thoughts had gone to other places? They liked their daydreams better than your speech."

"Well, no."

"You didn't invite them to get on board. You didn't set their seats on fire or incite them to take up arms and march."

"It was that bad, huh?"

"I didn't evaluate your speech as much as your audience. The hecklers sat quietly in the back. Think about that for a while."

Senator Fry laughed. "My mother would probably agree with you. I might be able to use a coach like you to boost my campaign."

Henry's face saddened. He looked down toward the floor, and his hands covered his face. "I miss my mother." Everyone stopped talking and stared at Henry until he walked out.

"Excuse me, everyone." Mr. Banes followed Henry out of the room.

Senator Fry stood looking at the team members. "Do you think he's right?"

"We're sorry, Senator. Henry is a bit unstable and has some issues," Kevin explained.

"But, do you think he's right?"

He searched from one team leader's face to another. None of them offered eye contact or replied.

"You do. You all think he's right, but you won't admit it." Senator Fry continued to study the faces of the team. "As scathing as his evaluation was, he was brave and kind enough to be honest... unlike the rest of you. And I think he was very close to being right. He did me a favor. You didn't."

"Senator," Kevin pleaded.

"Goodbye," Senator Fry said as he abruptly left with his aide following. Kevin turned his head away with a disgusted look.

In the conference room, Ginny was passing out stacks of portfolios to the seated team leaders.

"Lastly, next week we have a client coming in to see ads for his family fitness business," Mr. Banes said.

"You all know what to do, and you know where my office is," Kevin added.

Each person took a portfolio and held them closed. Henry opened his and began to read it as he made his way through the chatting group and out the door.

Henry and Cathy sat at a table at a nice restaurant and looked at each other's candlelit face.

"Cathy, why do you like me?"

"Because you're intelligent, sensitive, and complex, but not complicated. Why do you like me?"

"You're sweet and happy. You have great qualities like my mom... had."

"You love her, don't you?"

"Very much. You're the first person I have really wanted to talk to about her."

Henry grinned and leaned forward. "When I was a boy, at night my mother used to put a white bed sheet over her and chase my friends and me around our yard."

Cathy smiled. "That sounds scary fun!"

"It was! We knew it was her, but it was still scary! She would make ghost sounds! And other times..."

Henry's team was seated at the table with portfolios. Written on top of the flip chart on the easel was Fun Family Fitness.

"I feel this commercial needs to be light and funny without losing its message. I'm not inclined to be light and funny."

"Some of us are."

"We can definitely help," Steve said.

"Actually, you'll have to take the creative lead role. This is the direction I'm thinking about," Henry said as he stepped to the easel and took a marker. "A family who doesn't exercise, so they get someone or something to do it for them."

"Like robots?" Cecilia asked.

Henry grinned and pointed to Cecilia. "Like robots. I love it! Robots!"

"Scenes of normal life activities," Rick offered.

Rebecca added, "Being done by replacement robots."

Henry turned to the easel and began to quickly write the ideas as his team erupted into noisy suggestions.

"Keep them coming!" Henry said as he scribbled them on the flipchart.

It was presentation day for the Fun Family Fitness. All of the team leaders were, with the client, viewing the proposed commercials they had created.

"And now, Henry's ad," Mr. Banes announced.

The commercial came on, and the scene began in a family living room. Robots with human-like faces stood smiling.

The TV Pitchman began, "Introducing, Robo-Me! Robo-Me will make a robot that looks just like you!"

The next scene was a backyard where Robo-Me replicas were playing badminton.

"Why do all that exercise, when you could use your Robo-Me to do it?!"

The real family sat expressionless in the shade, eating chips, drinking soda, and wearing blood pressure cuffs.

The TV pitchman, still with enthusiasm said, "Make hiking and jogging, a thing of the past! Who wants to be 'that' active?!"

There were muffled chuckles in the presentation room.

The next scene was a human woman driving a golf cart down a hiking trail drinking a very large cup of soda. The woman's Robo-Me was ahead of her, hiking with a backpack.

The next scene was of a human boy standing on a moving skateboard talking on his cell phone. He was being pulled by his Robo-Me who held a lease with a dog.

The TV pitchman said. "Walking your dog outside in the fresh air?! C'mon. Who wants to do that?!"

The Fun Family Fitness client laughed out loud.

The TV pitchman said, "Order in the next thirty minutes, and we'll throw in free books for your Robo-Me family to read while your family can just sit and watch endless hours of TV!"

The next scene was a human family staring at their TV while eating bowls of chips, candy, and ice cream. All of them had drip bottles on IV poles. There was a defibrillator nearby. On the other couch, the Robo-Me family was reading books.

The TV pitchman continued, "Bicycles, canoes, and scooters are way too much effort! Team sports? Let Robo-Me play for you, so you don't have to run!"

The scene changed to a kid's soccer game. Robo-Me players were playing while the real kids sat in their uniforms on the sidelines playing on their cell phones, not even watching the game.

Students at Dance class sat slumped in chairs while their Robo-Me's were dancing.

The TV pitchman said, "You can watch your Robo-Me, or, you don't have to be there at all!"

The TV announcer's voice said. "Get your Robo-Me today! Just call 1-800..."

A spokesperson from Fun Family Fitness stepped into the screen, turned off the fake commercial with a remote control, and said, "That was funny and silly. Each one of us has to earn, maintain, or improve our health. But you get the point. Fun Family Fitness has a workable and flexible program that will set up your family for fun and fitness."

The video ended with the team leaders chuckling.

The client laughed. "I have never seen anything like that! But this time I might go with Marcel's ad. But keep Henry's for our second campaign.

"Very Good!" Mr. Banes replied

"Robo-Me! Blood pressure cuffs and drip bottles!" The client laughed as he stood. "Wait. I'll get back to you in two days for my final selection."

"See you then. Thank you," Kevin said.

"And thank all of you."

The Fun Family Fitness client left the room and could be heard laughing down the hall, "The boy just 'stood' there on the skateboard!"

Mr. Banes knocked on Henry's door before he walked in. Henry was at his desk coloring. Crayons were scattered around.

"Hi, Henry."

"Hi, Mr. Banes."

"Coloring, huh?"

"Yes. I've always loved to color. It's simple therapy."

Mr. Banes stepped forward to see the picture of an upside-down rainbow in a narrow valley landscape.

"Mr. Banes, what if rainbows were arched up?"

Mr. Banes smiled. "That's not the way nature does it."

"But, what if? That's always an important question."

Mr. Banes sat in the chair in front of Henry's desk. "May I?" He placed his fingers on the picture and spun it 180 degrees.

"If rainbows were arched up as you have this one, you wouldn't have found the end of yours."

"What do you mean?"

"My friend, I've seen a change in you. Your Fun Family Fitness ad surprised me, and everyone else. Lately, you seem happier."

"I let my team go crazy on that ad. I mostly just stepped aside. It was fun."

"It was funny and happy. And, if you'll pardon me, it was out of character for you. Something is changing in your life, Henry."

"Yes. A lot of things are changing for me."

"For the better?"

"Yes," Henry replied. "For the better."

"I truly hope it continues. You deserve to be truly happy. And I'm so glad you're here," Mr. Banes said as he stood and left.

"Me too."

Henry looked thoughtfully down at his picture, and said to himself, "Now it's a regular rainbow, and the valley became a mountain. Nice." He leaned back in his chair and tilted his head back. "What if I finally have found the end of my rainbow?"

Henry and Cathy stood alone in the museum, viewing a painting of a woman.

"Henry, what do you see? What do you feel?"

"I see a beautiful sweet woman full of grace and charm. I feel I want to know her better."

"What would you say to her?"

"I would say, Cathy, I'm developing some strong feelings for you."

Cathy turned with a smile and a look of adoration.

"Henry? You're so sweet to say that about me." She leaned her head against his shoulder.

Lee walked into Henry's office. "Hey, Henry. I've got a tough client coming in at three o'clock this afternoon. I'd like you to be at the presentation if you can."

"Sure, Lee. I'll be there."

Henry sat off to the side in the presentation room. His eyes moved up and down the client as he quietly studied everything about him.

"Listen, I've already been to four of these places, and none of them caught my vibe," the client complained. "I need you to do much better."

"We appreciate the chance to show you what we have," Lee replied

"Let's see it. I've got things to do."

Lee already had the commercial cued, and it began with a video of the company's building and their sign, then showed the inside offices and staff.

Narrator: "They say that our new company is different, unconventional, and overly ambitious. They write that we are too confident and our ideals are too futuristic while they complain that world is moving too fast. We're already looking into the future."

The video ended with a lingering silence. The client leaned back and locked his fingers behind his head. His face had no expression as he looked up.

"While they complain that world is moving too fast," the client repeated. "We're already looking into the future. We're already looking into the future. Hmm." He began to slowly shake his head. "Uh..."

Henry jumped in, "They complain the world is too moving fast. You better believe it is! And we're riding that big wave right into the future!"

The client quickly looked over at Henry and pointed.

"That's what it needs - a confident zinger! It's spicy. That's my attitude! You nailed it! Bam! I'll take it."

"Beautiful. I'll get the contract written up," Lee said

The client snapped his fingers. "Hurry it up. I want to sign it and get this moving. Bring everything to my office. You've got two days." He walked directly out the door.

"Henry, how did you know to offer that?!"

"His expensive clothes, jewelry, body language, his eyes, and the volume and tempo of his speech. Your client is a brash, mover-shaker, type A."

"So?"

"A brash client needs a brash ad. Think about that for a while."

"I'm going to split the commission with you!"

No, you're not, Lee. You're my friend. You already had everything there. I just took it up a notch."

"But you saved it. You 'are' going to get an assist."

Henry shrugged his shoulders. "Fine then."

In his motel room, Henry walked around in his pajamas flying his model airplane. He stopped and looked at it in thought.

"No. I'm done with this... Maybe."

Henry and Cathy were holding hands as they walked on the beach. Henry had his same clothes on, but the bottom of pants was rolled up. He was carrying his shoes and socks. Cathy wore casual summer shorts and blouse.

"I really enjoy our time together and look forward to a lot more," Cathy said.

Henry stopped and turned to her. "Cathy, I need to ask an important question."

"Okay."

"Will you try to fix me like everyone else does?"

"Fix you? Only if you don't want to have puppies."

Henry grinned. "Cathy, Seriously, I don't want to be someone else's broken project."

"That's easy for me because I don't think you're broken."

"Do you think I need to be saved or rescued?"

"Henry, a bad past doesn't have to mean a bad present. We should make new wonderful memories for a greater future."

"That's the best therapy I've ever heard."

"I just want to support you. And I need you to support me. With all of our imperfections," Cathy assured him.

Henry paused in thought. "Yeah, I like that. Warts and scars too?"

"Warts and scars too."

Henry kissed Cathy on her cheek. They continued to walk, holding hands.

It was the day of the month when Mr. Banes met with the corporate president, Mrs. Desmond, and the three board members. After brief handshakes, everyone was seated.

Mrs. Desmond opened the folder she brought. "There was a very nice uptick in sales last month, Mr. Banes. Great job."

"Thank you."

"I see a new Henry Newsome name on a good number of contracts. And some assists."

"Henry is extremely talented, and I like him. He has some psychological issues that he's working through."

One of the board members asked, "He's not violent or dangerous, is he?"

"No. Henry has times of deep mental darkness. But other times his creativity blossoms into absolute brilliance; sometimes instantly."

"Are you managing him?" Another board member asked.

"Yes. He respects me. Henry isn't his best in front of strangers but get him in front of a computer and he creates brilliant ads. Sometimes right on the spot."

"Consider hiring him and splitting his job into two areas - his own ads and training," Mrs. Desmond suggested.

"Great. I've already hired him and gave him his own team. He's done near miracles with them and saved their jobs."

"Everyone should pass through his training," A different board member said.

"Mr. Banes, do you think this arrangement might benefit the company?"

"Yes, I certainly do, Mrs. Desmond. And I'm sure he'll look forward to it."

Back in his office, Mr. Bane's said to Ginny, "See if you can find something that would help us understand why Henry is the way he is."

Ginny took a folder from under her arm and opened it. "I was going to share this with you. His parents were killed in car wreck when he was eight years old. He somehow survived in the back seat," she said as she pulled out old newspaper clippings and documents and handed them to him.

"It's easy to understand how a little boy could grow up to be a withdrawn adult and suffer the way he does," Mr. Banes said as he looked through the papers.

"It gets worse," Ginny replied. "He was passed around from relatives to foster homes. He was mostly in special education classes and never graduated from high school."

"It seems to me that parts of Henry's development were held back while other parts grew past the average person's abilities. Or, maybe he has always had the gifts of insight and creativity."

"An intelligent adult with a child's disposition. Mr. Banes, it's a wonder how Henry got this far in life."

"But look how far he's come since the day we first met him. Some people just need a fresh start."

Ginny replied, "Others need a whole new life."

Many of the company's employees were seated in the conference room. In front of each of them were boxes and bags with a small pile of unusual items. Henry slowly walked around the room.

"Remember, what we don't want are items that lead our minds to analysis. Where do we want our minds to go?" Henry asked. The employees hesitated. "Someone from my team?"

"Emotion and imagination," Ramon replied.

"Right. Emotions and imagination. We want to think abstractly and wander away from the concrete, the predictable, and the obvious. Contrary to what you might think, it takes discipline to let your thoughts wander freely."

Kevin laughed. "What are we doing, writing soap operas?"

"No, but we could. We want to see and think about things that pull raw emotion to the front; finally, engaging both sides of the brain."

Henry and Cathy were sitting across from each other at a table, reading at the library. Henry took a piece of scrap paper and wrote, 'I love you. Do you love me?' He folded the note up and slid it over to Cathy. She opened the note, read it, and placed her hand over her open mouth. Then she wrote on the note and slid it back to Henry who unfolded the note that read, 'Yes, I do love you!'. Henry looked up at Cathy who was tearing up. He smiled then extended his pinky half-way across the table. Cathy reached her pinky out and locked it with Henry's.

Henry walked into Stan's office. He was sitting at his desk with his fingers locked behind his head.
"How are you, Stan?"
"Not so good. I need something for this large auto mechanic company, but nothing's come to me yet."
"You might not know about little transistor radios. We had to carefully tune stations in until the static became music."
"Never had one. Way before my time."
Henry sat down next to Stan. "Let me take a look at the portfolio."
After reading it over, Henry said, "What car repair company most people use says something very important about that company. 96% of our customers return to us. That says something even more important, doesn't it?" Henry looked at Stan. "The question at the end forces the mind to agree."
"How do you do that?! I've been staring at this for hours, and you come in and have it within a minute!"
"When nothing comes to us, we have to look at it differently and find the 'something' in the nothing. Think about that for a while."
"I'll use this if you don't mind. I'll even split the commission with you."
"It's your ad and your commission Stan. You're my friend. Good luck."
"But I am giving you an assist."
"Only if you want to."
"I do."
"Okay. Thank you."

Henry walked into Mr. Bane's office, carrying a full box of items from his office.

"Hello, Mr. Banes. I'm leaving now."

"Leaving? Leaving where?"

"Back to the library and park. They're peaceful, and quiet and I can think."

"You're quitting?!"

"In your terms, yes," Henry answered.

"Why? Why? What's the problem?"

"Stress. When a job is no longer fun because some people aren't nice, it's just work. And I'm not a good worker."

Henry sat a compact disk on Mr. Bane's desk, shook his hand, and left. Mr. Banes stood and watched him with a confused and surprised look.

The Monday morning meeting started as the last team leader was seated. One chair was empty. Mr. Banes' face betrayed that something was wrong.

"First, I want to announce that we lost Henry. He quit. Something happened here at the agency. Does anyone know anything about it?"

The mumbling team members looked at each other, shaking their heads.

"Henry is a great guy. I have no idea," John said.

"Marcel said, "A real team player. Helped anyone whenever he could."

"Let's get real," Kevin said. "Yeah, he was nice and good at what he did, but we have to admit, he was a square peg in a round-hole world."

"All that might be true, but he changed this agency and many of us here," Ginny replied.

Moments after the meeting, Mr. Banes, and Kevin were alone in the hall.

"Kevin, you didn't have anything to do with Henry leaving, did you?"

"Listen, I didn't like the guy, but I didn't chase him away."

The next day, as the two of them were chatting, Mr. Banes said to Kevin, "Oh, by the way, Mrs. Desmond asked that you come with me for our next monthly meeting."

"Great! How come?"

"She thinks it's about time you were introduced to the people we work for."

Kevin smiled confidently. "Very cool."

"Mr. Banes and Kevin walked to the door of the corporate boardroom. Mr. Banes lifted his hand to knock.

"Hold on a second." Kevin took out a small piece of clean blank cardboard from his hip pocket and put it showing in his suit jacket pocket. "Okay. Ready."

Mr. Banes knocked on the boardroom door. Mrs. Desmond opened it. "Hello. Please come in."

Mr. Banes and Kevin entered the boardroom. Mrs. Desmond closed the door.

"Mrs. Desmond, I would like to introduce our VP, Kevin Gillam. Kevin, this is our corporate CEO, Mary Desmond, and our board members."

"It's good to meet you, Kevin," Mrs. Desmond said.

"Likewise, Mary. I've looked forward to meeting you for a long time. Thanks for inviting me."

"My friends call me Mary. You may address me as Mrs. Desmond."

"Of course. My apology."

Mrs. Desmond pointed to the three people seated at the table. "These are our governing board members."

Kevin nodded in the board member's direction. "How's it going?" The board members didn't respond.

"You address me by my first name and the corporate board members with, "How's it going?" Interesting."

"Please have a seat, gentlemen," one of the members said.

Mr. Banes and Kevin sat. Mrs. Desmond took a folder from the table and opened it.

"Gentlemen. You had another great month in sales. I see new names on new contracts. Healthy movement and growth."

"We're very pleased with the continuing surge," Mr. Banes replied.

"Mr. Banes, how much of this can you attribute to Henry's teaching?"

"I certainly don't think it's a coincidence. He was the top salesperson and a great mentor."

"How's that, Mr. Banes?" a board member asked.

"Henry trained everyone, including Kevin and me. And even made us all populate our work areas with items to induce creativity."

Kevin added, "Some of us now carry a small piece of cardboard in their shirt pockets like Henry had, to capture thoughts."

Kevin took the small piece of cardboard from his jacket pocket. Mrs. Desmond noticed that it was clean and blank.

"Henry was a bit of a problem child, but we all loved him," Kevin said.

"You're both talking in past tense. Why?" Mrs. Desmond asked.

"Did something happened?" a board member asked, looking confused.

"We lost him," Mr. Banes answered.

"Mr. Banes, you lost Henry Newsome?"

"Yes. Sadly."

Mrs. Desmond asked, "How? What happened?!"

"I think he finally realized that he just didn't fit in," Kevin said.

"He just walked into my office and quit," Mr. Banes said. "I tried to persuade him to stay."

A board member leaned forward with a frown and looked at the two men. "Did he say why?"

"He cited, 'stress' but wouldn't elaborate."

"Really. Even though I learned to love Henry, supported him, and always treated him well, we'll do just as well without him," Kevin said.

Mr. Banes reached into his suit pocket and took out a DVD.

"Henry left me this before he walked out."

Kevin looked at Mr. Banes with surprise. "You didn't tell me about a DVD."

Mr. Banes shrugged his shoulders.

Mrs. Desmond sighed. "Well, let's see what's on it."

She took the disk and put it in a player. The video began on the large wall monitor. Henry was sitting in his chair in front of his computer. "So that's why you'll enjoy eating at our family restaurant."

Kevin walked straight in and closed the door. He wasn't aware that Henry was recording himself through his video camera on his computer. Henry turned to look at him.

Just off-screen, Kevin was angry as he spoke. "Henry, you sign a couple of contracts, and they hire you. Is that how it works around here? You live in a motel. You came here from some state program, and they make you a team leader?! To become a team member, I went to an expensive college and you went to the public library!"

"Mr. Banes just wanted to try something different."

Kevin's voice became a violent whisper. "When Mr. Banes gets fired, and I get to be the president, the first thing I'm going to do is fire you!"

"Why? What did I...?"

"Because you're a freaking oddball. You wouldn't even be here at all if you weren't a welfare project!"

"There's no reason for you to feel that way about me, Kevin. I've never..."

Kevin brought his face close to Henry's in front of computer's camera and pointed his finger very close to Henry's face.

"You just watch yourself, idiot. Because I'm watching you! Your day is coming."

Kevin turned, left, and closed the door hard. Henry turned back to the computer screen, reached down to his keyboard and tapped a key. The video ended. Mrs. Desmond reversed the video and froze it at the point where Kevin's face was next to Henry's, then looked intensely at Kevin. "You're the reason we lost Henry! You were the source of his stress!"

"Kevin," Mr. Banes said, "Henry was an irreplaceable asset, and you finally drove him out."

"But I..." Kevin began to say.

Mrs. Desmond interrupted him, "You have jeopardized the company's sales, incomes, as well as the confidence of the stockholders that I have to answer to!"

One of the board members said, "All because you just didn't like an employee and felt like you had to get personal and even threaten him."

"And you're disloyal to me," Mr. Banes said.

Another board member found her place to say, "I can't begin to tell you how unprofessional that is, especially for a vice president."

"You're the one that doesn't fit. You're the problem child," Mrs. Desmond said. "Kevin, you're fired!"

The boardroom door immediately opened. Two security guards entered the room and escorted Kevin out of the room by his arms. As he was leaving, he turned his head back and said, "The guards were waiting outside. You already saw the video! I was fired when I walked in!"

Mr. Banes replied, "Wrong, Kevin. You were fired the day Henry Newsome walked in. Think about that for a while."

The security guards escorted Kevin out and closed the door.

Mrs. Desmond asked, "Mr. Banes, is there 'any' chance you can get Henry back?"

"I'll try, today. I know where he usually hangs out."

Mr. Banes walked up to the park bench with a bag where Henry sat quietly with half opened and distant eyes. A small piece of cardboard and pencil sat on his lap with his autographed paper lunch bag at his side.

"Hello, Henry. It's good to see you... Henry, hello."

Henry jolted slightly to attention. "Hello, Mr. Banes!" He stood and shook hands, dropping his cardboard note and pencil to the grass.

"We miss you at the agency - everyone does."

"Except for Kevin. But I miss my friends. You're my friend too, Mr. Banes."

"Of course, I am. Kevin is gone. And I bought you a present." Mr. Banes opened the bag, took out a laptop, and handed it to Henry. "This is for you so you can work right here in the park, take it to the library, or work from home."

"Thank you."

"We all would like you to come back," Mr. Banes said as he sat down next to Henry. "You don't have to be a team leader if you don't want to, and you can go back to your cubicle if you like."

"Thank you, but no. I like to spend time here and go to the library when I want to."

"Henry, you need expressions for your creative gift and your penchant for teaching." Henry nodded. "How about if you worked just one day anywhere you want and come to the office just on Mondays?"

"OK. That's fine. I do like to be creative and help others."

"One more thing. I want to talk to you about a book."

The next Monday, Henry walked up to the front desk. "Hello, Ginny."

"Henry! It's so good to see you! Mr. Banes is in the conference room. I'll take you."

Henry walked into the room behind Ginny. All of the employees were there. Henry appeared stunned at first, then looked around at each of them.

"Henry, all of us are so happy that you're back!" Mr. Banes said.

"It's good to see my friends again. I missed you all."

Mr. Banes announced, "As a result of Henry's success and many other contributions, I have created 'The Henry Newsome Sales Award.'"

Mr. Banes held up a glass picture frame labeled, 'The Henry Newsome Sales Award.' Written at the top was Henry's favorite saying, 'Think about that for a while.' Attached in the center was just the small piece of torn cardboard with the ad for the charity that Henry slid across the table to Mr. Banes on his first day.

"Also, we will be helping Henry publish a Book called, 'A Henry Kind of Gift' with chapters including, 'Breaking Down Inhibitions', 'Look For What You Don't See', 'Think About That For A While', 'Selling Has Little To Do With What's For Sale', 'Know Your Customer', 'You're Not Selling - They're Buying', and 'That's Why I Have These At My Desk'.

Everyone in the room clapped, smiled, and cheered as Henry looked around at each of them, smiling.

"I'm going to have a book published, and people are going to learn," Henry humbly said.

Mr. Banes said, "It's because you are a kind and specially gifted person, Henry."

"Thank you. And I'm not an idiot. I wish my mom were here to see this."

Cathy walked over to Henry and stood by his side. "She would be very proud of you, as I am. And I love you." She kissed Henry on his cheek.

Henry smiled as he raised Cathy's hand and showed an engagement ring on her finger. Everyone suddenly looked surprised and cheered. Henry smiled and put his arm around her.

Henry was seated with Mr. Banes in his office. "Henry, our corporate President, Mrs. Desmond, would like to meet you at 11:00. We can take your car or mine.

"Meet me? Why?"

"Probably because you're doing so well here."

"I don't have a car or a license."

"Okay, then we'll take my car. We'll leave at 2:00 o'clock."

The door of the corporate boardroom was closed. Mr. Banes knocked. Mrs. Desmond opened the door.

"Hello, gentlemen. Please come in."

Mr. Banes and Henry walked in. "Hello everyone. I would like to introduce Henry Newsome. Henry, this is Mrs. Desmond our president and our distinguished board members.

"Ma'am. Ladies and gentlemen. My pleasure."

The board members smiled at Henry's polite charm.

"Please, both of you take a seat." Mrs. Desmond gestured with her hand to two empty chairs.

"Thank you," Henry said as he and Mr. Banes sat.

"Henry, you're doing so well at the agency, and everyone there speaks fondly of you," Mrs. Desmond said.

"Thank you."

"Henry, we want to offer you the position of vice-president, working with Mr. Banes."

"You mean Kevin's old job?"

"Yes. That's right."

"I'm... I didn't expect this." Henry looked at Mr. Banes. "What do you think?"

"Actually, Henry, I recommended it with my full confidence."

One of the board members said, "With your sales skills and love for mentoring, you've helped push the agency forward."

Another board member said, "And the revenue, upward."

"I didn't like the way Kevin performed his job as the VP."

"Neither did we, Henry. That's why he's gone."

"I would have to re-define the position to have a more active role - more like a coach than a superior."

"That sounds like a great idea," a different board member said. All three board members nodded.

"That's the first condition," Henry said.

Mrs. Desmond grinned. "Okay. What's the second one?"

"The second one is that this corporation sponsors a new kind of orphanage."

"A new kind, Henry?" A board member asked.

"One that specializes in orphans with severely traumatic childhoods like mine."

"Anything else?" Mrs. Desmond asked.

"Yes. I want to be the director. And work there one work day a week and live there with my wife and staff."

Mrs. Desmond grinned. "Gentlemen, would you excuse us during the lunch hour? We'll all meet here afterward.

"Of course," Mr. Banes replied.

Mr. Banes and Henry left the room, closed the door, and walked away.

Mr. Banes chuckled. "Well, you laid down a big second condition."

"I know. But it's important to me. It gives me the chance to help and maybe provide some needed therapy."

"Yeah. I can't imagine what some kids have gone through. Therapy will be good for them."

"The therapy will be mostly for me."

"There's a cafe downstairs. How about we have some lunch?"

Minutes later Mr. Banes and Henry had seated themselves with their trays of food.

"Henry, I know you and I will make a great team."

"I know we will. But if I had to choose between the VP of the agency or the director of the orphanage, I'd choose the..."

"Orphanage."

"That's right. I hope I can do both."

An hour later everyone met back in the boardroom. Mrs. Desmond began. "Well, Henry your first condition of re-designing the VP job was agreed to with enthusiasm. But your second condition induced a lengthy discussion."

"Do you have any questions?"

"No," Mrs. Desmond answered. "We understand your requests."

A smiling board member said, "We would love to sponsor the orphanage and help raise money."

"And we would like you to run it and be there at least one day of the work week and live there," a different board member said.

Mrs. Desmond smiled. "The only question we have is, will a million dollars be enough to start?"

Henry looked around at the smiling Mrs. Desmond, and the board members in silence then looked at Mr. Banes.

Mr. Banes asked, "Well, Henry?"

"Well, sure. Of course! Wonderful!"

Everyone clapped. Mr. Banes and Mrs. Desmond shook Henry's hand. The board members stood and walked over to shake Henry's hand.

The beginning of the long driveway offered a sign, 'Henry House.' A large Victorian house with a long, deep covered porch sat on a spacious green lawn with mature trees, sidewalks, and a playground. Three news vans parked in the lot brought anxious reporters with their equipment for the Grand Opening. A hundred nicely dressed people and homeless looking people stood in mixed pairs and small groups, drinking punch and wine and being served appetizers by the staff under large white tents. Rows of empty chairs on the lawn sat facing a portable stage and podium. A large yellow ribbon was stretched across the front of the stage. The entire first row was marked, 'Reserved for Special Guests.'

Henry was dressed in a new suit. His wife, Cathy, stepped up on the stage and stood in front of the microphone. She announced, "Ladies and gentlemen please find your seats. Ladies and gentlemen, we are about to begin. Remember, a tour will follow. Thank you."

The guests broke their conversations and moved toward the chairs.

"Honored guests and speakers, please come to the platform. Children, please take your seats," Cathy said into the microphone.

Mr. Banes, Ginny, the team members from the advertisement agency, Mrs. Desmond, all three board members, Mayor Patterson, and the librarian climbed the short steps to the platform. A somber line of quiet, serious-looking children emerged from Henry House escorted by two adults and took the reserved seats. Six homeless looking people from the park also sat in the front reserved seats. The guests were all seated and quiet.

"Mayor Patterson, Mrs. Desmond, board members. Thank you all for coming. I would like to introduce the director of Henry House and my husband, Henry Newsome."

Henry stood and walked over from one of the chairs behind the Podium and kissed Cathy. She returned to the empty chair next to Henry's. The guests applauded.

Henry gestured toward Henry House as he spoke into the microphone, "This wonderful thing... this miracle... this special and unique home is a gift from all of you. You are changing lives and will continue to do so; mine foremost. Thank you. May I present a man who gave me a big chance; my good friend Mr. Banes."

Mr. Banes walked to the microphone, hugged Henry, and gestured for Ginny to join him. Henry returned to his seat.

"Henry is the single most remarkable man I've ever met. A soul challenged with such adversity and formed by the same to become the great man he now is."

Ginny leaned toward the microphone. "And here he stands as the director of Henry House... to help ensure that other children won't endure the same adversity."

"This might embarrass Henry," Mr. Banes said. "because until now, we haven't told him. We first met Henry in the park, weeks before he came to the agency."

Henry raised his head higher.

Ginny said, "He was sitting on a bench. Mr. Banes and I saw him and brought him breakfast and just gave him the ability to re-start his life."

Mr. Banes turned back to look at Henry. "Do you remember that day, Henry?"

Henry nodded, with a slight mesmerized look.

Ginny said, "When he got to the agency the first morning, we didn't recognize him, nor he us."

"Until he pulled out his familiar little piece of cardboard and used his signature phrase, 'Think about that for a while,'" Mr. Banes said.

Ginny continued, "The small investment that we sowed that day, has reaped ten thousand-fold. 'Your' sowing will do the same for the children in the front row and every future child who will call this house, their home."

Mr. Banes ended with, "Your donations of money and time are well placed at Henry House. Thank you, all."

The seated guests clapped.

Cathy stepped to the microphone. "And now, the ribbon cutting. Mayor Patterson, Mrs. Desmond, board members, Mr. Banes, and Henry. Please stand behind the ribbon."

A large pair of scissors was handed to Henry. Mr. Banes, Mrs. Desmond, and Mayor Patterson held it with Henry and Cathy. The board members stood at the side. Pictures were taken by the reporters.

Mayor Patterson said, "Together, we dedicate Henry House to the present and to the future."

The ribbon was cut. The guests clapped. Reporters took more pictures and continued to film.

Cathy walked back up to the microphone. "Ladies and gentlemen and children, please join us at the tables over there under the white tents for refreshments."

As the crowd moved from their chairs, Henry stood, quickly looking around to see as he silently counted the children in the front. A cameraman noticed and followed him as he quickly made his way through the crowd, breaking away from quick conversations, as he nervously looked around. He ran through the parking lot and across the lawn to Henry House.

In Henry House he rushed through the rooms, searching frantically as the unnoticed cameraman waited near the Family Room recording until Henry burst through the door slightly out of breath to discover the small missing boy was sitting on the couch with a toy helicopter on his lap, staring and disconnected. Henry remembered being that boy, and every other child there. He took a deep breath opened a closet and removed his model airplane. Walking over to the center of the room, he flew his model airplane through the air while making airplane sounds. The small boy watched with blank eyes. Henry moved closer to him and sat on the floor still flying his model airplane.

"Do you want to play with me? Please?" Henry asked.

The boy hesitated before slowly sliding off the couch. He held his model helicopter and watched Henry without expression, who was still giving life to his airplane as he slowly dipped and rose it while making airplane sounds. Lifting his model airplane above his head, the boy continued to watch Henry.

"My name is Henry. What's your name?"

"Tommy."

"I like your helicopter. C'mon, lets fly!"

The little boy responded softly, "Okay."

"Do you know how to make helicopter sounds?"

Tommy faintly shook his head.

"You put your lips together and blow air out like this." Henry demonstrated his helicopter sound. "Try it!"

The boy softly made the sound.

"That's good! Ready?" Henry stood and slowly walked. "C'mon, follow me. Let's fly!"

First reserved, and then louder, the small boy made helicopter sounds as he followed Henry throughout the rooms, while Henry made airplane sounds.

Mr. Banes, Ginny, and Cathy arrived in the doorway and watched smiling with teary eyes.

"If anyone ever doubted whether Henry would make a difference, they would need to see this," Mr. Banes said.

"He's the kindest and sweetest man I've ever met," Cathy said.

The sun was shining through the tall wide windows of the Family

Room where the children were coloring. Henry, Cathy, Mr. Banes, Ginny, the board members, and Mrs. Desmond had volunteered to sit at tables and color with the children.

Later that evening, the live-in staff quietly cleaned up empty glasses of milk, used napkins, and small crumb-covered paper plates from the large table. Henry and Cathy sat on a couch. The children were seated on the floor in pajamas with stuffed animals and blankets.

"Now, whose turn is it to sit on the couch with Cathy and me tonight?"

Three children raised their hands.

"Come on. And bring your blankets," Cathy said.

Henry and Cathy slid apart. One child sat on either side of them, and the third child sat between them. Henry began reading a children story book to them, often turning the book around for the attentive children on the floor to see the pictures.

At the end of the story, Cathy said, "Okay, children. Bedtime. Upstairs, please. Brush your teeth. Henry and I will be up in a few minutes to say good night."

Some staff gathered the children and led them upstairs, holding their hands. Henry and Cathy sat back on the couch. Cathy leaned her head on Henry's shoulder and said, "From, once upon a time to, they all lived happily ever after,"

"Someday, our children will also use that phrase to tell their own stories. Well. It might be our bedtime too."

"Yes. Let's go up and say good night," Cathy replied.

Henry stood, took Cathy's hand, and helped her up. They went toward the stairs but stopped at the large picture of young Henry and his mother, hanging on a wall. Henry kissed the tip of his finger and touched the lips of his mother.

"I love you for what you mean to me."

Cathy spoke to the picture, "And I love you for what Henry means to me... and to our children."

They began to walk up the stairs, Henry said, "I love our children."

"Me too."

Revenge for Revenge

Jerry was in his late twenties with a face younger than his mind.

Sleeves rolled up to his elbows of his lose buttoned shirt hinted that this man wasn't vain. Grabbing his large olive-colored military duffle bag off the airport baggage carousel, he walked out the airport doors and hailed a cab.

Anyone who had been deployed for six months having seen what he saw and done what he did would be looking forward to all the familiar comforts and conveniences back home that they were denied. And even though all of his favorite restaurants sped past his window, along with the theaters that had new movies he wanted to see, and his favorite sports bar, Jerry's only thought was getting back home to his wife, Stephanie. She was the source of his strength and the reason he wanted to do his job and go home. And his only fear was what he might find, or not find. Was he to expect a 'Dear John' letter on the table? He didn't think so because they were very much in love; at least he thought so. Of course, being with other troops overseas, he witnessed the damage that time and distance can have on a lonely wife and the inconsolable devastation of the soldiers who sat reading such letters. But everyone one of his and his wife's video calls were charged with love, joy, and her constant teasing about starting a family he wasn't sure he was ready for. Those connections were unbreakable, he thought.

Beyond the skills of recognizing patterns and behavior, and beyond the discipline of keen observation regarding changes and details, is the gut, a sense, a feeling, an intangible and internal radar. It warns you of danger even when the visual facts of safety permit you to let your guard down and when the eyes conclude that what is seen is all there is to know. When looking at calmness, your blood-pressure rises and your order the men you command to stop or take cover. It's an eerie feeling that rises from within without logical justification. It's instinct; a third eye that has saved the countless men who felt it and instantly prepared themselves for that which was waiting for them hidden and silent. Jerry had it. And it had saved him in forward positions when there was no luck, no hint, no military intelligence, or warning. But he had no bearings in this new landscape regarding his wife suddenly going dark.

This soldier returning home desperately needed to find out why, lately, his wife hadn't answered his calls from the mid-east, and why in the last few days did he suddenly stop getting his daily letter from her. During the long flights, he thought about every kind of surprise as he played different scenarios in his mind. He pushed back the worst ones. This surprise return will tell all. This soldier never imagined the surprise he would find.

Jerry stared at his house as the cab slowed to a stop at the curb. In that early afternoon, all of the shades were pulled down. He took his bag from the driver standing at the open trunk and paid the fare. Walking past his wife's car in the driveway he noticed the faint film of dust that covered it. The front door was slightly ajar. He quietly pushed it open while noticing the pry marks and scratches around the lock. He stepped around a small pile of mail under the mail slot and gently pushed the door to the edge of the jam, stood and listened. Probing the small pile with the toe of his boot, he saw a couple of his letter of his to his wife among the advertisements and bills. The air was stale. As he carefully placed his long green duffle-bag on the floor next to their dining table, then his eyes searched the room in vain for a letter and were relieved that he didn't find one.

While not taking his eyes off the stairs, he reached under the lamp table next to the door. The faint unsnapping sound of the mounted holster attached to the underside allowed him to pull out the hidden .45. After confirming that the magazine was still full, he silently pulled back the slide and chambered a round. If he finds anyone robbing his house, he'll beat them. If there is a man in his bed, he'll kill him.

He quietly cleared the kitchen, half-bathroom, small laundry room, and office while searching for some indication of a reason for Steph not being there but found none. The pictures of the two of them still hung where they always did. The limp fading leaves on the plants in some of the windows suggested they had not been watered for a week or two. Why? Jerry stood at the bottom of the carpeted stairs. Maybe it was the angle or maybe the light, but it was then that he saw drops of blood on the brown carpeted floor. He turned around with a double-take. The inside of the front door and the knob were smudged with blood, and his eyes followed the trail going up the stairs.

Cautiously climbing the stairs with his pistol in front of him, he avoided the one spot on the seventh step that always gave a little moan when bearing his weight. Swinging his weapon into the bathroom, this young husband recognized his wife's makeup on the vanity and special shampoo in the shower. There were more blood drops on the landing and still more near the bedroom door. He took in every detail as his eyes looked across the narrow hall into the bedroom. The light-switch was off. Their bed was unmade. Her pillow was the only one with an impression.

A pencil was next to an opened cross-word puzzle magazine on the bed. Something else caught his eye. His head snapped around to the wall next to the bedroom door. A bullet- hole, about a foot above the height of the doorknob. Another bullet hole circled with blood was in the middle of the open bedroom door. A wide bloody streak led down to the floor. Turning to the partially open louvered doors of the closet, he saw that the louvers were shattered in two places. And there was something disturbing on the floor; a bare foot of his wife just inside the almost closed doors. Jerry hurried over to the closet and pulled the folding doors open. His wife lay on her side with her face away from the room in her nightgown among the scattered shoes, the fallen pile of extra linens, and splintered fragments of white-painted wood. He knew the look and the color of death, and now that he was close, the smell. She still had the .45 kept under his nightstand, loose in her hand. Two empty shell casings were on the floor next to her. Jerry fell to his knees. Crying, he rolled her stiff body over. Two bloody and dry bullet holes on the front of her confirmed what he already knew. He gripped the closet door to stand to his feet. Then he noticed through his sobbing; the killer had shot his wife through the partially closed doors as she barricaded herself there and shot the intruder. Gathering what senses he could, Jerry found four shell casings around the bedroom door. He picked one up with the point of the pencil he found, next to a crossword puzzle book on their bed, then took another. Looking at the bottom of an empty casing, he confirmed that they were from a 9mm. A wave of shame takes him over. How could he have imagined even for a moment that his wife had left him or was having an affair? He played the scene out in his mind. Jerry pictured his wife with her weapon in front of her just inside the closet door and her eye trying to find the sights. She was scared but courageous. Maybe she was shaking but composed enough. The intruder must have cautiously stopped in the doorway, holding his gun. Maybe he thought she was hiding under the bed, and when he turned his attention to look, she took the opportunity and fired. Did her first shot miss, or the second one? One of her shots got the intruder center mass, knocking him against the door before he slid down to the floor. Jerry confirmed that the bulb in the lamp was loosened. That was the first thing he had taught her in the case of a home invasion; get the home-court advantage. Don't let the intruder know where you are, and if possible, never let him see you. That way the intruder, in effect, would be walking into an ambush you set. Further, turning a light on will temporarily blind you until your eyes adjust. There

133

had been just enough light in the bedroom coming from the streetlight for her to see the silhouette of the intruder; just like the ones on the large sheets of paper at the shooting range which they had spent time at.

Hurrying back down the stairs, while being careful to not step on the blood drops, he went to the kitchen and found two sandwich bags and ran back up to the bedroom. Without touching the sides, he placed just two shell casings into a bag. Jerry took a credit card out of his wallet and scraped some dried blood from the carpet fibers near the bedroom door into the other sandwich bag. He stuffed the bags into his socks then called the local police station.

Before the operator could get through her short, scripted greeting, Jerry interrupted her. "Sharon, is the Chief in?"

"Yes, he is. May I ask who's calling?"

"Jerry Grant."

"Jerry! I didn't know you were back! When did…"?

Jerry cut her off. "Karen, I need to speak to the Chief, right now. Please."

"Okay. I'll transfer the call."

"Jerry! How the hell are…"

"Chief, I just got in. Steph's been murdered in our home."

"My God. I'll be there in ten minutes."

As of that moment, his life had no context except as a hunter. His face was set to one place, to one final moment, and one unfamiliar person. Envisioning his last act, he would look into the set of eyes as the light of life, by his hands, left the murderer.

The ambulance arrived right behind the three police cars. The County Coroner arrived ten minutes later. Neighbors across the street came out of their homes to watch from the sidewalk as an officer walked a wide roll of yellow tape around the small trees in the yard. The phrase, 'Police Line. Do Not Cross,' flew out of the spinning roll. Officers carried kits through the front door after giving compassionate looks at Jerry.

A neighbor yelled over from across the street, "Jerry! Steph okay?!" Jerry turned slowly to look at the small crowd of familiar friends staring over at the scene; a scene which brings dread to every neighborhood. He shook his head.

The Chief of Police, Jerry's former boss, hurried out of his squad car and over to him.

"Jerry, where is she?"

"Upstairs in our bedroom closet."

"You wait here. Let us take care of things."

Another officer came from around the corner of the house and said, "Chief, the outside phone line was cut."

While Jerry waited outside, it wasn't difficult for the team of crime scene investigators to determine what happened. An intruder forced the front door open and went inside. His wife was upstairs, or else she would have grabbed the gun under the end table in the front room. From her bed, she heard him, placed her crossword puzzle book down, took the bedroom gun and went into the closet, leaving the door slightly open. As the intruder stepped into the bedroom doorway, she shot him before or during the gunfight. She got shot twice, and the intruder got shot once. The wounded intruder fled, leaving a trail of blood downstairs to the front door, across the lawn and was concentrated on the curb where the blood trail ended. Those were the facts at the scene. But the 'who' and the 'why' were still out there somewhere.

Chief Brown, opened the front door and stepped outside to speak to Jerry. Right behind the Chief, a gurney came out. The E.M.T.'s were careful on the steps. A blanket covered the black body-bag containing the rest of Jerry's life. The gurney was pushed into the open doors of the ambulance waiting at the curb of the street in a perfect middle-class neighborhood. Their neighbors just starred; some with hands over their mouths.

"Damn shame that a soldier should come home to find this," the Chief said. "I'm very sorry. It seems clear what happened. The only mystery is that we found only two shell casings from the murder weapon. Hopefully, we can get a print from them. Maybe the intruder being shot could only manage to find two of them before had to get out. He was bleeding a lot. I have the team dusting for prints. We'll try to find a DNA match for the blood."

"You'll tell me if you get a print and a name, right?"

"Of course, my friend. Jerry, we all miss you at the station. You're family around here. We'll check all the hospitals for gun-shot victims over the last few days. The coroner said it's been about that long. You've got friends, neighbors, and a few relatives around the area. Find someone to stay with for a while." The Chief put his face close to Jerry's and whispered, "Jerry, I know something about your military training, and can only imagine some of the shit you had to do over there. Please don't do that kind of shit here in my city."

"If your wife was murdered in your home, what kind of shit-storm would you make?"

Chief Wooley knew that he couldn't keep Jerry still. He also knew that he should give the expected 'police' answer to let them handle it, but he didn't. Instead, he tightened his jaw before he whispered, "The quietest kind of shit-storm you ever saw. And the kind that close friends can help with." Jerry watched the Chief turn and drive away.

Jerry's life was now a mirror that had fallen and laid shattered on the floor with each piece reflecting a uniqueness from the others and never to be whole again. Today his life had little context. His wife, his home, and his future are gone and he, himself will likely die in his pursuit of the man who took them. The death of the thief in the night will also be quiet and private. He doubted that the man will be as brave as his wife was. But he was determined that the murderer must feel fear and terror before he dies, and Jerry will watch his face until the murderer's pathetic life passes before his eyes and the light of life is snuffed out. His wife is gone and took all of their dreams with her. Jerry had one last dream; to kill the man who murdered his wife.

Standing there, zombie-like, he pushed morals and ethics to the place in his mind with everything else he didn't want to think about at the moment. Morals? Hunger, poverty, and pain can open a person's mind and put their morals up for sale. Comfort and a full belly keep morals so righteously and tightly held. But the history of human nature assures that a man will murder for far less than survival, and even cannibalize to sustain himself. Most people don't know what they would do to survive and will never have to find out. They think they couldn't bring themselves to doing 'such things.' They believe they would never go 'that' far to stay alive. Jerry believed revenge is different; it's the son of justice and the two can't be so easily separated.

Another issue that soldiers like Jerry didn't think about was the family of the one he killed in his duties as a soldier. Further, he didn't care enough to consider the relatives of the murderer he might kill.

Revenge is an unequal exchange for murder; an act of violence wherein despair has turned into deep hatred and helplessness into focused action. There is no fair and sufficient payback, and the score is never evenly settled. Vengeance is a lustful and second-best matter when the victim who couldn't prevail is replaced by another who must. To many, honor is tandem to revenge and not easily separated. But the news of justice can't be given to the fallen. And their sleep won't be any sweeter, nor their title of 'victim' taken away. Retribution, honor, justice, or dignity are not concerns for those have been murdered. And what about the one who kills the killer? Is there a creed for such cold killing? Will the revenger be granted a final satisfaction? Is a momentary devilish sigh squeezed through heavy grief the only reward? None of this mattered because of Jerry's verdict. No other logic or emotions present or future could trump the law. It was Jerry's law. After all things were considered, the logic of the law was simple for Jerry. A man entered his home, came into their bedroom, and murdered his wife, and now, Jerry decided to hunt him down and kill him for it. How much simpler, obvious, and dutiful could the equation of his revenge be? It would be a matter of personal design, however, as to how the man would die. After, there would be no justification to hash over or second-guess to nag him. Revenge will be a done thing; finished.

Whether the justice is immoral, or the justice is savage, or the justice is illegal, it's justice nonetheless and not governed by dignity or decorum. And sometimes justice has to be served out of public view, and without public knowledge, at the tip of a knife, from the end of a rifle, or the thick end of a baseball bat. Jerry didn't see the splash but he sure as hell will follow the ripples back to whoever threw the rock in the middle of his life.

A murderer is a cursed man who can't return the murder or restore the life. Not even his own life can be a payment. The coward's murderous soul is stained; if not by some divine decree, certainly by the hunter. The curse must play out and finally be satisfied. The curse must run its course and cannot be revoked unless the cursed one kills the hunter.

That foreign man, that arrogant bastard didn't expect that his prey would fight back. Once again, Jerry played that night out in his mind. He taught his wife that if there ever was a home invasion, to turn the lights out so the intruder, unfamiliar with the layout of the house, would have to search for her in the dark. Or, if he had a flashlight, she would see his movements. Also, he taught her not to lock the .45. Trying to find the small key to a trigger-lock in the dark, then fumbling with it under that kind of pressure is a dangerous waste of time. Jerry further imagined the intruder finally entering the dark bedroom and his panic at the unexpected flash and roar of the .45 exploding from within their closet. Jerry grinned to himself as he pictured the man being knocked against the wall and the pain that erupted from his belly as he was knocked back and slid down the wall. And finally, the blood that hurried to leave him as he turned and stumbled down the stairs holding his hand over his oozing wound before he staggered out the door to a waiting car.

"Good job, Steph. Damn good job, babe. You kept your head, and you got him."

Over in the next town, Jerry held a bottle of beer as he sat in his brother Greg's living room. Jerry and Greg were different men. While Jerry was a disciplined and structured man, Greg usually wasn't shaved and spent most of his time in sweatpants and loved his bachelor's life. He worked mostly from his home that generally wasn't clean, and he didn't pick up after himself. Greg had no idea what was in the big box Jerry brought in and sat on the floor.

"So, what are you going to do?" Greg asked.

"I'll wait to see what the Chief comes up with from the DNA and the prints. He's a good man... I should have called you to check on her."

"I checked on her every week. This must have happened in between checks."

Greg took a drink from his bottle. "What now?"

"I'm going after the son-of-a-bitch."

"Not without me, you're not."

"I have to go alone at first. One person can usually be harder to track. Plus, with what the military taught me; it'll go better. However, you need to follow me because I'll need you. Greg, the government is going to be watching you too. I want them to."

Greg sighed. "The funeral is tomorrow. Are you going be okay?"

"Yeah. I'll make it. Want to sneak into a cemetery tonight?"

"And play, Devil in the Graveyard?"

Jerry replied, "Yes. A version of that old game." He stood and opened the box he brought in. "This is what we'll use to try to find the devil in the graveyard," he said as he pulled out a plastic gravestone and sat it on the floor.

"Okaaaay."

"I got it from a Halloween shop a few years ago. We used to set it in our yard every year. It's hollow. I've mounted a motion-activated video camera inside. I want to know every car and, it's license plate that comes tomorrow. The kind of person who caused me this pain will likely want to see it again at the funeral. We're going to find the devil tomorrow."

"You think Steph's death was connected to you?"

"Yeah. It had to be revenge for someone who I helped send to prison or about someone's death in the Middle-east. Whoever is responsible will wish to God they never messed with me."

Jerry knew that his brother had no military training and that as a number, he would be a zero in the plan. But even a zero at the right side of any single digit increases the value of that digit ten times and becomes 90% of the new bigger number. He needed his brother.

The middle-aged woman sitting at the reception desk stood to her feet and awkwardly smiled as Jerry walked into the police station. She came around and hugged him.

"It's so good to see you, and I'm so sorry about Steph. She was a good and lovely woman."

"Thanks, Sharon. The Chief called me in."

"He's back there in his office. Go on in."

Jerry walked back to the Chief's office and knocked on the door.

"Come in."

Jerry opened the door and walked in. The Chief was behind his desk.

"Hello, Chief."

"Good to see you, Jerry. Have a seat."

The Chief pointed to the chair in front of his desk. Jerry sat and looked across the desk with a hint of excitement.

"So, what's up? What did you find out?"

"I found trouble. The government is involved in this. I sent over those 9mm casings for fingerprints. They kept them and the results. The same with the DNA and told me to back off. The sad news is that I visited your house. Someone cleaned it. I mean really cleaned it. All the carpet that might have had blood on them are gone; pulled right off the floor. The bedroom door is gone and large pieces of sheetrock. There is no for DNA. The perpetrator is either related to a foreign embassy, or in a witness protection program."

Jerry lifted up each pant leg, removed the sandwich bags, and placed them on the desk. The Chief stared at them.

"A second set of samples," Jerry announced.

The Chief grinned and picked up the bags. "I don't know how you had the frame of mind to gather them."

"If you had worked with the kinds of people I did, you find the frame of mind and stay a step ahead."

"Roger that. I have a connection with a private lab, and my source will keep our business under wraps. I'll drive to them in my personal car. Should take about a week or less. Jerry, we haven't talked about who might have wanted your wife dead, and why."

"She was a regular girl who has never even been out of the country. Someone killed her to punish me. The only places I've ever been is, here in the states and the middle-east."

"But you've been a cop and now a soldier. We need to find out what part of you they wanted to punish and why," The Chief said.

At the cemetery, parked cars lined the narrow roads as mourners sat in folded chairs. A few soldiers in their class-A's sat together in the group. Jerry sat with Greg in the first row. The new headstone at Steph's grave looked far nicer than the fake one that the brothers had placed nearby last night. No one seemed to notice it, much less, the small hole that the camera lens was in. The service was nice, and the conversations were sincere. There were a couple of foreign-looking men who Jerry didn't recognize; one of them pushed the other in a wheelchair.

Before the closing prayer, Greg got up and stepped away from the group. He activated the video-recorder on his cell phone which was hidden in a bouquet of flowers and casually walked around until he was close to the two men of interest who stood close together and talked in a foreign language. He was able to capture their faces and conversation and watched them walk to the dark car with diplomatic plates. Arrogant bastards protected by their diplomatic status. Did they really think that they were so safe as to attend the funeral of the woman they murdered?"

Two days later, Jerry had his stuff laid out on his bed in his brother's spare room. He had small hand-weapons that most people didn't know about and better versions of a few things they did know about. He looked at the small vial of a drug used to temporarily mimic serious health issues when ingested and decided to take it. He would take the other vial too. That drug will kill a man if injected yet leave no trace. He threw a few syringes into a bag. Although most of his items were illegal, he also brought a standard lock-blade knife, paracord, his specially designed belt with a hidden knife sheath and a weighted buckle. He gathered some spent 9mm casings and one of his 9mm pistols with the serial number ground down and wiped his prints off. He'll take the wigs, hats, and the old dirty overcoat while making sure that his makeup kit was still in order. He packed everything under the false bottom of a large ice cooler and left for his meeting with the Chief.

"I've been busy," the Chief said to Jerry and Greg from across his desk. "And I've some things I shouldn't have. I wouldn't have done them for anyone other than you."

"I appreciate all your help, Chief," Jerry replied.

"We pulled the footage from some of the traffic cameras in the vicinity of your neighborhood. It seems that we had a speeder around the same night as your home invasion." The Chief laid some enlarged pictures on his desk. "Here's one of their faces. The passenger was slumped forward so we can't see his face."

Greg took his cell phone and presented the photos of the two foreign men at the funeral. As he held them next to the traffic camera pictures, his and his brother's eyes jumped back and forth until they were satisfied.

"It's them," Greg announced.

"Sure is," Jerry confirmed. "Since this man was driving that night, then the other man was the killer."

The Chief took the phone and spun the traffic picture around. After a few quiet moments, he responded, "Yep. And the car is connected to the Afghanistan embassy in D.C. That's probably why there were no DNA or prints on file. I'm sure the CIA has them, but they keep those things to themselves."

Greg took the camera back and advanced the pictures until he got to the one of the rear of the diplomat car at the cemetery. He held it out to the Chief. "Just to confirm, This one?"

After looking at a form on his desk, the Chief replied, "Yep. Same plate."

Jerry's eyes changed the instant he heard that. The look on his face seemed to be one of diabolical satisfaction as if he had already been granted his revenge. "I know who you are now, you two sons of bitches."

In D.C., Jerry paid for two weeks in cash for a motel room and gave the front desk instructions that no one was to enter his room; not even to have the linens changed. After loading his cooler and bags of supplies into his room, he opened his notebook and his laptop. All the information that he researched was saved, so he didn't need the internet. He reviewed his carefully made plan. Since he already found his enemies on social media, he knew personal information about them. First, would scope out the place where Aarif Nabi and Habib Khan lived. Next, he would understand their travel patterns and places they frequented. He stepped outside and quickly taped a single thread from the door to the jamb. If the thread were broken when he returned, he would know that someone entered his room.

On the wide city sidewalks this morning Jerry was well camouflaged as an older man among the blurry crowds of expressionless faces whose unsynchronized heads slightly lifted and fell with each step toward redundant destinations. He never allowed himself to forget that he was likely being watched. After all, both the FBI and the CIA knew who he was, the skills he had, and what had happened to his wife, and figured he would be in D.C. He determined to go as far as he could with his plan. The only things that could stop him were his capture or his death.

He had a number of things to concentrate on. First, get the job done while evading the probing eyes of the government. But getting the job done would come after he sufficiently prepared the situation with psych-ops techniques. His goal was to let the two men see him, to let them know that he was in town. From the media reports and pictures in response to the murder, he was sure they already knew. It was likely that the embassy knew too. An order to murder a wife of a US soldier on US soil had to be approved and handed down the line.

In his training, Jerry was taught about the power of observation. It became more and more obvious that he was, in fact, being watched. Since the government knew he was there, they must have a plan to prevent the revenge. Possibly, they had contacted the embassy and told them of the imminent danger the two men were in.

Jerry noticed that the tires on the car in front of the middle-eastern shop were straight as they should have been. The driver appeared to be casually reading a newspaper as he held the two unfolded sides out from the sides of his head. He didn't want to be seen. Jerry stepped into the shop for a minute then walked out. The wheels on the same car were turned toward the sidewalk. He noticed eyes following him at other places, but he didn't give the graveyard glance – a look for too long that says, 'I see you watching me.'

What Jerry didn't see was the pair of binoculars watching him from inside the open window on the third floor across the street. The man dressed in a suit jacket lifted a radio to his mouth.

"I've got eyes on Subject 45." 'Subject 45' was the CIA's code name for Jerry Grant.

"Continue to monitor his activities."

"Will do."

On the third day, Jerry began his psych-ops. He planned to kill Aarif, but not until he worked his way to him, taking that which was dear to him.   He watched the two men enter a café with two women. One of the men walked carefully with a cane, slightly bent forward with his hand on his abdomen. As they sat at the table drinking tea, Jerry stood outside the window and stared at them until one of the women noticed. Her eyes turned down to the table, then back up to the window. She spoke to the man next to her who was the one waiting in the car while the other went into his house. Now, Jerry knew who which woman which man's wife was. The two men whose backs were toward the window, turned around to see the clear image of Jerry raising his finger and pointing at them. Suddenly, they all started to nervously talk at once. Jerry left the window, turned into the alley and quickly put on his old clothes. He laid down next to an empty bottle of booze and pulled the hood over his head just in case they searched for him, but they didn't. The two men and their wives stepped out onto the sidewalk and looked around. After deciding that Jerry had left, they returned to their table. Lifting his napkin from the table, Habib stared in fear at the two 9mm casings that rolled out. A wave of panic fell on the table. They swung their heads around the room before quickly leaving. Once they were outside, Aarif took out a cell phone, dialed, and began to talk frantically. When he knew they were gone, Greg in disguise, stood from his table and met Jerry in the alley.

"That scared the hell out of them," Greg said.

"What I have planned next will be much worse," Jerry replied, as he sat up.

Aarif, a liaison from the embassy, routinely took a cab from his residence to the university library. He was nervous as he walked on the sidewalk, not holding his arms at his sides in a normal way, they hung loosely. He stopped and hailed a cab. His nervous hands flicked as if they were being harassed by flies.

On the second floor, an older man with gray hair walked slowly up the empty staircase to the top floor of the library, grasping the rail with each labored step. Each footstep taped a slow meter that echoed against the painted cinder-block walls. Aarif flew up the steps. Just as he was

143

passing Jerry, who had stopped to rest on the top landing, Jerry grabbed him from behind, choked him until he passed out and dragged him into a maintenance closet. Jerry had already been in that closet and prepared it. He gagged Aarif, tied his hands behind his back, then slapped his face to wake him. When he came to, his eyes bugged out in terror as he recognized the man who looked down at him. Jerry seated himself on Aarif's chest, placed both hands on his throat, and squeezed until the man's life flashed before his eyes. In mere moments, his mind quickly turned the pages, looking for a memory or a reference to associate with this crisis to so he might know what to do to save himself. If any ideas did come, none of them were good enough. Neither were his panicked eyes or struggling body. Jerry held the grip until he was dead. Next, he took off his sweater, revealing a tee-shirt and disguised himself with a fake beard and long wig, before stuffing the items of his disguise into an old backpack. After wiping his prints, Jerry took Aarif's wallet and credentials to make it look like a robbery, opened the door, and walked down the steps.

As he stepped outside onto the sidewalk, a different man in a suit jacket watched Jerry from inside a car. Without looking at the man seated next to him, he said, "I think I see him. Can't make a positive ID."

The other man replied, "Stay with him," as he lifted his binoculars.

Jerry noticed them. With his sunglasses on he could look at them with his head pointed just off to the left or right. Besides, whenever two men sat in the front seat of a dark, full-size newer car, he noticed. He wondered why they hadn't grabbed him yet, having both the opportunity and the manpower. It bothered him.

After the death of Aarif, Habib didn't go anywhere by himself. Usually, there were two or three men with him. When he did go somewhere, he still moved gingerly. It's a wonder the .45 that passed through him didn't kill him.

Greg didn't go far from Jerry either. Often, he walked behind him half a block. Other times he would create a distraction so, if someone was watching Jerry, they might look away for the moment Jerry needed to duck into an alley or change his disguise.

The players connected to the embassy who were involved in Steph's death got together to find Jerry. They feared that he might come after them too. That plan wasn't going to be easy unless the CIA helped, which they did. They had their reasons. Although they weren't actively involved in Aarif's murder, they were passively involved by not stopping

Jerry, and glad to know it happened. Both he and Habib were protected by diplomatic status, and they had taken advantage of it, doing crimes and suspected of committing other murders. Deep intelligence suggested that they were a pair of hit-men. Their arrogance and recklessness constantly disturbed some in the CIA. The two men could only be sent home as a maximum penalty. This was an unsatisfactory option and this is where Jerry Grant came in. He would do what the CIA didn't want to do. Being in any way connected to killing to murdering was not an option. But they were damn sure happy to assist someone like Jerry to do it. It was time for the CIA to step up to the line.

Greg sat in the back seat of the dark SUV, in the middle of two men in suits. The driver and the other man in front didn't talk. Minutes ago, the two men on either side of him had approached him in a bookstore as he stood in an aisle holding an open book.

"Greg Grant."

Greg turned around to face two of the suited men who held out their credentials. "Maybe. Maybe not."

"We know you are. We have some unfortunate news about your brother, Jerry. He's been killed."

"What? Killed?"

"He was attacked by a group of people and left in an alley. We'll take you to him."

"Oh, my God! Uh, sure. Okay."

Greg calmly followed them out of the store and into the waiting SUV because the story made sense and was something that he and his brother talked about possibly happening. "Well, at least he got one of them," he thought to himself.

Their SUV turned and stopped in front of a large warehouse door that was opened from within. The vehicle pulled in and parked close to another one just like theirs. The doors of both SUV's opened at the same time. Greg slid out of his seat at the same time his brother slid out of the other vehicle.

"Jerry! They said you were dead!"

"They said the same thing about you! What the hell is going on here!"

An older man in a suit explained, "Sorry, but we thought it was the only way that each of you would come peaceably. We have Habib Khan behind that door," the man announced as he pointed to a small gray door on the back wall.

"Damnit!" Jerry shouted, driving his thumb into his chest. "He's mine! I have the right to finish him! He murdered my wife!"

The same suited man replied, "That's why we brought you here. Both of you, follow me."

He started walking to the gray door. Jerry and Greg followed as the other agents waited.

Inside the room, sat Habib, tied to a wooden chair and gagged. The agent flipped the light switch. Two white suspended florescent fixtures began to hum as the room was flooded with light. When Habib saw Jerry, he struggled and tried to talk.

"He's yours now. Do what you have to do and go home. We'll clean up the mess." He handed Jerry a knife.

Jerry knew it could be a trap to frame him for murder. He looked around the room but didn't see anything but blank walls. He also knew that the agent beside him could have a hidden video camera. But he hoped that his friend, the Chief of Police in his town, who was also in D.C. had followed them and was at least videoing the front of the warehouse. The CIA never suspected he would be in the equation, but Chief Wooley wanted to help.

"Untie him," Jerry said.

"Untie him?" the agent asked.

"He's got to have a fighting chance like Steph had."

The agent in the room turned to the warehouse with a hand signal and directed two agents to enter the room.

"Untie him," the older agent ordered.

"Sir?"

"Do it."

One of the two agents held a gun pointed at Habib while the other one untied him. After Habib painfully pulled the tape from over his mouth stood and instantly began to make threats. The agent still holding the rope punched him in his face. "Shut up."

Randy tossed Habib the knife in his hand and took one out hidden in his belt. "Everyone, out," He ordered. "You too, Greg."

The two agents that had just untied the murderer looked at the older agent who tilted his head toward the door. They walked out the door in front of the older agent and Greg, who closed the door.

Two men stood opposed to each other in the room. Habib had served revenge for someone else, and Jerry wanted his own.

Publicly, Habib was mostly out of the reach of the US government that graciously accommodated him and the embassy. Most of the laws that all of our citizens were subject to, didn't apply to him, and the penalties for breaking laws that would be given to citizens here, simply didn't apply.

Habib stood defiantly holding the knife and asked, "Do you think my embassy will not know that it is you and the CIA?"

"Did you think I wouldn't find out that it, was you? We have the home-court advantage. This is our house."

Habib picked up the wooden chair and threw it at Jerry, who just stepped aside. The chair landed next to him, on its side.

"If you were smart, you would have used the chair for defense, but now, I have it."

Jerry brought his foot down hard on a thick square leg of the chair and broke it off. He picked up one of the legs.

"Now, I have my knife *and* my club. I can already tell that you're not very good at this kind of thing. You couldn't even carry out a simple order to kill someone without almost dying yourself. You must have graduated at the bottom of your class at Jack-ass university."

"I will kill you like I killed your wife."

That confirmation made Jerry angry but he didn't show it as the two men began to slowly circle the room, tightening the circle with small steps.

"And if you were intelligent, you would have known your target better. You ignored one of the most basic rules of engagement. Never underestimate your enemy, especially if it's an American. What were you thinking? That a young woman alone at home would come at you with a broom for her defense? You're not brave. You're not even a man. You're a coward. But she surprised you, didn't she? Oh, yes. Didn't expect her to fight back, did you? How's the stomach? How did that report to your boss go when you stumbled back to the embassy?"

Jerry did an impression of his opponent. "I got shot by a little, young woman in her pajama's, and I'm going to die unless you get me to a hospital!" Jerry laughed. "I thought she was a sheep, but she was a lion!"

In a different voice, he did an impression of Aarif's boss. "But Habib, you are the greatest assassin in all the middle-east! You can kill a chicken with only your hands!"

Habib, still feeling the humiliation of the actual report which probably wasn't much different than Jerry's mockery of the interview, took a step closer. Jerry was baiting him to lose his temper. It worked. As Habib lunged with his knife, Jerry knocked it out of his hand with a simple strike of the chair leg. The knife slid across the floor. Habib looked at him with terror.

"Pick it up, great assassin."

Habib scrambled to retrieve his knife. His eyes were wide and his breathing, heavy. His face was glossed with sweat.

Jerry tossed him the leg of the chair. "Take this and try again."

He knew that an unskilled man having two weapons is often less effective. Not knowing how to use them together can make each one each one less dangerous.

Habib held the weapons apart and looked at each. He charged at Jerry who dropped to the polished concrete floor and swept his attacker's legs out and stood up. Habib landed with a crash, held his stomach, and groaned before slowly standing to his feet. He picked up his two weapons.

"Take your time. Catch your breath," Jerry calmly said. "And say a prayer if you want. You'll be dead within the next thirty seconds."

Habib dropped the chair leg. Screaming, he ran at Jerry with his knife held above his head. Jerry grabbed his arm, twisted it, and forced it behind him before slamming him face-first into a wall. Jerry ended up behind him pressing tightly against him, pinning his arm. He placed his head on Habib's left shoulder to avoid Habib's other arm. Then Jerry slid his right arm under Habib's jaw and lifted it. With his left hand, he placed the tip of his knife under Habib's chin, drove the blade all the way up, and left it there before turning the murderer around and watching the life fade from his eyes. Jerry stepped back and allowed the body to fall to the floor.

"That was for my brave wife, Steph. And I hope you're on your way to hell."

The men out in the warehouse were standing close to the door as it opened.

"It's done," Jerry announced, as he came out.

No one knew what to say. The older agent looked into the room. Habib was lying on the floor, faced up with open eyes, and the handle of the knife stuck under his chin.

Greg asked the older agent, "Why did you guys need Jerry? Why couldn't you have done that?"

"If we were ever under oath or on a polygraph, we could deny doing it. But mostly because we all finally agreed that if it were any of our wives, all of us would want to have personal revenge. You two are free to go home. I'm sorry about your wife, Jerry. We'll take it from here. There won't be a trace left behind, and we already have a solid cover story."

As the two brothers walked out the door, Greg asked, "Feel any better?"

"In a way. But now that it's over I can already feel the sorrow that I held it back by revenge, beginning to swell."

Greg asked, "What is better to endure, the sorrow of a loss with helplessness, or the sorrow of a loss with the satisfaction of revenge?"

"I'll take the second," Jerry answered. "You're a pretty cool brother. You need s haircut though. And a housekeeper."

"Move in with me, and I'll have a live-in housekeeper," Greg replied.

"If I took the job, I would have to bounce a quarter off your bed."

"Would that mean I would have to start making it?"

"Roger that."

"Yeah, well never mind."

They walked a block before they noticed that headlights from a parked car flashed twice.

"There's our signal. The Chief."

Just Imagine This Life

A desperate old voice from darkness cried, "Hello? Hello! Can you hear me! Hey! I'm in here! Get me out. I'm trapped. Help me. I'm very sick. Why can't I move? Why couldn't things have been different? I'm lonely. I wish I had a family."

———

"Mom, can I play in the shed and pretend that it's a fort?" Billy asked his mother as she stood at the kitchen sink wiping a plate with a small towel.

"No, Billy. That's where dad keeps the lawn mower and other dangerous things that a nine-year-old boy shouldn't be around."

"I don't have any friends to play with."

Mrs. Gertson pulled a chair out from the dining table and sat in front of her son. She looked at him with compassion before saying, "When I was about your age, I used to have an imaginary boyfriend named Rex who lived down the road. He had curly red hair. For years he would come over here and play in our backyard. He used to come inside the house, and we would have tea. He said he was safe in our house. I never knew what that meant by that. My parents didn't understand when I told them, and Rex never came back."

"Was he your best friend?"

"We loved each other. I decided I wanted to marry Rex when I was only nine years old. He was a perfect boy."

"Mom, how do you make magnary friends?"

"You just close your eyes and make them in your mind. If you try hard, they'll seem real."

"I'll make some magnary friends too!"

Billy ran out to the backyard. He had just closed his eyes and began to imagine what his new playmates would look like. Suddenly, two boys stepped through the tall wooden fence of snugged vertical boards that wrapped around the backyard. One boy was about Billy's size, and the other was bigger. The bigger one turned back and looked at the smaller boy carrying a blue rubber ball.

"C'mon, Peter! Dad told me not to lose you again, or else!"

"You walk too fast, Derek! Slow down! We're not even supposed to be here."

Billy's eyes opened, and he watched the two brothers approach.

"Who are you?" Derek asked with a bully tone.

"My name is Billy! And you're my new friends!"

"Whatever."

"You're brothers?"

"No, stupid. We're sisters," Peter replied. "What do we look like, girls?"

Billy just looked at them blankly wondering if the harsh answer was supposed to be funny or mean.

"Hey, come inside and meet my parents!"

"This should be fun," Peter mumbled to his brother.

Billy ran to the back door and held it open for Derek and Peter. Billy's mom was still in the kitchen.

"Mom! It worked! Where's dad?! I want to show you, my new friends!"

Mr. Gertson walked into the kitchen from the living room. "What's all the excitement about?"

Gesturing toward two empty places in the air, Billy introduced his imaginary friends, "Mom and dad, meet my new friends, Derek and Peter! They're brothers!"

"Glad to meet you," Mr. Gertson replied, awkwardly.

"Hello. Why don't the three of you go upstairs and play?" Billy's mom asked with a smile.

"Follow me!" Billy said as he ran toward the stairs and quickly climbed the steps. With a private hint of panic, his father watched him leave.

Mrs. Gertson smiled. "I taught him to do it. And he seems to be pretending very well."

In Billy's room, Derek and his brother didn't allow manners to hold them back from roughly handling his toys and models. Peter picked up his blue rubber ball and started to play catch with his brother across the room.

"We can't throw the ball inside the house," Billy informed them. "Mom said something would get broken."

"I think she's right," Derek replied as he reached his arm back and threw the ball hard at the lamp next to Billy's bed. The speeding ball knocked the lamp onto the hard floor with a crash.

Mr. Gertson quickly looked up from his book. Mrs. Gertson walked into the living room and stood at the bottom of the stairs. Her voice was clear and loud, "What was that?!"

"Derek threw Peter's ball at my lamp, and it fell over!" came Billy's little voice back down the stairs.

"Billy? If you… boys can't play by inside rules you'll have to play outside!"

His mom closed her eyes for a moment to remember not to damage her son's fantasy. "I'll bring up some snacks in a few minutes!" She turned and winked at her husband.

As she entered Billy's room, Mrs. Gertson held the tray level, so the three small plates of tuna-fish sandwiches, the plate of cookies, and small glasses of milk didn't fall over. She looked over at Billy sitting alone on the edge of his bed while noticing impressions on his left and his right.

"Thanks, mom," Billy said, as she placed the tray on the card table.

"You boys are welcome."

Billy looked to his left and right. "You're supposed to say, 'Thank you.'"

Mrs. Gertson picked up the blue rubber ball saying, "I'll take the ball downstairs until you go outside. Wait. Billy, this isn't yours."

"I know. It's Peter's," he answered matter-of-factly.

As she quietly made her way down the stairs, she wondered where Billy got the ball while listening to him speak to Derek and Peter about their lack of manners.

An hour later, Billy's mom went back up to her son's room to collect the tray and lunch items from the card table. Billy's plate was bare as was the cookie plate. The sandwich on the second plate hadn't been touched. A few bites had been taken from the sandwich on the third plate. All three glasses were almost empty.

"They don't like tuna fish, so they ate all the cookies," Billy informed her as he sat at the card table.

Mrs. Gertson began to worry and hoped that her son would pass this phase soon. His ability to pretend and act out astonished her.

Mr. Gertson whispered to his restless wife as they sat at the kitchen table, "You heard what Dr. Marcos said. Don't make a big deal about it. Don't worry. It's a common phase and perfectly normal. He'll outgrow it."

"I know, but it seems as if he believes they're real."

"Well, of course, he does. That's the point of it."

"Do you think he'll be okay?"

Billy's dad nodded. "I'm sure of it. He's a good boy. And you're a good woman to be married to. I love you."

"You tell me all the time, but I never get tired of hearing it."

"I say it because I love my family."

As Mrs. Gertson left to go to the kitchen, her husband stared in thought, then closed his eyes, and slowly shook his head.

Billy came down the stairs, passed through the kitchen, and headed towards the back door.

"Billy, here's the ball. Remember, it's only an outdoor toy," his mother said as she handed it to him.

"Yep!"

Mr. Gertson looked at his son with a proud smile. "I love my family."

Later in the afternoon, Billy's mom stood at the kitchen window with her cup of tea, watching her son play in his sandbox. There weren't any toy trucks near him. The toys, pails, and little shovels were in two groups on the other side of the sandbox. He spoke to the spot where another boy might sit and acted as if other children were there.

"Give it back!" Billy demanded as he looked sternly across the sandbox. After a moment of silence, he shouted, "I hate you both and wish you were dead! You can't come here anymore!"

His vivid arguments with his imaginary friends made her wonder if her son was especially gifted with a clear imagination because his monologue was quite convincing. She walked across the yard to the sandbox, with concern for her son's tone and language.

"Billy, are you okay? How are you getting along with your new friends?"

"I hate them! They're always mean and causing trouble! I want another friend - someone nice."

With that, he jumped up and hurried to the back door. She followed him into the house and sat at the kitchen table to finish her tea.

As his mom turned back to the window, Billy quietly opened the back door and peeked at the sandbox before deciding that Derek and Peter were too busy playing to notice him. He closed his eyes to create another imaginary friend.

"Someone nice and friendly," He whispered.

He opened his eyes to see that a pretty little girl about his age was walking through the yard. She walked over to him and smiled.

"Hello, my name is Nellie."

"Hi. I'm Billy," He said with a smile. "Are you my new friend?"

"Uh huh."

"I see you've met my brothers," she said, looking toward the sandbox.

"They're not my friends anymore. They're mean."

"They're not supposed to be over here. Daddy is going to get mad. I need to get them home before he finds them here."

As the words left her mouth, a man with curly red hair entered the yard.

"Rex!?" Billy's mom exclaimed under her breath as she lowered her cup from her face.

Derek and Peter suddenly looked toward the fence. "It's dad!"

"Daddy?" Nellie exclaimed to herself as she turned.

Rex walked over to the sandbox with a purpose. "You two. Get your ball and let's go. I told you never to come into this yard!"

Derek scrambled to get his ball before their dad grabbed him and

Peter firmly by the back of their shirts and led them toward the fence. Billy's mom continued to stare in disbelief from the kitchen window before she hurried out the back door and met Rex in the middle of the yard.

"Rex? Wait! Are you...Rex?"

"Yes. You look wonderful."

"We're all grown up now," Mrs. Gertson said. "I miss you. I'm so sorry. I told my parents about you. You never came back."

"I can't remember why or much of anything after that. We had so many wonderful times at this house. I'll make sure they don't bother you again," He said as he looked down.

"Bother me? Who?"

"I have to go now."

"Honey?!" The voice of Mr. Gertson called from the back door. "Who are you talking to?"

"Just myself!"

Mr. Gertson wasn't convinced. Her monologue was too realistic. He knew someone was there with her. After going back into the house, he took a few deep breaths and said to himself, "I think I'm starting to lose control of this."

Rex continued to escort his boys back toward the fence. Nellie followed. She turned and blew a kiss to Billy. He slowly raised a sad hand good-bye.

As the four of them faded into the boards of the fence; Billy asked his mom, "Was he your maginary boyfriend?"

"Yes, but let's not tell your father," she said, staring at the fence. "I wouldn't know how to explain it."

About a dozen years had passed undisturbed in regards to Derek, Peter, Nellie, and Rex. But Mrs. Gertson didn't forget about Rex and Billy never forgot about Nellie.

One evening as dusk was setting in, Billy, now in his early twenties, sat with his parents around a small fire pit in lounge chairs in their backyard. Suddenly, the same blue rubber ball from Billy's childhood rolled across the lawn. Moments later, three adult figures walked through the fence. It wasn't clear at first who they were as they came from the dark edge of the yard, but as they came closer to the fire, Billy realized that they were Derek, Peter as adults, and following quickly behind was Nellie. Billy looked past the brothers to stare at Nellie. She was grown up and beautiful, and she was looking at him too.

"Well, well. Look at big Billy now," Derek said.

"Don't start with him," Nellie demanded.

Peter laughed sarcastically, "Oh, you still love your boyfriend."

"What do you want?" Billy asked firmly as he stood up.

Mr. Gertson asked, "Who are you talking to, son? And what are you looking at?!"

"Seems that the old man can't see us. This will be fun," Derek said with a deviant smile.

"Dad, remember my imaginary friends, Derek and Peter? They're here and grown up."

"What?! How did that happen?" Billy's dad exclaimed. The look on his face might have seemed like confusion, but his feeling inside was dread.

Derek walked over to the fire pit. "Nice little fire you have here. But we need a bigger one."

He took the magazine lying by the lounge chairs and put the edge of it in the fire until it ignited. Next, he walked over to the wooden shed and tried to catch it on fire.

Nellie shouted, "Derek, stop! When daddy finds out about it, you're in big trouble!"

"Dad's old. He can't whip us anymore," Peter said.

Suddenly, Rex came through the fence and headed for the shed. "Hey! Get away from that shed!"

"Rex is here now," Mrs. Gertson informed her husband.

"Rex?! Who is Rex?"

"My imaginary childhood boyfriend."

"The old man's here!" Peter announced as he stepped in front of his dad. "And this is the day when you stop giving orders."

Rex looked at Billy's mom. "I'm here to stop my sons."

"What do they want?" she asked.

"Trouble. They're just bad seed; always have been."

Mr. Gertson looked around the yard like a man who couldn't see as Rex pushed by Peter and hurried to the shed. Peter followed behind him. Rex grabbed the burning magazine pressed against the shed from Derek. Derek punched his dad in the face just before Peter jumped on his dad's back.

Rex looked at Billy in panic. "Get everyone inside and keep them there!"

The two brothers brought their dad to the ground as Billy quickly ushered Nellie and his parents through the back door. They watched the fight begin through the kitchen window. Billy ran back out to help him. Nellie followed. Rex managed to stand but was immediately punched again. He staggered back, landed at Nelly's feet, and looked up at her with blood on his mouth.

"Don't interfere," Rex whispered. "If I die, they might too. Get back inside and stay with Billy. Stay inside until this is over. Please! Go!"

Nellie explained, "My dad wants us to go inside!"

Billy stood for a moment; torn between helping Rex and honoring his request. He turned and looked at the kitchen window where his parents were watching. Billy ran back inside.

Rex fought hard as he tried to protect himself from the hard kicks and punches, but he was outnumbered and outpowered. Finally, Derek managed to get on top of their dad and began to choke him with both hands while Peter struggled to hold his arms. Soon, Rex became limp. A moment later, Derek and Peter stood and headed for the back door.

"They killed my daddy!" Nellie exclaimed, crying.

"Rex is dead," Billy announced.

Mr. Gertson closed his eyes. Rex vanished where he died on the grass and his sons vanished as they stepped up on the porch reaching for the doorknob. Billy's mom cried.

Mr. Gertson just closed his eyes, shook his head, and asked, "Does someone want to explain this whole thing to me?"

He had a pretty good idea what was happening by now but wanted to know what everyone else knew. Maybe he could explain it all away, and life would get back to normal, or maybe he wouldn't be able to.

He pulled his chair out from the kitchen table and gestured toward the other chairs. They all sat down.

"Rex was my imaginary boyfriend when I was a girl," Mrs. Gertson began. "I imagined him living just down the street. Suddenly, he just quit coming." She smiled at her husband. "Then I met you."

"Mom, how is it that I can see and hear imaginary people?"

His dad sighed then answered softly after glancing at his wife, "Billy, you are our imaginary son."

His mother immediately added, "But we love you as a real son."

"What?! Then how did I go to school and grow up?!"

"Your dad and I imagined those memories and experiences for you."

"Oh, that's wonderful," he exclaimed, throwing his hands up. "I'm not even real, and you both programmed my mind!"

"I'm so sorry, Billy," Nellie said.

"Thanks," Billy said, looking at the empty chair next to him.

"Thanks for what?" Mrs. Gertson asked.

"Nellie is in the chair next to me and feels sorry for me. She knows how I feel."

Billy's mom gently added, "But, fortunately, when your father and I die, you'll inherit this house as I did. However, when we die, you'll die too, unless you are in this house when it happens."

"Actually, it's when 'I' die," her husband said, with a quiet sadness. He knew this was the moment that it would all start to come to a close and he would die alone.

Mrs. Gertson looked at her husband. "Honey, I thought it was when the last parent dies."

He looked away in silence as his wife studied his solemn face. Suddenly, she realized it. Her mouth dropped, and her eyes opened wide.

"What?! I'm your imaginary wife?! Oh, my God!" Her hand quickly moved up to cover her mouth.

"I wanted to tell you so many times, but I didn't know how. I'm so sorry."

She sat back in her chair and allowed the stunning revelation to settle. Then questions began to swim through her mind. She asked, "Then why couldn't I see Nellie's brothers?"

"Because you didn't imagine them, but neither did Billy. Something in my failing mind sparked their appearance. I don't know what it was. It was getting too complicated, and I lost control. And I never imagined this 'Rex' episode." Tears began to form in his eyes. "And I sure as heck never wanted to have this conversation with my family."

After the terrible silent awkwardness subsided, Nellie asked Billy how her dad and brothers died.

"Dad, Nellie wants to know what happened to her family."

Mr. Gertson sighed, "When you said your brothers were coming to the house, I imagined them both gone. I didn't want any more trouble. This was supposed to be a peaceful life for me!"

"What's so special about this house that makes it safe?" Nellie asked Billy.

"Nellie wants to know what's so special about this house."

"Nothing. It's imaginary," Mr. Gertson replied in a defeated tone. He decided that he had to continue to be honest.

Mrs. Gertson jumped to her feet and raised her voice in frustration, "Our home is imaginary?! Is nothing real?!"

"No. Nothing at all. While you're looking at the thirty-five-year-old imaginary me, I'm actually a sick old man of eighty-three in Orlando lying in a hospital bed in a coma. And when I die, all of you, this house, and this life will be gone." He began to cry deeply. "Oh, God. I never wanted to say that to you! I love you both! I don't want to lose you!"

Quick looks of confusion were exchanged across the table as Mr. Gertson stood sobbing and began to make his way around the table to his wife and son with his arms spread to hug them. Suddenly, his mouth dropped open, and he gasped for air. His eyes became wide as he placed his hand over his heart and fell on the floor. No one moved as they became filled with terror because of what he told them will happen to them when he died.

At the same time in an Orlando hospital room, a doctor lifted his eyes from Mr. Gertson's chart as the heart monitor signaled a long 'Beeeeeeee' warning. Instantly, the nurse turned her head to look at the elderly male patient lying in his bed.

"Let him go, nurse. Remember the 'Do Not Resuscitate' order."

"Yes, doctor."

"Did Mr. Gertson have any family members to contact?"

"No," the nurse replied. "He never married. No children."

The backyard of the Gertson home and the house faded into blackness.

Epilogue

With every detail carefully thought out in silent darkness, Mr. Gertson's perfect imaginary life was the final creation of his failing mind. A parting gift to himself. This dying lonely man was comforted in his imaginary life until his weakening mind could no longer manage it. And, although he finally had to confess the painful truth about the world around them, he was able to tell his wife and son that he loved them; another event that his real life did not provide him.

What Jesse Wasn't

The living room in the middle-class home was dark except for the two electric night-lights on opposite sides of the room. Jesse stood there in his pajamas. His lack of a fresh shave made the thirty-two-year-old look unkept. But the lack of focus in his eyes made him look absent in mind. He was a sleep-walker. After several minutes of blankly staring he slowly and trance-like, laid down on the floor and closed his eyes.

Awaking the next morning on his side, he looked over at the legs of the coffee table and shook his sleepy head slightly then walked toward the hall to his bedroom mumbling, "Damn. It's still happening."

The next day, Jesse came through the front door of his parent's house carrying an urn of ashes. He gently placed it on the middle shelf next to his father's ashes and the framed younger picture of him. The framed portrait of his mom also in much younger days, awaited its companion urn. Their only son stood there at the little shrine still not sure which was harder on him; his father who had died without notice, or his mother's long battle to the expected end.

"Now, you can be together… I suppose. And I get to be alone."

Now the house was his and all of the contents. Looking around the living room, Jesse thought to himself that the walker and the wheelchair wouldn't be needed anymore. He planned on donating them someday.

Over the years Jesse's parents had furnished their home with nice items. His bedroom, however, was always his to design and maintain. And he did so with super-hero posters, video games, a bed that was never made, and scattered clothes. The dirty plates and glasses were stacking up because his mother wasn't around anymore to take care of them.

Jesse was a single man. He tried dating but failed to find a woman who could follow, much less enjoy his philosophical thoughts and conspiracy theories. Those that did tolerate his lengthy topics found them to be a distraction from the romantic possibilities they were interested in exploring.

His shaky relationship with his latest girlfriend finally ended in a booth in a restaurant when he passionately presented to her his theory, "I'm telling you that Big Foots are real!" he emphasized with moving hands and excited eyes.

"Jesse, can we change the subject? This is supposed to be our first monthaversary date."

"There are actual pictures and videos! They're real!"

His new girlfriend slid to the end of the bench and stood. "I'm going now. I can't see you anymore. I'm sorry, Jesse. You've gotten weirder lately."

She walked to the door as Jesse watched in confusion.

"It's true!... Come back."

He had a job but took too much time off. It wasn't that Jesse was lazy, it was that he needed frequent breaks from the uninteresting conversations in both his job and the carpool that picked him up and dropped him off back home. He felt that the conversations in the front seat were shallow; full of self-interests and self-promotions with the occasional slivers of flattery that were exchanged as the passenger put on her make-up.

People at work gave Jesse extra room knowing that he had recently lost his mother to a long battle with cancer and his father's passing was only two years before that. They had agreed that his apparent depression and general weirdness was well founded and he would just need some time and space to work through it. After all, they determined, his work required only that he maintain the facility. Mopping floors and emptying trash cans required little more than redundant mechanical motions which allowed him to be perpetually lost in thought as he mumbled down the halls pushing his cleaning cart or mop pail.

One morning as the car-pool moved along the sluggish interstate, Jesse was in his usual place alone in the back sitting silently and observing the scenery of poverty, barred windows, and commercialism as he always did. Without anything interesting being said, the conversation in the front seats became muffled and lured him into deep thoughts as he closed his eyes and leaned his head against the window.

The young man driving asked the young woman in the passenger seat, "Did you see what happened on our show last night?!

"No. I was getting a piercing at the mall. What happened?!"

"Oh, my god! You're not going to believe this!" the driver exclaimed as he glanced at the passenger. "They broke up!"

"Shut up! No! I knew he was going to!"

"No! She broke up with him!"

Jesse was not aware that he started to think out loud. Further, he began in a rare time of silence in the front seat.

He mumbled, "We're going to our meaningless jobs. We have work to do. We will perform our designated functions for one-third of our day, then leave to travel the crowded lanes with the other mice to take our cheese home. We will come back tomorrow to do our dead-end jobs again."

The driver and the passenger in front looked at each other. Then, the driver looked in his rear-view mirror.

"Jesse, what's your problem? You have an easy job. You're just a janitor."

Jesse kept his eyes closed. The two commuters in the front seat didn't know if he had heard the rude comment or not. He hadn't.

That afternoon the car routinely stopped in front of Jesse's house. He got out and blandly said, "Thanks. See you tomorrow."

As he closed his door, the young woman in the passenger seat rolled her window halfway down. "Jesse, we're sorry, but you can't ride with us anymore."

She quickly rolled her window. Jesse watched the car drive away.

"Fine. You're both shallow and immature anyway."

It was on a late Saturday afternoon that the family lawyer knocked. Jesse opened the front door wearing his regular sweatpants and a t-shirt to find the familiar suited man holding a large yellow envelope, standing on the porch.

"Hello, Jesse."

"Hi, Mr. Lang. Come in."

"How are you?" Mr. Lang asked as he stepped in and closed the door.

"As expected, I guess," Jesse answered.

"You should start getting your trust fund deposits in your new account very soon," Mr. Lang said, as he gently patted Jesse on the shoulder.

"That's good because I got fired. We had a heated discussion in the breakroom about the moon being hollow. Well, I guess I need to learn how to do a budget and pay bills now… and start the washing machine."

Mr. Lang handed Jesse the yellow envelope. "Jesse, this envelope has been in my possession for some time. Your mother gave it to me to be given to you after she passed. So, here it is. It's good to see you."

"You too."

"Take care of yourself. Call me if you need anything," He added as he stepped back to the door.

"Ok."

Mr. Lang gave a grin of compassion and nodded before he closed the door behind him.

Jesse was obviously curious about the contents of the envelope that his mother had withheld from him until now. After tearing open the sealed part, he pulled out a letter, a stapled three-page form, and a small book. He read the letter out loud.

"Our Dearest Jesse,

Your dad and I agreed never to tell you what you are about to learn while we were alive. We feared it might somehow change your view of us or cause you to wonder how we thought of you. Along with this letter, you will find some forms from an adoption agency. Jesse, you were always our son, but the truth is that we adopted you as a baby. You were discovered at the entrance of a hospital, sleeping in a box. Also, inside the box was the enclosed strange book. As you can see, nothing is written in it. It's the only clue we know of as to where you came from. We're sorry that it isn't much to go on if you ever want to try to find your biological parents. There might be enough money in the trust fund if you ever want to go to college. Your loving dad and mom."

Jesse stood numbly as he took the adoption forms and confirmed what was in the letter.

"I was adopted? Found in a box outside a hospital?" Next, he picked up the hard-cover book and fanned through the blank pages. "With only this book?"

It felt and looked strange with no printer name or retail markings. He took the book and sat on the sofa to re-read the forms and letter. Resting his head back and closing his eyes to absorb the emotions and new information, Jesse dozed off.

When he awakened, it was dark. He turned on the lamp, picked up the book, and opened to the first page where he saw strange new symbols. He read them out loud, "Kornik, begin now your observations of the humans now." He paused. "I've never seen this kind of writing, but I understand it. Is it for me to write in? Am I the one that's supposed to fill the pages with my observations? It seems so."

He began his entry, reading it out loud. "Modern life is a literal maze of streets and buildings in which we must obediently scurry or crawl to work to get our bite of cheese so we can work to get our next bite of cheese. If we have enough cheese, we may choose the maze we would like to explore and the wheel we would like to run inside of. We're rodents nonetheless. Often, to get our cheese, we must do something we don't want to do, over and over. We sell portions of our short life in slow traffic going to a place we don't want to be, to do tasks we don't want to do, with people who are not true friends. We are told to push harder, reach higher, drive on, suck it up, work longer, focus on that big house, envision that expensive car, proclaim our success. Items, titles, corporate recognition, compete, go for them! Materialism! Life is about filling our short existence with whatever we can. Life is servitude to vanity, survival, and labor. Success isn't measured in what you become; it's measured in what you have acquired."

He closed the book and slid it under the cushion. Before he walked down the hall to go to bed, he routinely checked the door to make sure it was locked.

It was afternoon as Jesse, still drugged with sleep, carefully staggered down the hall in his robe. In the kitchen, he made hot chocolate from a little packet of powder and took a sip before placing the empty envelope with the rest of the trash on the counter.

Looking into the living room he saw that the book was on the coffee table in front of the sofa. He stared, trying to remember if he had placed the book under the sofa cushion until deciding that he had. He was nervous thinking that maybe someone had come into the house during the night and moved it but nothing else seemed to have been disturbed. Entering the living room, he walked by the table and went straight to the front door. It was still locked. Turning back to look at the book, he decided to sit on the sofa and drink his hot chocolate. What was he to think? He knew he placed the book under the cushion last night and there it was right in front of him. Thinking what he would write in it next, he picked up the book and opened it. He was alarmed by more symbols. He placed his fingertip in the center under the symbols and slid it to the right. After placing his fingertip in the center again, he slid it to the left and read the new entry out loud.

"Kornik, why do the humans labor for greed?"

Jesse looked up and controlled his panic. His eyes darted around.

"Someone is talking to me," he whispered. "Why do they think my name is Kornik? What the hell is going on?"

He tilted his head back and blew air and hurried to his room to let his internet friends in their chat-room know what had happened.

Dashing back to the sofa, he grabbed the pencil and replied in similar symbols while reading it out loud to himself.

"After all our intelligence, sophistication, education, and clothes are peeled back, we are still animals with all the same needs and urges. We easily forget and dismiss the fact that we humans still own the most basic primal components along with our animal citizens. We should address some of our social issues as being connected to our primal desires. The strong urges that nature has given us to survive, must be controlled. You address me as Kornik. Why?"

Jesse closed the book, looked around, then hid it in the back of the oven. While in the messy kitchen, he opened a bag of chips and took a can of soda from the nearly empty refrigerator. He walked down the hall to his room and sat at his in front of his computer to chat with his friends about the book, the unusual writing, and the mysterious entries he told them about. Some of his geeky chat-room friends thought he was just playing and went along at first. It wasn't long before most everyone left the conversation because he got upset when they tried to discredit his story or add to it thinking it was the beginning of a community sci-fi fantasy story.

The anxiety became overwhelming. That night Jesse tossed and turned in his bed between dozing off and waking up. He figured that he would go back to the sofa and watch some TV.

"Damnit! What the hell?!" he shouted as he rounded the corner of the hall.

He went directly to the book that he left in the oven but was now back on the coffee table. He picked it up and opened it to new symbols. Jesse slammed the covers together, sighed, then sat down to read aloud what was just written.

"Why then do humans kill each other for no reason? The name Kornik was given to you by our leader, Mlowkic before you were placed on the planet you call, earth."

Jesse shook his head. "The earth might be a penal colony where I'm expected to labor among these common workers who understand and accept the expectations of the mortal struggle inside this petri dish. They think their universe is infinite. How the hell can they know? Arrogant humans. Your little petri dish is among many, many others," he said to himself.

He put the tip of his pencil on the page and began to vent his critical entry as he rapidly formed the symbols.

"They don't even consider that anything might have gone wrong inside their brains other than it just took a very long time. They think that our evolutionary process is complete and they are, intelligent and have a clear and bright future, and best of all, they are complete. They never considered that any genes were deviant in the process. They don't talk about the truth that something in our DNA persisted in keeping the animal within us. Or, that, because they have survived so far, these perversions of nature are now out of danger. Oh, yes! Mother Nature took off her apron and left the kitchen after she made the homo sapiens. They don't say it, but they think they are her favorite recipe and the best thing she ever made. She served the delightful dessert to the rest of the inhabitants. Humans are good, they say and just need to address a few more issues. They believe that education is the answer. You know; more information, some facts they didn't know, maybe a few charts to create, or a final discovery that will make everything perfect. But some of the most educated are the ones who got us into this mess!! While technology increases, civilization decreases!"

Jesse sat silently before realizing that he had changed his pronouns from 'we' to 'they.' He was gladly losing identity with his humanity.

That night in his bedroom, Jesse got under his covers and closed his eyes. Later, he opened his eyes to find himself without blanket or pillow lying on the sofa. It was the middle of the night. After realizing where he was, he adjusted his pajamas and returned to his bedroom mumbling, "I have to get my meds changed."

The next night, in his bedroom, like a patron at a museum, he stood viewing his gallery of super-hero posters by the light from his bedside lamp. "I never really considered myself to be fully human. I'm like most of you. Except I just realized that I'm an alien of a royal breed, who found myself in this stupid existence living on this stupid planet. Or, maybe I'm not like any of you. I'm a special agent sent on a mission to spy and understand this race and report back. In any case, I now know the reason I'm here is to observe these earthling's stupidity."

Jesse sat at his desk and put the empty foil tray from TV dinner he had eaten for lunch on top of the overflowing trash can and began to type a message in the chat-room.

"I'm not from the earth but a spy from an alien government. Aliens placed me as a baby on the steps of a hospital to grow up in society and give reports about it."

Instantly, the chat room blew up with comments. Jesse took a potato chip from an open bag and watched his computer screen to answer any questions.

"Am I Jesus? No, you idiot. Oh, 'I'm' the idiot? You all are idiots! I'm going to tell the aliens about you fools!"

People called him 'the spacey spy.' One insisted that the box Jesse was found in a manger. Another in the chat room asked if he was currently in Bethlehem. Most thought that he was just a psycho-idiot. After reading the flurry of insults and sarcasm, Jesse wrote back in anger that it was up to him and what he wrote in his next entry that would decide if they were all going to be eliminated by the aliens. He hurried down the hall to the sofa, flopped down, and took his pencil.

"Do it! Destroy them!" he shouted as he wrote in his book, quickly filling the lines with the unusual symbols. "The fools have ruined the planet! The wars, crimes, and hatred have ruined the earth! The earthlings deserve to die! Do it! Done!" Jesse closed the book and tossed it on the coffee table. "Idiots. They'll see."

Sleep came and left as Jesse lay in his bed trying to calm down. Finally, he whispered, "Maybe I shouldn't have written that last one. What have I done?!"

He flew out of bed, flicking on light switches as he ran to the sofa saying, "I have to erase my last entry before the aliens read it!"

He dropped himself on the sofa, grabbed the pencil, and turned it around to use the eraser. As he found his last entry, Jesse panicked when his eyes fell on a new entry.

"They already read it and answered!"

He studied the symbols as he mumbled the translation, "Kornik, you have done well to gather the necessary information on the humans. Your official advice to terminate the dying specie has been agreed upon by the Council."

Jesse's eyes grew big. He flipped the pencil around and began to write using the symbols.

"Do not destroy the humans! They have resources that we need to study more; like emotions and imagination!"

He looked up at the ceiling, "Oh, my God! They're coming!"

Jesse ran to his bedroom and quickly got dressed in his only nice set of clothes. In the bathroom, he hurriedly wet his hair and tried to smooth it down in the mirror above the sink. He ran to the living room expecting to be translated from there since that was where the book always was.

Jesse nervously fumbled with the remote control until he found a news station on the TV. A reporter stood below the night sky pointing up to three strange lights that hovered.

"Apparently, several groups of UFOs' like these have been reported around the world…"

As more reports came in, Jesse also grabbed the book and read the reply. "We have decided to delay the destruction the earth until we have studied the subjects of imagination and emotions. You will be returned now. Another will be sent for further study."

On TV the three UFOs' left the night sky. The reporter continued to try to explain the event. "We're not at all clear as to what just happened, or if there is any danger. Stay with us for more reports."

Jesse bent over and placed his hands on his knees. "Oh, God. That was too close."

Suddenly the remote control and the book dropped to the floor as Jesse fell dead. The book vanished.

A week later a nurse walked from the dark parking lot to the hospital door. There she noticed a box near the door and carefully looked inside to find a baby and a mysterious-looking book.

"Looks like someone just dropped you off and left. C'mon, baby girl. We'll take good care of you."

She picked up the baby, and the book then walked toward hospital door.

Epilogue

Perhaps the aliens could have chosen a better person. Or, perhaps Jesse was the perfect spy, having had an honest heart, a simple open mind, and acquainted with rejection and loss. Further, he was conditioned with sensitivity having often been judged unfairly. The one thing that saved the earth, at least for the time being, was a final passionate plea from what might have appeared to be an unqualified source; a man who was all human but gradually came to realize that he was also an alien.

Two Fevers, One Lust

Gold fever could be described as a deep and spreading lust whose roots have squeezed down through the folds of the mind. A psychological virus from which few men recover. The lite version is an obsession that gives promises to dreams and pulls the imagination toward visions of what life will be when a prospector finally reaches their hand down to grasp that first nugget. The worst degree of gold fever is when the gold becomes not just a means to an end, but a single end itself.

Old Jake left his ranch-hand job with a different kind of fever. He didn't begin to get the gold fever until he set out toward the desert to find some. His personal fever was getting his own cattle farm, and maybe even share it all with a wife for his old age. For years and years, he worked for someone else. And at the end of the long day of hard labor, he would watch the owner return to his nice house while he, himself stiffly staggered through the food-line of beans, a small piece of pork, and hard bread with the other dirty, tired men. Finally, he would fall into his sleeping spot in the straw in the barn with most of the other laborers.

Jake was older and didn't want to die without giving a final thrust toward the dream of owning his own property. The old ranch-hand had already spent years thinking about it, especially when stood in line to collect his small weekly pay. He saved his money to buy tobacco chew, salted bacon, dry beans, and an old pistol from another ranch-hand. Hardtack was cheap. He wasn't an explorer or an adventurer. Jake was a destitute old man after an entire hard life had denied him even a meager crumb of convenience. His fever wasn't necessarily attached to gold but hoped that gold would be the means to his ranch. He had a pretty good notion that he wasn't going to return to his ranch-hand job without gold. Truthfully, Jake didn't want to. Why should he? To eventually have the other hired hands find him dead in the barn on his nightly bed of straw? Then to have a few stuttering words said over him by crude men, struggling to create even a momentary sense of religion before his body is placed in a distant shallow grave and forgotten? To have an old board with his misspelled name etched on it and stuck in the ground to become the only source of knowledge and memory of the man beneath? Another ranch hand would quickly fill his place. And how could not go off on his own when the rumors of gold baited men such as him to abandon kin and community to trek through the desert mountains and valleys in search of the source of such rumors? Even if you didn't see where the rock hit the water, you could just follow the ripples back. Such was how the rumors of this coveted yellow treasure played out. Having no one and nothing to return to provided old Jake just one plan, to forge ahead for as long as it took. Gold was said to be in a particular area and search for it he would until he found enough for himself or died trying. This plan, although having just the two extremes, had its rationality. But gold fever that many considered an actual disease of the mind would not permit most men a compromise anywhere in the middle. Once the fever entered the mind of men, who had already found a fair amount of gold, it would begin to ask subtle questions like those spoken to Eve in the garden. 'Are you sure the gold you found is enough'? 'Why not dig behind that big rock too'? 'Why not stay another month'? How much gold is enough? The usual reply in the prospector's mind was, 'Just one more nugget.' But in the minds of the men who hadn't found any gold and were completely committed to doing so, there weren't any questions or suggestions and no subtlety. The burning fever gave loud orders to work harder and longer, often making violent threats before it weakened then attacked his pride, mocked his labor as futility, then finally announced that the results were a matter of life or death. On the day that Jake set out he began to hear the initial echoes of the approaching threats.

The wide brim hat did its best to hide Jake's tan leathery face from the intense glaring sun which he often cursed. His white beard hid most of the etchings on his face and protected it from more wrinkles. The blue bandana tied loosely around his neck caught most of the sweat that trickled down his neck, but the dark gray shirt couldn't conceal the permanent large wet area of sweat outlined by a border of dried salt.

Likely, his mule was as nearly as old as he was. Jake had bartered a week of labor for her. The name Scarlett given to it had a note of contradiction and humor. That a beast so homely was granted such a lovely name of dainty grace but was assigned to carry packs and tolerate the ropes that secured them to her sides, probably seemed funny to her first owner. Her name and the sun-bleached bow attached to her long lead rope might seem to be her only sources of pride. Whenever Jake thought to keep his strength, he would stiffly throw his skinny leg over her back and ride his companion as the noisy complaints began and the bottom of his worn leather boots nearly dragged on the ground.

It had been a month since Jake set out and he finally decided that the area he was in was a good place to begin. He didn't miss the ranch; just the bacon that he had run out of yesterday. Not interested in working a claim, he thought it best to test the area from spot to spot. If he panned any gold dust, he would work there. His old pic-ax and shovel were somewhat rusty, and his one tin pan designated for panning gold also served to hold the wet beans that he pushed around with the tip of his hunting knife over an open fire. Together with leftover bacon grease, there was enough moisture to soften his hardtack. Although most folks wouldn't call it a meal, it was an event that happened twice a day; morning and evening at least for the time being.

Having only five bullets, he kept his sidearm loaded and resting in his holster. He decided to use them only when threatened with loss of life or limb and hoped that the mere sight of the weapon might detour anyone with bad intentions he might come across. It was easy in the open wilderness, void of witnesses, to rob and kill, especially by men with gold fever - men like he was becoming.

Two weeks later, old Jake's supplies were finally diminished to the point where he had to hold the panic back, especially because he was alone and far back into the desert mountains. Now, he regretted not having accepted a partner from the ranch, although six other men had offered.

It was another hot month of leading Scarlett through the washes, stopping, and putting his pan in the water to scoop out enough sand and rocks to pan out. Without exception, he ended up throwing remaining sand and black dirt out with a frequent curse after not finding even a speck of gold. However, he took these opportunities to refill the metal canteen that he used at the ranch.

It was time to find a new spot along the narrow stream and to continue the crunchy march of hoof and heal on the sand and stones as the uninterested passing mountains stood safe and content. Jake didn't understand why they allowed themselves to act so proudly when they possessed very little on their stone faces. The stray cacti and ugly stiff bushes were their adornments. It was as if nature stood on the mountain with a hammer and slowly chisel pieces off that slid down the tall narrow rock slides. But the proud mountains had thousands of years before they could no longer call themselves mountains, while Jake might have just days until he was dead.

As the two, walked side-by-side, Jake was alarmed by the sudden thought of starvation that flashed in his mind. He looked over at Scarlett as he slowly walked beside her. Could he if he had to? She was old anyway, and by then he was tired of hearing her rhythmic hooves crunching the gravel as she, as if on some march, effortlessly continued on through the still air, hot and dry while he was hot, miserable, and often without water. He snapped his head away from the vision of killing and eating his mule, half disgusted with himself.

Jake pulled Scarlet's rope and led her for nearly an hour more when suddenly, she stopped and pulled to the left, moving her legs anxiously as she stood in place. Jake knew enough to heed the mule's mysterious warning and wondered if there was a mountain lion close by. Laying his bony hand on his side-arm, he began to study the motionless landscape carefully and listened to the silence. Finally, his attention was drawn to a quiet rattling sound down in the pebbled sand on his right side where sat a coiled rattlesnake not more than four feet away. Most folks would slowly detour around such a dangerous creature, but Jake wasn't most folks. He was very weak and starving. If things went well in the next few minutes, he would have tonight's dinner. If they didn't, he might be dead in the next few hours. After taking his shovel from the pack, he carefully approached the coiled snake and extended the shovel in front of it. The rattlesnake didn't sense that the shovel was warm flesh and didn't strike it. Jesse began to circle it hoping the snake would leave its angry coiled posture. As soon as it stretched out to escape, old Jake landed the flat side of the shovel directly down on its head twice. He knew that a writhing and twisting snake could be just as dangerous as a coiled one. For that matter, so could a dead one. Bringing the pointed end of the shovel down hard behind the snake's head caused its death, but danger remained. The mouth opened and the fangs fell into place as if still attached to its body and searching for warm flesh to inject its venom into. Jake flicked the head away with the tip of his shovel, dug a quick shallow hole, and buried it as the rest of the snake continued to writhe in the sand. As he picked it up with a shaking hand, the thick, headless body of the snake wrapped around his arm. It can take hours for the body of a snake to quit moving and this one still twisted as if in great agony and looking for revenge. As Jake put it in an empty grain bag and tied it to the pack, Scarlett became more nervous and stiffer, but Jake talked to her gently and walked beside her holding the rope. Even if he didn't find gold that day, Jake enjoyed the vision of forthcoming six-inch portions of a skinned salted rattlesnake on sticks leaning on rocks toward the flames of tonight's campfire. It was snake meat, but it was meat and would be the featured item next to the little remaining half-crunchy beans and the few pieces of old hardtack remaining. He pushed back the thought that when the meat was gone his food supply would be almost gone and this rare feast would give way to the complete famine, he would very likely face.

One day as Jake led Scarlett, he noticed that the mule was breathing in a different way as if she was smelling the air. Soon enough, Jake picked up the scent too; rotting flesh and the faint sounds of birds squawking. Twenty yards away, two bodies lay in the gravel and sand. Jake scared the birds away as he approached. He figured that the men had been dead for at least a week. One man had a bullet-hole in his head and the other a large dark blood-stain on the front of his shirt. Although the bodies had begun to bloat under the hot sun, and it was clear that the birds and coyotes had been feeding on them, Jake wondered if he might be able to loot anything at all. Finally, as he stood as near as he could without gagging, he realized that the boots were gone from both corpses, their packs had been gone through, and there were no tools or hats. He spotted a small leather pouch with a draw-string lying near the man who had been shot in the head. Jake dropped the mule's rope and held his nose as he stepped closer while swatting at the buzzing cloud of flies before he picked up the pouch. He hoped that it would be filled with gold nuggets. The open pouch held upside-down over his palm confirmed that it was empty. It was clear to him that there wasn't anything useful or valuable left. Whether the two men had shot each other in a dispute and later robbed, or whether they were killed by someone wanting whatever they had, wasn't clear. What was clear was that he would walk away with nothing at all, and there might still be killers in the area. With a careful look at the area, Jake wondered how he himself might die as the fever nudged him ahead. Had he quietly crossed the path of death unnoticed, or had he been on death's trail from the start? It was hard to know. But the dream of having his own ranch had been mostly been replaced by the irresistible vision of gold. So, he forged ahead.

A week later, old Jake came around a bend in the wash that had a narrow and shallow flow of water. He decided to leave Scarlet there by one of the few trees to graze among the few weeds near the bank. After taking her lead rope and quickly tying a knot to a branch, he walked ahead about fifty yards. Behind a large boulder, he pushed his shovel into the shallow water with his boot and removed two small loads of material then dipped his metal pan into the bottom and scooped out sandy gravel. The larger stones had to be removed first after a quick rinse. After fifteen minutes of playing the pan toward the sun and swirling the water around, he had just sand. Again, there was not even a spec of gold. He violently cursed at the stream. Suddenly, a terrifying bawl mixed with angry growling came from behind him. Jake dropped his pan and began to run back to his mule yelling while drawing out his sidearm. Scarlet was lying on her side kicking as a mountain lion's jaws were clamped on her bloody throat. The lion wasn't about to quickly release her prey and waited until Jake got within thirty feet to flee. He fired at it but missed. After the lion ran off, Jake stood over his bloody mule and stared at its bulging eye as it frantically tried to pull in the gurgled air. With nothing he could do for her, he used another bullet to end her suffering. The bag that held his last handful of dried beans had come open in the attack and now were scattered in the dirt. His old canteen had been crushed under the mule as it fell. As Scarlet lay still, it seemed to him she was both the symbol of his failure and his dark future. It was in that place and at that time that the heat of the gold fever began its final stage of attack on his mind with desperation and feelings of doom. The irreversible regrets of coming there and the finality of that tragic decision bore down on him. Jake believed he would die there without compassion, kind words, a grave, or marker. The old prospector looked at the gun in his hand and raised it to the sky in anger and screamed, "You don't want no gold! How many men have you scorched?! Cooked their brains until they cried?!" He staggered a few steps and fired his gun into the air, then dropped his head and then shot a round into the water. "I know you got it and you're hiding it! Why?! What good is it to you?!" After turning, Jake fired the next bullet into the ground and shouted, "You have no use for it, but you keep it anyhow! Damn you! Damn you all!!" He looked down at his dead mule and cried as he softly said, "And you left me when I needed you the most." He sat down against the mule. Although it had taken everything, the fever still would not release him. But the hope of his ranch that had recently become a stranger now fled altogether.

Jake would not allow himself to starve to death and now with his mule dead, he had no way back. And without his canteen, he couldn't make it a day. He quickly rejected the image of himself standing on top of a hill and screaming for help. While crying, the old prospector placed the barrel of his gun against his temple and pulled the hammer back while the cylinder advanced. He closed his eyes and squeezed the trigger. The hammer came down with a click on an empty chamber. All of the bullets had been fired.

"Ahhhh!" he screamed, as he stood and threw his worthless gun as far as he could. After violently wrestling the pic-ax from the ropes that held it to his mule, Jake charged the small bank along the stream with curses and fanatically began yelling and hacking dirt until a large pile of dirt and rocks formed at his feet, and he became exhausted. He stood quietly and numbly let the pic-ax fall from his hand. All expression and emotion left his face. The fever that had taken everything else had now taken his mind and pushed him to climb over the bank and stagger out into the great span of the flat desert under the glaring hot sun to his certain death. The same hungry mountain lion who had not yet satisfied itself with the flesh of the mule stood up and watched him from the top a large boulder. It would choose between a freshly dead mule and an old dying prospector for today's meal.

A small amount of dirt from the bank loosened itself and gently cascaded down the dirt pile to rest against the pic-ax. It carried a gold nugget resting on top as if the fever, for its own sadistic pleasure, got the final satisfaction of killing and mocking yet another prospector.

The Third Button

The hurried delivery driver pushed his hand-cart carrying a tall box down the sidewalk. He didn't notice the faceless mannequin posing in the narrow store window as he passed. Hardly anyone did. Taking a left turn through the door of the clothing store he announced, "Delivery!"

"Can you put her in the back room please?" Mrs. Baxter asked.

Mrs. Baxter was the owner of the clothes store. She was young and promoted the latest styles and fashions.

"Gary, please show the driver where to put it. Thanks."

"Okay."

Gary wasn't an employee but a nephew of one the investors. He was an older simple-minded man with what some might call, 'a few issues.' Gary's presence at the store was an unwritten clause in the contract, a favor, a wink in a verbal arrangement to help Mrs. Baxter to get the financing she needed. It was understood that she was to allow him to be in the store and help her with whatever he could do. He enjoyed spending his days there where he did light cleaning, stocking, and dressing the mannequin named Audrey. Gary had announced her name to Mrs. Baxter on his first day at work. When she asked why it was her name, he replied that the mannequin had told him.

Gary waved to the driver. "Follow me."

Once inside the backroom Gary asked, "What is it?"

The hurried driver glanced at the shipping label and replied, "Probably a new mannequin."

"A new mannequin? What will happen to Audrey?"

"Who is Audrey?"

"The woman in the window," Gary answered.

"Don't know, buddy. Sorry. Not my worry."

He placed the box on the floor, spun his handcart around, and hurried out to get a signature from Mrs. Baxter.

Gary had dressed and undressed Audrey many times, always talking to her flat vague face while looking into the blank places where eyes should be, asking if she liked the new outfits and if the new purse that hung from her shoulder felt comfortable. When he fitted her with a new scarf or wig, he complimented her and answered back for her.

"Gary, would you take her out of the box, please!" Mrs. Baxter asked from somewhere inside the store.

"Okay!"

Standing in front of the big box, Gary took out his box-cutter and slid out the tip of the blade out just far enough to cut through the cardboard. He made a cut across the top, and a cut down along the sides and pulled the flap down to the floor. He looked inside, took a step back, and stared. She was beautiful and stared back at him with a confident and flirty look with her life-like glass eyes, long eyelashes, and perfect brows. Her detailed pierced ears, an elegant nose, and full lips were far more than what he expected as he quietly gasped. She stood confidently with naked breasts and bare slender legs. The way her arms were positioned made it look as if she was anxious to get a hug.

"Hello. My name is Gary. What's your name? Raquel? That's a pretty name."

Gary explained how things worked. "First, I have to get you dressed in something nice. Then you'll get to show off new clothes. Mrs. Baxter will decide where you will stand in the store."

Just then Mrs. Baxter walked into the room with new clothes on hangers. "Wow. She's hot and sassy. Nice upgrade. Dress her with these things and put her in the window. Leave open the top two buttons on the blouse and push them apart. She's got cleavage."

"In the window? That's Audrey's place."

"Gary, look at her. She's modern and more realistic. Change Audrey's outfit and place her back by the clearance rack. Try putting some sunglasses on her and maybe a scarf."

"She's not going to like that," Gary said as Mrs. Baxter was leaving the room. "I'm not going to like it too."

Mrs. Baxter, who had known Gary for several years, said, "Gary, she has been in that dark box for who knows how long. The sunshine in the window will do her some good."

"Okay."

After he dressed Raquel and adorned her with accessories and a wig Gary carried her through the store to the window and stood her on the floor near the display window. Next, he removed Audrey from the place she had modeled for years and stood her opposite to face Raquel so he could change the decorations in the window. Raquel glared at the vague white face of Audrey.

"Raquel, that wasn't a nice thing to say to Audrey. You're in, but she's not out. Don't be upset, Audrey. I still love you, and we'll get to see each other more when you get to stand in the store. You're using bad language, Raquel. You don't even know her. She's nice."

As soon as Gary finished with the decorations, he placed Raquel in the window and made last adjustments while avoiding her eyes. He turned to go and suddenly stopped.

"Oops. Thanks for reminding me." Gary quickly peeked around the little wall at Audrey before he opened the two top buttons on Raquel's blouse. Whispering, he said, "Yes, I like what I see, but you shouldn't talk that way... No. Mrs. Baxter said 'two' buttons." Just inches away, he looked into her eyes. Moments later he said, "Okay." He gently unbuttoned the third button and pushed open the top of the blouse before nervously forcing himself to step out of the window.

Gary carried Audrey to the back room and began to change her. Noticing moisture on the mannequin's cheek, Gary looked up at the ceiling wondering if there was a leak.

"Please don't cry. I'll try to find a way to make you even prettier than you are. Maybe a different wig... I know. But you have to go there for now. I can blow a kiss to you anytime I want."

At the clearance rack, Gary gently placed Audrey on the floor, but couldn't bring himself to look at her vague white face while managing to put the sunglasses on her and tie the scarf loosely around her neck. He started to walk away, stopped, and slowly turned his head and looked at her.

"But I have to go to put bags behind the counter... I love you too," he whispered.

Suddenly, he hurried back and hugged the mannequin while the two nearby shoppers watched with confused grins.

On the sidewalk, Gary approached the store the next morning. As he walked by the window, he suddenly stopped and turned his head. Raquel stood as if waiting just for him. Her relaxed eyes, long lashes, and arched brows were seductive, and her lips lured him. A wave of weakness overwhelmed him. The more he stared, the more he was pulled in. He didn't realize that Audrey was facing the window from her station back by the clearance rack.

"Good morning, Gary," Mrs. Baxter said as she came from behind him. Gary twitched as he was pulled from the trance.

As Mrs. Baxter held her coffee in one hand, she searched through her purse for the keys to the store she noted, "She's beautiful, isn't she? Very expensive but we've sold three of those satin blouses since we put her in there. And a lot of accessories. I think it's the eyes," she added, not noticing that the third button was opened.

"Her name is Raquel."

"Is that the name of her model? I didn't see it on the packing slip."

"No," Gary said looking back at the mannequin. "She told me."

Mrs. Baxter looked at Gary with surprise and then at the mannequin.

"Okay. Raquel, it is," she agreed as she walked to the door. "Come inside and let's get the day started."

"Okay."

Mrs. Baxter unlocked the door and disabled the alarm panel on the wall. Gary headed to the clearance rack to say 'good morning' to Audrey.

"No, I didn't kiss her. I had to get her ready... Yes, I thought about kissing her, but I didn't!"

"Gary! Get the lights on please!"

"Okay!"

Even though Gary wasn't highly intelligent, he knew he had a problem. He had known Audrey for a long time and grew to love her. But Raquel was sexy and beautiful. And even though he didn't know why she flirted with him, he liked it. But this could work, he decided. His two ladies were apart from each other, so maybe he could pacify them both without either one knowing. However, Audrey always stood at the back of the store watching him work. He could feel her looking at him, and he began not to like it.

As Gary was straightening folded sweaters on a shelf, Mrs. Baxter walked up to him and said, "Gary, I've selected new outfits for both of the mannequins. Can you take them both to the back room? I need to look at them together and design an ensemble for each. Thanks."

"Together in the same room? Gary replied with a sense of panic.

"Yes. And make sure I can get to the wigs and costume jewelry."

"Okay."

"Hello! Welcome!" Mrs. Baxter greeted the customer that had just walked in and went to meet them.

Gary stood dazed before he walked back to the clearance rack to stand in front of Audrey. He looked around, and whispered, "Audrey, I'm supposed to... oh, you heard... I can't make her put you back in the window... I do care."

He wrapped his arms around her, picked her up and carried her into the back room as he said, "I know you hate her... Don't get mad at me... I 'have' to go and get her... No, I don't have a thing for her! I love 'you.'"

Gary left Audrey in the storage room, walked to the display window and stood in front of Raquel. He knew Audrey couldn't see him wrap his arms around her and put his cheek against hers. He paused to enjoy the moment as he smelled the hair from her wig. Without planning it, he kissed her on her lips.

"Yes, I've always wanted to do that," he whispered in her ear. "Do I love Audrey? Not right now."

Gary carried her across the floor to the back room while seeing that Mrs. Baxter was fully engaged in a conversation with customers.

As he came through the door, he could feel Audrey glaring. He sat Raquel down several feet away facing her.

"Raquel, it isn't funny! Don't make up lies... I didn't say... Audrey, I didn't kiss her!" He closed the door. "Raquel quit laughing! Audrey, I can't hear what you're saying when she's laughing! Now you're both yelling and being mean to me!"

Gary placed his hands over his ears and closed his eyes as the loud, angry voices blended and echoed in his mind.

"No! Stop! Stop! I didn't say it! I can't hear you! ... I don't know!!" Gary reached out his arm and grasped at the air as he fell to the floor.

Mrs. Baxter heard Gary yelling and quickly excused herself from the customer, ran to the back room and swung open the door. Gary's lifeless body laid between the two expressionless mannequins. His eyes stared blankly at the ceiling. Mrs. Baxter quickly took out her cell phone and called 911.

If anyone was to look closely at Audrey's cheek, they might notice the tiny tear. And on the proud lips of Raquel's beautiful face, a faint smirk.

The Coal Mine's Canary

As dim light announced the morning, the group of twenty men with clean faces, smudged caps, and blacken clothes quietly emerged from the group of tents and walked to the cook's wagon where breakfast was ready. The foreman who had already been up for an hour walked through them with a birdcage toward the entrance of the coal mine. The yellow canary chirped delightful sounds and seemed always to be forming some new random melody. The routine early morning delivery had to be done with caution and vigilance. A quick walk past where the light from outside ended, place the cage on the floor and quickly leave. If later, the foreman brought out a dead canary it likely meant that gas was present and there would be no work that day, but it usually wasn't the case.

One of the miners named Marc, had an interest in the concept of the canary. Although it was subject to the same dangers, every day the caged bird would sing its way into the mine and continued to chirp throughout the day while he and the miners broke their backs. Its only job was to do that which was natural; that which it loved to do. Neither the dimness or the sharp sounds of the axes against the coal discouraged its songs. Also, its sweet notes brought comfort to the miners. As long as it chirped the miners knew that there was no deadly gas. But even when it suddenly stopped singing to fluff its feathers or groom itself, some of the men stopped and looked at it until it chirped again. Birds generally have shorter lives than people, but at least their lives had meaning Marc noted while wondering what his was.

The men watched as the foreman walked by them. The waiting shovels and axes leaned against the hill next to the wheel barrels piled with strong metal pails.

The foreman was a good boss and insisted that it was always he who entered the large dark hole framed just inside with timbers. Jim stared until his boss's silhouette was swallowed by the darkness. Minutes later, the foreman reappeared without the cage. Jim stayed at the entrance listening to faintly echoed chirps. If the bird died now, the day was lost. Inside a working mine if the bird, being more sensitive, ever became sick from the gas the men would immediately snuff their flames and evacuate.

A cave-in was altogether a different scene. Not only could one open up a new seam with deadly gas in it but any amount of rocks could come crashing down with little to no notice. The skeleton of support timbers offered no guarantees but gave the men hope.

"Okay. Let's get ready. Jim, pass out the candles and matches for those who need them."

Jim gestured for another man to take his place as he opened the lid of the wooden crate and knelt. Each man stepped up to request the number of thick beeswax candles and wood matches needed. Two candles might be enough to get a man to the noon meal. But, sometimes in the blackness, a candle would be dropped and lost. Each man's cap had a small spike sticking up in the front. The candles were forced down over them. Other candles were placed into lanterns to be hung on vertical timbers where the men worked which was always dim at best.

At the end of this preparation, the foreman walked to the entrance of the mine.

"Still chirping?"

"Yes, boss," the man standing there answered.

The foreman turned back toward the men and shouted, "Jim, let's go! Send them in!"

"Let's move!" Jim ordered as he took his place behind them to make sure, that every man worked and at the expected pace.

Most of the miners walked toward the side of the entrance to grab a pick and shovel to throw into the wheel barrel before they entered the mine. One man went in carrying two pails of drinking water with ladles. They all stopped to light each, others candle and each man brought up a hand to shield his flame from blowing out as he entered.

The foreman turned and beckoned Jim over. He lowered his voice and leaned his head toward Jim.

"When I went in this morning, I kicked away a few new rocks that had fallen on the floor last night. More than usual. There's some ground moving above. Keep an eye open and get the men out of there at the first sign of trouble."

"Got it, boss," Jim replied as he started toward the entrance.

Some of the men employed by the mine just shoveled coal into buckets and carried them to the constantly moving wheel barrels for the whole day. Others spent their time pushing and dumping the wheel barrels. Marc and two other men were diggers, swinging their pic-axes against the black walls and breaking up larger pieces of coal that wouldn't fit into the buckets. The canary was always near them because they were the ones breaking into new coal. If they were going to hit gas, it would be there.

Later in the day, Marc's two companions had gone over to the water buckets for a deep drink from the community water pails and drank from ladles of cool water. Marc was alone when the rumble came. All of the men froze holding their tools and looked up at the black ceiling releasing columns of dust and sand. Next came the panic.

Jim yelled, "Get out! Move!"

He swept his arm as if pulling the men toward the main tunnel. No one had time to snuff out the lights as flickering candle flames made their way toward the mouth of the mine. As the rumble got louder, some men fell over rocks and tools as they scrambled on their hands and knees. Then the mine shook with a terrible roar and released tons of rocks that the earth had stored above for tens of thousands of years and was held up by the vacant coal that had been there for millions. Jim followed the last survivor out.

Marc flung himself against the wall, pulled his knees to his chest, and locked his fingers on top of his head cap. This was his only defense against the thundering crashing rocks and the swooshing air. Some of the timbers snapped, and some fell. His candle had gone out, and the air was thick with coal dust. After most of the rocks had settled, he stood and felt his way around to discover that he was trapped in a place about ten feet across with no light and no sounds. There were matches in his pocket, but he knew better than to strike a flame. If his burning match didn't ignite the gas that might be present, it would soon burn the oxygen in his prison. Marc knew that the foreman would order anyone that managed to survive to wait until they were sure that the mine had ended its tantrum before attempting a rescue. Suddenly, the canary chirped a crisp note. Marc was glad to hear that it had survived and at least he had a companion.

It seemed that silence passed for an hour only perforated when the canary chirped and offered its broken melodies. The only other sound that he was conscious of was his breathing. This trapped miner could have been crushed like he imagined others were, or he could have found himself alone without even the company of the bird. He imagined that he was better off than most men there, even in his little prison.

As Marc sat on a boulder, he noticed that the canary chirped less often and the chirps became strained. Panic began to set into his mind. The canary fluttered its wings and made a squawk. The miner froze. For years and years, this was the sound that sent many miners rushing back outside like crazed cattle. Suddenly, the canary fluttered as if trying to fly, then stopped, chirped, fluttered lightly, and went still and silent. Marc stood, felt his way to the cage with extended arms, and fumbled with the small door. He reached into the cage to find the motionless canary on the bottom.

"Heeeeeey! Gaaaas!" Marc called out in alarm.

He barely heard some rocks move. The men on the other side of the cave-in worked desperately tossing aside chunks of coal until they heard Marc's warning, "The canary is dead! Get out! Gas!" He managed to choke his last words out as he fell to his knees and then onto his back.

Two miners stopped and looked at each other. One turned and shouted to Jim, "Someone behind the cave-in just shouted, 'Gas' and 'Get out. The canary is dead'!"

"Everyone out! Snuff the flames!" Jim repeated the urgent evacuation order in every direction. The sixteen rescuers scrambled toward the main tunnel and down toward the entrance, regretting to have left a man trapped.

<u>Epilogue</u>

Marc succumbed to the gas alone in the sealed dark chamber. He could have used his last amount of contaminated air to plead for an impossible rescue, demanding that the other men risk their lives for him. But his final sacrifice, like the canary, was to announce a dire warning that saved other men from death.

The military gives medals for such brave and selfless sacrifices. Perhaps in the industry of mining, there should be a posthumous award for the people who, in a moment of danger, had deeded over their lives to other miners so they could live. It would seem fitting to call the hopefully rare and sacred recognition, simply: 'The Canary Award.'

Witching Stick

The stagecoach, pulling a cloud of dust, finally came to a stop in the main street of the dry wooden town as the driver commanded, "Whoa," and set the brake. Gentle snorts came from the four-horse team for the break after hours of pulling. They had learned that the water trough was just minutes away. The man seated next to the driver placed his rifle down then climbed to the top to untie the luggage while the driver climbed down to set the crate under the door for the passengers. A few men who were waiting reached up to receive the luggage from the man handing them down and set them together as a crowd watched in the background waiting with hope to see what the woman who might save their town looked like.

After the driver opened the door, a nervous woman wearing a long blue dress and a matching bonnet stepped out assisted by the driver. Her little boy was next. They were immediately welcomed by a nicely dressed man in a new brown cowboy hat who stepped out from the small waiting group of those there to welcome the passengers. He picked up the boy and the family walked away in conversation as his wife glanced back at the coach, pointing and sharing private words about the third passenger. Mayor Watson stood next to Sheriff Kline as they looked into the coach at the last passenger. She was an older woman dressed from head to toe in black. Her denim pants were worn and common as were her shirt, boots, and wide-rimed hat. Her dark wrinkled face held a stern expression while her sleeved arms protected the forked branch on her lap. The only ornamental things about the woman were the beaded necklace made from small turquoise stones and held together by a leather string, and the same styled band around her hat.

"She's an Indian," one spectator quietly said.

"No, she ain't. She's a witch," another man announced in the same low voice.

"Maybe, she's both," the first spectator added.

"Ms. Birdsong?" the mayor asked with a smile as he and the sheriff stepped toward the door of the coach.

"Yes," came the reply as she stood up as far as the ceiling would allow and stepped to the door. Mayor Watson reached his hand to take her branch which she denied by tucking it under her arm. She offered her other hand which the mayor took as she stepped onto the crate then onto the dirt road. Taking off her hat allowed the two long gray braided ponytails to fall over her shoulders, then she wiped her forehead with her arm sleeve. Her black gun belt added to her odd and serious look, allowing the lady spectators to silently wonder why she needed a gun and the men to question how fast she was.

"Is that uh, a witching stick?" the sheriff asked looking at it as if she was holding a snake.

"Yep," she replied confidently. "Is that a problem?"

"Uh…. No. Not really. We just didn't expect… Well, we didn't know… Never mind."

"Did you expect me to find water with a shovel?"

"Of course not," Mayor Watson replied with nervous laughter.

Some of the women in the crowd shook their heads in disapproval as she took out a slender cigar from her pocket, bit the end off, and spit it on the ground. After striking a wooden match on the bottom of her boot, she brought it to the tip of her cigar, then drew the flame into it with quick sucking sounds.

The mayor pointed to the building across the street. "Ms. Birdsong, we have a room for you at the inn. You can have your meals there too. The town will pay for all of that. Got any luggage, ma'am?"

"Nope. Where's the horse I'll be using?"

"Ready for you in the stables," the sheriff replied.

"Half up front and half when I find water, Ms. Birdsong said as she held out her flat hand."

"Of course," Sheriff Kline replied. "You have quite a reputation for finding water," he announced loudly enough for everyone to hear. He reached into his pocket and withdrew a stack of paper money folded in half. An uneasiness stirred the crowd as he counted out $150 into her open hand. The two men looked at the skeptical crowd then began to walk toward the inn with Ms. Birdsong.

"No need. I can manage," She said as she tucked the money into her hip pocket and walked toward the inn alone, leaving puffs of cigar smoke over her shoulder like a departing train as the town folks stared.

The next morning Ms. Birdsong came out of the inn carrying her witching stick and walked to the stables as folks going about their business pretended not to be watching her. It was bad enough that three hundred dollars were taken from the town's general fund, but worse, it was given to what some folks thought was a witch. However, because of the drought, most folk's wells had gone dry, so the debate was quiet at least for now.

The town's run of misfortune started when the Indians in the area were among those made to relocate to a distant reservation. Eventually, some were killed after refusing to leave, and some of the white folks and soldiers from the town had lost their lives too. The hardship continued with the drought. Water was what they desperately needed, so the town sent a wire and hired Ms. Birdsong. Whether she was a witch or not, this situation called for them to pay her fee, bite their tongues, and turn their heads.

The town's Preacher wasn't too happy about the whole thing and publicly said so from his pulpit. His voice was the only public voice against it and the only man on the town council who voted against the woman coming. He was suspicious of the woman who believed she could find water and thought the money they would have to pay her should go to better places. The rest of the council insisted they wouldn't have a town left if they didn't find water.

The following morning, Ms. Birdsong mounted her assigned horse; a chestnut-colored mare and came out of the stables. She put a cigar in her mouth, wet the end, and lit it, holding her smooth forked willow branch in one hand and the reins in the other. She trotted down the middle of Main Street leaving dust behind as even the spectators who despised her silently wished her luck.

Ms. Birdsong worked close to the town. She could be seen walking back and forth with her arms extended holding out the witching stick straight and level. Seeing her do that caused some those who didn't want to believe that she was evil, decide she was. And when she came back in at the end of the day having found no water, most people decided that she was altogether a fake.

The agreement was for three days. If she didn't find water, she wouldn't get the other half of her fee. If that happened, it would be the town's only satisfaction, and the preacher would be happily vindicated although it didn't seem as though his prayers for rain were working either.

The second day Ms. Birdsong came out of the stables and walked her horse over to the public water trough in front of the saloon. After her horse drank what she wanted, Ms. Birdsong stepped away with the fork of her stick held in her hands. She held it out and level, as she walked toward the trough. As she got to the water, the end of the stick dipped down noticeably. Some of the men in front of the saloon mumbled their disapproval at what they believed to be an obvious trick or an act of the devil. She mounted her horse and rode farther out of town and out of sight.

As she walked around for the day in the sand and rocks, Ms. Birdsong didn't get even a slight movement from the end of her stick until she poured a little water on the ground from her canteen and passed her stick over it. She confirmed that the stick was working and began to believe that there was no water to be found.

When she rode back into town, the Sheriff and the Mayor came out to greet her.

"Any luck, Ms. Birdsong?" the Mayor asked, eagerly looking up at her on the horse.

"It ain't got nothing to do with luck. Either there's water or there ain't. So far, there ain't."

"Well," the Sheriff said, "Let's hope tomorrow brings us good news. In any case, you already have your ticket home."

"Won't be needing it."

"Why?" the Mayor asked. "Are you staying?"

"Nope."

Ms. Birdsong clicked from her cheek, and the horse walked to the stables.

Of course, the rumors and opinions of the town folks became louder and more aggressive. The saloon was the worst place because the tongues of drinking men get lose as they did when Ms. Birdsong walked in one afternoon with a cigar in her mouth, looking and walking like a man. And not only did she look like a man, but she also stepped up to the bar and ordered a whiskey. The bartender nervously looked past her to the staring eyes of the men at the tables and the showgirls that often flirted with them. Ms. Birdsong dropped her coins on the counter as the bartender slid a whiskey glass in front of her and filled it. At this point, he couldn't refuse any money for the failing tavern in the shrinking western town. She brought the glass up to her mouth and sat the empty glass back on the bar.

"Another," she ordered before the glass was refilled.

At one particular table a cowboy said, "Ah, she ain't noth'in but an old woman who took us for fools."

"And now, she's a lot richer," another man at the table added.

"Ya think she'll find it?" a cowboy holding cards asked in a lowered voice.

"What? Water?" another man asked in a whisper.

"No, you fool. You know," the soldier at the table whispered.

"Oh. I don't think so."

"But she's got that stick!"

"That stick don't work. Might as well be a rock. Neither one will find water unless you drop them in it."

None of the men got up to challenge her even though they believed her to be a fraud and stealing from the town in broad daylight. First, because society wouldn't allow it. She might be downright strange, but she was still a woman. And secondly, because any woman walking around with a gun belt around her waist and a holster strapped to her thigh, might just know how to use it. None of the men in the saloon wanted to be known as the man who challenged an old woman to a gun fight and lost.

It was the morning of the third and final day. Ms. Birdsong did the same routine of the previous two. The only differences were that day she took two canteens of water and started before the sun had a chance to show itself.

About six miles from town, Ms. Birdsong had worked herself up against the bottom of a rocky hill. As she walked between rocks and bushes, she felt slight pressure from her stick and stopped. It dipped about an inch. The movement was not enough to certify the presence of underground water, but enough to make her pay keen attention.

Walking a few yards in different directions caused no movement from the tip of her witching stick until she came close to a narrow opening of a deep dim pit among the large rocks. There, the tip of her stick pulled her hands down remarkably. It was then that she noticed fresh blood on a few rocks around it and a broken Indian bow. A few beads were scattered around a single moccasin. She knelt down to look into the pit but immediately pulled her head back at the putrid smell. Holding her nose while looking down again, the daylight that did make its way inside revealed a dark glossy surface at the bottom, but it wasn't water. She found a long branch in a nearby wash and brought it back to the pit. After extending it down with her arm, she felt around before pulling it out. The end of it was covered with fresh blood.

Most of the town-folks had already gathered as she rode into town that late afternoon. A lot of them were waiting to scorn her and run her out of town. Some of the men held rifles just in case. Others were ready to demand that the town get their money back.

Ms. Birdsong stopped her horse in front of Mayor Watson and Sheriff Kline and puffed her cigar. The Preacher stood behind them with his arms folded.

"Any water?" the Mayor asked.

"Nope," she replied looking down at them. "And I don't suppose Y'all be getting none neither."

A rumbling immediately set in as the folks began hurried conversations with one another.

"What are you saying?" Sheriff Kline demanded.

"This town is guilty, as the blood of Indians will testify."

She took the leather strap from off the saddle horn and pulled up a canteen as all eyes watched. Taking the top off, she raised it and poured a long stream of fresh blood onto the ground. Everyone stepped back as it splashed on the dirt before she dropped the canteen into the puddle. Noisy comments swelled from the group.

One soldier tipped his head to cowboy next to him and whispered, "That can't be fresh Indian blood. We killed them over five months ago."

Under his breath, a soldier said, "She found the pit."

"My witching stick found where you dumped the bodies of them you slaughtered," she proclaimed as she looked over the crowd. "How many women screamed as you shot them?! How many terrified children watched afore you murdered them too?! This town is cursed! Y'all won't never get no water again!"

One man at the front of the crowd had enough of her witchery, her looks, and now her accusation began to raise his rifle. With the speed of a rattlesnake, Ms. Birdsong's gun was out of its holster and pointed right at him with the hammer back before he could even get the stock of his rifle up against his shoulder.

"What's it gonna be?" Ms. Birdsong asked. "You wanna sleep in yer bed tonight or rest in a long wooden box?" The folks around him pushed themselves away.

Sheriff Kline ordered, "Sam, put it away."

The man looked shy and slowly cradled his rifle in his arms.

Ms. Birdsong got off her horse, holstered her gun, and walked out of town with just her witching stick and $150 of the town's money. When she got about a mile away, some of the folks said that her image got blurred then lost in the distorting heat of the desert. Others watching claimed that she just vanished.

Half an hour later, the scheduled stagecoach came in. The Mayor went out to meet it. "Charlie, did you see a woman dressed in black walking on the road?"

"No, Mayor. Didn't see no one."

Epilogue

Nowadays there isn't anyone living in that forgotten western town. There hasn't been for a long time. If someone had the interest, about six miles out from the main street in an unknown direction, they might find the pit with some bones of an ancient people who proudly resisted the white man's aggression. And the blood is still fresh.

Just One Last Thing

There are at least two times in a person's life when the biological alarm clock inside us goes off. One of these times is often referred to as a 'mid-life crisis.' It's a prompting from within that demands that we stop and look back over our shoulders to review what we have accomplished and experienced now that we are half-way through our lives. If our list is short, a degree of panic and irrational changes can happen. The second phase of this first alarm bell is an urge to look ahead to consider any changes that need to be made and to get done what we haven't yet done. The other alarm goes off toward the end of our lives when we don't have much more road to travel, and we know it. This is a chance to cross off any remaining goals from our bucket-list, or to satisfy any suppressed urges that we could not have risked expressing when we were younger. This was the discussion that brothers, Steven and Robert were having were having as they sat in cushioned chairs that somewhat faced each other on the front porch of Steven's upper-class Florida house. They were old and close in age and had stayed close throughout their lives. Both of them had married twice, were widowers, and retired. Having been successful in their careers and well-traveled, it would seem that they had led full lives, after having done everything they wanted to.

As they enjoyed an afternoon cocktail, Steven said, "You know, I've done a lot of exciting things, like sky-diving, running with the bulls in Spain, and climbing Mt. Rainier. But there's one thing I've never done that I sometimes still think about doing."

"Really? What's that?"

"I've never killed a man."

"You... want to kill someone," Robert replied with emphasis hoping to make his brother's statement sound as crazy as the idea was.

"Not just anyone. Someone who deserves it."

"Like, shoot somebody?" Robert asked as he held his glass motionless.

"No. That would be too easy," Steven replied.

"You, senile old fool. Why not give life to someone instead?"

Steven seemed not to hear his brother's rebuke as he looked out over the manicured yard and continued talking as if he was actually committing the murder. "To feel the hot blood on your hand as the blade is pushed to its limit, and watch the light in his eyes goes out, knowing they deserved every inch of it."

"Hey! Come on. Snap out of it!"

Standing to his feet, Steven leaned against the porch rail and pleaded, "Why not? There's no one left in our lives to care what we do. Robert, we're both going to die soon. Even if I get caught, what will happen to me, life in prison? That won't be very long for me. I'll be in hospice soon, anyway. Right? And yours and my portraits will be stuffed into a box with other junk and donated to some thrift store. Someone will buy them for the frames. That's our legacy. Right now, we're both standing in the long shadows of a quickly setting sun."

Robert asked his question gently, "Is this the cancer talking?"

Steven paced in front of the porch railing holding his glass.

"Probably," came his quiet and honest reply. "And I'm pissed-off because of it. Six months max." His voice got angry, and his chin quivered. "I'm a good and generous person! And if I have to go, I'm taking a dirtbag with me! It'll be my final contribution to society."

A long pause set in. Robert loved his brother and knew that when he died, he would have no one else in his life that was dear to him. And it was important to Steven that he did this one last thing.

"Okay, if it means that much to you. But I'm going to help."

The two brothers looked at each other with the same look of assurance they had exchanged since they were kids. It was a special look; a silent bond of commitment that said, 'I'm with you even when no one else might be. Even though the situation is difficult.'

The two dark hooded figures in sweatshirts and faded jeans were out of place in the dark streets of the bad part of town. Steven had his father's old army knife tucked into his belt, out of sight while his brother, Robert had his worn .38 snub-nose revolver hidden in his belt for back up.

A young man leaning against the wall of a warehouse in dim light caught their attention. He had just made a quick hand-exchange with a passerby.

"There's a drug pusher," Robert said. "And he's by himself now. What do you think?"

"Yeah. I'll do him."

The two brothers put their hoods up walked over to the thin young man leaning against the wall.

"What's up, my fine gentlemen? You're too old to be cops and too old to be users."

"We need drugs," Steven answered as Robert stood beside him.

"I ain't got no drugs, man."

"My granddaughter badly needs a fix, and she's too sick to come herself. She told us about you," Steven said.

"And we watched you sell some just a minute ago," Robert added.

The young man looked at them in silence before he grinned and said, "What the hell? Twenty, cash."

As the man reached into his pocket, Steven reached behind his back as if he was getting his wallet and pulled out his knife. Instantly, he raised it up and thrust it into the man's heart. Before the tip was an inch into the man, he grabbed Steven's hand with both his hands. Robert, seeing the moments of impasse, quickly pushed his hands hard on the end of the handle and leaned in which was enough to drive the entire blade into the man. Steven paused and looked at the blood on his hand, then at the man's eyes of panic and waited for the death-stare which came in moments.

"Pull the knife out and let's go," Robert ordered in a hurried whisper as he looked up and down the street.

Steven pulled the knife out as the man collapsed onto the sidewalk. The two brothers fled as fast as their old legs could back to their parked car and drove away in silence.

The next day they sat on Steven's porch as Robert asked, "So, did you get what you wanted last night?"

"Not really. I mean it was okay but different than what I thought it would be. Hey! You want to rob a bank with me?"

"Did you just think about that right now," Robert asked, "or is it something else you've always wanted to do?"

"No. I just popped into my mind."

"Then, the answer is no."

"Then how about you help me sell my house and get things arranged before I have to go into hospice?"

"I thought you'd never ask."

Nothing-talkers

Some people have admitted to the experience of getting into their cars and suddenly arriving at their destination without memory of the trip. Joyce's experience was similar that day except she didn't remember getting into her car or even knew where she had arrived. But she found herself in a remote dinner along the side of a country road that she had never been to before and sitting at the end of the counter on a mounted swivel stool.

Although there were the usual small tables, the full counter wasn't rectangular as most are, but oval with stools that provided every diner a view of every other patron who sat there. The sign on the wall read, 'We reserve the right not to listen to nothing-talkers.'

Joyce, plus eleven other customers ate their breakfast and sipped their coffee as the man in the middle, dressed in a white stained apron and disposable paper hat took orders, delivered plates from the window on the back wall, and topped off coffee cups. Joyce sat in curiosity and confusion, trying to figure out how she got all the way to her stool.

"Okay," the Server announced. "Real life doesn't have background music, so the jukebox goes off." No sooner had he said that the lights on the jukebox went out and the soft murmuring at the counter stopped. "Most of you know how this works. Now that I've gathered all of you together, who wants to start with some original thoughts or insight on a famous quote?"

Just then, a young man with a shadow of a beard and wearing a sports cap came through the glass door into the diner.

"Back again?" the Server asked as the young man approached the counter. "I hope you have something rich and meaningful to say this time."

"Yeah, I've got something. I'm so sick of politics! Did you hear…"

Some of the other patrons looked at him and slowly shook their heads. Apparently, they knew something that Joyce didn't.

The Server in the paper hat interrupted, "We can't benefit from your opinion about politics. Turn around a get out. I'm tired of you coming to my counter and repeating headlines. You ought to be ashamed that most of your knowledge is written in large print."

"What?" the young man complained. "It matters! There are problems."

"The 'problem' is people like you who think that politics are both the problem and the solution. You're not looking for answers or a civil dialogue; you just want to regurgitate popular opinions. Get a better view of a question that pertains to the betterment of humanity before you vomit in my diner."

"We just need to elect…"

The Server reached his arm out and pointed to the glass entrance door saying, "Go back out there. Your worldly contributions are never worthy of this counter. This was your third invitation. You're not getting any more."

The young man got up and stood defiantly. "I AM coming back and with other people with signs to protest this place!"

"Get out now you angry nothing-talker, or I'll come around this counter with my own protest."

Joyce watched the young man walk to the door as the Server sarcastically said, "Just text all your protesters an emoji. Never mind a 'face-to-face, look into their eyes' communication! Who has time for that?"

As he opened the glass door the roar of noise that came through was deafening. Immediately, the young man began shouting against the strong wind of noise toward what looked like a murmuring sea of movement across the street. Talking faces shouting accusations, protest signs, and megaphones as far as could be seen came up through the rolling layer of newspapers, magazines, and other debris, then back down. When the young man got close to it, he simply waded out until the sea swallowed him. The Server hurried over and closed the door to mute the deafening sound.

"It used to be just a pond back in the day and a lot farther away. I miss the days of old men sitting on chairs in front of the general store telling stories and exchanging bits of wisdom and ladies gathered together to sew and make quilts as they talked about their families and the latest happenings in the town. I really miss it."

To Joyce, the Server seemed to be a moderator of a discussion in which the customers were subject to rules. But she would learn there was only one simple rule; share something deeper and more meaningful than the quick and shallow exchanges that have replaced rich, engaging, and personal conversation. She decided to stay quiet and let the mysterious scene unfold.

"Is there anyone who wants to share what's in their deep and honest hearts; something meaningful and insightful?"

Joyce could tell by the nervous movement at the counter that some people were struggling with the courage to talk. Finally, the older man sitting next to her took off his red plaid cap and raked his fingers back through his long thin hair and began. "My wife's dying. She's only forty-six."

The Server looked at him with compassion. "We're so sorry. What does that say to you about life?"

"It's too damned short! You only get a sliver of time!" He pushed his face into his open hands. "It's overrated. You get whatever you can before it's just taken away."

"Thank you for your sincere contribution to us all," the Server said as a moment of mumbled condolences arose and fell. Joyce and all of the other customers watched the older man take off his glasses and wipe his eyes in the silence of the counter.

"Anyone else? Wisdom? Truth? Philosophy?" the Server called out as he wiped the inside of a glass with a towel.

Another man in his thirties complained to the Server, "Listen, I have a right to say whatever I want."

The Server replied, "And I have the right not to have to hear it at my counter." He pointed to the sign on the wall. "Go to the tables."

The man shook his head in disagreement while stepping off his stool with his glass of orange juice. As he walked over to a vacant table, he mumbled, "No one tells me I can't give my opinion."

"Quiet!" the Server demanded. "Don't you people notice that the water has come up to the edge of the road since the last time I gathered you together? Once, it came up to the door, and I had to pick up all the junk after it receded!"

A middle-aged woman gave her thoughts, "I want to say something. This new generation is just going to ruin this country. They…"

"Stop," the Server exclaimed as he pointed. "To the tables, you nothing-talker."

Confused, she picked up her plate without a word and walked toward her own little table.

"Such is the superficial talk that people exchange without really taking the time to think profoundly and share a meaningful perspective that many other people could benefit from," the Server said as he topped off coffee cups. "Ma'am, maybe you will listen and learn. Likely, you won't. You've already been here twice."

Joyce continued to watch and listen. At least, she was beginning to understand what was required by the Server and wondered if she had any thoughts that met his expectations.

After taking a bite of his scrambled eggs, a man wearing dark-blue polo shirt said, "Thinking banished to the surface of the mind with the simplest of human topics. Worldly interests effortlessly maintained with quick words and shallow conversation."

The Server turned to him smiling. "My thanks to Mr. Grayson, our resident philosopher." With an 'open-mic' invitation the Server looked at the remaining patrons and asked, "How about something from Socrates, Plato, Jesus, Buddha, King, Mohamed? Someone please at least share a line from Shakespeare! Anyone?"

A quiet conversation between two patrons became contentious and caught the attention of everyone at the counter.

The Server stepped up to the counter and asked the two arguing, "Okay, what's the issue?"

"Nothing," the first man said. "This guy was making fun of the people who had to leave the counter. I told him to mind his own business."

"The Server laughed and repeated, "Mind your own business. Now that is an ageless bit of wisdom! If you added that to the Golden Rule and sat them both beside the three monkeys of see no evil, speak no evil, and hear no evil, how much better would the world be?" He laughed again.

The second man defended himself, "I just told this idiot that if I were told to go to the table, I wouldn't."

"That's where you should be. So, go."

"I'm not going anywhere until I'm done!" he said as he took a bite of his toast.

The Sever took his plate from him. "You're done now. You have to leave. I'm withdrawing your invitation."

"I never even got an invitation to come here."

"Yes, you did. You all did but didn't open your minds to read them, so I took your non-answer as a yes."

"Leave? C'mon. Where am I supposed to go?"

The Server lifted his head toward the glass door. Out there to re-join the masses of other nothing-talkers. Go."

The remaining customers watched as the man walked over to the door and pushed it open. Again, the thunder of commotion burst into the diner. After stepping outside, he turned back and looked at the diner while mouthing insults before running to dive into the troubled sea of protests and opinions. Joyce quickly got off her stool and closed the door.

"I'd like to say something about religion," a nicely-dressed young woman said as she held a brochure.

What about religion?" the Server asked.

"Well, our church believes that…"

"That's enough," the Server interrupted. "Go sit at a table."

"But I haven't finished!"

"Oh, you're finished alright. Leave the counter."

The young woman took her plate, walked a few steps, and stopped. She persisted in finishing. "What I was going to say was…"

He lifted his hand, and the woman was unable to speak.

"Go!" Joyce urged her. "Or you'll have to walk out the door!"

The nicely-dressed woman could only cough as she continued to a table with her plate.

This process continued until more customers at the counter had to sit at tables and others had been forced to walk out the door. Only the older man whose wife was dying and Joyce remained at the counter.

"Well Joyce," the Server said. "I'm not sure if you're still at the counter just because you're afraid to say something or because you have nothing good to contribute."

"Where am I? What is this place?"

The Server wiped the counter as he replied, "The question is, "What do you have to contribute? Something that would heal and give life? Do you have any wisdom from the gray-haired, or don't you have the patience to listen? Have you gotten anything from suffering people after having sat quietly and listened? What new perspective did you take away? Have your words ever made someone stop and think, then thank you? You didn't even have a comforting word for this man sitting right next to you whose wife is dying."

196

It was clear that nothing had come to her mind. She dropped her head. The Server came out from around the counter and walked to the small the tables. "Has anyone learned anything?!"

Their common subjects of religion, politics, and complaints quickly swelled into a noisy crescendo.

The Server stepped over to the door and pulled it open and waved his arms toward the door. His voice could barely be heard as he shouted against the rage of the noise, "Out! All of you! Go back and rejoin the mass of nothing-talkers! Come on! Get out! Dive back in or jump back in; I don't care. Come back another time when you've got something meaningful to say."

One by one the people at the tables stood and filed out the door still talking about their favorite topics. Once outside, they all headed for the troubled water. The Server held the door as Mr. Grayson, and the old man held their hands over their ears. He looked at Joyce, pointed to her, and shouted, "Come on. You too!" he shouted.

"But this is my first time here!" she shouted back with pleading in her voice.

The Server closed the door so they could hear each other and said, "Oh, you may come back when I invite you, but just make sure you have something helpful to say at my counter."

"When we have nothing to say, just listen and breath," Joyce replied as she stood and walked to the door.

"Like that."

"How will I find this place?"

"I'll send you another invitation. And by the way, you had a second chance to comfort that man whose wife is sick, but you got off your stool and walked away without even saying goodbye. What does that say about the kind of person you are?"

"How do I even get home?"

"You 'are' at home and your alarm clock will soon wake you. You'll be back."

He opened the door for just long enough to let Joyce out. She walked away from the diner to the edge of the turbulent sea and stopped. She looked out at the bobbing heads shouting and complaining among the floating debris but couldn't hear what anyone was saying.

"Well, at least she stopped. She'll learn," the Server said to himself as he watched through the large glass window and flipped over the sign to the OPEN side. "Yep. That one just might learn."

Joyce slowly stepped into the turbulent mass and looked back at the diner and walked further into the frothy sea of nothing-talkers until she couldn't be seen.

Her eyes opened as she laid in her bed and she stayed there for another hour just thinking.

Sergeant Buckley

The skirmish didn't go well for the cavalry after the soldiers were caught by surprise. About an hour before, an Indian warrior had slowly made his way up the rocky hill where the Army lookout was casually sitting but not giving too much attention. His job was to survey the desert landscape for any Indians although none were reported to be in the area. After the stealthy warrior killed him, there was no one to announce the coming attack. Their only break was that a lieutenant had walked away from their campsite for privacy to relieve himself and happened to spot the cloud of fine dust rising about a mile away and hurried back to the camp to announce it.

Without hesitation, orders were shouted out. Soldiers who were lounging in shaded places in the rocks jumped to their feet and grabbed their rifles. Others who were cleaning their rifles without the tops of their uniforms on pulled up their suspenders and got quickly ready. Only a few of the twelve nearby horses were saddled up which delayed their readiness further. Finally, the small regiment charged out to intercept the dust cloud. And they didn't have far to go.

The Indians had split their war party into two to conceal their true number of nearly thirty warriors. It wouldn't have mattered to them because they wanted to fight the soldiers of the white government. But they didn't want the much smaller group of soldiers to retreat and scatter at the sight of their larger enemy. Pushing their horses hard to chase down fleeing soldiers wasn't what they wanted because water to refresh them wasn't anywhere near. What they wanted was a tight battle with all the soldiers together. And that's the fight they got.

The two sides started firing their rifles and arrows from moving horses before they could get a good aim. Very few are killed in this first stage of a battle. Sometimes a horse will fall having been the unintended target of a misdirected bullet.

That distance was very soon closed as the horses from one side merged with the horses from the other side. Indians gave war cries, and officers shouted orders as guns fired and arrows flew in the dusty and smoky battlefield. After the other group of Indians came around the rocks, it didn't take long for the braves to cut down the cavalry. The Captain ordered a retreat as he and a Private turned and fled on their horses leaving behind five dead Indians, nine dead soldiers, and one wounded soldier; a sergeant by the name of Buckley. He was a red-bearded Irishman known for his clever mind, hot temper, and eagerness to fight. He wasn't wounded badly, but Sergeant Buckley had taken an arrow in his left thigh which had stopped at the bone. But he continued to shoot and fight until his horse was hit with the second arrow and fell to the ground sending his rifle flying. He couldn't move fast enough to get another horse to join the ordered to retreat. Actually, he hated the thought of running from a fight.

As the sounds of the battle died down, four warriors on their horses quickly gathered around Sergeant Buckley with arrows pointed down at him. At a time when other men might have surrendered, the heavily-breathing, red-faced Irishman raised both fists and shouted profanities up at them. He had plenty of fight left in him, and the Indians knew it. His bravery and toughness earned him respect from the Indians, so they didn't kill him. Instead, they wrestled him to the ground, removed the arrow while he growled in pain, and wrapped his hands in front of him with a long leather strap. After putting the worthy opponent on a horse, the Indians took him away with them along with all of the surviving cavalry horses and the guns that laid near the dead soldiers on the battlefield.

Although being deemed a brave warrior, Buckley was still an enemy and wasn't treated well in the five days of riding back to the Indian village. A drink of water, twice a day and a bit of dried meat was his portion. But Buckley was a hard man so when an Indian brave sought to fight him or taunt him; he would stand to the challenge with a red face and both tied fists extended out and let out a long string of cursing. The Indians would laugh and taunt him more but secretly respected his warrior attitude that he was willing to fight even with a wounded leg, tied hands, and no weapon. It was his temper and defiance that kept him from getting killed on the journey.

The soldier's horses tied together and trailing behind them were constant reminders of the defeat and deaths of the men he knew. And most of those men had been his friends. Buckley privately mourned them as he pictured their scattered bodies still lying out under the hot sun and was determined not to share their end.

After the five days of riding hard, the warriors arrived at the Indian village, whooping and hollering with their weapons raised over their heads and displayed their rewards of winning the battle. Indian men and woman, young and old, and children came out from teepees to welcome the warriors back and to celebrate. The front of the procession stopped at the Chief's teepee where he and the Medicine Man stood outside the buffalo-skin door. Buckley watched as the head of the returning party got off his horse and communicated with the Chief using native language and gestures.

After several minutes, the Indian who had led the party, spoke to a warrior who brought Buckley, still bound with his hands in front of him, to stand in front of the Chief. The escorting brave roughly cut off Buckley's dark-blue uniform shirt with a knife he withdrew from his belt, leaving the captured soldier with only his white short-sleeved long-johns and blue pants. Their Medicine Man silently took notice of the Shamrock tattoo on Buckley's arm and spoke to the Chief about it.

The Chief spoke through an Indian interpreter, "They say you are a brave and fierce warrior. You killed two of our warriors."

"Yeah. So, what?" Buckley replied with intensity in his thick Irish accent. "And I'm not even done with ya."

The interpreter listened to the Chief before speaking to the sergeant, "The Chief is glad that you do not beg. He honors your proud spirit."

"Beg, me arse!"

"But our Medicine Man says that you must die because your heart still fights even after the battle has ended. He wants to know what that symbol means," he said pointing to the Shamrock.

Buckley, knowing the Medicine Man had an obsession with spiritual matters, used it to his advantage by replying, "It's the symbol of me ancient god who fights within me. He's older than the wind and stronger than the mountains! He's angry with the lot of ya!"

After listening again to the Medicine Man, the interpreter replied, "You still must die now."

A Brave stepped forward with a knife and held it against Buckley's neck. Buckley looked at the Medicine Man and said, "Go ahead, but the god within me will come out of me dead body and make his home inside yer head until the day ya die!"

As the interpreter repeated the warning to the Medicine Man, it was easy to see the sudden look of concern on his face as he spoke to the Chief.

"You will be taken far away," the interpreter said. "and left in the desert to die. We will see if your god keeps you alive. The Braves will return to you there after five days to see if you are still alive. If you are, you will be given supplies and a horse and will be free, and we will honor your god."

Immediately, two of the same Braves put Buckley on a fresh horse and mounted their own. His blue army pants were torn with a streak of dry blood beneath them. He hoped that during the ride his wound would heal enough to altogether stop the slowing blood flow.

They led Buckley for two more days of hard riding, giving him the same meager rations as before until they got to an area in the desert of small mountains and rocks. They trotted into a narrow canyon ending in a six-foot dry waterfall that had been polished smooth over thousands of years of rare flash floods that had hurled themselves over it and into the canyon. He figured the Braves wanted a reprieve from the sun, and the breeze that flowed through was refreshing after the long hot ride. The two captors helped him off his horse. After mounting their horses, one of the Indians threw a knife on the ground. The other Indian put an arrow in his bow and drew it back as the sergeant stood defiantly preparing to die. At the last moment, the Brave lowered his bow. The arrow was released with a 'thwang' and embedded itself into the ground at Buckley's feet. The Indians laughed as they rode away. Buckley watched them until they disappeared into the distance before taking the knife and carefully cutting the long leather strap that had held his bruised wrists together for the last seven days. After rubbing the deep red indentations, he pulled the arrow out of the ground hoping the arrowhead was made of flint. It was, and he kept it. He also took the leather strap and the knife before finding a nearby wash and starting to dig in the lowest area to try to find water. Between the little amount of water he found, three feet down into the sand next to a Cottonwood tree, and the moist flesh of a fishhook barrel cactus, he managed to get enough to survive in his desert exile for at least a day.

Back in the narrow canyon, the Sergeant paced back and forth looking down at the sand as he considered his situation. He knew the odds of survival were very much against him, and the Indians knew it too.

"C'mon Buckley. Ya've been in tough spots before," he said out loud. "Whatcha gonna do, ya stubborn Irishman?" Lifting his head, he eyes fell on the three tumbleweeds laying against some boulders that the wind had blown it. His eyes shifted back and forth, then up the walls and back down. "That might work. That just might work."

That night Sergeant Buckley squatted in front of a little cove that nature had carved out from the canyon wall and prepared a small pile of dry grass and twigs before carefully striking the back edge of the knife against the arrowhead which was hard to hold. It was a frustrating and tedious task and perforated with vulgarity, but finally, a single spark jumped onto the small pile. Gently he blew on the pile. Smoke began to thicken inside the little bundle before it erupted into fire. He sat it inside the circle of stones he had prepared and added twigs.

It was dark as he listened to the distant sound of coyotes patrolling for food. Buckley lay inside the little cove enjoying the breeze that flowed through the canyon and thought about the last week. Finally, he remembered that in four days two Indian braves would return. They were his only way out, so he had to set an ambush.

Insects and the occasional lizard were his diet for the next two days as walked around favoring his stiff leg and winced in pain when he forgot to. He was always hungry and thought about the coyotes. It wouldn't be the best meal, but he decided he would kill one.

After half a day of poking in between hot rocks with a pointed stick, and frequent trips to the waterhole, he managed to get eight lizards. That night he would eat three and save the others for the coyote trap.

It was finally night as Buckley sat sunburned and hidden in a different place in the narrow canyon. There were enough tracks going in and out there to make him believe it was a regular path for coyotes. Next to him was a pile of hand-size rocks he had gathered. The sergeant had made a knotted loop in the leather strap at the end of a long stick that lay on the ground. In the middle of that loop was a small pile of dead lizards. No coyotes passed through that night.

The next night as he waited crouched down the same big rock, Buckley heard faint yelps and gripped the long stick with both hands. His heart began to pound as the yelping drew closer. The three hungry coyotes were cautious and curious as they came through. Although they were drawn by the smell of the dead lizards, they also smelled Buckley's odor which enticed them further. All three hunters approached the leather knotted loop. As the first coyote lowered his head to eat the lizards, Buckley quickly lifted the stick as the loop tightened around the neck of the coyote. Immediately, it began to yelp and fought the noose. Buckley tucked the end of the stick under his arm and grabbed a rock which he threw at the other two. He threw three rocks before they turned around and scampered out of the canyon. Buckley grabbed another rock and hit the coyote he had snared. He threw another rock and another until the coyote went down. After setting the stick on the ground, he walked on it over to the twitching coyote, drew out his knife and cut the coyote's neck and let it bleed out. It wasn't much different than dog meat, he imagined, but tonight Buckley would have his belly full of campfire-roasted protein. For the next step of his plan, he saved the bones.

His schedule was completely different the morning after. Buckley was feeling a little stronger and optimistic. The goal was to collect tumbleweeds. It took him all day, but he managed to bring back dozens to his little canyon. In just two days the Indian braves would be returning, and he had to be ready.

It was the day of the expected arrival. Sergeant Buckley had been busy the day before preparing the narrow canyon. He was almost naked in his white long-johns and black socks. He had placed most of the tumbleweeds against the canyon walls about fifty feet from the dry waterfall making them look to have been naturally placed by the breeze that channeled through. The other tumbleweeds were up on the canyon wall a few feet from the hot coals where Army Sergeant Buckley waited and watched. Shading his eyes from the sun, he finally noticed three approaching horses; two of them with riders. His trap was baited and set. Two Indian braves had one fact to establish; either the sergeant with the marking of his god was dead or alive. It would be wise to return to the chief with real evidence, like a scalp.

The two Braves stopped their three cavalry horses at the entrance of the canyon because they didn't want the sand trampled, and walked in.

They didn't take their rifles as they thought they would immediately find what they were looking for within just a short distance. But the sparse trail of luring clues drew them further into the canyon and away from the horses. Twenty-five feet from where they stood was an army boot buried half-way in the sand. They went over to it, then looked ahead to see another boot sticking out from behind a rock. The coyote tracks and the bones from his feast that Buckley had scattered were enough for one of the Indians to lift his head and start walking toward the blue army pants wrapped around a stick near the dry waterfall. When the two Indians passed through the narrow opening between the two piles of tumbleweeds, it was Buckley's cue. Standing out of sight forty feet above his enemies he took the first tumbleweed and placed it on the coals. It quickly caught fire, and he threw it down into the canyon. As it fell, the breeze coming through the canyon fueled the flaming ball as it hit the piles. The sergeant tossed another flaming tumbleweed as the confused Indians were backed up to the waterfall by the heat and watched the piles of tumbleweeds erupt into a wall of fire. Another tumbleweed went over on fire, and then he quickly dropped the rest without the fire. Each one floated down and toward the trapped Indians who tried in vain to climb up the polished wall of the waterfall. Berkley scrambled down the rocks to the horses as the flames were at their highest. Through the flames, the two Indians watched helplessly as Army Sergeant Buckley grabbed a rifle from the long leather sheath attached to the side of a horse. He lifted the rifle to his shoulder and walked toward them.

"I told ya I weren't done with ya!" His voice echoed loudly against the canyon walls as he reminded the trapped Indians before shooting them dead. After gathering his boots and pants from the sand, he took the decorated sheathed knives from their bodies as proof of his wild story he would later have to tell as he reported to some army officer at the closest Army fort.

Next, he selected a piece of blackened wood from the embers which he used to draw a huge Shamrock on the canyon wall. He tried to imagine the reaction of the Indian search party when they came into the narrow canyon to find their two warriors lying dead underneath it and wondered what the Medicine Man would think. He grinned.

After putting on his pants and boots, Buckley tied the reins of two horses to the saddle of the other which he mounted. As he rode out of the narrow dead-end canyon with three army horses, two army rifles, and plenty of supplies, the red-bearded Calvary Sergeant laughed loudly and shouted, "Beg me arse! Ya never fought an Irishman, did ya!?"

A Journal's Journey

Almost everyone has said, "Someday, I'm going to write a story." My name is Matt, and I'm one of those people, but I'm very determined to write one. I need to find a place be alone with my thoughts; alone without people, noise, or disturbance to find inspiration to write one. Other people might just sit home waiting for an idea to come to them for a story to write. Not me; I'm going out to find mine. After kissing my supportive wife good-bye, I left with a backpack, some money, a blank notebook, this journal, and hitchhiked to the mountains.

A pickup truck with tools and a ladder in the bed stopped just ahead of where I stood to hitchhike. The driver looked through the passenger door window and asked, "Where're you going?"

"As far up the mountain as I can."

"Well, I'm going about three-quarters of the way. I've got to open some seasonal rental properties now that winter has passed. Put your backpack in the back and hop in. Do you have a place to stay up there?"

"Well, no, but maybe I'll stumble across something. I'm only staying for a week or less."

The man looked over at me from behind the steering wheel and announced, "You're a writer."

"What? How do you know that?"

"Well," he said, "you're alone, so you're not going up there to party, you have no hunting or fishing gear, and I don't think an easel would fit in your pack. It's just simple deductions."

"You're right. I am a writer."

When I heard him say it and when I said it out loud in the present tense it validated me. It felt as though the universe certified me and I quickly agreed. I thought to myself, "Yeah, I'm a writer. Yes, sir, I do writing. Writing is what I do."

"But you haven't gotten very far on your work, or else you wouldn't be up here so good luck." The driver held his chin and thought for a moment. "There's an old cabin near the top. No one ever goes there. Why not? Follow this road until the pavement ends and take the dirt road to the left. You'll enjoy the scenery."

"Thanks," I replied.

When I arrived at the cabin my brain couldn't reconcile the vast distance between the mountain that I was standing on and the next one, so my brain asked my eyes to look and wait a few moments until it could. I was concerned that this magnificent vision would often distract me from my objective but still believed that some inspiring epiphany for my story would come to me at any time. While wondering what the easy whispering wind was saying as it wrapped its hands around the sides of my head and mumbled in my ears, I closed my eyes and seemed to be suspended, small and vulnerable in the hugeness. A distant eagle's screech made me open my eyes again. It was gliding on the air with smooth confidence; comfortable with itself, comfortable being here.

The cabin was old and seemed to have been without a visitor for years. Thankfully, many things were still inside including the woodstove which I lit after filling it with short broken branches, just as darkness settled in. This place up here, this little remote, rustic cabin is the dream of many people. For even a day or two most anyone would love to stay there and maybe reconnect with themselves, someone else, or with nature. I came here to connect with my inner literary artist which still hadn't announced its title or for that matter, its content.

My notebook was propped up on my knees as I sat on the old bed. Hard, wood slats pretended to support the mattress that was deteriorated down to the coils. The dim lantern cast a faint light on my first page as the anxious tip of my pencil was pressed down on it like a runner in a starting block. Out of the corner of my eye, I watched a mouse climb up the leg of the table across the small room and sat sniffing my pack then disappeared into it. "Get out of there you little rodent," I said with a laugh then walked over the old plank floor and gently shook the pack until the mouse ran out and went back down the leg of the table. But it didn't hide. Instead, it stopped near the wall and sat on its back legs, holding its front legs like a dog asking for a treat. I felt no malice toward it. There was no reason it shouldn't enjoy the warmth and food so; I broke off a good size piece of a nutbar and placed it on the floor. Moments later, the mouse came forward to eat it. I smiled and watched it for a long time before I realized how much time had gone by, and I was tired so, I climbed into my sleeping bag and fell asleep thinking about my unborn story and expecting to have a dream or a vision to direct me, but nothing came in my sleep.

Early in the morning, I woke up in the dark with a clear mind. The cabin was cold, but I lay there in the silent stillness. This was my best hope for an idea for my story I decided and closed my eyes to think.

The morning light woke me up an hour later as the cheery voices of birds announced the day. I was hungry and still in dire need of inspiration, so I got up off the squeaky and wobbly springs.

Usually, distractions are noisy or visually disturbing and try to wedge themselves into my already congested mind, but not there. Distractions were cousins to attractions; the bear walking along the riverbank, the sun setting on the last large chunks of ice floating in the bay, and the almost primitive feel of these untamed mountains. There, in the mountains, serious thinking conceded to dreaming and imagining and writing stepped aside for watching and listening. I concluded this was no place to be for a wanna-be writer like me who needed to focus, so I left a handful of trail mix on the floor and started the long walk back to the main road and hitched another ride to the truck stop a few miles back.

The desert was my next destination and its desolation my best hope so, I thought. Surely, the desert was the place for me to start my story.

I met a chatty trucker at a truck stop who offered to let me ride the four-hour or so trip toward the desert. He said he would appreciate the company.

He started off even before we left the parking lot, "Yep. I've been nearly everywhere it seems. Seen a lot of things and places. People often tell me, 'George, you ought to write a book!'"

I turned my head toward my window and rolled my eyes. "He's another one of *them*," I thought to myself. The odds are that he will never write a book, but I told him, "Yeah, maybe you should."

"My name's George, but my CB handle is Smoke'in George. Some folks call me Barbeque George. But I won't tell you what my wife calls me." He winked, laughed too loudly, and reached over to casually backhand me on my arm with an, '*If you know what I mean*,' wink.

"I'm Matt, glad to meet you and thanks for the ride."

"Don't suppose you have a handle, not being a truck driver."

"No. You're right." I thought to myself, 'If I did it could be 'Bitter Writer.'

"So, where you head'in?" he asked.

"Somewhere in the desert where there are no people."

"It's about four more hours. If you don't mind my asking, whatcha gonna do there?"

I told him 'bird watching' so I wouldn't have to lay bare the very bare fact that I also wanted to write a story but had no idea about what.

"What's yer favorite desert bird?"

I had to think quickly. "Probably… the Brown Bobble-headed Thrush." "Aw, heck,' I thought to myself. "I may as take this lie all the way." So, I cupped my hands around my mouth. "It makes a peculiar sound like whad-d-d-d-errrr. Ever hear one?" I asked with authority after having made the name up and the bird sound because I didn't remember any real desert bird names in the short time I had.

"Nooo. No, I never did hear noth'in like that. Sounds like its saying, 'water.'"

"Yes, it does. That's what people say," I replied, nodding.

"I like the Roadrunner."

I wished I had remembered that one. I would have made things much easier for myself, but it wouldn't have been as fun. The conversation dropped off.

During the Country Music songs on the radio, I thought about how the listeners were denied so much in regards to the introduction of the songs like you hear on public radio. The movement, key, name of the symphony, the history, the composer, and every other detail sprinkled with foreign names the listeners will never remember and don't need but enjoy the feeling of culture and sophistication they grant. Laughing to myself I imagined a country song actually being introduced with these elements by a slow, older, calm, and sophisticated voice of a woman who clearly holds a Ph.D. in Music Introduction but had recently lost her job at the public radio station. Because for the first time in the history of public radio, they actually didn't reach their fund-raising goal and had to close leaving cases of promotional coffee cups from the fundraiser on the floor of the studio. Unfortunately, she had to take a job at a local radio station in West Virginia whose support came from the ads of local feed and hardware stores. I made up her introduction to a country song for my own amusement. She begins in her smooth and flowing voice, "Our next selection is by artist Jed Willy, an American vocalist from the southern region of the United States, performing the fifth movement of his 'Lost Love' Sonata in the key of G major accompanied by a fiddle, an electric guitar, an acoustic guitar, and percussion. The fiddle dates back to the early 1960's. This musical piece was written and composed by the vocalist in a drinking establishment in Nashville, Tennessee in 2008 just as the Great Recession was beginning. In recent years, other artists have performed various renditions of this ballad but have been judged by critics to have unsuccessfully communicated the depth of the despondency of the author. One cannot accurately communicate the tragedy of having run out of beer on a Friday night unless one has personally experienced such despair." Finally, I imagined Country Music fans yelling at the radio, demanding, "Lady, just play the damn song!"

After listening to some radio talk shows, enduring a few coded CB chats, and attempting to sing along with him with the radio, I said, "Smoke'in George, anywhere along here, please."

The trucker geared down pulled off the road and set the airbrake. I stepped into the sleeper to get my backpack.

"Good luck now and be careful hiking. I hope you see a lot of birds! What was the name of your favorite bird again?"

I had forgotten what I told him. "It's in the thrush family. The females are a darker brown than the males. Thanks, George," I said as I turned around, stepped down, and closed the door.

After hoisting my backpack and adjusting the straps, I waved goodbye and started walking. Smoke'in George gave his last goodbye with generous blasts from his air horn as he pulled back onto the road.

The desert has its own unique beauty; I realized as I stood staring at the landscape. At the same time, it wasn't welcoming. Maybe it was that I had just stepped out of air conditioning, but the heat greeted me like the hot towel after my barber cuts my hair.

After an hour of walking, I found a large cleft in the side of a mountain to stay in. This place was intensely hot, dry, and bright. But the cooler nights came alive with Coyotes and indiscernible sounds that, at times, were a little too close and unnerving. I decided there shouldn't be much there to distract me although it was an ancient place with memories held on the surface of every rock.

The next morning, I climbed down from my uncomfortable stone nest that my sleeping bag convinced me would be enough padding against the hard floor, but it wasn't. After a short hike, I stood before the rocks asking them to tell me what they saw and heard over the centuries. But they wouldn't respond to my interview.

"Alright, I get it; you're all nervous but there's nobody else here, and I'm not going to record anything. I'm just asking if any of you are willing to talk to me about what you've seen over the years." No response. "Maybe you don't speak English. Como Esta? Do you speak Indian?" I asked, as I made up crazy hand sign movements. "It's OK. I understand. We haven't warmed up to each other yet. You see, I really need something to write about and, well… I'm between a rock and a hot place." I laughed out loud at my joke. "I thought that was funny, but you're just sitting there looking at me all stone-faced." Tapping an imaginary microphone in my hand while mimicking the sound of loud screeching feedback, I laughed again and walked away not even caring if they were offended. Those rocks didn't have to treat me like that.

After further exploring the area, I found strange 'stick-men' images on some rock walls; wagons and Indians on horses, and hazy prospectors. Suddenly, a lizard ran up on a rock and stared at me then bobbed its head up and down. I allowed myself to believe that it was a spiritual acknowledgment that there on that spot is where I would find something to write about. But I didn't take the bait. Petroglyphs will not be the subject of my story. A Big Horn Sheep casually looked down at me from a ledge above. He wasn't impressed with me. Neither was I.

All of this felt very strange to me and even a bit supernatural. I didn't like it, but I was determined to go one until either I found my elusive subject, or I clearly didn't. So, I took out my notebook and my pencil and made myself sit down in some shade and think of something. Forcing my pencil to write against its will, a word appeared - 'society.' The pencil flipped over, and the eraser assaulted the word. I swept off the pink rubber crumbs, and my pencil returned back on point again. 'Politics' formed on the paper and without hesitation, my pencil slashed a dark line through it. I sighed, paused, shook my head, and wrote a title for my story, 'I'm an Idiot and Can't Even Write'. "That's the title I deserve." My pencil agreed by adding an exclamation mark. There was nothing here in the desert for my story I concluded and walked back toward the highway and began to thumb a ride to the coast.

After two rides I found myself walking down the side of the interstate. A state trooper car pulled behind me with the police lights flickering. The car stopped, and the horn honked. She got out wearing sunglasses and ordered me to step over to the front of her car as she leaned her head to speak into her radio attached to her shoulder.

"It's against the law to solicit rides or walk along a state highway. Do you have any weapons or drugs on you?"

"No, ma'am."

"It's 'officer'. You don't have any knives, guns, or explosives?" she asks with the disposition of a bayonet.

"Well, I have a pocket knife."

"I thought you said you didn't have any weapons?" the officer replied as if she had caught me in a lie.

"Doesn't the word 'weapon' imply 'intent'? My pocket knife is for hiking and camping."

She held out her hand as if she hadn't heard me. "Let me see it." I reached into my pocket. "Slowly," she warned, placing her right hand on her yellow Taser attached to her wide black belt. As I wondered if she also had a bayonet handy on her police belt, I carefully took out the pocket knife and slowly handed it to her. I was scared. The officer opened it and inspected the blade by gliding her thumb perpendicular over its edge. "It's legal but dull. This thing couldn't cut a fart in half."

Taken by surprise by her colorful assessment of my knife, I chuckled in relief.

She looked up at me over the top of her sunglasses. "Is there something funny?" she asked dryly.

"No. Nothing. Sorry," I meekly replied while a small surge of fear swelled up.

"Where're you going?"

"To the ocean," I announced. "I want to get out on the sea and work on my story."

"I want to see the story."

She was clearly suspicious and smart. She wanted me to open my backpack so she could look into it for contraband. Already being warned about moving too quickly, while she carefully watched me, I slowly took off my pack, set it on the ground, and produced the notebook from a large zippered pocket. The officer read the word 'Story' on the cover out loud and opened it to the first page which had only the one sentence I had written. She read it out loud, "I'm an Idiot and Can't Even Write." The officer looked at me with a 'got-cha' expression. "Do you want me to believe that you're actually writing anything? All you have is the word 'Story' on the front. That's not even a real title, and the sentence on the very first page leads me to believe that you're not a writer. She fanned through the rest of the blank pages and stared at me in disbelief.

"Yes, I know. I have writer's cramp. Uh, swimmer's block. No, wait, I mean, writer's block! I have writer's block. That's it. That's what I have." I said the last sentence nodding with emphasis to make it sound truthful and final.

She squinted her eyes as if trying to look into my mind for the real truth then handed my notebook back to me but kept the knife. "Wait, right here," She commanded after taking my driver's license and getting into her car.

After a couple of minutes, she came back, handed me my license and said, "You can't be walking along the highway. I'll take you to the docks where you can get a boat. Get in."

She opened the back door of the police car. "Watch your head. If you forget to watch your head, then watch your language."

I chuckled again, believing that she had thawed a bit.

"Is there something funny?" she asked. "Because I'm not a comedian."

"No ma'am…officer."

The uncomfortable trip was perforated with police radio codes and sentence fragments. The dispatcher always mumbled in the lowest and quickest voice, and the officer matched it. I wondered if there is a class at the academy were the candidates have to learn low volume mumbling over the radio. But there was no conversation between us in the police car until we arrived at the docks.

The officer got out and opened my door. "Here, and stay off the highway," she said as she handed me my knife.

"Thank you, ma'am." I got the last jab in as a payment for being questioned and searched.

"It's 'officer.'" she corrected me as the police car pulled away.

"Okay, lady. Whatever you say."

"If you're going to charter my boat, I charge by the day and round up to the hour. All meals, gas, and fishing are included in the price. I'm the cook, bartender, and guide. This is a good time to go. The ocean should be relatively calm this week," the captain told me as we stood on the dock.

"Okay. It's a deal. I just need a few days of peace and quiet."

We began our two-hour trip out to the ocean. Dolphins playfully swam next to us; breaking the surface and darting back into the water over and over.

Later, a curious whale spotted with white barnacles rose to the surface and blew, sending a fishy smelling mist into the air, then listed slightly to look at me with an enormous eye before sliding back under the water. I recalled the story about Jonah and instinctively braced myself, so that I wouldn't fall in.

Eventually, the captain cut off the engine, and we drifted. I pulled out my notebook and journal and placed them on the white table mounted on the deck and worked with my fingernail to flick off three large fish scales that seem to be glued down. Now I was ready to write but was compelled to lean overboard and look into the water at the expansive and haunting deepness.

"You're guarding secrets and hiding hundreds of forgotten and anonymous shipwrecks under the deep sediments," I whispered, wanting the sea to understand that I knew this.

"Seasick?" the captain asked me from the doorway of the cabin.

"No. Just looking."

"At what?"

"The dark depth." I glanced up at him with my slow and distant answer and turned back to continue staring down at the water. "The countless lives lost in storms; tales told among the crews... lost treasures beneath."

"Oh." He quickly brushed my spacey sentiment aside. "Want to do some fishing?"

"No thanks. I came to write in silence," I politely answered.

"So, what are you writing about?"

"Oh, here it goes," I mumbled under my breath. Didn't I just use the words, 'in silence'?" I looked at him. "Uh, I don't know yet. I'm just... you know, thinking about it. I have a few ideas that I'm developing." I didn't. I still had zilch.

"Alright. You think about your story. I'll be down in the galley fixing lunch. If you need anything just let me know."

I turned again to my blank page smudged by my excessive fingering and hesitant dots that my pencil tip never got to move from. To win a small and pitiful victory, I connected the dots to form a fictitious constellation and name it 'Frustracious Boredialis.'

"There," I proclaimed.

My meditation was perforated by the small waves knocking against the side of the boat as if to invite me again to look down blankly into the water again, which I did. My mind drifted to battles fought and was pulled to visualize lawless pirates attacking merchant's vessels. Visions of anxious wives standing on their watch, searching the horizon for their husband's ships formed in my mind. The demanding blank page on the table tugged for my attention against the dark mystical sea. The former required me to think about my story which now seemed like the chore of an academic assignment, but the latter felt dreamy, ancient, and alive.

Later, the captain came up to the deck with scraps of food and threw them overboard. "Ready for some company?" He asked me as if I were a bored tourist in need of entertainment.

Moments later, noisy seagulls hovered above us, and all I could do with my deliberately looking manufactured smile was watch and wait for them to leave.

At night in my bunk, again I was aware of the lapping waves against the boat like quiet taps at my mind's door. I couldn't think. I didn't want to. The rhythmic waves and the gentle rocking of the boat gave me the mood to write in my journal before they lulled me into a deep blue sleep.

At the end of the three days at sea, I was still without inspiration. As the captain slowed the boat toward the dock, I ceremoniously tore off the smudged page and threw it in the water, giving it a burial at sea. Hopefully, I will begin my story on the next fresh white page somewhere else.

"I need a cave," I thought to myself as I sat in the internet coffee shop. "I need a deep and dark space below the surface of this crazy earth with no noise or distracting activity." So, I searched the internet, asked around, and finally found out about a place not too many miles away that promised to be my refuge.

"Just know, there are some weird stories and rumors about that area of caves," The friendly man told me. "People have claimed to have seen ghosts walking around in the dark in old tattered clothes whispering to themselves."

"I'm all over that!" I thought to myself.

My flashlight searched the mouth of the mostly concealed cave entrance before I stepped inside and began to tear off little pieces of yellow flagging tape. Measuring ten steps, I dropped one along the wall of the cave to find my way back out when the time came.

Immediately, I began to notice symbols on the walls of deer, horses, and the sun among others and imagined a Neanderthal named Thog standing in this same spot thousands of years ago, maybe at the very inception of written language. I stopped and stared at the ancient wonder before deciding I would gently touch the symbol. Then it was as if I was whisked back to stand next to the hairy author.

As I walked on, hanging from the ceiling were hundreds of bats that stirred but didn't fly as I slowly walked underneath. However, two of them somehow knew that I really wasn't a writer; just a fraud on a futile journey so they christened me with guano. "Those two are the intuitive ones," I thought. "They know what kind of writer I'm not."

Further along, large beautiful stalactites hung down; that over the years had grown downward and joined themselves to stalagmites on the cave floor below them. I was mystified by them and allowed myself to stand there and look until my mind suggested that maybe they were long barred teeth and I was actually in an enormous mouth of a monster.

"You definitely need braces. And do something about that stale breath. It smells like a musty cave," I told them as I ripped off another piece of tape and dropped in on the cave floor. Abstract thinking might be my only quality as a pre-writer. Inspiration sure wasn't. Finally, I was beyond the reach of the light from outside.

Creeping about seventy yards of turns further, I found a little nook to sit in with my battery-operated lantern to finally start my story. The silence was disturbing but acceptable. But tiny disguised sounds that interrupted sporadically had the same effect of those you would hear in the dark woods at night. They brought enough tension to make me try to figure out what they were. A drop of water falling onto the wet floor? Two bats competing for the same spot to hang upside down? But the loud sound of my breathing reflecting off the cave wall right next to me, diverted my ability to concentrate most of all and made it feel like there was another person with his face too close to mine who didn't seem to be bothered by it like I was.

Just as I opened my blank notebook to write about nothing, I was startled by soft footsteps then a whispered, "Hello?"

I thought, "What in the world now?" And whispered back to the entrance of the alcove, "Uh, hello."

"Looks like we have a new neighbor, doesn't it?" The quiet voice came back from the dimness.

"What are you doing here?" A different voice asked.

I turned my flashlight on and shined it at the voices to see half a dozen or more, bearded, messy-haired men of different heights who instantly covered their faces from the brightness while complaining about it. I quickly turned my flashlight off. The light of my lantern was barely enough to see them as they stepped forward with what I thought were clubs but turned out to be unlit torches.

"I'm sorry. I came here for a while to work on my story and didn't realize there were other people here. I expected to find ghosts."

"Ghosts?" one of them asked.

"Yeah. There are rumors that people have seen ghosts walking around in the dark out here."

Another voice replied, "Ain't no ghosts here. Must'a seen *us*. We walk outside most nights. That'll keep people away though."

"Writing a story, huh? About ghosts or hermits?"

Another silhouette chimed in, "He can't write no story about us! People will read it and find us and ruin everything!"

A different man offered, "If he writes about ghosts, no one will want to come here cept those darn ghost-chas'in people with the cameras and lectronic gadgetry."

"I bet we could give them a show!" another man said.

"No. No," I said with extra assurance. "Let's slow down. I'm not writing about ghosts or hermits. Uh, you know what? Pardon me for my intrusion, I'll leave now, and I promise not to tell anyone where this place is." Returning my notebook and journal to my backpack, I stood to leave as they watched. "I thought hermits were private and reclusive?" I commented out loud.

"We are." came the answer back. "Each of us has our own private area way back in the cave but we talk with each other sometimes, or else we would go batty."

I stopped and turned my face toward them expecting a response from the obvious use of the word 'batty' while in a cave with bats, but none came from the staring faces, so I offered, "That was very clever."

"*What* was very clever?"

"It's funny to me that you would use the word 'batty' in a cave with bats," I answered with a smile, then thought, "Maybe this very cave is where the phrase 'going batty' originated."

"Oh, yes! Now I get it!" the man replied with delight. "Batty! We would go batty here in our cave with bats! Did you get that, gentlemen?!"

Echoing laughter broke out until one of them hushed the rest, looking nervously around. "Shhhh… someone might hear us!"

"Oh, by the way, you might have a hole in your pocket," one of them said as he smiled and held out a handful of small pieces of yellow flagging tape. "I collected them for you."

I took them. "Yeah. I dropped them as markers, so I would know how to get back out…so."

"We'll take you back!" A whispered chorus insisted that the hermits guide me back to the entrance.

Carefully and slowly making my way past the small colony of hermits I whispered, "No thank you. I can find my way out. Goodbye," and walked back toward the entrance of the cave wondering if, next, I would meet a lost girl named Alice. Maybe *she* could give me a thought for my story.

Following the lead of my flashlight, I came across some familiar rock formations and kept walking through other corridors and turns until nothing looked familiar. It's said that when you are lost, the best thing is to stop and wait to be rescued. I was certain that a rescue attempt was not coming. Suddenly, panic set in. I asked myself, "Am I in some catacombs where looser authors come to die? Will my skull be tossed onto some pile with the others?" Instead of running and screaming like a crazy man which was my first impulse, I sat down on a moist boulder and turned off my flashlight to preserve the batteries. "Easy, Matt. Breath."

"Oh, your name is Matt? I'm Stewart. Welcome to my home," the voice whispered as I jolted and fumbled my flashlight. My frantic beam of light finally settled on one of the same hermits I had left an hour ago.

"Aim that to the floor!" Stewart whispered as he covered his eyes. "This is my little place," he proclaimed as he swept his arm toward a heavily blanketed cot, stacked crates, and a shelf with cans of food and candles. A small fire pit glowed dimly several feet away.

"I'm so sorry. I'm lost."

"You were lost, but know you know where you are. How about I take you to the entrance?"

"That would be so kind of you, Stewart."

"Let's follow the deer," he said, as he took my hand to point the flashlight at a painted deer on the cave wall. "I'm the deer." He led the way for about a half hour quietly explaining that every hermit chose an animal image and painted them to find their way around the cave. My connection with the Neanderthal whom I had named, Thog, vanished in a puff of private embarrassment.

The faint glow of natural light from the outside informed us that we were approaching the entrance.

"There you go, Matt. Goodbye and good luck."

"Thanks, Stewart," I replied, offering him my flashlight. "I have a spare." I reached into a pocket in my backpack and handed him three fresh batteries.

"Wow. Thank you!"

"You're welcome," I replied as I walked right past the group of painted symbols that I first saw without even looking at them while wondering if all the symbols painted on cave walls around the world were actually painted by colonies of hidden modern hermits snickering behind cave walls while archeologists inspect them with the same sacred awe I did. A colony of hermits? I shook my head and grinned at the contradiction. My contradiction was that, although I daily filled my journal with pages of details of my days, I had made no progress on my story. I just have to find someplace different to get this story started. Maybe I should write a story with the title, 'The Mystery of the Hermit Ghosts.' I could spice it up nicely. Nah, I told them I wouldn't.

Thinking that a quiet cemetery would be the best place to write, I checked out of my budget motel room and took an early morning walk to a local country cemetery.

Sitting among the differently-shaped stones, I opened my pack, took out my notebook and begin to search for a theme or subject. "What a setting," I contemplated. "Above, the sun shines bright and warm and below the dead lie under the ground and I'm in between."

In a moment of searching for my next thought, my eyes wandered and stopped on the gravestone in front of me. Cut in the stone were the man's name, dates of birth and death, and the phrase, 'We shall be reunited.' I wondered what kind of man he was and the life he lived. On the stone next to his was a woman's name. The two stones shared the last name, and the dates were close. Her stone also had the same phrase. "They must have been husband and wife," I thought, and mused over the shared phrase. *Had* they been reunited after death? My heart hoped so. But even if they weren't, their mutual belief that they would, gave them hope that made their deaths easier to accept. Whether faith reunites the dead is not certain to me, but that it grants hope and joy for the living, cannot be denied and is worth having.

I got up off my knees and looked out over the rows and rows of similar stones and suddenly felt like one; the only live one and the only one who could still change anything about the dash in between the dates.

What would these deceased, change given the chance? My attention was drawn to my chest and as if it was a blank gravestone. What can I change still having the chance? I stood and searched other stones for clues to on how they lived and the beliefs they held until it occurred to me that I had wandered away from the spot where I intended to work on my story.

The nature of this cemetery along with every other, firmly determines that the emotion in their presence will be solemn, and will allow only thoughts of life, death, and eternity.

I returned to my spot and gathered my notebook and journal, realizing that this place was not the place to find a subject for my story. Quietly I made notes of my thoughts and feelings in my journal and left - almost sneaking; while being sensitive not to draw attention to myself that I was leaving and they who were resting there, could not. Moreover, I didn't want to betray to this sacred throng that where they abode was not suitable for me to start a story.

The distant sound of an approaching lawnmower, starting on the other side of the cemetery, confirmed that it was time for me to go. I nonchalantly walked out through the gated stone arch that had watched an unknown number of dead and mourning pass under it.

I just wanted to walk and get away from traffic, buildings, and people so I did; through fields and pastures for miles in acute frustration under darkening clouds. I was ready to yield to the thought that there is no place on earth that I could go to start my story as I came upon a wooden cover on top of an old well. Weary and exasperated, I sat down on it to rest and think of where I could find the quietness and stillness to think about a theme or subject for my story. Then, it was as if my stubborn mind tapped the chip on my shoulder making me believe that the well under me might be suitable for a few hours of serenity. I would soon wish I had heeded the tap on my other shoulder that told me I was being stupid and shouldn't do it.

While mumbling curses under my breath, I discovered that the cover was easy enough to slide aside and the coiled rope, still appearing strong, promised to let me down but probably not all the way. Dropping a rock to the dim bottom, I expected to hear a splash, but a quiet 'thud' swore that the well was dry. Wonderful! I tied knots in the rope for handholds then climbed down and dropped about a foot to the bottom where I stood for a moment before taking out my pencil and notebook. The rain gently began and quickly rained hard. Doing my best to ignore the raindrops thumping on my hat while protecting the white page of my notebook, I had to think out loud to keep my thoughts from scattering. "I should have covered the well before I climbed down," I said out loud and cursed. So, I climbed up the rope using my shoes against the wall, moved the cover back over the well, and climbed back down. Finally, sitting there thinking about a subject to write about while defying the feeling of the water soaking through my pants as the dirt slowly turned into mud. Water began to seep through the stone wall and trickled down to join the forming puddle that I was sitting in.

"Aaaah!" I yelled, before repacking my things and began my climb out. The rope that seemed honest enough when I climbed down waited until that moment to suddenly brake above the first knot dropping me back to the bottom with a muddy splash. Jumping up and down a few times, I was able to reach the second knot that dangled teasingly and prayed that it would hold me, then the third knot, finding footholds on the stones, and the fourth, until I reached the top and climbed out. In the most frustrating moment of my journey, I hurled my backpack in anger at the rain with anger at my stupid decision to go down into the well. After gathering my composure, I retrieved my pack and quickly rummaged through it to find my thin orange rain poncho, then covered the well and walked away in disgust and embarrassment making a firm commitment, that this embarrassing episode will be in my journal but never will be in my story. My story? What story! I'm done with it! The only words for my story are, The End!

Finally, after a series of rides given to me in which I had to answer probing questions with lies that sounded much better than the truth, I returned home to my anxious wife. After a shower and shave, we sat at the kitchen table with our coffee, my journal, and the virtually blank notebook.

"All I've come back with is a month-old beard and a full journal of my attempt and failure to write a story. I'm no writer. I just don't have it in me. Put my name on the long list of people who say they want to write a story but never do."

My wife insisted that I read my journal to her. At the end of several silent refills of our coffee cups, she looked at me over the top of her coffee cup with an expression of someone ready to share a secret. She lowered her cup and rested her finger on the notebook.

"Matt, you left to write a story…" She moved her finger slowly to the journal. "and you came back with your journey to do so. You may as well just exchange the label 'Story' with 'Journal.'"

I stared at my journal then at the notebook and smiled. I *did* write a story! "Honey, you can move my name over to the short list of people who have 'actually' written a story.

"Do you have a title for it?"

"Not yet. But I'm thinking about, 'Writing Warrior!'

"Matt, how about the title, 'A Journal's Journey?'

"I love it!"

When Sam Whitmore Fell

Since he was a little boy, Sammy had worked many long and hard hours on the family farm. By the time he had reached fifteen the routine wore on him. He wanted something else – anything else. The farthest that he had ever journeyed was small town a few miles away, and he wanted to know what was further. Eventually, a young man's many desires will cause him to look beyond the barn and fences to wonder what and who is out there. Finally, he will go, because he must; it's natural and expected.

Other young men stayed on their family farms being content, while knowing that they would take it over some day, Sammy had no such aspirations.

He realized that he wanted his freedom, one day, as he was fishing in the small, mountain pond. Looking at the water as he waited for a fish to bite his worm, Sammy thought of himself as the water trapped in a mountain pond, dreaming of cascading down the mountain to become part of an exciting waterfall, and eventually finding the great ocean.

Two nights later, Sammy snuck away from his father's abuse on the family farm with his gun and hat, and set out for the adventurous job of working on a cattle drive. Walking down the dirt road with the farm behind him and the road illuminated by the moon, Sammy had joy and uncertainty conflicting in him.

Almost thirty men showed up for a job on the appointed morning near the herd of three hundred head of grazing cattle, and the two wagons hitched to oxen. One wagon was the chuck wagon; a large wooden box with a large hinged serving window attached to two spoke-wheeled axels. The supply wagon was similar.

When Sammy arrived, he stood as the shortest and youngest applicant in the line of tough and tanned grown men; some of which couldn't find decent work elsewhere and others who had worked with cattle all of their lives.

There would have been more applicants if it weren't for the fact that this cattle drive was led by the infamous, Mr. Wallace and his righthand man, George. They were two stern men who didn't tolerate rule-breakers or foolishness. There was too much at risk, and the long, hard trek didn't provide for it. It was well rumored that Mr. Wallace would hang a man, or make someone walk back alone, no matter how far, whenever they thought such punishments were justified. No one ever knew if the man ever made it back alive, but the chances were less than slim.

George, it seemed, had never allowed a smile to form on his face. His two, permanent deep, vertical lines of scowling between his brows were permanent, suggesting that he may have been born with them. He sat under his cowboy hat, with his Winchester rifle lying on the table next to him, asking qualifying questions of each man as they stepped up to the table while Mr. Wallace stood by, studying each one. It was he who ultimately decided who would be added to the small group of men already hired, and standing behind the wooden table, next to the supply wagon.

Young Sammy's only expressed experiences were that he was raised on a farm and knew his way around a horse. So, when his turn came to talk to George, he wasn't very impressive. This boy, who wore a tattered broad-rimed tattered hat, and suspenders that held up patched pants that were too big, was younger than anyone else but, he was strong. The old Colt Paterson Revolver which he wore on his hip, seemed too big for his thin frame. Finding a left-handed holster wasn't easy, so Sammy had made a crudely-stitched version which he used for the rest of his life.

When he finally got a spot in front of the table, he promised George that he was willing to do whatever was asked of him from the list which included cattle guards, scouts or, a horse rustler, while ignoring some of the grown men in the line behind him complaining out loud about the notion of the 'boy' even applying for a man's job. After all, it was the grown men who had families to feed.

Finally, one frustrated man, who appeared not to have had a history of hard work, as betrayed by his portly frame, stepped out of his place and abruptly went to the table complaining, "C'mon, now! There are family men like me back there needin' a job! What's this runt doin' takin' up my time?! He couldn't even get his gun out of its holster if he had to!" He gave Sammy a hard push away from the table. Sammy stumbled backward before falling onto the dirt.

He stood, and brushed himself off promising, in a voice that had not yet changed from that of a young man, "Mister, if you try to push me again, I'll show you just how fast my gun can come out."

Chuckles and laughs of doubt broke out from the line of impatient men.

"Teach that boy a lesson!" a voice called out from the line.

Another man yelled out, "Get that whelp out of the way!"

"Oh, is that right? Are you callin' me out?" the man replied with a grin as he suddenly reached for his gun.

Before it cleared his holster, Sammy had drawn his sidearm with uncanny speed. He quickly stepped up to him holding his gun at the man's face, but didn't fire. The man froze looking down at the barrel in front of his face, and let his gun drop back down.

"That's enough!" Mr. Wallace exclaimed. "What's your name, son?"

"Sammy Whitmore, sir," he answered as he stepped back and holstered his gun, never taking his eyes off the portly man.

Mr. Wallace stood and looked at the embarrassed man with his hands still raised. "Go home. I don't need you."

"But I can..."

"You heard, Mr. Wallace!" George said, moving his hand to his rifle. "You're not a man for this drive, or any other! Go!"

As the rejected man walked to his horse, grumbling, Mr. Wallace pointed to Sammy. "Get behind the table. It seems that you only have one good skill, but we'll need it. You're hired as my horse wrangler."

"Thank you, sir," Sammy replied with a wide smile as he took his place among the much taller hired men.

Privately, Mr. Wallace began to like young Sammy, who he thought was brave enough to apply for the job, and scrappy enough to defend his turn at the table. But Sammy's true worth, he noted, was the speed and accuracy with which he used his gun.

"Sign here," George instructed, before Sammy added only his first name to the column of first names, X's, and just a few full names.

The array of the twenty different men that was hired for the drive, and the wide-open land, over the next six weeks, formed Sammy into a man. He, like most boys, wouldn't have become a man at the farm. After everything else fails, it's adversity that will make a man from a boy.

"To the rest of you," George addressed the men not chosen, "thank you for coming. We'll post the next drive at the mercantile and hope to see you back here."

As the disappointed men turned their horses around and dispersed, Mr. Wallace gathered his hired men together. "St. Louis is a long way from Austin," he announced as he slowly paced in front of them. "Men, this drive will take about six weeks. We can't push the herd too hard, or they'll lose too much weight, but time is money. For you, new men; you need to know that likely, we'll run into problems. We usually do. These problems could be in the form of Indians, rustlers, bandits, or farmers. Every one of you needs to be sharp. Some of you might die, so give George the names and towns of your next of kin. I don't care how old or young you are, or if you are experienced or not; you'll pull your weight and then some, or suffer the consequences. When we get to the end of the drive, all of you will get paid according to what I and George decide you were worth. If you don't like these terms, you can leave right now." He waited a few moments, still looking at the faces of his men whose silence agreed to the arrangement. "George, here is my right-hand-man. He's your boss too. George, do you have anything to add?"

"Yes, sir. Most of you have heard that we have rules out there. We keep them because we have to. When you're given an order, you obey it. When we give you a job, you do it. When you address Mr. Wallace, you'll use 'sir.' Men, we need to average twelve miles a day, and it's my job to see that we get it. That's all. Mr. Wallace, at your pleasure."

Mr. Wallace cupped his hands around his mouth and shouted, "Move 'em out!" The cattle drive began.

Two men walked over and climbed up into the seats of the wagons. Five others mounted their horses and trotted to get behind and beside the herd, whistling and shouting as the reluctant cattle began with complaints, their first steps of a very long walk. The goal was to use just enough skill and motivation to get them walking but not create a stampede.

Sammy looked at the twenty-five spare horses that he was suddenly in charge of, hoping that he would do a good job taking care of them. The position of Horse Wrangler was the lowest in a drive, but he was determined to do what he had to. After all, that was his very first paid job.

Most days were long and hot on the drive, and the starry nights were often cold with coyotes howling and yelping in the dark. They knew that a full-grown cow was too big to bring down, so rabbits and other small animals were constantly being hunted.

Meals from the chuck wagon were predictable; beans, coffee, a little chunk of meat, and a hard biscuit. The portly cook, Fred, standing in the serving window, wore a dirty white apron and gave no heed to a visual presentation as he dropped spoon-fulls of food onto round tin plates, which often mixed everything together before the cowboy could find a place to sit.

When camp was set up in the late afternoons, Sammy took saddles and blankets off the horses brushed them, checked for rocks in their hooves, and made a make-shift corral from rope tied to the wheels of the wagons kept near the campsite. Also, he made sure that all the horses were fed, watered, and kept safe from the dangers in the night.

Every man was given a mandate by Mr. Wallace to be armed. Because, although the US Army seemed to be winning the war with the Indians, there were still factions of remaining tribes determined to roam the desert mountains and go on raids. Being of whatever color or culture, whoever believes that what they have is sacred, whether land, creed, or deity, defends them as such, or tries to take them by force. When these sudden skirmishes happened on a cattle drive, every cowboy needed not to *get* ready, but always to already *be* ready. Of course, the other threat was cattle thieves who would come in the night, silently rope as many cows as they could and lead them quietly away in the darkness. Like all crimes, it wasn't without risk, as every night the perimeters of the herd were guarded by four different men of the drive who rode horses while carefully observing the resting cattle.

A week later, the camp again enjoyed the smells of fresh coffee, and frying bacon that had greeted the sleeping men who reclined on their bedrolls with their hats tilted over their faces. As they slowly arose from the ground, Mr. Wallace, casually reached down to gather up his bedding among the gentle murmurings and stirrings of the drowsy men. About thirty feet away, Sammy, preparing to leave as well, suddenly noticed the rattlesnake that had silently entered the camp and was coiled near the warm fire, ready to strike the reaching hand of Mr. Wallace. Young Sammy quickly drew his sidearm and from the hip and shot the snake with only moments to spare. It jumped off the ground and landed dead in two pieces, still twisting. Of course, the loud gunshot instantly alarmed the men who scrambled to get their guns but didn't know why until their leader held up the back half of the dead writhing snake. He slowly turned his head toward young Sammy and stared. "Thank you, Sammy."

"You're welcome, sir," he humbly answered as his returned his Colt to its plain leather holster.

"I didn't even see it, and if it was rattling, I couldn't hear it. That was a long shot. You're fast, son, and dead on. From now on your name is Sam. You're a man." He looked around at the other men saying, "Y'all hear me? His name is Sam. He's earned my respect and appreciation."

Heads nodded, and a few men mumbled, "Yes, sir."

"Sam, you've just been promoted to join the scouts. I need your skill. Talk to George about the schedule."

"Yes, sir. Thank you."

Mr. Wallace looked at George. "Who's the next youngest?"

"Bill, sir."

"He's your wrangler now."

"Yes, sir."

Bill did his best, but the expression on his face betrayed his dissatisfaction with his demotion.

Later that day, George offered Sam a Winchester rifle for his new position.

"No thank you, George. I never fired one."

"You never fired a rifle?"

"Nope. I'll stick to my Colt if it's all the same to you," he replied as he patted the holster strapped to the outside of his left leg.

"Okay, fine. You've already proved that you can use that."

Sam's reputation as a quick-draw didn't need to spread among the men because everyone was there and saw it. But jealousy made its way through whispered conversations over the next few days until it found Bill who was a few years older than Sam. While the crew sat eating their dinner out of tin plates around the evening fire pit, Bill called him out. Having spent most of his pay for a fancy black holster, belt, and silver gun, it was clear Bill had plans to be a gunfighter.

The few mumbled conversations abruptly ended under the dimming pastel sky of sprayed oranges, yellows, and reds. Music from a lonesome harmonica stopped on a flat note as Bill, on the other side of the fire, said to Sam, "Sammy boy, I know yer a quick draw when it comes to snakes, but how about when the snake has a gun of his own? I already killed me a man in a draw. I bet I'm faster than you."

"Could be," Sam replied as he circled his biscuit around his tin plate. "Why don't we find out?"

"Nah," Sam replied after a bite of soggy biscuit. "If ya wana be called the fastest, then yer the fastest. Happy now?"

"I'm callin' you out, Sammy boy," Bill continued with his hands on his hips. "Now, you ain't got no choice; that is, unless you ain't a man like the boss thinks you are."

Bill sat his plate down, walked over to Sam, and knocked his hat off as the other men watched. Getting his hat knocked off was something that Sam's stern father regularly did when he felt his son didn't do a chore right or said something foolish. Sam hated the humiliation; it was part of the reason for leaving the farm. It was also part of the reason he finally accepted the gunfight with Bill.

Sam stood, being a full head shorter. "Alright," he replied. "In the morning before the drive begins, we'll face off. Ya might write a letter to yer mama tonight cuz tomorrow will be your last day on earth. And the devil don't deliver post."

"We'll see about that, little Sammy boy."

Sam called over to George, "George, do you know where to send Bill's effects?"

"Yes, Sam, I do."

Mr. Wallace just grinned. Again, impressed that Sam, being younger and smaller, would be so confident. He wondered if anyone ever told Sam that he wasn't a giant.

Sam had never before killed anyone, neither had he spent much time shooting cans. And because his father wouldn't let him ever use the only rifle on the farm, Sam had to hunt with his pistol – that's when he discovered he was good with it. He learned to shoot both still, and moving game.

Usually, the gentle mooing of the contented cattle kept the mood calm. But breakfast was tense the next morning as Bill practiced twirling his silver pistol off to the side of the chuck wagon while Sam quietly ate with his eyes on his plate. Sam never twirled his gun because he wasn't a performer by nature, and it had nothing to do with his draw.

"Well, snake killer, ya ready?" Bill asked with a confident grin.

"Yep," Sam replied as he put his plate on the ground. "Ya knocked my hat off last evenin'. Ya really shouldn't ah done that."

All of the other men stood off to the side as Bill walked to a spot a few yards outside of the camp while twirling his pistol. Mr. Wallace allowed the gunfight, believing that Bill was bad seed and Sam would win. Once Sam got to his place, about fifty feet away, he stopped, and the stare-down began until a finger on Bill's gun hand twitched. It was all that was needed for young Sam to throw his right hand out from his side a little, while reaching for his gun with his left. The movement was fast and fluid. Sam's muscle-memory had directed his index finger precisely into the trigger guard which was a second in front of Bill who had just gripped the handle of his gun. Sam's gun cleared his holster while his opponent was still pulling his gun up. After leveling his gun, Sam's bullet found its place; exploding the hammer of Bill's silver gun as he was about to level it. He yanked his hand away and yelled with shock as his gun fell to the dirt. Sam quickly walked toward him with his gun at eye-level as Bill raised his hands.

"Sam," Mr. Wallace calmly said.

"Sir?" Sam replied intensely without looking over at him.

"It's your choice, and you have the right. But I need every man and his gun. We're heading into hostile territory."

Standing directly in front of Bill, Sam looked up at him and promised, "If you ever call me out again or knock my hat off, I'll put a hole between your eyes," before he backhanded Bill with his pistol.

Bill got himself off the ground then turned to walk away with his broken gun, damaged pride, and his life. It was a rare time when a gunfighter had lost and still lived. Unknown to Bill, Sam appreciated his silver gun – it was easier to see and follow.

"George," Mr. Wallace instructed. "Get Bill a Winchester and see to it that he doesn't get ahold of a sidearm."

"Yes, sir."

Bill walked by as George reached his hand out to accept the pistol.

From then on, Bill kept his distance from Sam, and Sam kept his eye on him. No one ever asked Sam if he had actually aimed for Bill's gun, but remembering the rattlesnake having been cut in two, gave the men confidence that he had purposely aimed where his bullet hit.

Three days later, Sam was on schedule to ride out with Frenchie to scout out ahead of the drive. It was the routine to have three sets of two men who would fan out in different directions. The scouts usually rode for half a day with the job to draw out danger, take note of tracks, detect the smell of campfires, find missing cattle, and listen for whistle-sounds by which the Indians communicated. On that first ride out, Sam was hunting-mode quiet, and thought Frenchie should be too. But Frenchie felt it was safe enough to talk, because, so far, the cattle drive had been uneventful. However, Sam was aware that this new different territory, with canyons and rocky hills were perfect for other stealthy scouts to hide in, observe, or attack from.

As the two men passed through a dry wash with high rocks on each side, Sam continued to allow Frenchie to talk because he decided that his accent provided a little entertainment, and to display to anyone who might be watching, a sense of unsuspecting normalcy. But, once they had ridden through, Sam directed his horse to turn right around the end.

He stopped and whispered to Frenchie, who was looking at him in confusion. "I saw movement in the rocks. I'm going around the other side and circle-back. If someone is in the rocks, they're getting ready to attack us, so I'll come up behind them. I need you to be quiet until I get back. When I whistle, come to me with the horses."

Frenchie looked over at him. "Oui, okay. But, why? What are you going to do?"

Sam's replied with a polite, "Shhhh," before leaving his horse, removing his boots, and silently hurrying around the end of the rocks.

Halfway back, he passed two saddled horses and five cows with the familiar brand from Mr. Wallace's drive. He stopped quickly to search in saddlebags where he discovered a different branding iron.

Climbing the rocks on all fours until he could peek down at the wash below him, just twenty-feet down were two whispering cowboys cautiously standing and looking down toward the direction that Sam and Frenchie went.

Sam stood and announced, "You men stole some of our cattle. Get your hands up."

The men quickly turned. One of them drew. Sam drew and shot him in the chest. The thief slumped dead over a rock. The other man raised his hands and froze.

"You wana try me too?"

"No."

Sam whistled to Frenchie, then instructed the captured man, "Come on up here. And do it with caution. Your life depends on it."

That evening, just before sunset, supper was interrupted by a guard at the sight of Sam and Frenchie riding back into camp with one man on his horse with his hands tied together. The flopping body of the other thief was tied and slumped across the saddle of his horse. Frenchie had tied a rope around the neck of one of the five cows, and the others followed.

"Last scouts are back!" a voice from within the herd announced. "And they have cattle!"

Mr. Wallace stood in front of all of the gathered men who had put their plates down as the scouts arrived.

"Well, gentlemen, what did you bring me?"

"Sir, we have one cattle thief; the other one is dead, five cows, and the branding irons to prove that they're thieves," Sam replied, as he dismounted to present the branding iron to Mr. Wallace.

Frenchie helped the man stepped out of the stirrup, and stood him in front of Mr. Wallace.

"Well done, gentlemen. Which one of you killed the other rustler?" Mr. Wallace asked as George removed the rope from the cow, allowing all five to merge back into the herd.

"It was Sam," Frenchie answered. "Truly, Sam gets all of the credit. I was not even there for that part."

"No, Frenchie. You had just as much part in the whole thing as I did," Sam replied.

"Sam?" Mr. Wallace asked. "What should be done with this other man?"

"Please!" the man begged.

"Shut up!" George ordered with a backhand that violently swung the man's head to the side.

"Well, sir, we're too far from the law. We would have to take him the rest of the way. Someone would have to watch him, and we would have to share our supplies. His fate is in your hands, Mr. Wallace. But I'll bet he's part of a bigger group that's been trying to pick off our herd. His life might be spared for some information. Other than that, we could hang him now or shoot him."

"Or, drag him along behind my horse," George offered with a growl.

Mr. Wallace walked over to the man. "Get Down. Those are the choices. We can hang you, shoot you, drag you, or, you can talk."

"I'll talk! I'll talk!" the distraught thief insisted.

"How much are they paying you for each cow?" Mr. Wallace asked.

"Ten dollars, sir."

"And where are the rest of you?"

"About ten miles beyond where we were watching from the rocks.

You're heading right toward them. You can expect an ambush. They'll know you're coming."

"Just like you and the other man were going to ambush us," Sam noted, out loud.

"Hmm," Mr. Wallace said as he nodded his head and looked around the area. "No strong trees." He took out his sidearm and shot the rustler in the chest. The thief collapsed to the ground with a thud. "Gentlemen," he exclaimed looking around at his men. "We do this to make a living! I despise cattle thieves! They take money out of all our pockets and from our families! We only get paid for the cows that we deliver. Bury them and mark the graves, 'Cattle Thieves.' He turned to look at his right-hand man, "George."

"Sir?"

"In the morning, let's get the herd well around that ambush."

"Yes, sir."

Of course, Bill saw all the attention that Sam was getting and the obvious heroics attributed a man younger than him. And the humiliation of his defeat in the gunfight was still as fresh in his eyes as the day it happened. He wanted another chance to prove that he was faster than Sam. After secretly buying a gun from another man for much more than he should have, Bill thought he was ready.

Camp was just set up, and the men were trying to find good places on the ground to lay their bedrolls. Inside the chuck wagon, the sounds of pans being moved inside indicated that the cook was beginning to make supper.

Breaking both the movements and the talking of the men, Bill took off his coat to reveal a different gun in his holster.

"Well, Sammy, let's try this again. I still think I'm faster than you, so get ready to draw, right here and right now."

George grabbed his lever-action, chambered a round, and brought it to his shoulder. "Put it down, Bill! Mr. Wallace forbade you to have it. Put it down now, or you're dead. I've got you in my sights."

"It's alright, George," Mr. Wallace, said. "If he loses against Sam, he's dead. But, if he wins, he's banished from the camp, and he'll leave on foot." He looked over at Sam. "Son, this time, get it done."

Sam nodded to the boss and took his jacket off.

"It wouldn't be fair for Bill. He's got a new gun that he's not familiar with."

"Shut up, Sammy, and get ready to draw. And, this time, I ain't going for your trick of moving your other arm to distract me," Bill exclaimed as he tossed his coat to the ground.

The men stepped back several paces. In the moments it took to get in position, Sam could only think about Bill's antagonistic mouth and decided where to shoot him. He also knew that his opponent expected him to throw his right arm out a little before he drew, so this time he wouldn't.

Finally, squared off against each other, Sam just drew and shot Bill through his throat. The bullet lodged in his spine, making his death instant. Bill's bullet slammed into the ground between them, kicking up dirt.

"Bury him before it gets dark, and collect his effects," Mr. Wallace ordered. "Now, who gave him the gun?"

No one answered.

"Everyone, get in a line and show me their guns, now," George demanded, as he walked over and stood before the forming line.

Each man took his gun out and held it up in the air. All of the sidearms were accounted for.

George turned and looked over at the chuck wagon. "Fred?!"

Fred stepped down out of the wagon wiping his hands on his stained apron. "I ain't got mine. I'm a cook and don't need it," he said with apprehension. "Sold it to Bill."

"You heard the boss's order that Bill wasn't supposed to have one, right? Along with the order that every man be armed? You disobeyed two orders."

"Yes, but he paid me a lot of money for it. Can I please get it back?"

Mr. Wallace stepped forward. "Yeah, you can get it back. Then you'll start walking. If those terms are unacceptable, I'll shoot you now."

The line of men didn't move as George walked over to Bill's body and picked up the gun that lay next to it. "Alright, men. Put them back in your holsters," George ordered.

"Just one bullet, George," Mr. Wallace ordered. "And one canteen."

"Yes, sir."

Five shells dropped into George's hand as he turned the cylinder with the barrel tilted up. He walked the empty gun and one bullet over to the cook. "Put the bullet in it when you're well outside of camp."

"Walk," Mr. Wallace instructed. "And if I see you again near this drive, I'll shoot you in the back or front. Makes no difference to me."

"But, it's almost dark, sir!"

Mr. Wallace placed his hand on his holstered gun, "Walk or die." After looking around at the men with a look of dread, Fred started his walk back.

It wasn't likely that Fred would survive for more than three or four days. If he didn't die from lack of water, he might get killed by outlaws or Indians. As much as anything else, he would think about the value of his one bullet. He could take his chances at shooting his single bullet at game, but if he missed, he would have nothing else. And with one bullet he couldn't protect himself in any kind of attack. But, if he had the mind to, he could end his own life in any situation. Most of the men decided that it would be exactly what they would do.

The cattle were finally delivered in St. Louis, having been prolonged by the detour around the ambush, and ended up two men short. Every man was paid according to what Mr. Wallace and George determined. Some of them were pleasantly surprised, and others were disappointed, but none of them complained. Sam got a little extra because he saved Mr. Wallace from the rattlesnake, and brought back five cows. Also, Mr. Wallace gave Sam an open invitation to join him on future drives, which he accepted for the next half-dozen or so.

Many of the other men rode their horses directly to the nearest town to get everything they had wanted during the last six weeks. Although poker was the favorite evening entertainment on the trail, whiskey was rationed, and women were altogether absent. They would be denied no longer, and gladly paid the price for each pleasure whether at the card table or in a private upstairs room with a woman who made it worth the cowboy's money.

Sam visited a saloon but was, at first, denied service. It was only because the other men complained to the bar keep, that young Sam was allowed to drink. He played some poker, drank whiskey, then returned to Texas with Mr. Wallace and George, and most of his pay.

His reputation for being fast with his gun followed him back through rumors and stories that each man from the cattle drive told, enhanced by the whiskey they drank. Some of the area gunfighters dreamed of buzzards circling above Sam. But the birds wouldn't be gathering for this new name, Sam Whitmore. Those to whom the dream was given, never imagined that it was a bad omen for they, themselves.

As a full-grown man, Sam wasn't big. He stood just below medium height at best, as just a regular looking man. His modesty and decency were paired with a natural gift: he was lightning fast with his gun and a deadly aim that enabled him to keep on living for as long as he did. Certainly, he could be put among the painter born to paint and the singer born to sing.

Had it not been for this ability, he and his name might have found themselves in a life of some common labor, living, at best, in mediocrity in every respect. Sam would have been fine with that.

Some men, by choice, or not, are pushed to a place in life that they find themselves not wanting to be in. Sam managed a balance of being a regular man, while answering the call of a gunfighter who wanted fame.

God was never with Sam, it was said. Luck was often close by his side, many believed. To the religious, Holy Divinity wouldn't be thought of as the source of his gift of killing, though the devil might take the credit. Nature's balance in all things seemed to be the easiest source to agree with. Depending on which perspective was chosen, Sam was a neutral sentry of sorts to protect small towns and vulnerable folks, or an attraction of bad men. In any case, gunfighters were somehow drawn by their evil to stand in front of his old Colt Paterson Revolver.

Each cocky young gunfighter had traveled at his own expense and risk to find and challenge him, having promised in saloons along the way, that he would take down the one-and-only, Sam Whitmore. Most of the patrons would ignore the brash predictions, while others, who had heard of Sam's reputation, gave stern warnings. But a fool is a fool and they rarely take advice or rebuke. Lacking the perspective of age, full of opinion s, and scarce on judgment, the reckless glory-seekers just talked louder before they drank their last shot of whiskey, and rode on toward their untimely deaths.

Most of his challengers, like himself, began as hard-working and well-mannered farm boys. But, once they heard there was a way to get off the family farm, travel, and make easy money, many did so. Others just wanted to make themselves a name and became a different human species as a gunfighter. This kind of young man sought out the death of another; not in revenge, or justice, or protection, but simply to establish himself as dangerous and to put fear in the hearts of others. It's the cheapest kind of respect when the foundation is the fear of a gun. Many would suggest that respect is nowhere near the such men.

A man considering to be a gun-fighter is like faith nesting safely under the protective wings of inactivity - they both chirp loudly of their need and value. But push the chick into the air and the gunfighter into the street and watch to see what happens. The graves of others that were brash, impatient, and not quite ready can be found in cemeteries in most any town in the territory. In time, what would remain are bones, dust, and the lead bullets from another's gun which was just a moment faster.

Just knowing how to shoot and being fast wasn't enough to stay alive in the mining camps, cattle-drives, and dirt streets of the Old West. Sam had a system which included a solid and balanced stance, standing just a step to the left of his opponents, dry hands, and most of all, he knew his gun and holster as if they were attached to his left hip at birth. He kept the technique of throwing his right arm out just a little from his side as he drew with his left, believing that this unexpected motion would draw his opponent's attention, and confuse them for a split-second. The process seemed to work. In a fight that's usually over within two seconds, distracting the mind of the men who wanted to kill him, added to his success of defending himself.

One way a gunfighter could survive an 'off' day was when the other gunfighter had one too. Oh, Sam had been grazed several times over the years. Once, he even took a bullet to the shoulder opposite of his gun arm and had favored that arm for the rest of his life.

Sam determined if his challenger had just arrived in town. If he had been on his horse for a long time his back might be stiff and his arms sore from holding the reins for days. If he had traveled alone, he might be tired from broken sleep as he strained to listen for sounds of danger in the night as the light from his camp fire blinded his eyes from whatever could be watching from within the darkness.

As best as he could, Sam kept count of how much the challenger had drunk from the bar. If the visiting gunfighter weren't much of a drinker, Sam would send him a drink anonymously through one of the women serving them.

There were a few saloons whose bartenders liked Sam, and unlike other folks, considered him to be a decent man. After serving drinks for as long as they did, the bar keepers could spot a new face coming through the doors and determine if the man's gun was common, or new and fancy like gunfighters wore. These bartenders would make sure that they gave the visiting gunfighters a free drink or two as a welcome gift for being new in town, and kept the bottle close by. It was the bartender's way of softening up the challenger's minds and slowing down the reflexes.

All of the gunslingers of different skill levels had stood face-to-face with Sam with a gun of their own and the intention to kill him. All thirty-one of them had died in dusty streets.

The only time that Sam called out anyone was the time he confronted two gunfighters as cowards for shooting a couple of unsuspecting and unprepared ranch hands who casually cradled their rifles. The two young gunfighters had bragged about it in the saloon that afternoon and had publicly added them to their kill count. The local Sheriff couldn't do anything about it because the witnesses confirmed that the two ranch-hands were holding guns and heated words were exchanged.

Sam looked up from the five cards in his hand, and stood from the round poker table. The saloon got quiet. He made his way to the bar and confronted both of the gunfighters.

"So, you two killed two men holding rifles? You do know that gunfighters don't use rifles, right?"

"What's it to you, old man?" one of them snapped as he turned to look at Sam.

The other gunfighter added, "And what are you going to do about it?"

"The first thing I'm going to do about it, in front of all these people, is to call you both cowards. Some of us here knew those men. They were hard-working, family men. Easy targets for the likes of you."

The first man asked, "You calling us cowards?"

"No."

"You better not be," the second gunfighter warned as he took a threatening step.

"You're not regular cowards. You're chicken-shit cowards. And chicken-shit cowards only shoot when the odds are heavy in their favor. So, I'm going to invite you two cowards out into the street and challenge both of you all by myself. Two, against one. How do you like those odds?"

"You got it, mister," the first man replied, laughing.

The second one gave a wide, satisfied smile as the two gunfighters placed their empty shot glasses on the counter, dropped two silver dollars, and followed Sam out into the street. As usual, everyone else trailed behind while trying not to look too excited.

It wasn't until some spectator whispered the name of Sam Whitmore that the two young men began to fear for their lives. They had heard of him but didn't realize that the older, skinny man had who called them to the middle of the street was the infamous gunfighter. The rare left-handed holster that they suddenly noticed, confirmed it.

As the two stood opposed in the main street, Sam raised his voice, "Do you like these odds?! Two, chicken-shit cowards against just one old Sam Whitmore?"

The gunfighter on the right nervously whispered to the other, "Jimmy, one of us is gonna die! We gotta back out of this somehow."

"No! We can't back out and keep our pride too!"

"He was right, you know. There ain't got no pride in us killin' those ranchers."

Sam yelled over to them, "C'mon! Quit your mumbling! I've got a poker game to get back too, and I got a good hand! Draw when you're ready! The first of you to draw will be the first to die!"

Sam knew the two men were full of nerves and their movement would be too hurried and clumsy. Suddenly, the gunfighter on the left went for his gun. Sam killed them both in the time it took for him to draw, shoot, fan his hammer back, and shoot again. It was the first time that a single gunfighter stood against two others and remained standing, howbeit with a bullet-torn sleeve.

The Sheriff who stood with the town-folks, was privately pleased, and the undertaker made extra money from the town by building two coffins. Where a trial and noose could not bring justice, a legal and quick draw of revenge did.

Some people called Sam 'the fastest,' while others claimed he was 'the greatest.' None of the accolades mattered to him, and he never boasted about his kill number. Sometimes when Sam was asked for his kill number, he would say, "Does the jack-rabbit care that it is named such, or that it lives in one territory and not another? Do these things matter to it at all? No. He just lives, minds his own business, and watches out for the coyotes hunting it. And that's what I do." Once, he added, "But having men hunt for me is like a rock in my boot. I feel it with every step I take."

The names of the men who had called him out had faded with time. But it was the faces that still looked at him in his dark sleeplessness. He thought about the mothers and other family members who might have cried at the news, and those who would stand before graves, holding flowers, year after year. But the visions didn't stay poised for long as he reminded himself that they had come to kill him. Judging those who have been backed into a moral corner is left to those who have never stood in one.

Some of his challengers were wanted men whose names were on posters tacked up outside of the town jails. They sought Sam out because he was the ultimate prize. And the extra notoriety of having their names in the newspapers of being the one who killed Sam Whitmore was the goal. They came and challenged him. Sam often kept the reward money.

Sam Whitmore should have quit a decade ago while he was his fastest; when most of the young gun-fighters thought it best to leave him alone until the slowness of age came to him. So, they kept on shooting old cans from fence posts that couldn't shoot back. If you practice on cans too much with no one around, you might become the best can shooter in the West, but it's not the same as the having the murmuring crowds watching while life and death wait in a stare-down and the heart beats so strongly that you can hear it in your ears. Further, target-practice can get boring and prematurely send an impatient gun-fighter to stand opposed to a better one in a main street somewhere.

In gunfights, many wild bullets went past the fighters and down the main street or occasionally into a watering trough near a hitching post. Once, an oblivious spectator got hit crossing the street a block away and limped to the other side. But, so far, no other gunfighter had ever got that perfect shot into Sam; the shot when at the instant the critical place on the front of the shirt pops open, and the blood comes instantly. It's the shot when everyone knows that the fight is over including the looser in his remaining moments of life.

Sam tried to ignore most young gunfighters who had stepped up to him at the bar or poker table, wanting to give the challenger the chance to just blow off some steam and walk away. The other patrons appreciated his tolerance as far as it went. It wasn't that he wanted to kill anyone, he didn't. But, like most good men, he could only be pushed to his limit. He often remained silent, hoping the young fools would just laugh and brag. However, his patience found its limits on occasion as he never could bring himself to try to talk his way out of a challenge, especially when certain demeaning tones were used. Once a new gunfighter started taunting Sam in a loud voice or, worse, touched him, the other patrons would close their eyes for a moment and shake their heads at the thought of another needless death of a foolish young man,

238

who, maybe on a different life path, could have gotten married and raised a family.

Probably, Sam shouldn't have visited the woman nicknamed, Daisy Mae, upstairs in one of the private rooms of the saloon just before he joined the poker game downstairs. After such activity, a man can become tired and relaxed too much. But Sam's ego was always stroked hot as he believed that he impressed her as she pretended that she was taken to sensual delights that only he could take her to. She routinely let him believe it as she did for every man who walked into that private room because in her business it's far worse to tell the truth than to lie. The extra silver dollars they usually left on the bed, like Sam did, confirmed the rare saying. It was common for a cowboy, rancher, or miner to find the services of such a woman, and develop affections for them. The wise women would pull them in just to the point to ensure they would become regular customers. Some of the lonely men even offered marriage proposals. But those experienced women of ill repute knew that their customers were not in love but in need. It's a big difference that not everyone understands.

The next day, the newspaperman who witnessed the scene wrote an article titled, 'When Same Whitmore Fell.'

"Yesterday, in the afternoon, as it had happened many times, the swinging doors of the saloon were pushed open, and a hot, dusty stranger walked in. He stood for a moment to look around, then continued toward the bar. His expensive-looking gun belt indicated that the visitor was a gun-fighter as did the notches carved into his holster. Patrons couldn't help but notice his arrogant stride as he looked at each man standing at the bar or seated at a table. The stranger ordered whiskey. The bartender filled a shot glass.

"I'm looking for Sam Whitmore," he forcefully announced.

The bartender, knowing exactly what the gunfighter was looking for, answered, "Haven't seen him today."

"Oh, I think you have. I'll bet he's here right now," the stranger replied as he drank down his whiskey and turned around to face the poker tables.

At that moment, a young woman serving drinks walked by with a bottle of whiskey. The stranger grabbed her arm and stopped her.

"Which one of these men is Sam Whitmore?" he rudely demanded.

The young lady turned away and pulled her arm out of his grip, saying, "Hey! Don't touch me, you pig! I hope you do find him! You'll get what's coming to you!" She abruptly hurried away.

Sam and every other person in the saloon watched the stranger from the corners of their eyes as he walked through the tables with his gun drawn, pushing folks and turning over a few tables.

"Which one of you is Sam Whitmore?!"

"I'm Sam Whitmore," Sam replied flatly as he continued to study the five cards in his hand through the smoke of the cigar he held in his mouth. "I'll take two, Bob." Sam removed two cards from his hand as the dealer took two cards from the deck and laid them face down on the table.

The saloon got quiet as the stranger wagged his shiny gun and started to make his way over to the table where Sam sat playing cards with three other players.

"Who said that!"

"Right here. I'm Sam Whitmore," came the calm reply. Sam pursed his lips as he tried not to show expression while he considered his new cards, and added them to the three he was holding.

The stranger stood over the poker table. "You can't be him. You're an old man and shorter than I imagined."

"Ask anyone here. Go ahead," he said, nudging his head toward the staring patrons.

The stranger looked around the nervous saloon at gently nodding heads. "Well, well. Finally, I get to meet the territory's most famous gun. An old Colt and a homemade holster," he laughed. "How can that be? Not what I expected. No, not what I expected at all. I'm Clay Matthews. Ever heard of me?"

"Nope. But we've met many times. You're just another man pushed to his death by arrogance and violence. Same man, different face."

His challenger looked around at the hushed group. "Ever heard of me? Clay Matthews. You have, haven't you?"

Already disgusted with his brutality and arrogance, the poker players choose to embarrass him by shaking their heads and shrugging their shoulders.

"I've got fourteen kills, but your thirty-one beats my fourteen all to hell," Clay said, as he flicked Sam's hat.

"It's not a game, but I've killed thirty-two. All of them were just like you; worthless fools," Sam said, as he dropped a silver dollar into the poker pot. "I'll raise."

"Oh, it's thirty-two now?" he asked, with a sarcastic grin and raised eyebrows.

"Will be in about five minutes," Sam replied before he silently poured his shot of whiskey down his throat, then laid his cigar and cards down. He slowly stood and looked up at Matthews in his eyes and proclaimed, "You might be Clay Matthews, but I'm Sam Whitmore, and you're number thirty-two. I'll kill you anyway, but you never should have touched my hat," before he gestured with his head toward the saloon's swinging doors. "Let's go."

Hunting Sam Whitmore while dreaming about the gunfight might have seemed adventurous at the time. But, then to finally stand next to the fastest man known, brought reality to the forefront of the challenger's mind and pushed its way into his eyes. Taken back at the strong confidence of this smaller man, the stranger smiled with a twinge of nervousness and holstered his gun.

The rustle of boots on the wood floor and soft murmurings swelled as the customers, who didn't intend to mimic a hurried herd of cattle, followed behind the two gunfighters, vying to get a good spot on the board walk to watch as they all pushed out through the swinging doors.

Most every spectator believed that today's gunfight might not go well for the aging Sam, as they did on his recent fights. Mostly, because Sam walked out of the saloon stiffly and slightly hunched. His sleeves were rolled-up to just below his elbow, displaying slender arms lined with muscle and tendons.

He had known his challenger for just minutes, but enough to already hate him. Sam had had compassion for some of the other men who stood opposed, and ensured that their deaths were instant and painless, but there was no such mercy for Clay Matthews. Sam would have liked to fatally wound him and watch him writhe in the dirt in raw pain with a depth of suffering that rips away facades of toughness and brash pride before death; the level of pain that had forced some men to cry out for their mothers. But he couldn't risk Matthews taking a second shot at him as some did in the past. Sam decided to make the kill instant as he paused under the shaded wooden sidewalk. There, he took off his hat, wiped his face with the back of his arm-sleeve, and pushed back his thick gray hair before putting his brown hat back on. Then, he stepped into the bright dusty street with a routine deep breath. Whether this was an act or not, it gave many of his opponents too much confidence and excitement for what some thought of as easy pickings. Some challengers in the recent past had even displayed playful behavior and taunting which added to their demise as their focus was divided between humor and killing.

Even in gun-fighting, there are rules. After walking safely to their places and standing for a few endless moments with their hands next to their holsters, almost at the very same moment, both guns were lifted just after Sam had thrown his right arm out. But his shot was released first as he didn't allow his challenger to shoot before he did. Together, fifty feet apart, both Sam and his wide-eyed challenger, Clay Matthews, fell. Matthews was dead before he hit the ground. His motionless body and the bloody bullet hole in his forehead left no doubt that his was an instant death. Like the others who had stood opposed, his last vision of the senseless life he chose, was the image of Sam Whitmore's drawn gun.

Sam fell hard to his knees after Clay Matthews' bullet popped open a piece of shirt near his heart. He slowly placed the barrel of his smoking gun on the dirt to support himself. After he looked over at his fallen challenger, the folks rushed over from the wooden walk-way to his side. His chin fell to his chest before he fell on his back to mutter his last words, "And now I'm free… No more coyotes"

Perhaps his final moments on his knees were given to him to make amends before he toppled over to his side and died. Most say that Sam was the winner the moment the challenger died. Other folks had decided that there were no winners, just two dead losers.

Sam Whitmore's death reminded me of an old bell which had fallen from a crumbling church steeple, tarnished and buried halfway into the ground by its own weight. At the moment he died, Sam Whitmore's name became a sacred relic of his best days and continued to be a legend for all other gunfighters.

When most men die, their eulogies cast a bigger shadowed legacy of their much smaller life. But the story of Sam's life will not be like a proud statue in some noble poise of someone who they never really were. Because, Sam Whitmore is on record to have removed from society, thirty-two men fair-and-square, men who needed to die.

It isn't until our death that the sum of all we have said, experienced, and done can be given as the answer for who we finally became. To the critical minds, Sam was just another gunfighter whose overdue death was welcomed. To others, he was a hero of sorts; perhaps a divine man in some way who stopped thirty-two men of violent bloodlust with the silent proclamation, "I'll stop you here and now, on this dusty street."

Having been a friend of Sam Whitmore who I knew for many years, my epitaph for him is the following. "If the contest of gunfighting ever had a good man, and if that good man ever had virtue, his name would be Sam Whitmore.

The Dead Writer

"I'm sorry to tell you, Mr. Norman," the doctor said, with an unconcealable sadness as she held a folder. "The tests came back. Peter, you have pancreatic cancer. It's terminal."

Mr. Norman, fifty-nine years old, with mostly gray hair, stood from the comfortable chair in the waiting room, studying the eyes of the doctor. "How much time do I have?"

"Weeks. Four to seven. I don't have to tell you how sorry I am. Now, is the time to send letters, make phone calls, and get things in order."

Looking as if he was just placed in a trance, Mr. Norman replied, "Okay. Thank you."

"Do you need to talk to someone? We have counselors here for you, and a hospice program where you'll get personal care and great support."

"No, thanks. I can't die that way. I have a lot to do first." He silently nodded his head for a moment with busy thoughts behind his eyes. "Okay. I have things to do. Goodbye." He walked toward the door.

"Mr. Norman... Peter!?"

Peter Norman didn't stop or reply. And he wasn't going to use up his precious remaining time in a hospital. He had stories to finish writing.

The desert trail wound through rocky hills and open areas that featured a variety of plants. Dry breezes came and went. Two friends, Carmen, and Judith, busy in a conversation between sips of water from the tubes of their camel packs, and laden with high, aluminum-framed backpacks, spotted the end of a short, hand-painted green bus parked well off the nearby dirt road. The bus's position suggested that it was intentionally meant to be hidden within the cluster of large rocks next to the hill. Since there seemed to be no activity, the young ladies cautiously approached, calling out unanswered greetings. They knocked on the bus doors without an answer, and couldn't see past the cardboard and bed sheets that were taped to some of the eight, slightly-opened windows.

"What is that smell?!" Carmen asked, holding her nose while looking wide-eyed at her friend.

Judith replied, "I hope it's not what I think it is," as she pulled the doors apart.

Immediately, the odor increased, causing Carmen to gag. Judith covered her nose with the bandana around her neck. She took note of the papers and trash met them on the steps, and placed her foot on the first step and stopped on the second to swat a few flies. Looking around through the dimness at the messy, smelly scene, she discovered that most of the seats had been removed. The bus floor, white foldable table, the small bed supported by the two remaining seats, and forward-facing desk were covered with empty water bottles and hand-written papers, melted candles, loose batteries, empty food cans, a cooler, paper cups and plates, pens, two lanterns, and empty prescription bottles. The bed sheets on some of the windows, fought to be freed from the duct tape with the help of the gently moving breeze to offer a sense of peace within the tragic scene. Finally, Carmen pressed up to Judith's back, noticed through the candle, and empty water bottle on the desk, the top of a graying head of hair belonging to the seated figure slumped over the desk toward them.

"Look!" she whispered and pointed over Judith's shoulder. "That's a person!"

"We have to call the police," Judith announced with resolute sadness.

It took an hour for the police and ambulance to arrive where the two hikers waited on top of a large boulder with their backpacks next to them. As the vehicles approached, leading a cloud of dust, the girls stood and waved.

"Hello. I'm Officer Palmer," the first officer said after talking into his radio. "How are you two girls holding up?"

"Fine," they unconvincingly replied together. "I'm Carmen, and this is my best friend, Judith."

"Good. Well, lead the way."

Fifty yards further down the wide, vague path, the two officers, two paramedics, and the two hikers stood near the bus.

Officer Graham noted, "Looks like the person inside didn't want to be found."

"Did you girls go inside?" Officer Palmer asked.

Carmen answered, "Just to the second step."

"That was far enough," Judith added, still emotional from what she saw.

While one office took pictures of the bus from multiple angles, the other one pulled out surgical masks and rubber gloves from her pockets.

Placing the masks over their mouths and putting on thin rubber gloves, they opened the school bus doors and slowly walked up the steps. There, they took a couple of pictures before disappearing into the bus.

The coroner pulled up to the police car and ambulance and followed the footprints to the bus, as the officers stepped back out with an empty prescription bottle and read the label under the sunlight.

"George, we have one deceased male in his late fifties," Officer Graham informed him. "He's been there for a while. This bottle might help you identify him."

"Okay. I'll go inside and do my thing. But I'll need help getting him out," he replied as he put on his own rubber gloves and mask.

"Sure thing."

Officer Palmer took the hiker's information and thanked them. "We don't want you to be around for the rest of this, and I'm sure you don't either. We're sorry that you had to see it. You both can continue on your way."

The two hikers hoisted their packs onto their backs and quickly continued on their hike, talking in low tones.

After the ambulance left with the body of the victim that was carefully placed in a black body bag, the commercial tow truck backed in as far as it could. The driver in light-blue overalls and a matching cap got out and pulled a thick metal cable to the front of the bus as the officers watched. By adjusting the levers, the cable dragged the bus ahead until it was close enough to the tow truck.

The bus was taken to Central Salvage Yard, holding piles of cars, and various vehicles snugged together inside the acres of the walled fortress. Narrow dirt roads with tire tracks that usually held water divided the different futures of every vehicle. Although it looked like the vehicles were randomly placed, there was a specific order to it all, including an area for vehicles that were pending legal or insurance decisions. The short, green bus was placed there.

At the police station, the brother, being only family member had already confirmed the bad news by identifying that the body was his brother at the morgue. He signed a form that he didn't want the old bus or its messy contents. The prognosis from the doctor and the forms that his brother signed were the first steps of a long conclusion of the death of Peter Norman, a private man whose passion was being alone and writing unpublished poems and stories.

At Central Salvage Yard, the next morning, employees parked their cars and went into the office. The owner, Bill, made a pot of coffee while explaining to his three employees that a tow truck brought a short, green bus and was parked in the 'hold' area, in the back of the yard.

"The police called. I had to come back in last night. So, we can't touch the bus until the police conclude the cause of death regarding the man found inside. Other than that, it's a regular day."

"Where did they find it," Jim asked, taking his turn at the coffee pot.

"Somewhere out in the desert. He was living in it. It's full of trash."

"And he died in it?" Monica's question had the feel of a sad announcement as she stared at Bill.

Chester decided out loud, "Man, I am not going to go that way."

"Yeah, that's what I was told by the driver. The man lived in it. Gabe took an unusual interest in it. He actually put his college books down and went outside to watch it being parked by the tow truck. I'm not sure how much actual security he provides at night, but at least he's getting some college work done."

"Gabe is a good kid," Monica said, as she reached into the refrigerator and withdrew a carton of cream. "He's just been under some stress to find a subject for his thesis."

As the employees prepared to leave in the late afternoon, Gabe stepped into the office wearing his security jacket and hat. With a large flashlight in one hand and a backpack in the other, he began his routine night shift. 'Hello, Gabe' and 'Have a good night,' were traded as Bill, Jim, Chester, and Monica each collected lunch filed out the door.

At the coming of dusk, the few scattered lights came on in the salvage yard. Gabe had his books laid out on the folding table with a view of the yard. He was supposed to make irregularly timed rounds out in the yard, but that ability to choose when, and his homework, often allowed him to forget.

In the middle of the night, Gabe sighed as he laid the open book on the table. He picked up his flashlight and walked out the door into the dim streets of the colorful city of metal.

A beam of light swung back and forth from Gabe's flashlight as he walked down the dirt road, avoiding the puddles of water. He had gotten used to the constant smell of oils and other automotive fluids.

His route would take him to the end of the salvage yard where he would turn right, and walk back toward the office, where he would turn left to go down that road, and so on. After this process, he would go back to the office.

Arriving at the end of the first road, Gabe shinned his light into the section where vehicles were being held for their pending releases. He saw, sitting in front, the little green bus with cardboard and sheets still in the windows. The story that Bill had told him, the night the bus arrived, gave Gabe enough intrigue to walk over to it.

His light swept back and forth over the side, stopping only to absorb the clues and little parts of the story; the windows slightly opened to adjust to the temperature, the lack of plan and provision indicated by thin sheets and cardboard, and the hasty paint job, clearly intended to hide the underlying bright yellow. Illuminating the two narrow doors that folded together, Gabe noticed they were ajar. As he stood in front of the doors, only able to see the driver's seat, his heartbeat increased. Gabe knew that the door was not just one to allow him into the bus, but a door that would permit him inside the thoughts of a reasonable man who decided to spend his last living days and moments in a place he knew he would die. What caused the man to become so desperate? He had to know. He had to pull the doors open. Ghostly metal quietly screeched out his intrusion, like that of a haunted house. The smell, although being weaker than it was, reflexively brought his empty hand to cover his nose while his brain urged him to withdraw. But his quest to understand pulled him inside and up the three steps. His flashlight quickly zig-zagged across the scene, trying to detect any threat; natural or unnatural. Trash was everywhere. Papers in the aisle had been trampled along with other trash.

Taking his phone out from his hip pocket, he pushed his camera icon and set it to flash. He stood there and took pictures of the windows, floor, makeshift bed supported by the only two seats on opposite sides of the aisle, the white foldable table, the opened cooler with the contents of three empty ice bags, and the desk. Gabe stood there to allow his eyes to catch anything else among the debris until he noticed a paper on the floor with what appeared to be a title and hand-written words beneath it. Page 17, was at the bottom. Other stacks of papers had come from an absent printer. Gabe decided that the dead man had brought them with him.

At 7:00 AM, the next morning, the employees arrived one-by-one to begin the day's routine. Short, tired greetings were exchanged. Chester made coffee. Monica filled her cup and sat at her desk to check her email.

"Bill, the 20014 white Chevy, and the green bus were released."

"Thanks."

"I want to clean out the bus," Gabe announced before every head turned to him.

"What?" Bill asked. "You're a leased security guard, not an employee. You don't have to do it."

"I want to clean out the bus before you do whatever you plan to do with it."

"Well, why?" Monica asked.

"The man who died inside was a writer. I found an empty prescription bottle and looked up the pills. He was dying and in a lot of pain. He bought the bus and hand-painted it. By the receipt I found, he stopped at one store to buy what he needed, then drove it to a secluded spot in the desert, to write as much as he could before he died. It's a story. And at the risk of sounding like I'm taking the boots off a dead man, this story might turn into my thesis." He looked around at the silent, attentive faces. "I want the stories he wrote. I want to write a story about Peter Norman and his stories. Please, Bill."

"Okay," Bill replied, nodding. "Do you want the bus too?"

"Why would he want the bus?" Jim asked.

"Yeah, why would I?"

"I'll tell you what. I'll keep the bus where it is, and I want you to imagine where you can take it on a flat-bed trailer for your project. Take the bus too, Gabe."

"You never know," Monica said. "You might want to drive it, for publicity."

Gabe smiled with a, "Thank you," then took the empty box from under the folding table and walked out to the bus.

The green bus gave a completely different feeling as Gabe approached it in the morning's light. He was happy that the unknown writer could become posthumously famous, and that the same writer could be the subject of his college thesis.

This time, Gabe imagined that the doors squeaked in an exclamation of shared excitement. It took hours, but every square inch of the bus was photographed. Small pieces of numbered masking tape, were placed by each item and logged in his notebook. Finally, after labeling and collecting the trash, he then put the puzzle of the papers together to complete each story. However, the writing on the sweat-stained page sitting on the desk, became less legible as it moved down the page and stopped in the middle of a sentence. The last words that Peter Norman wrote were, "Please publish."

The college contacted several publishing companies, all of which agreed to publish the biography, pictures, and stories that Peter Norman wrote. Gabe put his college on hold for a semester to work with the editor.

Gabe built a website to honor Peter Norman. Included, were the titles and short excerpts from each of the twenty-seven brilliant stories. A digital photo presentation, a short video of the site of the bus's discovery, and a biography of the writer were all displayed inside the short, green bus that Gabe drove to the college. Students and faculty lined up to enter and view each piece of the exhibit while they slowly shuffled through the bus. Select framed papers, including the last one he had written on, hung in different places. The last feature near the back was the desk and chair permanently mounted in place where a previously unknown, and unpublished dying man had spent the last weeks of his life doing what he loved the most. Some of the students paused to sit at the desk for a few moments to take the experience further.

A small set of steps were placed out on the ground for the visitors to exit the back door. As they stepped down, each person was given the chance to reflect on their own passion and commitment, and decide what they would do with the last weeks of their lives.

The faculty at the college determined that the entire presentation qualified as Gabe's thesis.

The Sacrifices for Oak Mill

As the angry residents gathered nosily inside the church for the impromptu town meeting, they believed that the stranger had committed the crime. But, no one, without doubt, could produce evidence or testimony. They wanted to believe that the bewildered negro seated alone in the only cell at the jail had murdered the young Sally Green, although he firmly denied it. Each resident expected that just the accusations they hurled, and the mere curious arrival of yet another transient, would be enough to gather unanimous consent for a hanging. None present had the intention to refute the absence of evidence or calm the crowd, who every Sunday, sweetly sang hymns in the same wooden pews. The residents took turns standing to extend their arms with pointed fingers at the Sheriff, and Mayor Russel, who were seated at the vacant communion table on the platform, passionately demanding a judgment of death as women with bowed decorative bonnets and shaking hands dabbed their angry eyes with laced-lined kerchiefs.

Very early, that morning, the Sheriff had yelled out for a doctor from an alley between the mercantile and the small saloon at his discovery of Sally's body having been found during a routine walk around town. Men casually walking in the streets, became alarmed and ran toward the alley as one man ran for the doctor. The stranger, who called himself Josiah, standing across the dirt street, in front of the feed store, was immediately apprehended and considered guilty even as he was being pushed toward the jail. He had to have done it, they believed, because, undoubtedly, none of them had killed her. Everyone who lived in Oak Mill knew each other, and many of them were related. So, it left only him who was instantly passed by the labels of a witness, a suspect, and an accused, to be roughly treated as guilty.

Josiah had wandered into the wrong town looking for work. Arriving in the morning after having walked in the safer dark, he prepared a promise to do any kind of work no matter how low or hard it could be; this was how he got as far as he did. The paper he carried with him, officially guaranteeing that he was a free man, explained to the many soldiers and sheriffs who stopped him, why he was traveling without a white man.

After he left Georgia and headed north on foot, some of the work foremen hired him on because Josiah always offered to labor the first day without a wage. With his family in mind, this eager man worked nearly twice as hard but got paid less than what the white men got. When work ran out, or the threats and violence got to be too much, Josiah collected his pay and moved on. Of course, the relatively large amount of money that he saved that was found on him by the town folks at Oak Mill, raised even more allegations. And the three books, also in the bag he carried, fostered accusations of thievery. However, the books were meant to be gifts to his daughter to ensure that she would learn to read. Having been separated from his wife and daughter after he sent them from the tumultuous landscape of the South to Indiana, he always thought of them. This family, like many, were unaware that elements of state's rights, slavery, and the continuation of national cohesion were joining to form the forthcoming Civil War.

It didn't matter that young Sally Green had often been seen flirting, even with some married men on the church steps after the service. The general disgust of her conduct wasn't brought up at the meeting in the noisy church. No one ever questioned why this unmarried woman bore two children or inquired as to whom the fathers might be. And the fact that she was pregnant when she was killed, just added more disappointment to her poor image. Such things in the town were overlooked, as these kinds of public wounds would scab over with time and become simply, unmentionable. Soon, the looks of her toddlers might become similar to any man in the town, but no one will mention that either. The only facts that mattered were that she called Oak Mill, home, and was murdered in a dark alley.

Most of the citizens of Oak Mill had a history of secretly loathing while tolerating violations of high moral and civic expectations. Being a close-knit community, no one was ever publicly punished or shamed. However, all of their frustrations and disappointments were easily attached to every unsuspecting, and vulnerable stranger who experienced the misfortune of crossing into the town. A section of their cemetery contained the victims whose eleven graves were marked with a name if the town knew it and the date of their hanging. The different spans of time and various crimes were enough that residents never questioned why almost every different kind of stranger who visited over the years had ended up on the gallows.

Like any good mayor, Mr. Russel patiently kept his finger on the pulse of the town. He had no tolerance of anyone disrupting the good moral standing of his town and decided that it was again time for some cleansing. Once again, with one stone he had killed two birds. It was easy for him to frame Josiah, and it was just as easy for the Sheriff, who was the only one to suspect the Mayor, to remain silent. After secretly luring Sally Green into the alley with a promise of a sexual encounter, he murdered her. Then, the Mayor gave the town Josiah to pile their frustrations on, having never made the initial accusation himself. All that remained was to watch the residents follow their usual violent course.

The heated discussion inside the church grew to unintelligible shouting until Mayor Russel repeatedly slammed down the gavel. As the noise quickly subsided, a guilty verdict was pronounced by the Mayor. Josiah would be hanged at noon, the next day. The sentence would be carried out on the innocent man, and the sense of justice enjoyed would weigh heavier than the sorrow of losing Sally Green.

For months, the town Oak Mill was settled and peaceful until typical rumors about an adulterous relationship formed and spread along with the rumor that another one of its residents, Lawrence Bowman, had gone out, stole some horses and took them to his little ranch just outside of town. As usual, to keep the peace, no public investigations or accusations were made among the private whisperings in the sewing circles and poker games. But Mayor Russel took note, and again waited for the next innocent stranger, a scapegoat, by comparison, to arrive in his small secluded town of Oak Mill to be sacrificed on the gallows and buried, ending the troubling sins of a mysteriously murdered resident who will rest on the other side of the cemetery.

Dreaming of Nightmares

The residents gathered around the tables in the cafeteria of the Placid View assisted living facility. Those who couldn't walk unassisted had been gently pushed to the tables in their wheelchairs by caregivers. Others who couldn't walk unassisted parked their walkers near their seats.

After lunch, the residents slowly dispersed. Some went to their rooms for naps, while others went to participate in the scheduled activity of watercolor painting, or sat at the tables in the common room to complete puzzles, or to watch television.

To seventy-three-year-old Martin, walking with his cane throughout the daily routine was just a necessary fill-in between bedtimes. In general, life had become an inconvenience as his mind and body surrendered more and more to old age. It was after the lights were turned off and his roommate had fallen asleep, that his other life began.

Smiling to himself, while pulling up his covers, he looked forward to becoming young again. His detailed episodes of romance that weren't just imaginations or fantasies. Martin's dreams presented themselves in vivid details with every episode being a continuation of the previous one. Best of all, he helped direct them. At the center of his dreams was the beautiful young princess who, at the castle, had introduced herself as Princess Catherine. Immediately, they fell in love.

Almost every morning, Martin woke smiling from the night's romantic dreams. Wondering how he as a young man found himself at the castle, where he got his horse, and how he knew his way to the meadow, were the small questions. How he and a beautiful young princess fell in love was the large wonder.

The staff at the assisted living facility carefully helped the residents in wheelchairs and walkers to their seats around the tables. All of the normal background sounds and smells of dinner were present. Seventy-three-year-old, Martin sat down in a chair and leaned his cane against the table waiting for someone to bring him tea and his meal, customized for his diet, while he looked around the cafeteria. He had spoken to most of the residents and was even friends with a few. But, in this final stage of life, the occasional loss of a resident was soon replaced with a new, unfamiliar face.

After each resident finished their dinner, they left the cafeteria and continued down one of the two halls toward their shared rooms. Martin slowly walked among the slow parade of walkers and wheelchairs with measured steps, placing the end of his cane where it needed to go to support his weakness.

In the light of the two bedside lamps, Martin's roommate went through the routine steps of preparing for bed. However, Martin wasted no time getting into his bed and turning off his lamp. With an excited smile, he closed his eyes, hoping, as with most nights, to find himself in the continuing dream.

The seventy-three-year-old, again, found himself to be the strong and handsome twenty-five-year-old carpenter standing with young Princess Catherine in a small meadow surrounded by trees. He was in love with her and presented his simple, handmade jade stone bound in a thin leather strap. Even though such a crude necklace would never be considered by a royal, Princess Catherine's eyes lit up as young Martin reached around her neck and tied the leather ends together. Her bountiful love for the giver made his simple gift lovely. The two secret lovers kissed and embraced. "I love you, my handsome carpenter."

And you have all my love, Catherine."

Wednesday evenings were scheduled for Bingo in the cafeteria. Martin sat alone, realizing that it was the same people, sitting in the same chairs, in the same tables. The only difference was, instead of plates and glasses, there were Bingo cards and Bingo chips. As the last game ended, the staff member standing at the Bingo cage announced, "Thank you all for playing. Remember, we play every Wednesday."

Staff members walked around collecting Bingo cards and chips from tables as Martin stood with his cup of tea. Sixty-eight-year-old Catherine walked by with her walker and noticed Martin's ring.

"Hello. We haven't met yet." She tilted up her face to look through the bottom of her glasses. "Now that's an interesting ring. It feels like I've seen it before."

"Thanks. It belonged to my father."

Catherine became wide-eyed. "Want to hear something funny? I think someone put a necklace on me while I slept! I woke up one morning and saw it in the mirror as I was getting ready for the day! Someone must have found it and thought it was mine!"

"I haven't heard about anyone losing a necklace."

"I've asked all around, but no one knows anything about it," she said as she pulled up a thin leather necklace to reveal a single jade stone. Martin stared in disbelief.

"It's simple but lovely. I dreamed that a young man gave me one just like it!"

"Is his name Martin?"

"Well, yes! What in the world?" she exclaimed with wide eyes. "How did you know?"

Martin replied quietly with mystery in his voice, "I'm Martin and you... You're Princess Catherine."

Catherine stared in disbelief.

"I gave you that jade necklace in the meadow. I made it myself. I'm Martin, your young carpenter!"

Martin and Catherine sat down in chairs and looked at each other with bewilderment.

Catherine whispered, "You are Martin. I can see traces of my young lover in your face. We share a dream."

"But how?"

"I don't know," she replied with awe. "But you are my Martin. You come to me on your chestnut mare."

"My princess waiting in the meadow."

She slowly reached her old, thin hand to his wrinkled face and rested her palm on his cheek.

"I'll see you tonight," Martin assured her with a smile.

Catherine and Martin stood with expressions of love and wonder, then walked out of the cafeteria in separate ways.

While love quickly grants many new exciting thoughts and strong emotions, it will often deny lovers their sleep. Such was the case with Catherine and Martin that night.

In the quiet dimness of separate rooms, each lover excitedly waited to be reunited with the other. Catherine closed her eyes as she listened in vain for the sound of quick hoofbeats approaching their secret rendezvous spot – a place where they shared the sweetness of stolen waters in a small meadow cloistered by thick trees. Her glowing clock gave the unpleasant news that it was 2:14 in the morning.

In his bed, Martin imagined riding, young and strong down the narrow dirt pathway toward the same meadow to kiss and hold her in a forbidden love. But imagining is not the same as dreaming in the way that hoping is not the same as having. He rolled over. His digital clock gave the frustrating news that it was 3:28 AM. Sleeplessness denied Martin and Catherine their meeting of passion in the meadow that night

Catherine and Martin arrived early at the cafeteria and sat alone at a table drinking coffee as the staff prepared the tables for breakfast.

"I missed you last night, my love. I couldn't get to sleep."

"Me either, my Princess. For hours, I imagined riding my horse and seeing you standing there in your beautiful dress."

"In my mind, the lunch basket was on our blanket under the warm sun spread out in the green grass. I waited for your kiss, Martin."

Martin teased, "I haven't decided if it's more romantic making love under the moonlight or in broad daylight."

"Stop that Martin!" she said with a grin. "Do you want to give an old woman a heart attack?"

Martine smiled as he placed his hand over Catherine's hand. Catherine quickly pulled her hand away with a look of caution before glancing around the dining room.

"Martin, we have to be careful."

"I'm tired of being careful; meeting in the meadow in fear of your husband finding out."

"He will be away from the castle for a month."

"Catherine, please try to sleep tonight. We both should ask the nurse for a pill."

"Good plan. I will wait for you tonight, my handsome carpenter."

"And I will come to you."

The next afternoon, Martin and Catherine were seated at the table with other residents putting a puzzle together. Martin looked at Catherine and winked. Catherine slowly brought her hand up to hold the leather strap of her necklace. Martin stood to leave. As he walked away with his cane, he blew a secret kiss to Catherine.

That night they both entered into their dream. A small meadow of grass sprinkled with wildflowers framed in by surrounding trees. A basket of food and a bottle of wine waited on the blanket. Martin and Catherine, in their twenties, lie together on the blanket kissing and embracing. Suddenly, they heard the distant sound of horses running, and snorting. Martin stood, adjusted his clothes while looking toward the path coming into the meadow. Moments later, a horseman burst through the tree-line.

Catherine quickly stood up by Martin. "My husband is here! He has returned early!"

The horse galloped toward Catherine and Martin and stopped near the blanket. A tattoo with the words, Prince of Nightmares" and a crown, was on his neck.

"So, it is true. My wife has found the arms of another lover. A common man, it appears," the Prince dryly exclaimed.

"My husband, please!"

The Prince put an arrow in his crossbow, and said to Martin, "Normally, I would challenge you to a duel if you had any status or dignity. But I shall simply kill both of you."

"My Prince! I beg of you," young Princess Catherine pleaded.

Martin suddenly turned to Catherine, took her by her shoulders, and gently shook her. "Wake up, Catherine! We have to wake up!"

Catherine's closed eyes fluttered as she lay under the covers of her bed. Deep, soft moans swelled inside as her troubled mind tried to escape from the dream.

The Prince shot at Martin as sleepy Catherine stepped in front of him. The arrow hit Catherine in her heart before she fell, lifeless onto the blanket clenching her necklace. Martin looked down at Young Catherine, horrified as tears blurred the sight.

In her bed, Catherine jolted and her old hand loosened around her necklace.

"No Matter. She was a princess whore. I shall find another wife."

"How did you get into our dream?!"

"I'm a Prince of Nightmares. You should run."

"Why? You've just took away the only thing in life I had left."

"Have it your way."

The Prince pulled the string back and placed another arrow in his crossbow while Martin stood defiantly with tears falling down his cheeks. Martin fell onto the blanket next to Catherine with an arrow sunk in his chest. In his last moment of life, he reached his arm over to his princess.

In his bed, Martin's body jolted moments before he reached his old arm out, and died.

In the morning, staff entered Catherine's room to find her dead. Her hand was loosely clutching her simple jade stone necklace. Martin's dead body was discovered around the same with his arm hung over the side of the bed. The staff would never connect the two deaths.

Sleeping on a narrow bed in a prison cell, Prince opened his eyes and sat on the edge of his bed with a sinister smile Mimicking shooting a crossbow twice, he laughed. "Thwap! Thwap!"

The young couple, James and Britney were asleep in their bed. In another bed somewhere else, a woman in her forties slept alone, also dreaming. Another communal dream would form and introduce them.

It was the time of the Old West. James, dressed as a cowboy with a gun belt, sat on the porch of a farmhouse in one of three chairs next to Britney in her long modest dress, and her mother. Each of them held a glass of tea as they talked.

Britney's mother took a sip from her glass and said, "Thank you, James for working on the woodpile."

"And thank you, both for that delicious dinner. A wandering man doesn't get one very often."

Britney smiled. "Your welcome."

"Since there isn't a man here on the farm, I think I should stay for a little longer."

"James, you're on your way to find work. You don't have to stay," Britney replied.

"But we would be happy if you would," her mother added.

"An outlaw named Prince is in the area. I'll stick around until he passes through."

Britney's mother asked, "Prince? Is that his name?"

"Seems so, ma'am. That's all it says on the wanted poster in town. He has a tattoo on his neck."

A horse and rider came down the dirt road and stopped in front of porch. As the man in his forties got off his horse, James quickly stood and fumbled to take his gun from his holster. He pointed it at the man who stepped toward the porch.

"Who are you and what do you want?"

"Easy, partner," the man said as he slowly pulled back the side of his vest to reveal a Marshall badge. "I'm a Marshall, and I'm in this dream too."

The Marshall looked at Britney and her mother. "Ladies."

Britney replied, "You have to tip your hat when you greet a woman here."

"Oh. You're right. I remember now from the movies." The Marshall tipped his hat again. "Ladies."

Britney's mother smiled. "I kind of like that. It makes me feel properly respected."

James asked the Marshall, "How did you get in our dream?"

"I don't know. But we have to stop Prince from his killing spree."

"You just got here. How do you know about Prince?" Britney asked.

"I've been tracking him. You can bet he'll be around. And I'll be watching."

"Thank you, Marshall," Britney's mother said.

The Marshall smiled. "I love hearing that. It's much better than my real name, George Nimrodel, Purchaser."

The coffee shop was beginning to get busy with morning customers on their way to work. Some stood in a line waiting for their orders, while others sat a table with their open laptops and tablets. James and Britney sat alone at their table.

Abigail, their friend, walked to their table carrying a tray with two coffee cups and two breakfast sandwiches. As she placed the items on the table, she said, "Hi. Sorry it took so long. I thought I would bring your order to your table."

"Can you take a break with us?"

"Sorry, Brit. In a few minutes, it's going to get crazy in here."

"Abigail, you wouldn't believe it, but James and I are in this dream together!"

"I've heard about people having the same dream."

James added, "It's not that Britney and I are 'having' the same dream...!"

Britney excitedly interrupted, "We're 'in' the same dream! With a mom and a Marshall!"

"Yeah, it's weird! We're like in the cowboy days! I'm a drifter who stopped at a farmhouse on my way to find work!"

"And I'm living there with my mother!"

"Sounds fun," Abigail replied as she watched the two excited faces.

"And there's a bad guy in the area!" Britney added with wide eyes.

"He's a killer! The Marshall is hunting him down! I saw the poster!"

Abigail smiled and looked around at the customers walking in. "Ooh, a dangerous adventure! I have one of my own right now. I'll check back in a few."

James brought the ax over his head and straight down on the end of a short log. The log split in two before the pieces jumped off the stump. In front of him was a large pile of short logs and a smaller pile of split ones. He took off his cowboy hat and wiped his forehead with the sleeve of his old, white button shirt.

Prince rode his horse down the dirt road, turned onto the dirt driveway, and shot his pistol at James. James quickly looked and noticed the tattoo on Prince's neck.

"Prince!" James exclaimed to himself, as he dropped the ax and dove behind the pile of split logs. There, he took his pistol out and looked over the top of the wood pile.

Britney and her mother ran out of the farmhouse and onto the porch. Prince looked at
at the two women and said, "James, I'm going to burn it down and take that pretty young thing!"

"You're going to have to kill me first!"

"I plan to!"

"How do you know my name?!"

"I'm a Prince of Nightmares! I know everyone in my dreams!"

James fired at Prince. Prince shot back, and grazed James in his left arm. His shirt sleeve was ripped and a little amount of blood began to appear.

Continuing to sleep, James groaned and placed his hand on his arm.

Prince got off his horse and walked toward James. He fired another bullet that splintered the edge of a short log just before James fired at him.

"You're not a very good shot!" Prince announced.

James looked back at the farmhouse porch, then frantically fired at

Prince until the gun clicked but didn't shoot. He was out of bullets. Prince walked to the wood pile. James stood, stepped back, and fell onto the woodpile.

Prince stood over James with his pointed his pistol at him. "Killing people in their sleep takes some planning, but it's so easy."

Britney screamed from the porch, "James! No!"

While Prince was looking over at her, James grabbed the ax and swung it up, hitting Prince in the head. Immediately, he fell to the ground, motionless. James stood as Britney and her mother hurried to him. Britney hugged James. He winced, pulled away, and looked at ripped, red stain on his arm.

"Oh, my God! I'm so sorry! You're bleeding!"

"He really shot me, Britney! I'm in a dream! It hurts!"

Unnoticed, Prince slowly reached for his gun and pointed it up at James. "And you never imagined that you could die in your sleep this way."

Suddenly, there was a loud bang. Prince was shot dead. James and Britney stared at him with wide eyes and open mouths.

In his prison cell's bed, Prince jolted in his sleep and stopped breathing.

The Marshall, holding his gun, walked out from behind some bushes to Prince. He looked down at Prince and pushed his body with his boot before he put his gun into his holster.

"I told you he would come around here."

"Thanks, Marshall. You saved my life."

"It's my job."

"These dreams are way more real than any regular dream," Britney said.

James sighed, "I'll call the police.

"That's me," the Marshall replied.

"But you can fetch the local Sheriff and collect the reward money," Britney's mother suggested.

"Yeah, right. The Old West thing."

"And while you're in town, James, take some shooting lessons."

"Very funny, Britney."

Everyone laughed.

In the coffee shop, James and Britney sat at their favorite table, drinking from mugs.

"How's your arm?"

James slowly lifted his left arm. "Getting better."

"It's nice that Prince isn't in our dreams anymore."

"Yes-sir-ree. I saved the farm and the women-folk from the outlaw, Prince."

"Yes-sir-ree? Women-folk? Really, James?"

"You gotta learn the jargon of the Old West if you're going to dream there."

"I wonder if there are other Princes of Nightmares."

"It might explain why some people just go to sleep and never wake up."

"James, are you going to stay at the farmhouse with my mother and me?"

"Ah, Britney! You want me to stay because you fell in love with me the handsome wandering stranger!"

"Not so much that. That woodpile isn't done yet, and the farmhouse needs to be painted.

"What?!"

Britney laughed, then James laughed.

In an aisle of a grocery store, a woman in her fifties took a loaf of bread and put it into her cart. She was professional looking, except for the tattoo on the side of her neck which read, *'A Princess of Nightmares' with a crown above it.

As a middle-aged couple pushed their cart past her, the woman with the tattoo watched them with a deviant smile.

The Laughing Man

"He is guilty of being a warlock!" the king proclaimed at the end of the short trial. Although the man kneeling and shackled before the throne wasn't a warlock, the religious leaders in the jury held to their suspicions that were fed by only rumors, but they were enough to convict him. Truth be told, the trial was fake; an event to convince the subjects of the kingdom that the goal was to find truth where justice would be served. The clergy wanted no more talk and no more gossip in their city about this man, and needed the people to be sure that no such devilry would be tolerated. As an example, the king having been bullied by the church once more, agreed that his death would be slow.

The defendant sat listening to one witness after another, telling lies about him until any hope of escaping death was finally gone. What is one to do in that case? Should he beg? Would a confession be enough for the court to forgive him? He knew better.

Suddenly, upon the king's pronouncement, the guilty man broke out laughing as if he had been told a joke. Everyone stared and then became angry. All other defendants had been devastated and begged, but this man laughed and wouldn't stop. His laughter was so deep and sounded so sincere that some in the jury smiled in amusement while others laughed too. Frantic orders from the judge to 'Be silent!' and 'Order!' were ignored even as the guards dragged him out through the doors where he would serve out his life sentence in the filthy, cold dungeon.

Two days later, shackled to the stone wall in his cell, the man was still laughing as he hung bleeding from the wounds of his wrists. Grins on the guard's faces had faded the day before as questions began to form in their minds. They wondered what he knew. Was he possessed? Had he gone insane? Was something going to happen to the kingdom? An attack? Had he conjured a malevolent curse to be realized at the moment of his death? Some of the guards did everything to comfort his and delay his death, while others were restrained by law from beating him to death.

Orders were given to keep the heavy wooden door to the dungeon closed and cloth to be stuffed around the gaps as the laughter echoing against the stone walls rose up the steps to disturb the royalty. It seemed that nothing could be done to mute the perpetual laughter.

At night the princesses, princes, and others of high esteem lay in their beds with pillows over their heads, begging for reprieve and praying for the death of the man accused of being a warlock.

Musicians were stationed in halls to play soothing music on harps, and singers to sing quiet slow songs. Some in the castle had their rooms moved to the tower to distance themselves from the never-ending laughter.

The beatings he endured weren't even enough to convince the bloodied man to stop laughing. The guards became dismayed that, although his body was ravished by the damp, cold, and lack of enough food, the laughter continued to flow with the same strength.

Three weeks into his sentence, the man still hung from one arm after one thin hand had slipped through its shackle. With his mouth barely opened, the laughter was as robust as the day he began to laugh in the courtroom.

A week later, while life still refused to abandon the tortured man, he became a spectacle of great interest as the residents of the castle and many of the clergy visited the man who was now barely conscious. With his eyes half-closed, and the other hand having slipped though the iron shackle, the condemned man lay on the cold stone floor among scattered pieces of straw. Yet the laughter was still as vibrant and loud as ever and continued to infiltrate every aspect of the kingdom's activities as his angry ghost took control of his unconscious mind and laughed defiantly, mocking and punishing the minds of all of those within its broad range, through the slightest movements of his mouth. Even while his unfocused bloodshot eyes, framed in drooping lids, the man laughed vigorously. The sound echoed against the dirty stones and up the stairs and out through the small window to the streets changing the feeling of what laughter should bring into a hideous curse.

The guards who at first were cruel, had begun to respect the endurance of their laughing prisoner, then privately began to turn their heads having become tortured by the laughter. Each one formed balls of candle wax and pushed them into their ears, and on his night-watch a guard privately cried in brokenness that the prisoner, mostly dead, was laughing.

Most among the royalty and clergy believed it to be a confirmation of witchcraft, while many of the common people in the streets remained convinced that the man was innocent and felt pity for the suffering prisoner. They took turns kneeling at the edge of the dirt road to peer through the cell's only window. Whereas, they had always heard anguish from that window over the years, the laughter seemed to be a defiance of the pre-determined trials and cruel sentences that too many in the kingdom had suffered. Silently, they cheered for him, and in the night, often dropped bread and flowers into his cell before running away.

Nearly two months after he was convicted, the prisoner finally died in the morning, and instantly the ever-present laughter stopped. The silence was so abrupt that many people in the streets and in the castle stopped whatever they were doing and lifted their heads to listen. Most people cried; some for the relief and others in sorrow.

The king's great relief was obvious to all. His mood changed to become friendly and benevolent. Never had there been a noble, a knight, or a threat of war from another country that caused him as much distress as the laughing man in his dungeon. He ordered haste in removing the body from the cell to be buried in the pauper's graveyard.

Normally, it was the undertaker's job to remove dead bodies, but the king had ordered four armed guards to carry the body to the graveyard, outside of the wall surrounding the castle. Dozens of town folks had quickly gathered around the freshly dug hole after someone spotted the guards approaching, each holding a corner of an old brown blanket, behind two priests. Clearly, it was a body that weighted the middle of it. Some of the people grabbed handfuls of wildflowers before hurrying to the cemetery.

As they came to the open grave, the guards stopped and looked down at the body whose thin bruised skin was loosely wrapped about the bones and the eyes were half-opened. The dreadful expressions they exchanged with each other assured them all that they each had just heard a moment of quiet laughter from the open mouth of the emaciated body.

A defiant old woman with missing teeth, wearing clothes that were little more than rags, called out, "That's right," e laughed. "We all 'erd 'em! Di-ent we?!"

"En doon't think eez doon laughin' either!" a man in poor clothes, pointing a wooden pipe at them, added. He, too, had followed the whole process, from the vague rumors about the man to that moment.

After tilting the blanket, the body fell into the hole and landed in the mud at the bottom with muted splash. As a precaution, the two clergy members uttered some words in Latin, crossed themselves, then nodded to the two men waiting with shovels. With every shovelful of dirt, the men refused to look into the hole, as they dropped dirt onto the corpse, unrecognizable from what their fellow citizen used to be.

The spectators waited until the last shovel of dirt brought the hole level with the ground before placing their flowers on top and mumbling last thoughts.

The grave would have remained unmarked, except that night someone had gone to it and placed at the head, a wooden board with the thinly painted words, Laughing Man.

It seemed that all was normal again in the kingdom for about a week, when the king's eyes suddenly opened in the middle of the night. He wondered if he had actually heard laughter, or was the laughter just a bad fragment of a memory that drifted into his mind while he slept. After drifting back to sleep, he jolted in his bed, believing he heard laughter again. He couldn't fall back to sleep as he listened with his eyes open for the rest of the night.

By orders of the nervous king, standing at the grave the next morning, one of the three priests sprinkled holy water onto the dirt as the other two said monotoned prayers and crossed themselves. Before they left, a priest ordered the keeper of the graveyard to remove the marker and destroy it.

Two nights later, there was no question in the king's mind that he heard laughter through his window. He jumped out of bed and shouted to his chamber attendant in the adjoining room if he had heard laughter. The young man quickly appeared in the doorway. Not wanting to upset the frantic king, he stuttered to answer as he kept his eyes to the floor.

"I order you to answer me!"

"Yes, your highness, I heard laughter from outside," the nervous attendant replied.

Clenching his hair with both hands, the king frantically paced back and forth. "He laughed! He is laughing at me again! He is laughing at the priests!"

"Your Grace," the trembling attendant offered, "might the laughter have been from a drunkard passing near the tower?"

"No! I know that laugh, having endured it for so long!"

This nightly event continued as more and more of the residents of the castle heard the laughter. The dread felt when the Laughing Man was alive was replaced with rumors that the dead 'warlock' was now laughing from his grave, or that the evil spirit was released by his death and now walked among the living. A nightly curfew was announced and the guards around the castle were doubled.

A heavy stone marker, buried half-way into the earth, stood at the grave bearing the carved words, "Laughing Man.' After the church had the dirt around the body removed, oil was poured into the hole and the remains were burned in place, while every applicable prayer was offered by the attending clergy. Before the men refilled the hole, a wooden cross was placed on top of the blackened bones that smoldered while the shovels dropped dirt over them.

The nightly laughter from the grave of the man never stopped. Those who lived near the castle, moved far enough away to where the laughter couldn't be heard. Most of the royalty took up residences elsewhere, leaving the castle mostly empty at night.

Finally, after months, the king had the heads of the clergy killed for their impotence in silencing the laughter. In fear for their lives, the rest of the clergy left.

The grip that terror had on the king's mind continued to tighten. Not being able to rule, he couldn't make wise decisions in the affairs of his kingdom. Eventually, a ruthless king from another country invaded. On the day the king was conquered the laughing stopped.

Always weeping and half insane, the former king found himself deep in the dungeon, shackled to the same wall that once held the laughing man; there he died the same long painful death.

Made in the USA
San Bernardino, CA
26 January 2020

63501556R00151